NIGHT OUT
IN FARGO

For Clarence citrus mobile
01-25-2012
Ernest Francis Schanilec

By Ernest Francis Schanilec

Also by

Ernest Francis Schanilec

Blue Darkness
The Towers
Danger in the Keys
Purgatory Curve
Gray Riders
Sleep Six

NIGHT OUT IN FARGO

Copyright © 2006 by Ernest Francis Schanilec

Author - Ernest Francis Schanilec
Publisher - McCleery & Sons Publishing

International Standard Book Number: 1-931916-44-6

Printed in the United States of America

ACKNOWLEDGMENTS

INVESTING IN MY SON CLAYTON'S CREATIVE WRITING education back in the 80's has proven to be a wise investment for me. This is my seventh novel and his expertise have not only guided me along, but educated me as well. I thank him for everything that he has done to make me a better writer. He has contributed his talents to this novel as well as others.

I thank my grandson, William Rusche, of Maple Grove, Minnesota. He is currently a ninth grader and a very avid reader. His read of *Night Out in Fargo* and comments were very valuable to me.

Mac Nelson, a high school student at New York Mills, has my gratitude for contributing to the descriptions of the Tae Kwon Do actions.

To Dr. Larry Morrison and his son, Dr. Michael Morrison, and the following members of their staff: Kim, Twyla and Tammy of Detroit Lakes, Minnesota, go my thanks for contributing their optometry expertise to some of the scenes.

I thank the management and ownership of the Fargo Dome, Cork and Cleaver, Doublewood Inn, Radisson Hotel, Holiday Inn, Sleep Inn, Fargo Country Club and Meritcare Hospital all from Fargo. Thanks to Sunflower Hill, Central Market, and Fireside restaurant in Detroit Lakes, and also to Brainerd International Speedway for the use of their facilities to imagine some of my scenes.

Thanks to my neighbor Scott Elke for the use of his land and barn not only for the cover photograph but several episodes.

Once again, Julie Schonhoff of J & M Printing has done a great job on the cover. Thanks, Julie.

DEDICATION

THIS NOVEL IS DEDICATED TO THE READERS of all of my books, whether they liked them or not.

1

SENATOR SEAN MCDOUGAL PUT A HAND UP to his right ear as the NASCAR leading competitor raced by with only three laps to go. He sat in the VIP section at Brainerd International Raceway watching the Elite Division race on a bright August afternoon.

The Elite Division is an integral part of NASCAR, home to some of the country's very best competitors. The 2,900 pound race cars powered by 350 to 358 horsepower engines tested their skill on the three-mile, 10-turn road course.

On the seventh turn, the red and white streaked car, number 245, almost spun out of control. The people in the crowd next to the senator cheered as the driver regained control, losing six car lengths to his nearest competitor. Most everyone in the crowd had stood up, reacting to the possibility of a serious crash.

McDougal, nearing the end of his sixth term in the U.S. Senate representing North Dakota, had promised his sister, Belinda, he would attend the event and watch her son race. She's a basket case about Paul and his racing, he said to himself. She's worried to death and can't bear to watch him drive so dangerously.

The man standing next to the senator clapped his hands lightly and turned toward the white-shirted politician. "Whew! That was close, Sean."

The senator forced a smile and nodded. He hitched his pants up a little, and stuffed an escaped section of his shirt inside the top back edge of his pants. The wide gray belt circled and contained his generous midriff, hardly noticeable because of his height.

His light green eyes twitched a little as he sat back down, exposing a narrow scar above his left eyebrow. The senator's head turned left gradually as those around him also did, focusing on number 245.

————

AN ATTRACTIVE BLONDE with sparkling blue eyes sat directly behind the senator. She jammed a hand over her mouth and held her breath as number 245 struggled to remain upright on the track. Along with others, she stood as the car regained its position, and then sat back down.

Her respectable waist and generous bosom attracted the glances of several men from the adjoining section. Julie Huffman had taken a job as a travel coordinator and special aide for Senator McDougal. She loved to travel and eventually became one of his most dependable and efficient employees.

Julie's mind drifted to her family, mainly her daughter who lived in Colorado. I need to visit her again, she thought as she watched race car 245 speed around the final turn of the second to last lap.

Loneliness had motivated her to place a profile with an Internet dating service. Early experiences in meeting new men had been failures until she met a man that lived in the lake country, north of the Twin Cities. They hit it off on the first date.

Julie had been born and raised in northern Minnesota, the land of bears, moose and wolves. She loved the country, especially the birds and wildlife, but the relationship didn't last. Julie loved to travel, and his interests differed in that he favored attending to his business and property in the lake country of Minnesota.

She whiffed exhaust fumes as a tightly bunched group of cars roared by, quickly followed by number 245, driven by her boss's nephew. Julie wondered why he didn't simply pass them on the outside. She saw a space wide enough for at least two cars.

The people in the row ahead of her stood as car number 245 passed the tightly stacked group and sped into the fifth turn of the last lap. The man standing next to the senator raised a fist into the air, his shouts lost in the roar of engines. "Go, Paul! Go!" she heard him yell.

The red, white-streaked car roared toward the finish line. She saw a man raise a checkered flag.

"BOOM!"

Fragments of metal and plastic flew in all directions. A massive fiery streak discharged into the air. Everyone in the stands stood, some of them screamed. Car 245's existence disappeared in a massive plume of smoke.

——

THE CAB'S TIRES SQUEELED AS IT TURNED THE CORNER. It came to a stop in the parking lot of a downtown hotel in Brainerd, Minnesota. The back door opened and a man stooped and placed the back of his gloved hand against the frame of the door as he stepped out. He wore a charcoal, broad-rimmed hat and trench coat.

He reached back into the cab and grasped a small suitcase. Using his other hand, he handed a bill to the driver.

The light fixture on a metal pole lit up the driver's dark eyes. "Thank you, sir," he said.

The man walked into the shadows of the parking lot and watched the cab turn onto the street, and disappear around the corner. He set down the suitcase on the asphalt surface and removed his gloves, sliding them into the pocket of his trench coat.

Cupping his hands together, he lit a cigarette, and exhaled a cloud of smoke. He watched a garbage truck drive slowly down the street. It stopped for a light and then rumbled through the intersection. He took a deep drag of the cigarette and listened to the lonely, fading blares of a freight train.

His figure tightened when he saw a police car stop at the stoplight. It turned left on the green and neared the approach to the hotel. He breathed a sigh of relief as it passed by, out of sight.

Tossing the butt onto the pavement, he stomped it with a boot and walked toward the hotel. After pausing at the door, he grabbed the handle and took one last look toward the street. He yanked it open, walking quickly toward the worn, mahogany counter. The short, round-faced bald man in charge didn't look up as he approached. The guest cleared his throat. The clerk's body jerked and his eyes opened.

"I need a room," the tall, dark-skinned man said, bouncing his knuckles on the counter, his small black eyes darting around the room.

The clerk staggered, grabbing the back edge of the counter rail to keep from falling off the stool. "Yes, sir, we do have an opening. It'll be thirty bucks in advance."

The tall man with the narrow beak-nosed face peeled off three bills from a wad in his left palm.

"Only one night, sir?" the clerk asked, his eyes widening as he noticed the man's left ear, most of it missing.

His guest nodded and reached out to grab a key that the clerk had removed from a wooden cubby hole behind him.

The clerk's round, brown eyes followed the man as he sauntered up the oak railed-stairway and disappeared around the corner. He looked at the registration: *John Smith.*

2

TOM HASTINGS ACCEPTED A TABLE in the corner of Lenny's Night Club in Brainerd, Minnesota. He smiled and nodded at the hostess as he pulled back one of the chairs and sat down. He thought about the first day of the computer seminar he had attended earlier. The event still had one more day to run. Tom had registered for two seminars this year, the current one, and a second in Fargo later in August.

The final session of the day had ended at 5:30 p.m. and Hastings looked forward to a pork tenderloin dinner. He ordered a glass of chardonnay and studied the menu. The young waitress, who had deposited a glass of ice water, scooted away.

He gazed around the restaurant, part of an old building, next to a strip mall on the outskirts of town. One of his fellow seminarians had recommended the place to him earlier that day. He looked up and saw rugged wooden beams spanning the entire length of the room...rough sawn oak, he said to himself.

His waitress arrived. "I'm Nancy and will be your waitress this evening. Anything to drink?"

"Yeah, a glass of chardonnay."

A minute later, she brought Tom's glass of wine and he ordered his pork loin. This is going to be one boring evening, he thought. I don't know a soul here and there's still about 3 to 4 hours of daylight left. He saw two men and a blonde woman enter. Tom couldn't believe his eyes...*the woman is Julie...Julie....*

————

JULIE FELT SLIGHTLY UNCOMFORTABLE BUT COM-PLACENT. Her boss, Senator McDougal, and his closest aide, Aaron, had insisted she accompany them to dinner. It was only hours after the race car exploded on the track, killing the driver instantly. You would think there would be more remorse, she thought.

She sipped wine from a glass, not paying attention to the intense discussion going on between the two men. Julie looked around the room, wishing she hadn't agreed to the dinner invite. Her eyes widened when she saw a familiar face. She gasped. It was her old friend Tom Hastings sitting over by the wall.

"Excuse me, Sean, but will you excuse me for a moment. I need to visit with someone I know."

The Senator followed her gaze. "Aha, it's that gentleman over there, isn't it?"

Julie nodded.

"You go ahead, young lady, but don't be gone long. We need to spend as little time here as possible."

Julie stood and said, "I'll be back soon."

She stood, generating an exaggerated wide smile and walked toward Tom's table.

"I can't believe my eyes, Tom. What are you doing here?" Julie said, accepting a standing hug.

"It's so good to see you. I see you're with the politicians."

"Yes, I work for a senator. How did you know that he is a

politician?"

"I've seen him on television before."

Julie held onto Tom's hand. "So how've you been?"

"Great, but I'm pretty bored right now...just waiting around for tomorrow's final session."

"You still in computers, Tom?"

"Sure am—how about you?"

"Actually, I'm Senator McDougal's travel itinerary manager. As you know, I love to travel—especially to Africa. We've been there four times this year."

"Africa! What's going on over there?"

"The senator's main committee is dealing with a small country. It has to do with developing electrical power in the rural areas where they produce phosphates."

"What country is that?

"Togo."

"I've never heard of that one."

"It's in West Africa, on the coast—small. I've got to get back to the table—oh, but what did you think of the tragic accident at the race car track yesterday?"

"Accident? What accident?"

Julie placed a hand on her forehead. She smudged away the gathering moisture in her eyes. "His nephew's car blew up on the final lap! It was awful! I've never experienced anything like it."

"Geez, I didn't watch the news last night and didn't pay any attention to the newspaper today—hmm."

Julie laid her forehead against his chest, trying to choke off rapidly growing sobs.

"Did you know the driver?" Tom asked, frowning.

Her voice choked slightly. "No, not personally, but he was the senator's nephew."

"Wow—that's tragic."

Julie took a deep breath. She stood. "Well, Tom, I better get going. Perhaps we could have lunch one day." She reached into her purse and handed him a card. "My cell phone number is on there. Give me a call sometime."

Tom took the card and placed it into his shirt pocket. "Yeah, I'll do that."

Julie made one step and stopped. "Tom, that's Paul Newman sitting over there! I heard that he might attend the races today."

Tom's eyes followed the direction of her finger. "Well, I'll be darned."

"See, I told you," Julie said and left.

———

TOM WATCHED JULIE WALK BACK to her table. He stared beyond her at a dark-skinned man who stood, looking down at the senator. They appeared to be engaged in strained conversation. They stopped talking when Julie arrived and waited until she sat down. The man standing bowed to her and stepped away. He turned and pointed a finger at the senator, then quickly walked away.

Geez, that's a weird looking ear—part of it is missing, Tom thought as he saw the strange looking man disappear around a corner. Now, there's one sinister looking character.

He thought about Julie's visits to his lake home five years ago and how she had enhanced his appreciation for birds and other wildlife. It doesn't surprise me that she has taken on a position that leads to a great deal of travel, especially of the international variety...ah, here's my dinner.

This is really good, he thought, as he bit into the first cut of his pork loin. Tom reached over and grabbed his wine glass. Ah, this goes down so good...so good. He glanced at Julie's table and noticed her smiling face. Feelings of warmth spread throughout his body. We really had some good times, he thought. I wonder if it would be possible....Naw, we had lived totally different lives. Neither one of us could change that much...yet....

His thoughts drifted to Jolene Hunt, whom he had befriended a couple of years ago. Her father was killed in a train crash...murder it was. She actually used me, in more ways than one, to prove that a scrupulous sheriff and his jerk nephew were responsible for the death. I still have feelings for Jolene...as well as for Julie. He shook his head. Somehow, I always end up just like I am right now—alone.

"Sir, would you like anything else?" the waitress asked.

"No, Nancy, I need my bill. Say, is that actor Paul Newman sitting over there?"

"Yes, it is. Would you like to match his tip...twenty bucks?" she asked, smiling widely.

Tom threw up his arms "What can I say?" He got up and walked over to pay his tab. He signed his credit card and handed it to the woman behind the counter, her name tag read, *Deb.* "I see you have Paul Newman as a customer this evening."

"Yes indeed. Mr. Newman is one of the finest gentlemen we've ever had at this restaurant. It's been a pleasure for me."

Tom cocked his head, didn't say a word and walked out the door. "Twenty bucks," he muttered.

3

AGENT TRAVIS SPEAKER OF THE FBI nodded to his partner, Bill Brown. They had driven to Fargo, North Dakota from their offices in St. Paul to question the senator regarding the explosion of his nephew's race car in Brainerd the past weekend.

The racetrack case had become his partner's first Minnesota case. Travis had moved to St. Paul from Cincinnati only two months ago. His new partner reminded Bill of the actor Gregory Peck, except for his height and a slight stoop to the upper back.

After parking on the curb near the office building that housed the senator's office, they got out and stood on the sidewalk. Bill looked around. Another downtown dying, he said to himself. I bet the local authorities are working the tax increment financing to the hilt.

Travis checked the number on his note pad with the one over the entry door. "This is the place, Bill...let's hear what the senator has to say."

Bill followed his partner into the building and looked up at the marquee. "Fourth floor, Travis," he said.

They rode the elevator up and walked up a short corridor to the senator's office door.

Travis opened it and led the way in. "I'm Agent Speaker and this is Agent Brown of the FBI. We're here to talk to the senator. We have an appointment."

The woman behind the desk peered over the rim of her glasses. "Just a moment, gentlemen, I'll tell him that you're here."

The woman frowned before she sorted a few papers and got up off her chair. She walked to a side door and disappeared. I wonder why she didn't call him on the intercom, he thought. "Travis, this could be a sticky situation for the senator—election coming up next year, ya know."

Travis walked over to a wall and gazed up at a huge framed photograph of the senator. The gray-haired politician stood in front of the capitol rotunda, a flag furled in the background, his hair disheveled by the wind.

Bill remembered seeing the senator on television, testifying at a hearing of one type or another. He thought that it had something to do with a small country in Africa. The woman senator sitting on the high bench in front of the microphone sure gave him a bad time. Yeah, they ended up shouting at each other...that's why I remember it, he thought.

He heard the door open. The receptionist returned, stepping into the room. "The senator will see you now. Please follow me."

They followed her up a short corridor. She turned right and led the two agents through an open doorway. Senator Sean McDougal stood by his desk. He extended his hand. Bill grasped the enormous fingers and looked up into his pale green eyes. "I'm Agent Brown and this is Agent Speaker. We'd like to ask you a few questions regarding the Brainerd race track incident a few days ago."

"Anytime you need some help, gentlemen, I'm available. Please have a seat."

Bill watched the tall man sit on the corner of his desk and take a drink of water from a glass sitting near him.

"Senator, I'll get right to the point. Is there any reason that you are aware of that a person or persons would sabotage your nephew's race car?"

The senator set the glass down. He stood and walked to the rear of his desk and sat down. He licked his lips. "I'm still in shock. We think it—the accident—was caused by a gas line leak."

Agent Brown nodded. His right eye narrowed. "Senator, our job is to look into the possibility that the explosion was actually a case of sabotage—and murder—possible terrorism."

McDougal's right eye twitched. "Gentlemen, my staff is working with the authorities, and thus far there is no evidence to support that theory."

The senator and the two FBI agents batted the details of the accident around in a circle for a few minutes.

Agent Brown scratched the front edge of his crew cut. "Sir, we have access to information which the CIA has made available to us regarding a foreign relations committee that you serve on. The agency is aware of a hostile group of people in the country of Togo who were not happy about a recent vote of yours."

"Sorry, men, but short of a subpoena, I cannot divulge any more information to you...many of my dealings with that country are confidential, but trust me....The explosion was an accident!"

Bill Brown tightened his lips together, recognizing the irritation in the senator's voice. He knew the interview had ended. "Thank you, Senator, for seeing us. We'll be in touch."

He nodded to his partner and led him out the door, through the receptionist's room and out into the corridor. When they got down to street level, Bill said, "Travis, we've been cut off for now, but this case is not over by a long shot."

———

SENATOR MCDOUGAL WATCHED THE FBI INVEST-IGATORS leave the room. He pressed a button on his intercom. "Betsy, would you get Aaron in here?"

The senator chaired a foreign appropriations committee which dealt with African nations. Ambassador Acoussoulelou Bodjona spent much of the past month attempting to convince the committee that a massive grant to his country would guarantee adequate power supply system to enhance their Phosphate exports.

Aaron Crier entered the office. He walked to the desk and looked down. "What's up, Sean? What did the FBI agents want?"

The senator reached over and pulled out a bottom drawer. Thumbing through a row of folders, he retrieved one and set it on the desk. He opened it and plucked out a photo.

"Do you remember that guy, Aaron?" He pointed.

Aaron, the senator's top aide of the gray-haired senator, squinted and nodded. "Yup, sure do. Listening to that raspy voice only once and feeling that perpetual smile lock on your own face, one doesn't easily forget." He stood two inches shorter than his boss, even though he measured six-foot-three on the height register. His face, dominated by bushy, thick eyebrows, rarely changed expression. Dark brown hair, streaked with gray, lay swept straight back on his head. It thinned at the top forming an oval of a whitish area.

"Whether you remember him or not, his name is Zudoo Mante. He's the go-between for me and the Togo government," the senator said.

"So what's the big deal? The Togo government is only a small piece of cheese anyhow."

"Aaron, I received a call last night after midnight. I think it may have come from this man. He insisted on me voting aye to fund their energy project. For a moment I felt like I was talking to Marlon Brando, the Godfather."

Aaron gasped and rounded his lips. "Oh, I wouldn't worry about that wide-hipped, rounded-cheeks creep. He can beg all he wants. What does he offer in return?"

"In a few minutes I'll tell you, but first you need to know what he said."

"What's that...what did he say?"

The senator looked up at the ceiling. "Using that raspy voice of his, he talked very slowly and deliberately. 'The explosion of my nephew's car was no accident.'"

Aaron gasped. "Wow, the FBI boys would like to hear that."

The senator stood. He shook his head slowly from side to side. "He also said, 'Others could die.' Then he hung up."

Aaron scratched his chin. "It sounds as if that man is going to be a problem for us."

The senator nodded. "Going to be? He's already a problem. My committee will be voting on their humongous request next week."

The aide tightened his lips together. He stroked his chin with two fingers. "Frankly, Sean, I'm worried for you. You're messing with some sinister people...dangerous as hell, too. Now what else were you going to tell me?"

––––

SENATOR MCDOUGAL PUSHED HIS CHAIR BACK far enough to stretch his legs and raise them to find support for his heels on the desk.

Aaron had left the room. Sean decided not to divulge his zillium secret at this time. The senator's thoughts deepened. Electricity for potassium, my foot, he said to himself. They want the loot to develop zillium mines. Sure, they'll lay some electrical lines...but the great majority of the money will fund their mining.

Can't say I blame 'em, though, he thought. Their discovery and its future development will change the world in a dramatic way. The senator visualized his last visit to Togo, when officials there demonstrated the potential of the OxyEngine.

They showed how a specialized computer chip regulating the flow of oxygen over plates of zillium, generated energy. Software controlled its flow through a series of tubes, eventually propelling the drive train of a vehicle. You can say goodbye to gasoline and diesel, he thought. My God, the vehicle was clocked at 600 miles per hour. My God!

Gasoline stations as we know them will become oxygen stations. The oil producing countries in the world will go broke. African nations, led by Togo, will become very rich. I will become rich. Move over Bill Gates.

Sean reached into a desk drawer and brought out a sheet of paper. He stared at a picture of the OxyBeast. It had four huge wheels, much like a crop sprayer. The middle section looked like a huge panfish lying on its side, the mouth opened, sucking up high-intense oxygen, concentrated in the top 12 inches above the corn. He had caught a crappie while fishing earlier in the year.

He turned the paper and studied the blue print diagram of the OxyBeast. The fish-like tank consisted of a high grade of plastic. An oxygen powered engine propelled the beast up and down the field. It was the closet thing to perpetual motion that the world has ever seen— and to top it all off, the engine does not emit toxic fumes.

Yes, it will make me very rich. I will own the patent on the OxyBeast, he said to himself. The senator smiled. He visualized driving his Mercedes to an oxy station and filling up with oxygen instead of gas.

The senator thought about the expression on the usual poker-faced aide's face listening to his story. The man's forehead became a field of furrows, deepening and expanding with each of his revelations. The senator smiled remembering the change in Aaron's facial expression when he had mentioned the word, *formula*. "Without a strategic formula, the Oxybeast will not function properly."

"Formula?" the aide had asked. "Are we talking about some kind of mad scientist?"

Senator McDougal chuckled. "We could be. The formula is the relationship between an oxygen compression number and the temperature of the air above the corn."

"Whew, this is really getting complicated," Aaron had said, his eyes glued on the tall senator.

The senator leaned forward. "Thus far the formula hasn't been a problem regarding associated dangers." He paused. "I've been told that the oxygen will explode in certain situations!"

Aaron flipped his hands open. "Don't take me serious, Sean, but it sounds like you're getting into some sort of War of the Worlds scenario. Gads, I remember that movie. It really stirs the imagination."

———

AARON CRIER PULLED ON THE HANDLE of a kitchen cabinet. He reached up and grabbed a whiskey bottle, setting it down on the counter. Aaron's eyes locked on those of his son's in the photograph on the wall.

He poured some in a glass and sat down on the couch, mindless to the movie playing on television. This is only my second year working for the senator and it appears as if it's finally going to pay off, he thought. The big man is going to come into a lot of money and I should benefit. I will finally be able to afford to send my son to a specialist in Europe for treatment.

Aaron grimaced thinking about the telephone call he had received that fatal night. His son had been severely injured in a motorcycle crash...Darin's life was spared but he never regained consciousness...it had been six years since the brain comatose.

The first swallow of liquid hit the bottom of his stomach, giving him instant relief. He thought about his life in the past. Darin's mother had been a heavy drug user and destroyed my stature in the community and credit rating. I don't care a hoot what happens to her, but I care deeply about our son. I will do anything to get him to Europe to that specialist, he said to himself.

Aaron lifted up the glass and emptied it into his mouth. He swallowed and held his breath for a moment. Aaron got up and refilled the glass. He felt his problems lessen with each drink, even though his intelligence sounded warnings—the good feelings from whiskey are only temporary.

4

TOM HASTINGS TURNED HIS VEHICLE onto highway 10 and headed west. His attendance at the computer seminar, which he had just completed in Brainerd, led to his chance meeting of his prior Internet friend, Julie. Geez, I could've gone to a dozen other restaurants last night...quite the coincidence, he thought.

He switched to the left lane at Staples, knowing that the highway narrowed within the city limits. Tom noticed the veterinary clinic on his left as he slowed to thirty-five miles per hour. A minute later, he saw an ornate light-brown brick building, which stood majestically on a corner lot, adjacent to the highway. I wonder how many years ago it was built, he said to himself. It's an antique place now.

A few miles beyond Staples, he slowed for the town of Aldrich. A restaurant on the western edge caught his eye. I've heard some good things about that place, but it's for sale.

When he read the warning about a speed zone ahead, he paid attention. He slowed his vehicle to a speed of 50 when he entered the town of Verndale. He remembered a black-and-white police car flagging down a driver doing about 55, just in front of him a couple of years back.

Two miles out of Verndale, he saw the Whispering Pines Log Cabins billboard along the highway. As he passed, he thought of the time when he and his wife, Becky stopped. They ended up signing a contract.

The narrowing of the four lane highway and two stop lights in Wadena slowed his progress for close to ten minutes. He heard and watched a Burlington Northern-Santa Fe freight train rumble through town, leaving a long line of vehicles at the crossing.

Beyond Wadena, the highway remained narrow for a few miles before it returned to its normal four lanes. A few miles ahead, he saw the water tower which belonged to the town of Yorktown. He smiled noticing a billboard announcing a string of girl's basketball state championships.

The highway bypassed the town and eventually led to an overpass over the double railroad track. Pangs of hunger led him to exit the highway and drive into Pine Lakes. Tom drove into the parking lot of the Locomotive restaurant, immediately adjacent to the railroad track.

It had always been one of his favorite eating places, and he looked forward to a healthy lunch. The clanking of train crossing warnings and the subsequent blaring sounds of a freight train locomotive announced its entrance into town.

He walked across the parking lot and watched the train rumble by, feeling vibrations in the earth beneath him.

"How many in your party? Smoking or none?" the smiling hostess asked.

Tom followed her to a booth across from a section of gifts. A revolving rack of books caught his attention. The intersection that Tom saw out the window had continual traffic. While waiting for his order, he saw a pickup pulling a trailer with four ATV's in tow. It's a new way of life, he thought. Hot engines and wheels to separate families from their money.

Tom ate a waist-watcher burger for lunch and twenty minutes later, he pushed his garage door opener button...I'm home at last, he said to himself.

———

THE MONDAY MORNING DRIZZLE didn't deter Tom Hastings from heading to New Dresden for the mail. He turned his SUV onto the county highway and headed toward town. He slowed and tilted his cap passing by the cemetery where his wife was buried almost ten years ago.

He glanced at the two tennis courts, a part of the four-story high-rise on the edge of town. He thought about the women who he had played tennis with the past year. One of them ended up in prison for killing five guys. "I was damn near the sixth victim," he muttered, remembering an incident at the gift shop in Chilton Mills.

I don't know why the woman thought that I was one of the men who abused her mother when she was a little girl. I hadn't even heard of this town, back then, so long ago. Anyhow, the police and sheriff saved me from being victim number six.

New Dresden, a small town in west-central Minnesota, was surrounded by lakes. As a result, during the summer months, thousands of tourist and visitors frequent Main Street every day of the week. The population within the city limits was between 300 and 400.

He bounced his vehicle across the railroad tracks and pulled up into a spot in the parking lot of Stillman's Supermarket. As usual, his first stop became the post office. The mail box didn't bring him much satisfaction. He threw all but one item into a wastebasket.

Main Street was lined with businesses including a bank, grocery supermarket, a hardware store, a realty office, bar and grill and numerous gift shops. A post office in the middle of the street was the center of attention by just about everyone who lives in the area because there isn't any mail delivery service within the city limits.

"Hi," Ellie, the supermarket checkout woman, said as he picked up a newspaper from a rack.

"Geez, look at this, Ellie. That Brainerd incident is picking up some steam. I was there that day when it happened, you know."

"You were there....Tom, there you go again."

"Hey, I had nothing to do with it. I wasn't at the track where it happened. It was just a coincidence, me being in town that day."

"Tell me another one, Tom. We've been through this before, right!"

"Uh-oh, look at this picture. The fire-flash is huge...whoa, the police suspect arson...sabotage, perhaps...murder...."

———

BORDER'S CAFÉ DIDN'T APPEAR CROWDED when Hastings entered. He headed for a corner table where his friend Henry sat eating his lunch.

"Have a chair, Tom. Join me."

"I'll do that. Have you seen the front page, Henry? Look at this picture."

"Wow! I saw it on the news last night. One of the senator is from North Dakota, I heard...a nephew got killed."

"You're not going to believe this, Henry, but I saw the senator and two of his staff members at a restaurant in Brainerd the evening of the day it happened."

Henry lowered his sandwich, resting his wrists on the edge of the table. "You *what*? You were there!"

Tom nodded his head.

Henry returned his focus to the newspaper. He turned a page. "Hey, look at this, Tom...a two-headed calf." He passed the newspaper to Tom.

Tom read for a few moments. "It says here that the calf was born on a farm near Pelican Rapids in the 70's."

"Oh, I thought the picture was current."

"No, it's a picture of a taxidermist's work. Hmm."

Henry stood. "I gotta get back to work." One of the quarters that he dropped onto the table rolled. Tom caught it just before it fell off the table and tossed it into the pile.

While driving home, a mile past the cemetery, he spotted two large, white, delivery-like trucks turning onto a private gravel roadway. Hmm, wonder what Stuart is up to now, he thought. Maybe he's building a new house on the old farmstead.

Tom thought about his new rural neighbor, who had clearly established a reputation for growing and maintaining the most beautiful lawn in the area at his current home, located on the east shore of Border's Lake, a short distance from Mary Ann's restaurant.

Vehicles often slowed down more than normal on the highway passing by Border's Lake, mainly to feast their eyes on the beautiful grass.

During a recent walk up his northern trail, which ran nearly parallel with his western property line, Tom noticed that the field of corn next to his border was so tall that the old barn wasn't visible. Since Stuart had purchased the property, Tom felt more secure, knowing and trusting his neighbor more than the previous owners.

5

JULIE HUFFMAN TURNED OFF OF U.S. HWY-10 onto a state highway which led to Border's Lake. Her boss, Senator Sean McDougal, requested that she spend a few days at his lake home to assist in planning the itinerary for their next Washington D.C. visit.

She would have much rather returned to her apartment in Fargo.

So much needed to be done, Julie said to herself. She had just moved to her new living quarters, located just north of the Holiday Inn, and the place looked a mess.

Julie thought about her old friend, Tom Hastings, and the time they spent together at his home on the same lake as her destination. Those were delightful days, but I'm not sure I want to visit him, she said to herself. I'd rather not get into another relationship again. He's nice but we're so different.

Julie glanced at the number penciled on her notepad, which lay on the passenger seat, as she drove up the state highway. She slowed approaching each of the blue signs on the north side of the road. Julie looked for *54430*. Ah, there it is, she said to herself.

She flicked on her right-turn signal. Wow, the roadway is freshly blacktopped. Her eyes fell upon a closed gate and a small cubicle. She stopped in front of the gate...a burley looking man exited and walked up to her car.

Julie opened the window. She looked into the whiskered smiling face of the gateman. His large, penetrating green eyes reminded her of a cat. "I'm Julie Huffman. I work for the senator." She handed the gateman her ID.

"Okay, lady." The man pressed a button and the gate opened.

She drove slowly down the sloped roadway toward the senator's home. Julie noticed a fork in the road, the left branch leading to a circular drive in front of a colonial style house. Four huge white pillars framed the entryway.

Julie drove up the right branch, which continued past a four door garage, and ended in a parking lot in front of what appeared to be the senator's office. Julie parked and got out of her car. She saw a young man dash out of a door. "Hello, Miss Huffman, I'm Peter."

"Hello there, Peter."

The high school senior smiled wide. "I'll help you with your luggage."

"Thanks—which way do we go?"

"Follow that sidewalk over there." He pointed.

She noticed a long motel-like extension of the office with a number over each door.

The young man said, "Your unit is number two."

Julie carried one bag and a purse. Peter followed behind with her wheeled suitcase. Wow, he's one good looking young man, she said to herself. He owns the softest brown eyes that I've ever seen. She noticed his fluffy, dark-brown hair, dark facial skin and a tiny surface aberration on his right cheek. He's high school age...way too young for me.

Peter stopped. "Right here, Julie." He pulled the cart up a short walkway and opened the door.

He proceeded into her unit and left the case in the middle of the room.

"This is really nice of you, Peter. Thanks for all your help."

Peter nodded. "See ya later, Julie." He walked out and closed the door behind him.

———

THIS IS REALLY CUTE, JULIE THOUGHT as she looked around her small apartment. It included a small mini-kitchen L-shaped counter with refrigerator, microwave and a toaster oven. A small table with two chairs marked the center of the area. On the other side of the door, a small couch faced a television set. The door between the kitchen and television led into a small bedroom with bathroom and closet.

She walked into the bedroom and turned the latch on a rear door. She opened it and looked down a steep slope of tall grass and wild shrubs. It's here only for an emergency, she thought. Peeking around the corner of the doorway, she saw that the senator had a railed deck which overlooked the steep incline and clusters of trees.

It's a little stuffy in here, Julie thought, and she walked over to the window next to the door. Damn, it's stuck. She jiggled the frame until it opened.

She placed a palm against her face to stifle a deep yawn. Julie stared at her bags. Oh, what the heck, she thought and lay down on the bed. I adore the feeling of this mattress. Her eyes closed and she lulled herself into drowsiness and eventual sleep. A light rap on her front door awakened her an hour later. Julie arose from the bed and rubbed her eyes. "Jeez, someone knocked," she whispered and got to her feet.

Julie turned the knob and jerked open the door. She looked up into the authoritarian face of the senator's secretary, Isabelle Franks.

"Hello, Isabelle. What's up?"

The secretary frowned. "Julie, the senator wishes for you to join us for a meeting on his pontoon boat. Could you please be ready to go in half an hour?"

Julie nodded. "I shall be ready...oh, which way to the dock?"

"There's a walkway beginning just beyond the senator's office...on this side of his garages. It will lead you to his boat."

The door closed. Julie hurried to the bathroom to ready herself. Half an hour later, she locked her door and followed the sidewalk past the senator's office. She found the wooden walkway. It led to a small railed landing. Julie stopped and gazed at the trees across the bay. She watched an osprey shift directions and suddenly dive head first into the water. She held her breath watching the bird emerged from the splash—clutching a fish in its talons.

Down below, she saw a large pontoon boat moored to one side of a carpeted dock. A covered speed boat, anchored to the other side gently bobbed up and down. Putting her hand on a rail, she cautiously walked the wooden steps downward. After reaching the bottom, she stepped into the pontoon boat.

Isabelle sat on a cushioned boat seat, next to a young, dark-haired woman. "Julie, I want you to meet Veronica. This is her first day, coming to us after graduating from high school in Bismarck, North Dakota."

Julie smiled. She saw a dark-brown eyed girl whose dark hair splashed around on her shoulders as she stood. "Hi, Veronica, I'm glad to meet you. I'm Julie."

They shook hands. Julie envied the young woman's narrow waist, somewhat exaggerated by a generous bosom.

Julie heard a soft, cooing voice. "I'm very happy to meet you."

Veronica sat down, and Isabelle said. "Julie, you need to get to know Veronica. For starters, she's going to be your assistant."

Julie smiled and looked up at the sky. "I need all the help that I can get."

———

TOM HASTINGS HAD TAKEN A SEAT ON HIS DECK CHAIR, bottle of beer in hand, and a pair of binoculars next to him. He saw a fishing boat approaching slowly from the east. Tom watched a woman, sitting on a revolving seat in the front of the boat, flick her wrist. Her lure sailed across a bed of water lilies and splashed into a weedy area not far from his dock.

A man sat on the rear seat. He appeared to be busy working on his tackle as she slowly reeled in her line.

Tom lifted the bottle to his lips, thinking about his upcoming plans regarding his trip to Fargo. The very next morning, he needed to rise at 6:30 a.m. to arrive at the computer seminar in time. "This little fella' sure hits the spot," he murmured and set the bottle down.

Focusing his binoculars on the boat, he watched with interest as the woman's body tensed, her fishing pole bending downward. Bet she's got a big northern, he said to himself. The pole angulated, shifting from side to side as she worked the reel. Her partner stood, left his seat and approached the side of the boat with a net. "They got a big one," Tom muttered, grabbing the bottle and bringing it to his lips.

He heard the metal handle of the net clang against the upper rim of the aluminum as the man attempted to slip it under the fish. His eyes sighted a larger craft approaching from well beyond the small boat. Wow, sure looks like a big pontoon boat, he thought.

The man held up a large fish and attached it to a stringer before dropping it into the water. His woman companion had resumed her casting activity. Tom focused on the larger craft, wondering who it belonged to. That's the biggest pontoon boat I've ever seen on this lake, he said to himself.

He noticed several people milling around and sitting on the huge watercraft and reached for his binoculars. "It's the senator," Tom muttered. He must be loaded with bucks, he thought. Uh-oh, there's Julie....

THE SENATOR'S PONTOON BOAT made a long, slow turn at the far end of the bay. Most of the staff members sat on the twin three-seat padded couches near the front. The senator remained in the seats to the rear of the operator. He stood and walked forward. "I need to talk to ya all," he said, setting his large fingers on Julie's shoulder. "First, I want you all to greet the newest member of my staff, Veronica Lewis. Let's give her a big hand. Welcome, Miss Lewis."

An enthusiastic round of applause frightened two nearby loons, sending them into a dive.

The senator continued. "As you all know, I'm flying back to Washington tomorrow. My committee is going to vote on the Togo allocation request. The project has had a ton of publicity. Under no circumstances do I want any of you to talk to the press."

He took a deep breath and looked up at the sky. "As of this moment, I plan on voting *yes*."

The senator placed his hands on the rail. "The issue, which I am voting on, could result in some negative publicity—right now as well as any time in the future. My opponents likely will attempt to make political hay of my support for the Togo government. My conscience is perfectly clear. I sincerely do believe that they are going to spend the money on their electrical power expansion. The beneficial result, which we may not see for a few years, will actually mean a narrowing of our trade deficit." The senator puckered his lips. "Any questions?"

Peter cleared his throat. "Senator, why would anyone want to make political hay of aiding a responsible government like Toko? Any financial gains by them will lead to a more financially secure Africa...and hey, HIV prevention and treatment will get a boost."

The senator chuckled. "Peter, I'm glad that you're going along when we fly to Togo in a couple of weeks. You'll make a good representative."

Isabelle laughed loudly, leading to everyone else doing the same.

The senator smiled and nodded his head. "Well, when we get back to shore, you are all free to spend the evening as you wish. Just remember, the van will pick us all up at 7:00 a.m. sharp for the ride to the Twin Cities airport. Well, all of you except Peter. He's not making the trip...has some things to take care of in Red Wing. He'll be back later in the week."

6

REAGAN AIRPORT TERMINAL IN WASHINGTON D.C. bustled with people who had just arrived from Miami. The PA system blared. "Now boarding flight 126 to Minneapolis-St. Paul."

Julie and Veronica stepped forward up the ramp after handing their boarding passes to the attendant. They were followed by the senator and his top aide, Aaron Crier. The hostess in the first class section pointed to her left. You two are over there in seven and eight. "Senator, welcome aboard. You and Aaron are in number one and two."

McDougal removed a handkerchief from his pocket and wiped beads of perspiration from his brow. "Do ya want the window this time, Aaron?"

"Naw, you go ahead."

The senator set his briefcase on the floor and sat down. He adjusted the seat and closed his eyes. "Wake me up when we're airborne, Aaron, I've got an interesting topic to discuss with you.

"Sure thing, Sean."

Half an hour later, a stewardess closed all the overhead compartments and the P.A. sputtered, "Prepare for departure."

The Boeing 317 roared up the runway, getting airborne smoothly, and banking gracefully to the northwest. The cabin stuttered a little as the three jet engines propelled the plane toward its cruising altitude at approximately 33,000 feet.

Aaron glanced at the narrowing Potomac River and nudged the senator. "I've ordered us a martini. You said that you wanted to talk."

———

"AARON, I'VE HIRED A GERMAN SCIENTIST by the name of Hans Mueller. He's known to be an international expert on the properties of oxygen, especially in a compressed state. He has been briefed on the zillium discovery in Togo. The good news is that he's one of those guys who will keep his mouth shut...."

"Okay, what's the bad news?"

"I had to wire him a million bucks up front."

"Whew! I sure hope he knows his stuff."

The senator's eyes narrowed. He turned his head toward his aide. "Doesn't cost us a penny, Aaron. The Togos have taken care of it."

"When's he comin'?"

"Day after tomorrow...Thursday...the late flight into Fargo Hector."

"Who are ya gonna have meet 'em?"

"Julie, and I may as well send young Peter along. He'll be back from Red Wing by then and needs the experience."

"Good choice, Senator."

———

JULIE TURNED A PAGE OF THE BOOK SHE HAD BEEN READING. She glanced at Veronica, whose head nestled in a pillow, long strands of dark hair covering part of her face. Her right eye remained partially closed, exposing a narrow, dark-brown streak. Julie wondered about the senator's new intern...why does she ask me so many unimportant questions? And why does she take so many notes?

She felt a slight tremor as the plane streamed through a bank of puffy white clouds. Julie felt her seat move slightly as Veronica jolted awake and stiffened against the backrest.

"Where are we? Why is it so rough?"

Julie laughed. "We're only about an hour from the Cities. The plane is descending and taking us through those big, puffy, white clouds out there. They're usually turbulent."

"How can you sit there so relaxed?"

Veronica buried her face between her hands. "I don't like this
—"

Julie sighed. "Oh...I've done this so many times...so many times."

Julie felt a hand on her shoulder and looked up. Aaron stood above
her smiling. "Julie, we'll be putting on our seatbelts real soon. There's
something the senator requests of you."

"What's that, Aaron?"

"He wishes you to meet a passenger at Fargo Hector Airport
Thursday evening...the last flight...gets in about 10:30." Aaron
staggered slightly as the cabin experienced another tremor.

"Sure, I can do that. Do I go alone?"

"He wants you to take Peter with you."

Veronica flicked her chin upward. "Oh, can I go, too?"

Aaron laughed. "I'll ask the boss. Well, I better buckle up. It's
getting a little rough."

7

PETER NELSON LAY ON HIS BED at his parent's home in Red
Wing, Minnesota. He thought about his high school graduation earlier
in the year. Most of his classmates had enrolled in colleges. He had
decided to continue working and traveling with Senator McDougal,
and to pursue his college courses via correspondence.

I'm not much more than a gopher right now, but eventually, he
thought, I can see myself sitting in one of the hearing rooms in the
Senate. Peter felt excited regarding the debate about the issue of
financial aid to the country of Togo. According to last night's news,
they had been granted three billion dollars in aid to build power plants
and lines. The black man who represented the country pleaded and
pleaded.

Peter felt excited watching the Appropriations Committee debate
and vote on C-span. First a nay, then two yeas. As expected the votes
eventually tied at seven to seven. Senator Sean McDougal broke the

tie, resulting in loud applause from the audience. He noticed that the Togo representative raised a fist in the air. *If it was me voting, I'd have gone for it, too...what's another billion or two to our budget anyhow?*

Peter didn't feel very enthused about the upcoming bus ride tomorrow. *It would take most of the day to ride from Red Wing to Fargo, North Dakota...so many stops...going through the Cities.*

I do need my own vehicle, he thought. *Just perhaps the senator will keep his word and reward some of us a bonus...we, who make the trip to Togo, Africa, later this month.*

———

PETER ROTATED HIS TORSO and listened to the public address voice in the Greyhound crackle, "Fergus Falls coming up!"

He felt grossly uncomfortable after spending most of the day attempting to find a comfortable position on his seat. Peter stood and stretched, twisting his torso from side to side. He sat back down and closed his eyes while the bus filled with new passengers at the depot.

Fifty minutes later, he saw the *Moorhead 12 miles* and the *Fargo 15 miles* signs. Sitting up, he began to place his reading and writing material into a briefcase. Peter looked at his watch. *Gosh Almighty, I've been in this tube almost the entire day. It's almost 6:00.*

At last the bus turned off the Interstate at the Hwy 52 interchange. As it pulled into the Fargo depot, he saw Julie Huffman standing on the sidewalk...*aha, I've got a ride,* he said to himself, feeling great.

Peter liked Julie. She reminded him of his mother...especially the warm smile that he saw on her face as he stepped off the bus. He especially liked her warm hug. "Hey, thanks for pickin' me up, young lady."

"My pleasure, Peter...how was your week?"

"Boring...I'm anxious to get back to work. Traveling by bus is not my favorite thing. I've been in that monster most of the day. How was the trip to Washington?" Peter asked.

"Anything but boring. The tension I felt during the roll call for votes was awesome. You should have heard the groans when Sean voted 'Aye.' Some nut in the back of the room yelled, "You'll be sorry!"

Julie turned her steering wheel to the right and drove into the parking lot of the Holiday Inn. She stomped on the brake to avoid colliding with a delivery truck that didn't yield. "You dirty—"

Peter ran his left hand fingers over his right wrist that had been jammed when he stuck out his arm against the dash to keep his body from flying forward.

"Did you see that?—the nerve of that guy!" Julie exclaimed.

She stopped her light brown convertible in an empty spot in the parking lot. "Well, it wasn't very smooth, but I got you here."

"You sure did...and I appreciate it," Peter said and exited the car, holding the door open.

Julie turned toward him. "I guess that I haven't mentioned it before, but the senator wants you to go with me to meet a plane tonight."

"Tonight! I'm ready to have something to eat and hit the sack. Meet a plane, huh. Who's on it, Henry Kissinger?"

Julie laughed. "No....Tom Cruise."

She emerged above the top of the car and quickly walked around to the front. "Peter, here's the key. You're already registered...room 242. You don't need to stop at the desk. Everything's been taken care of. Here's my phone number if you need anything. Oh, by the way, we're picking up a scientist."

She handed him a card. "Oh, what the heck, I'll walk with you to the stairway."

The door of the motel opened into a long, wide lobby, the sides lined with stuffed love seats and chairs. They all appeared empty except for a man sitting in a lounge chair reading a newspaper. Peter noticed two people behind the L-shaped check-in counter. Ignoring their stares, he walked toward the stairway.

"Don't lose my card. Better put it in your billfold," Julie said.

He smiled widely and said, "A scientist! Sort of like the Frankenstein one?"

Julie laughed. "I'll tell you more about him later, wise guy. Please be down in the lobby by 10:00."

"Will do," Peter said, pulling his suitcase toward the motel front entry, waving as Julie drove off.

As he turned the corner after the first few steps he turned and saw the man who had been reading a newspaper rise.

———

PETER STOOD UNDER THE ROOFED UNLOADING AREA and watched for the tan convertible. He admired the perfectly round, bright moon on this August night. He closed his mouth and inhaled deeply. The air as expected smelled of vehicle exhaust, but in momentary instances, he detected the odor of a farmer's harvest. Peter looked at his watch. Come on, Julie, where the heck are you? he asked himself.

A black Lincoln Continental pulled up and a portly, dark-skinned man got out the passenger side. He wore a pin-striped suit and tan wide-brimmed hat with a wide black band. Peter felt a chill while the man continued to smile and focused his small black eyes on him for a few moments. The wide forehead and puffy cheeks reminded Peter of a farm animal on his uncle's farm. Without saying a word, the man entered the motel.

"Ah, there she is," Peter muttered, watching the convertible take a left off Thirteenth Avenue and turn into the parking lot. The wheels squealed lightly before the car came to a stop. The passenger's side window came down.

Julie leaned over, her cheeks puffed as she smiled widely. "Okay there, young man, are you ready to go?"

Peter got in and slammed the door shut. "Here I go again. What adventure can I expect next?"

Julie chuckled. "We are picking up a famous German scientist." She turned her car onto Thirteenth Avenue and headed for I-29.

"Take it easy, Julie, you'll get a speeding ticket."

Julie's eyes danced with excitement. "Catch me if you can, copper."

"It's your skin," Peter said, checking his seatbelt.

Minutes later, the convertible turned onto the approach to

Nineteenth Avenue North. She took a left at the stoplight and headed toward the terminal. Julie parked her car at the curb in the unloading zone. "Let's go get the German, Pete," she said and jumped out of her car.

"Can you leave the car right here? The sign says, 'unloading only.'"

"There's hardly anybody around, Pete. Come on."

Peter followed Julie through the terminal door and onto the escalator. She carried a cardboard sign, reading *Senator McDougal.*

"Here, Pete. You hold the sign up over by the gate. I'm gonna take a peak into the gift shop."

Peter took the sign. The uniformed security guard standing next to the gate yawned deeply and covered his face with his hand. Peter walked over to him and said, "Long night, sir?"

The guard chuckled, looking down at Peter. "Looks like the senator's expectin' some one, huh?"

The PA blared, "Flight 405 has just arrived from Minneapolis-St. Paul. The passengers will be disembarking shortly."

Whatever gave that goof the clue, he said to himself. He anxiously looked through the glass and saw the first passengers enter the gate waiting area. His eyes fell on the fourth man in line, a short, stately built man with huge black eyebrows. His thick, graying hair, parted in the middle, stretched down to his ears. The man wore thick-lenses eye glasses with round, dark-brown frames.

Peter glanced toward the gift shop. Just as he had hoped, Julie approached. He waved and cupped his fingers over his mouth. "I think I see 'em."

Peter moved over by the gate and watched the short man's eyes. He saw them lock on the sign that he carried. "It's him, Julie."

"I am Hans Mueller. You are Senator McDougal, yes?"

Peter chuckled.

———

JULIE TURNED HER CONVERTIBLE onto Nineteenth Avenue North and headed west. She sped onto the approach to I-29 and exited on Main Avenue, continuing on to West Fargo. "Peter, would you check the directions the senator gave us?"

Peter grabbed a piece of paper from his breast shirt pocket. "Ah, let's see. You keep on going west until you cross the Sheyenne River. Then, take the second left. That should be Eight Street. Our destination is Kurtz Manufacturing—it should be on your right in the second block."

"Thanks, Pete." Julie turned her head. "How are you doing back their, sir?"

"Meen fine—thank you."

Peter smiled. "Okay, there's West Fargo city limits, Julie. Hmm, it shows here that the Sheyenne River is not far past Sheyenne Street, the main north-south thoroughfare through the business district."

Julie pressed the brake hard to prevent from going through a red light. "Aha, Sheyenne Street—the river should be there—straight ahead."

"Turn left at the next intersection," Peter said.

Julie slowed her car and peered at the buildings to her right. "It's supposed to be in the second block, you said?"

"Yup, and there it is. Kurtz Manufacturing!" Peter pointed.

Julie stopped the car and looked back at her passenger. She pulled on the trunk knob and turned toward Peter. "Would you help Mr. Mueller with his luggage?"

Peter nodded and got out of the car. He opened the back door and smiled. "Out you go, sir."

The scientist nodded his approval and exited.

Peter removed three cases from the trunk and set them on the pavement. "Hey, Julie, I'm gonna need a little help. There are too many cases for me to make in one trip."

"Sure seems quiet around here," Peter said as he set two of the cases down by the door with an overhead light. "Let's hope someone's home and lets him in."

Peter's eyes narrowed as he watched a black Lincoln Continental drive by slowly on the street. I wonder if that's the same one I saw at my motel? Sure looks the same, he thought. The door to the office opened.

Peter and Julie each made two trips, carrying the cases to the door. The scientist followed them on their final carry.

"Mr. Mueller, I presume," a deep-sounding voice said.

A tall, broad-shouldered person stood and smiled in an open doorway. The man's face remained in the shadows of the overhead light while he reached a long arm out to the scientist. They shook hands.

"I am Mueller," the scientist said. "Have I come to the right place?" he added.

"Yes, welcome, Mr. Mueller." The man motioned for the scientist to enter. "Just set the bags inside. I will see to it that they are delivered to his quarters. You two may leave now."

After Peter sat down in Julie's vehicle, he asked, "Do you see that black Continental driving by?"

"Yes, what about it?"

"That's the second time since we got here. Also, I think I saw it at my motel."

"It's not our problem, Peter. We did the delivery, and now it's time to go home and get some rest."

"I'll buy that. Drive on, James."

8

PETER SAT IN THE SENATOR'S OFFICE AND LISTENED to his instructions the next day. He nodded for a third time and noticed the senator's expression had changed. His smile had disappeared and Peter detected a frown. Peter raised his chin, his eyes following the tall man as he pushed his chair back and stood.

The senator stooped slightly and placed a key into the lock of a desk drawer, turned it and pulled the drawer open. He walked out from behind his dark brown oak desk, holding a large, brown manila envelope in his large, bony fingers.

"Pete, I need this to be delivered exactly at midnight to a location in West Fargo." The senator cleared his throat. "The address is written on the front. It's the same place where you and Julie dropped off Mr. Mueller last night."

"Why at midnight?" Peter asked, cringing, realizing that he had overstepped his bounds.

"Assuming you will be taking a cab, there shouldn't be any problem finding it."

"Cab?"

"Yes, I'll send one to your hotel. I want you to be in the lobby at exactly 11:30. I cannot emphasize the importance of the timing."

"No, guess not...ah, the cabbie is going to wait for me, isn't he?"

"Of course, Pete, but remind him just the same."

Peter grasped the envelope with both hands and nodded. "Yes, sir, I'll take care of this for you."

"I want you to go down to the street. Julie will be by momentarily to pick you up."

"Okay."

———

PETER STOOD OUT ON THE BROADWAY SIDEWALK watching the traffic move at a brisk pace at shortly after 5:00 p.m. Peter placed a hand over his left ear as an older model Dodge cruised by with the window open. That idiot has his speakers on full blast, he said to himself. I like loud music but not that kind. "Come on, move it along, moron," Peter muttered.

Looking up, he saw the number 230 above the entry to the office high-rise. "Here, let me help you," Peter said to an elderly woman who struggled to get out of the office building. He held the door open wide while she passed through.

"Thank you, young man," her ailing voice crackled.

"You're welcome," Peter responded and eased through the revolving door. He carried his blue tweed suitcase in his left hand, but clung to a black case with the inner part of his other arm. I can't let the senator down, he thought. I need to guard that envelope with my life.

He heard the honk of a horn and spotted Julie's car double-parked in the street. Moving quickly, Peter slipped between an SUV and a pickup to reach the waiting car. He opened the back door and tossed the suitcase onto the seat. After sitting down in the passenger seat, he sat down and clutched the black case on his lap. "Go," he said.

Julie took a sharp left onto First Avenue and drew a horn from the vehicle behind. Peter laughed. "Atta girl, you cut that fella off slick as an icy road in December—good job."

"Better fasten your seatbelt, young man. You haven't seen anything yet."

Fifteen minutes later, Julie turned her car into the approach to the Holiday Inn across the street from the West Acres Mall. She pulled into a parking spot between a blue van and a red sedan. Peter opened the door and grabbed the suitcase. "Thanks for the ride, Julie. I hope you get back in one piece."

He walked quickly across the lobby floor, paying no attention to two men sitting in separate chairs. They both lowered their reading material and appeared to be watching Peter as he took two steps at a time.

———

PETER HAD WATCHED THE NEWS ON TELEVISON. He worried about staying awake for the next hour and a half. He filled a glass of water in the bathroom and set it down on the stand by the bed. He propped up two pillows, making sure that he wouldn't fall asleep while watching.

The minutes crawled by and he continued to look at the clock radio on the stand. It's time at last, he thought, and jumped off the bed. He slipped his loafers on and put on a jacket. Peter grabbed the small black case from the dresser top and slipped his key card into his shirt pocket.

Peter walked down the steps and stepped onto the lobby floor. He wore a tan jacket and gray jeans—no hat. His eyes darted from side to side, scanning the lobby. Why am I so nervous? he asked himself. There's no one around, but why should I care?

Peter glanced at the large clock fastened to the wall behind the check-out counter. "It's only 11:30. I've got plenty of time," he whispered. He moved the black case from his left hand to his right, pressing the packet tightly against his waist, and proceeded toward the door.

The sound of loud voices caused Peter to turn his head. A man and woman had entered the lobby, coming from the direction of the opening in the wall which led into the bar. Peter passed through the first door and stepped into the small vestibule. He peered through the glass outer door, but didn't see a taxicab. The door behind him opened and the noisy couple entered. "Hello there, young feller...gotta big date tonight?" the man asked.

Peter smiled and shook his head. "Have a good one," the man added and guided his woman through the second door.

Here it comes, Peter said to himself, and tightened his grasp on the case. A blue and white taxi came to a stop in the roofed unloading zone. The driver's head emerged from behind the top of the cab, shielding his eyes with a hand. When he saw Peter, he waved.

Peter moved through the door and walked to the taxi. "Are you Peter?" the driver asked, holding a rear door open.

"Sure am."

"Get in, please."

The taxi turned right on Thirteenth Avenue and headed west. After moving through several intersections, the driver flicked on the wipers as drops of rain splattered the windshield. Peter glanced at the Applebee's sign and wondered why there was all the mystery and suspense regarding this delivery.

I know better than to question my boss, he thought. I just do what I am told.

Back at the motel, a second taxicab made a stop in the unloading zone. The driver, a short, round-faced man, got out and approached the door. He paused, looking around as if searching for someone. The driver opened the motel door and entered the lobby, remembering his instructions. The senator's aide was supposed to be waiting by the door.

His eyes rolled as he looked around. Shrugging his shoulders, he walked to the desk. "Have you seen a young man hanging around...about 18 years old...taller than me?" The cab driver placed a hand about 12 inches over his head.

"There was a young man around about half an hour ago. He left in a cab...different color than yours."

The cabbie took his cap off and scratched the top of his head. Now what the....

———

THE WEST FARGO CITY SIGN appeared on Peter's right as the taxi continued to head west. He saw the driver flick the right turn signal before coming to a stop. Peter recognized the street sign from the previous night, *Sheyenne St.* A short distance later, the taxi stopped for a red light—the left-turn icon on the dash blinking.

They crossed a bridge and the taxi slowed. It took a left turn and pulled up in front of a large building. Peter felt threatened for the first time. This wasn't the same building that he and Julie had delivered the scientist to the night before. It looks like a warehouse, Peter thought.

The cab driver turned his head. "This is it—the address they gave me. Doesn't look like anyone's around." He lowered his head and pointed. "That's it right there—number 304—the one with the light over the door."

Peter grasped the latch and opened the cab door. He cautiously stepped out onto the asphalt. Suddenly, without any warning, the taxi took off. "Hey! Wait! You're supposed to wait for me," he blurted.

The taxi took a sharp left and headed for Main Avenue. Peter's mouth, still agape, gradually closed. He took two deep breaths and softly said, "What the heck is going on here?"

He saw the headlights of the taxi disappear as it turned right onto Main Avenue and sped away.

Peter shrugged his shoulders and walked toward the door. He stopped three steps short and looked around. Low hanging clouds gave the area an eerie feeling. Why the heck did the taxi take off?

A pair of bright headlights startled him. They came from the direction of Main Avenue. A black sedan turned into the parking lot and approached slowly. Peter held the black case tight to his chest. The auto pulled up abreast and the passenger window slid down. The rear door opened. He heard a raspy voice. "Get in the car."

Peter took a step toward the vehicle and hesitated. This doesn't look right at all, he said to himself. He took another step toward the car. "I don't think so," he muttered and took off toward the building.

Peter ran hard, his thoughts flashing back to the days when he played halfback on the Red Wing High School football team. He ran for the corner of a high chain link fence, an extension of the building. He heard car doors opening and slamming shut. Without looking back, he ran along the fence as hard as he could, noticing a metal building to his left. He stopped to catch his breath when he got near the end of the fence, clutching the case in his right hand firmly.

Looking back, he could see movement, and heard running footsteps. "Jesus, help me," he muttered and continued to run, hoping that he wouldn't run into a dead end.

Suddenly, Peter realized that he had moved beyond the fence and the building. He stopped to listen. They're still after me, he said to himself frantically, and took a hard left, feeling lucky that he was out in the open.

Plodding southward, he came to the southeast corner of another fence. He could see two more commercial buildings to his left and the tops of houses straight ahead and farther south. Not certain if his pursuers were still following, he took several deep breaths and headed for the houses.

When he approached the back yards, he uttered, "Uh-oh," and stopped. That vehicle moving along the street ahead could be them, he thought. He squatted down on one knee and remained still to catch his breath and watch.

Moments later, Peter stood, trotting and angling toward an area of the street well behind where the black sedan had passed. He raced across the pavement and continued into the next block, eventually stopping at the rear of a garage. Peter cautiously walked onto the driveway and saw the front door of a house.

Gasping for breath, he pushed the doorbell. Nothing happened.

He pushed it again and heard the sound of footsteps. The door opened. "Yes, who is it?" a man said.

"This is an emergency. I need to make a phone call."

"Should I call the police?"

"Not necessary....If you could, sir, would you dial the number on this card?"

The man took the card. "You stay right here. I'll see what I can do."

He returned shortly and handed Peter a phone. "There's a woman on the line."

"Oh, God, thank you, sir." Peter spoke into the receiver, "Julie, is it you?"

"Hellooo, Peter, what's up?"

"Julie—Julie—I need your help."

"Peter? What's going on?"

"No time to talk. Could you pick me up? I'm at a house in West Fargo."

"West Fargo? What the blazes are you doing there?"

"Never mind! The address is 816 Fourth Avenue—oh heck, somewhere between Main Avenue and—"

"Seventh Avenue," the man added.

"Seventh Avenue...I'm still on the west side of the river."

"Just a second, let me write this down," she said. "816, Fourth Avenue—okay, I'll be there as soon as I can."

———

PETER THANKED THE MAN WARMLY and sat on a front step. The overhead light remained on and he felt concerned that his pursuers would drive by. He did need the light on to guide Julie when she drove up the street. At least, I hope she finds me, he thought. A vehicle approached from the west. He shielded his eyes with a hand and held his breath as it passed by.

Two more vehicles passed and he finally saw the headlights of a car which was moving along at a brisk pace. That's her, he said to himself. The car slowed and pulled into the driveway. The driver's side window opened and Peter felt greatly relieved seeing the smiling face of Julie Huffman.

He dashed around the car and opened the passenger door. "You're a sight for sore eyes, Julie," Peter said and reached out to tap her shoulder.

"I suppose that I shouldn't ask what the hell you're doing here in the middle of the night, and what's in that black case?"

"Julie, I've got a problem...not sure if I should head straight home to Red Wing or face up to the senator. He gave me this package late yesterday to deliver to an address here in West Fargo. Something went wrong. I literally ran away from what appeared to be serious trouble for me."

"The senator has a meeting at 9:00 in the morning—in his office. Perhaps after it's over—about 10:30, you can talk to him."

9

SEAN CLENCHED HIS TEETH. "Aaron, I didn't tell you this before because the committee may have subpoenaed you before the vote. You could have been forced into telling a lie."

The senator's top aide's poker face didn't change expressions one bit while he waited for more.

"The money—three billion—which has been appropriated for Togo is mostly not going to be spent on electrical power."

"Sean, is that Togo representative playing games with you and the committee? Are they going to spend the money on arms?"

"Aaron, it goes a lot deeper than that. Have you ever heard of an element called zillium?"

"No, can't say that I have."

"What's happening in Togo is the most exciting thing that I've ever heard of in my lifetime. The Togos really needed the money to develop a series of mines. The zillium that I mentioned earlier has a unique property. When you pass compressed, highly-concentrated oxygen over it, it generates controllable energy."

Aaron whistled. "I think I know what's coming next."

"Yes, Aaron, that energy has the potential to replace oil—goodbye to gasoline and diesel engines."

Aaron placed a hand over his heart. "I'm excited. Tell me more."

"Listen to this. I have a pending patent on a machine which sucks the high-intense oxygen from the narrow band of space just above a maturing field of corn."

The senator reached into his desk and pulled out a photo. "Look at this."

"Hey, it looks a lot like one of those big-wheeled farm sprayers."

"Yes it does, Aaron...but...but, instead of 10 foot wheels, these are two stories high. See that bluish looking tank beneath the axels. It's suspended with a hydraulic lift so it can be raised or lowered. The narrow screened, front opening sucks up the oxygen.

"Now get this. It feeds its own oxygen fueled engine. It can run up and down a field for close to a month—all on its own. All that the operator, seated in that small cab above, has to do is reverse the Oxy-Beast when it reaches the end of the field. Did you ever study *perpetual motion* in school?"

"Can't say that I have."

"You're looking at a picture of it right now. The best news of all—is that zillium has a long shelf life—darn near that of infinity. The exhaust from the beast is simply more oxygen. No toxic fumes—can you believe that?"

The senator grasped his coffee cup and brought it up to his lips. Setting it down, he smacked his lips together. He looked at his watch. "Damn, it's almost 10:30. Where the heck is that Peter? I sent him out to do a delivery last night. You know...what I'm talkin' about?"

"Oh, yeah...that."

"If the kid didn't do the job, he's gonna hear from me...big time...."
He turned his head toward the door hearing a gentle knock.

"Yes."

"Senator, Peter needs to talk to you."

"Send him in."

———

SENATOR MCDOUGAL'S CHIN DROPPED. His eyes glared at the black case.

"Sir, let me explain," Peter said, his voice stuttering.

The senator sat down and ran his fingers over his forehead. "Let's have it. What happened?"

Peter's face flushed. He talked rapidly and explained the taxi cab incident and the ensuing chase.

"Please take the envelope out and place it on my desk, Peter."

Peter sheepishly set the envelope down. "Anything else, sir?"

"I have another job for you later today. Please be here at 1:00."

"Yes, sir." Peter left the room.

After the door closed, the senator slumped back in his chair and looked at the ceiling. "Aaron...we have a problem."

A perplexed look came over his aide's face. His eyes narrowed as he waited for more words from his boss.

"We have a leak. Someone from my staff ratted on us regarding last night's delivery. I purposely set Peter up as a decoy. He got picked up by the wrong cabbie. Someone is on to us...."

"You mean that you deliberately placed that young man in danger."

The senator smacked the envelope against his wrist. "He really wasn't in any danger. They would have simply taken the envelope and let him go."

"How do you know that?"

"They can't afford to have the police looking for them. Besides, if anyone could get away from whoever it was, it would be Peter. That young man is a tremendous athlete."

———

AARON CRIER TOOK THE ELEVATOR DOWN and walked out onto the sidewalk on Broadway, his mind bustling, thinking about the senator's new revelation. I was confident of the Togo connection, but never totally sure, he thought. "Now I know for certain!" he muttered.

He walked to the corner of the block and waited for a green light. I need good thinking time, he said to himself. After crossing, he entered the Broadway Saloon.

An hour later, Aaron felt totally relaxed, escaping the internal tensions that pulled at him from different directions every single day. Should I toss right and wrong out the window, and do what I have to do...or do I stay within the framework of the law, and do the best I can? he asked himself over and over again.

I sure did one thing right, he thought. I have a new identity as of two years ago. Aaron smiled. It actually happened because of the nasty trail my wife had left behind us...debt and ruined reputation. Drugs ruined her and she almost succeeded in pulling me down, too. It's possible that the Federal Government will catch up with me, meanwhile....

10

TOM CROSSED THE RAILROAD TRACKS and rounded Purgatory Curve on his way home from New Dresden. He thought about the two large trucks which he had seen drive down Stuart Eldridge's farmstead roadway. I've got to stop and see what's going on. If he's building a new house, I need to know.

The gravel roadway to Stuart's property had a green streak of grass up the middle, showing it had had limited usage. The large *Dead End* sign jumped at Tom as he slowly drove up the road. He came to a fork where a *Minimal Maintenance* sign stuck to a crooked post. It probably refers to either one of the roadways, he thought, knowing that the county sets up its signs in that manner.

Tom drove onto the left fork, over a small rise and came upon a metal gate. To his surprise, two men leaned against the inside. Tom slowed his vehicle and noticed both of them wore camouflage clothing. They're either hunters or military guys, he thought, frowning. He touched the brakes and stopped his vehicle.

The two men watched him as he got out and approached. "Hi, guys. I'm curious to know if Stuart is building a new house. I saw a couple of trucks come in here earlier in the day."

One of the men smiled at his partner. "New house—I don't think so—sorry, but you cannot proceed any farther."

"What the heck is goin' on? I know Stuart. He wouldn't do this."

"I'd advise you to turn that thing around and leave immediately."

The smile on Tom's face widened. He scratched the sideburn in front of his left ear. His smile disappeared when he saw one of the men lower his hand to what looked like a holster. Without saying another word, Tom got back into his vehicle, turned it around and sped toward the highway.

Tom turned right on the county highway and drove to Stuart's house. He's not home yet, he said to himself. I'll stop by later. As he drove up his own roadway, Tom shook his head. What the heck is going on over there? he asked himself. This is weird.

He went to bed after downing two glasses of wine and fell asleep immediately. At 2:20, he awoke and couldn't go back to sleep. Tom's mind kept flashing the vision of military men at Stuart's gate. What? Why? he asked himself, over and over again.

———

TOM HASTINGS TOSSED AND TURNED UNTIL 6:30 A.M. He finally fell into a deep sleep. At 7:45 a.m., he awoke, startled. The dreams he had were too confusing for him to understand. *Stuart, his neighbor and friend, had joined the Foreign Legion. He was dressed in military getup, and warned Tom not to come one step farther, or he would shoot.*

Jerking and throwing the covers aside, Tom hustled down into the kitchen. He got the coffee started and walked over to his computer. He felt sad seeing a cat clutching the body of a baby rabbit between its teeth. Three weeks ago, a brood of rabbits were born in his flower garden. Tom made sure that Mrs. Bugs Bunny did not get disturbed during the process. I did all I could, he said to himself. He shook his head and muttered, "It's all over...the killer cat has murdered and ate the entire brood."

The deadly behavior of the cat reminded him of the people at the gate who he had come across yesterday. Armed guards! What the hell is going on? he thought to himself. Geez, this is America...Minnesota.

———

THE STRONG BREEZE COMING OFF THE LAKE splashed against Tom Hastings's cheek as he walked out onto his sidewalk shortly after 6:00 p.m. He turned to face the wind and saw the trees on the far shore light up from a lowering sun. He hoisted the strap of his camera bag across his neck. Tom smiled and thought about the cold bottle of beer packed in ice, next to his camera.

He walked up the path, past the tennis court, and into the woods. Tom knew exactly which trail he would walk. It led to an area where his property line adjoined that of his friend Stuart Eldridge. He caught a glimpse of a deer's tail on the far shore of a weedy pond, with just a little water remaining in the center.

Tom came to a small hiking bridge. He paused on top of it and looked down, kicking at one of the small planks. Darn, it's loose. Got to fix it, he thought. He walked onward, following a trail lined with aspen and tall oak trees.

Farther up the trail, it merged with a larger one, which led to a second bridge. The bottom of the planks barely escaped the greenish, still water underneath. The beavers had built a massive dam, blocking the normal flow of water from feeding a very large slough.

Tom walked on, knowing that he approached the area where the trail neared the property line. A clearing in his woods allowed him to observe his neighbor's field and normally the farmstead where an original barn stood tall and straight, surviving a century of changes.

He stopped and looked at the corn. Geez, it's so tall that I can't even see the barn, he said to himself. Nature had disintegrated most of the barbed wire fence, which Tom had stretched across this space many years ago.

A green colored metal fence post, bent at the base, held onto two strands of it. Most of the wire in the fence had disappeared, falling into the tall grass. He carefully pushed back the small branches of prickly ash bushes and stepped across the remains of the fence, working his way to the edge of the field.

Curiosity tickled Tom's brain cells as he stood next to the field of tall corn. He got a glimpse at two crows shifting their positions in a cluster of trees near the cornfield. They squawked their disapproval of his arrival. He studied the birds and the blue sky beyond them pondering his next move.

Tom took the plunge and stepped into the field, slowly threading his way through the extraordinarily tall corn plants. He found a slightly wider space between two rows. Looking up, he estimated the height at close to nine feet. Tom walked deeper into the field. He looked around and could see nothing but the ground, the sky and the corn.

Tom had walked across this stretch of land before. He remembered the distance between the property line and Stuart's farmstead as slightly longer than the length of a football field.

He stopped to listen, hearing a strange hissing sound. It seems to be coming from my left, somewhere near the end of the field perhaps, he thought. He looked down at his walking boots. They had accumulated an edge of mud at the base.

Tom thought about the gate and the two guards that had treated him rudely. He wondered what he would see beyond the edge of the field. The terrain changed to a slope, telling him that he wasn't very far away from the farmstead.

He stopped to listen. The hissing sounded closer. As he stood silent, he thought that it came from somewhere between him and where he had entered. Tom felt his heart thumping against his chest, imagining some kind of monster walking around in the corn.

Ah come on, get with it...this isn't a movie, he said to himself. He continued to listen, the hissing sound dissipating, moving away toward the north end of the field, and finally ending.

He walked cautiously, his muddy boots sloshing in the wet soil and the tassels above brushing against each other. Tom stopped and could no longer hear the hissing sound.

Tom moved farther, the terrain leveling off, telling him that the distance remaining between him and the farmstead narrowed. The roof of the barn emerged above the corn. He stopped and admired the new shingles which Stuart had installed by himself recently. The hissing sound returned, so did the thumping in his chest.

Tom took a few more steps. He could now see some of the outside wall of the barn, the small square windows dancing between the corn plants. He froze in his tracks hearing the sound of voices, dashing his hope that the farmstead would be unoccupied.

The voices sounded like a conversation between two men, one with a high-pitched voice, the other gruff. Cautiously, Tom walked forward. He could now see the entire barn.

Stop! he warned himself. Tom saw something large and white, not far away from the barn. As he walked closer and closer to the edge of the field, he saw a second large white object. His thoughts battled between two possible decisions: proceed to satisfy his intense curiosity, or get the hell out of there.

Tom walked southward, away from the barn and the two white structures. There's that darn hissing again, he said to himself, crouching and remaining quiet, until the sound disappeared.

He cautiously walked toward the edge. Only a few rows between him and the clearing remained. He stopped. One of the white objects near the barn became a truck. The side of the truck box had been raised upward like a canopy, exposing a vast array of electronic equipment.

He saw the other white object, parked beyond the first one. Just as he expected, it too had a cab and looked like a truck. Just ahead of him in a cleared edge of the cornfield, he saw a cluster of bushes and trees.

The left side of his brain won. He moved across the clearing very quickly, stepping over a sheep fence and taking shelter in the trees. Peeking around a large basswood, he could see the second truck more clearly. The opened rear end showed a long narrow ramp extending to the ground. He gasped when hearing the two voices again, this time much closer.

Tom didn't dare move, afraid of being discovered. He crouched slightly and saw the two men walking toward the electronics truck.

The taller and skinner of the men wore a white jump suit. The other, a short stocky figure, was dressed in fatigues. He saw the slighter of the two walk up a ladder onto the truck platform and flick a few switches.

Tom coughed. A gust of wind blew something into his mouth. He coughed again, attempting to suppress it by placing a hand over his mouth.

He peeked around a tree. Both of the two men stared in his direction. One of them pointed. Tom looked back at the cornfield, estimating the distance he would have to run.

Tom bent his knees. He dared another look around the edge of the tree. The two men walked toward him slowly. Uh-oh, looks like one of them is carrying a rifle, he thought. He made his decision and ran toward the cornfield.

Tom tripped on the sheep fence and plowed head first into a stand of tall grass. He got up and saw the two men trotting toward him. One of them yelled, "Stop!" Tom saw him waving a pistol over his head. The man dressed in fatigues had raised his rifle.

Tom reached the cornfield. He heard the blast of a shot and the zing of a bullet passing over his head. Tom crashed full tilt into the rows switching back and forth between rows. He didn't look back until he had almost reached the top of the slope. He could just barely see the barn, only the shingled roof showing.

He couldn't see his pursuers, but heard plodding footsteps behind him. Tom veered to his right, expecting his heart to blow up at any moment. He dropped to his knees. The trudging behind him had stopped. Tom felt pain in his lungs as his system panicked, attempting to draw in more oxygen.

Tom remained still, hearing nothing but his heavy breathing and the dark green leaves and tassels above tossing in the wind. My pursuers must have given up, he thought and stood.

Tom made a few silent steps toward his property and stopped. He heard the hissing sound again. It seemed to be coming from north of him and got louder by the second.

He heard the rigid crackling of cornstalks. The sound got louder and louder. Tom felt too frightened and confused to move. He had his head down between his knees. Peaking upward, he saw a bluish mass coming toward him.

Suddenly, the ground behind him crunched. He looked left and saw a huge wheel moving through the corn...it was too late for him to run. The bluish mass attached to it passed directly over his head. His head experienced dizziness from the incredible sounds...such as he had never heard before in his lifetime.

Tom placed a hand over his mouth and held his breath, watching another massive wheel...it followed the first one and passed by him, too. He looked up and saw blue sky again. Mercy, he thought, whatever the heck it was that ran over me is gone...I'm still alive and not hurt. The hissing sound faded into the distance. Tom stood and moved as fast as he could toward his property line. Just before reaching the field's end, he stumbled and fell. Pausing, his confidence grew...the frightening, unusual sound had not returned.

Back in his woods, he rested frequently to allow his heart rate to return to normal before walking his trail home. Ten minutes later, he reached his house. After entering, he locked the door and dashed up to his bedroom. He brought his deer rifle out of his closet and opened the breech to make certain that it contained shells.

Reaching up on a shelf, he grabbed his .380-caliber automatic. Tom carried his two weapons around the inside of his house as he looked outside through windows. He didn't see anyone. What do I do now? he asked himself, glad to be home safely, but troubled at what he had seen and experienced.

Tom looked at the phone. Should I call the sheriff? he asked himself. I've been shot at! Sure I was trespassing, but I wouldn't shoot at someone who trespassed on my property. He sat and thought for a few minutes. I think that I should talk to Stuart first.

11

THE TERRIFYING INCIDENT in Stuart's farmstead stuck in Tom's mind like mud to a boot as he backed his vehicle out of his garage and headed up his roadway.

A mere two miles from his home along a county highway, his former wife, Becky, lay in peace. She had been murdered several years ago by terrorist who blew up a passenger airplane. He drove by the city park where a large sculpture of a loon overlooked Loon Lake and the beach area. Farther down, across the street, he glanced at the baseball diamond, the three white infield bases standing out like popcorn on a short-weave carpet.

Tom drove across the railroad tracks and parked in Stillman's Supermarket parking lot. He entered the post office and fished out his mail from a private box. Tom walked rapidly toward Stillman's grocery store and bought a newspaper. He headed across the street to Border's Café , hoping to see his friend Henry.

Tom had been aware that Stuart worked for Henry's firm. There isn't too much news that occurs in the area without Henry knowing about it, he thought.

Yes...there he is looking at the menu. Tom scooted across the room and sat down at Henry's corner table. "I'd ask you to join me, Tom, but I see you already have."

Tom laid his newspaper on the table. "Henry, what looks good today?"

"The special is good," Henry said, taking another bite.

Tom glanced at the writing on the blackboard and nodded his head. He turned his head toward a waitress who had just arrived. "I'll take the special and a coffee."

The waitress jotted down his order and left.

"Henry, I drove out to Stuart's farmstead yesterday. The gate was closed and there were two men guarding it. What the heck is going on?"

Henry laughed. "Stuart has a great imagination. He's always up to something. I don't see him very much. He comes in early, gets his work orders and leaves. He keeps his private life to himself."

"What time does he usually get done at the end of the day?" Tom asked.

"It depends on how far away he is, but I would guess he is usually home by 6:00."

Tom decided not to share his harrowing experience that he experienced in the cornfield...not now...not just yet. "Thanks."

Henry finished his lunch, dropped a few coins on the table and advanced to the checkout counter. Tom watched him work his way around the other tables and walk out onto the sidewalk. Henry stopped to talk with a man wearing stripped bib overalls. He got a salute while doing so. Tom laughed. That's Edgar Sandvik out there, he thought...the community's number one, weird character.

Tom left the restaurant and returned to his vehicle. He drove over the railroad tracks and around Purgatory Curve. He slowed while approaching the roadway to Stuart's farmstead. Shaking his head, he decided to drive past and head for home. I best leave that whole thing alone, he thought.

———

TOM SAT ON THE DECK WITH A BEER IN HAND. He checked his watch. It read 5:55. It's time to visit Stuart, he said to himself. He walked toward his front door and heard the phone ring.

Tom stopped. He picked up the phone. "Hello."

"Hi, Tom, this is Julie."

The heat that he felt in his cheeks spread quickly. "Julie, great to hear from you. What's up?"

"I would like to take you out to dinner at Mary Ann's. Remember when we used to go there regularly?"

Tom felt his heart thumping. "I'd love to go there with you. What day do you have in mind?"

"How about tomorrow?—Friday?"

"It's a date. Do you want me to pick you up?"

"Yes, but I'll have to let the gate man know."

"I know where the senator's lake home is, but what road do I take in off the state highway?" Tom asked.

"The turn is about 3-1/2 miles off the county highway, coming from your direction. His home number is 45214."

"Okay, how about 7:00?"

"Sure, see you then."

Tom hung up the phone and stared at the computer screen. "Julie," he whispered. "It's been a long time—a long, long time."

———

TOM TURNED HIS VEHICLE INTO STUART'S DRIVEWAY. He noticed Stuart, dressed in shorts, spraying weeds on the other side of his house. He got out of his vehicle. "Hi, Stuart."

"Hey, Tom, what are ya up to today?"

"You know, I really admire your lawn. It's simply the best."

Stuart looked up and smiled.

"Stuart, I decided to take a look at that old barn a couple of days ago and drove up your roadway. I noticed a new gate...and there were two men guarding it. What's going on?"

Stuart pressed the lever on his sprayer and the mix hit a stand of grass next to the concrete foundation of his house. "Oh, that must be those government guys."

"Government guys? What are they doing there?"

"Ah, I've agreed to allow the Department of Agriculture experiment with my corn. Both me and my renter make some extra money."

Tom scratched the back of his neck. He decided not to share his terrifying experience and getting shot at. "Wow, I wonder why they chose your field."

"I don't know, Tom. Maybe, it's because of the seclusion."

"Yeah, that could be it. Well, just keep working on that lawn and make the rest of us look bad."

Stuart laughed and Tom returned to his vehicle.

12

TOM GRASPED THE STEERING WHEEL of his garden tractor mower and rotated it for the final cut, a narrow strip of grass ahead of him. Moments later, he muttered, "Ah, done at last," and pushed in the button to stop the blades. The cowl clattered as he drove the mower over the slight rise in the sliding door opening of his larger garage.

He turned the ignition key off. When the engine backfired mimicking a gunshot, he thought about his run toward the cornfield and the zing of a bullet as it passed overhead. Tom glanced at this watch and thought about Julie. I've got an hour and a half.

While walking toward his house, he began to feel more tension. He walked directly to the refrigerator door and opened it. Reaching in, he grabbed a golden bottle of beer. His first long draw of the brew lessened the tightness which had been building in his stomach. What am I so nervous about? he asked himself. I've taken that woman out before. Relax, buddy.

———

AT FIVE MINUTES TO SEVEN, Tom turned his SUV off the state highway onto a blacktopped roadway, making sure that the numbers he had written down matched the ones on the sign. The small trees and brushes between the road and field reminded him of his roadway. He hit the brakes when a small deer broke from the trees to his right and scooted across. I don't need an accident right now, Tom said to himself, concerned about being on time for his date.

Uh-oh, Tom thought when seeing a gate. How am I going to get through that? He stopped and watched an ugly, burly looking attendant come out of a small cubicle. "You must be Hastings. Miss Huffman told us you would be coming by. Can I see your ID?"

Tom shifted in his seat, drawing his billfold from his hind pocket. He handed the man his driver's license.

"Okay." The gate opened.

Tom glanced away from the ugly, large green eyes and grabbed his license back. Geez, a rattlesnake looks a lot friendlier than that, he said to himself. I'm glad he didn't ask to look into my glove compartment. The date would have ended before it started. He had placed his automatic pistol in there before he left.

Tom drove over a small rise and down a steep slope. He fixed his eyes on the massive six round pillars and the huge house. Colorful flowers and plants filled the island in the middle of a circular driveway. He kept his foot on the brake and arrived at a fork in the road.

Tom turned right, following the right branch, which led to a long motel-like structure. As instructed previously by Julie, he parked his vehicle in the lot across from the large sign, which identified the senator's office. He exited his vehicle and looked for unit number two. A tall man stood next to one of the pillars in front of the senator's house. Tom's comfort zone became threatened feeling the gaze of a pair of eyes.

Tom walked up to the door and knocked. Julie answered the door immediately. "Hi, Tom, it's so good to see you again."

Tom stared into her blue eyes. He grabbed her by the shoulders and gave her a massive hug.

"Whew, watch the ribs," she said, laughing.

She dressed in a medium-blue colored denim dress with a long row of buttons down the front. She wore her usual smile. Tom listened to the clacking of her black high-healed shoes as she walked to the refrigerator. He sat down on the loveseat and eagerly awaited his glass of wine. Why am I so nervous? he asked himself.

Tom lifted the glass to his lips and felt the liquid all the way down to the bottom of his stomach. This'll take away my tension, he thought. Julie looks just as nice as ever. She hasn't aged a bit.

"So how are things with the senator?" Tom asked.

"He's a super busy man. I don't get to talk to him very much. I communicate mainly with his secretary. Every morning, she has an itinerary ready for me. I take it from there. Well, I see your wine glass is empty. Should we get going?"

Tom nodded. He stood and gave Julie another hug. "You look so great."

Julie reached up with a hand, sweeping a tassel of blonde hair away from her eye. They moved apart. "We better get going," she said.

———

MARY ANN'S RESTAURANT SAT MAJESTICALLY ON A BLUFF overlooking Border's Lake. Two peninsulas about a mile away jutted into the lake. One pointed north and the other directly at Mary Ann's. Between them, the water mass narrowed to form a long narrow bay.

Senator's McDougal's compound could not be seen from the restaurant. It overlooked the long narrow bay about half-way between the southern peninsula and the far extremity of the water. Tom Hastings's home perched on a hillside on the northern slope of the bay, about a half-mile west of the senator's.

Recently, the restaurant had changed ownership. Harold and his wife Mary Ann sold the restaurant to Jeremy Hanson, a young man who lived in the New Dresden area.

"Look at all those cars," Tom said as he looked for an empty space in the parking lot.

"There's one!" Julie exclaimed.

"Oh, dang, I missed it."

"You gotta be quick to find a Julie spot."

Tom laughed. He remembered the method which Julie had used in previous years when she drove. She easily qualified as an expert at finding an empty slot as near to the restaurant as possible.

Tom opened the door for his date and they entered the long narrow vestibule. A group of four people stood in their path, between them and the hostess station. "Looks like a bit of a wait, Julie."

Fifteen minutes later, they were seated in a booth across from the bar. "Thanks for the good spot," Tom said to a tall, blonde hostess.

"You're welcome. Carrie will be with you shortly."

"Look at that bartender—he's all over the place."

Tom smiled. "Oh, that's Randy. He usually does the work of three people."

"Anything to drink, folks?" the waitress said as she stopped abruptly in front of their booth.

Tom looked up, breaking into a wide smile. "Hi, Carrie, are you our waitress today?"

"Sure am."

"Carrie, this is Julie Huffman. She's an old friend of mine."

"Hi, Julie, welcome to Mary Ann's."

Tom continued to smile. "We'll have a bottle of Kendall Jackson Chardonnay."

"Okay," Carrie said and headed for the bar.

Moments later, Carrie returned with their wine and took their dinner orders. She briskly moved away.

"We're lucky, Julie—Carrie is one of the best waitresses here." He noticed a sudden change in Julie's expression. Her smile had faded and furrows formed in her forehead. Tom watched her eyes, following their glare. He saw a short, wide-hipped, dark-skinned man standing near the hostess station. The man wore a wide-brimmed, light brown straw hat and sunglasses. His head moved slowly from side to side, scanning the people in the area.

"Who's that, Julie? You have that concerned look on your face—that look—remember what went on at the Towers?"

Tom referred to the year he had rented an apartment in a high-rise in Minneapolis, near Lake Calhoun. He and Julie had been seeing each other often back then. A serial killer, living in Tom's building at that time, disrupted their well being more than once.

"It's someone who I've seen Sean with." Julie placed a hand over her mouth. "This is all confidential, but I'm concerned about some of the senator's visitors lately."

Tom watched Julie bring a wine glass to her lips. He noticed the furrows in her forehead had deepened as she set the glass down. "Do you think it has anything to do with the race track incident? I was there that day, you know—in Brainerd."

"Yes, I remember that you were there," Julie said, continuing to glare across the room. "That was at Lenny's—sort of an off-the-beaten-track place," she added.

Tom lifted a glass to his mouth. "Later, I felt confused, wondering how the senator could take his staff out for dinner after losing a nephew in the explosion."

Julie's face relaxed. "Here comes the food. I'm hungry."

The dark-skinned man had disappeared.

They ate in silence. Occasionally each would glance toward other sections of the bar area. Tom wiped his face with a napkin. "Julie, I've got another story for you."

Her eyes opened wide. "Now what?"

He explained his cornfield experience. Her mouth opened and she slowly shook her head when he described the huge wheels straddling him as they passed over.

"I'm still confused as to what happened and what I should do about it, if anything," Tom said.

Julie narrowed her eyes. "It could be a job for the sheriff to check out—or—or the FBI. Who knows?"

"According to my neighbor who owns the property, the Department of Agriculture is conducting experiments there."

Julie smiled. "Hanging around you very long could be dangerous. You seem to attract trouble—worse yet, trouble attracts you."

Tom laughed. "Do you suppose that's why we met?"

————

JULIE PASSED A PLASTIC CARD TO TOM. He turned off the highway and drove toward the senator's gate. He opened the window of his SUV and slid the card into the gate slot. The gate opened and he drove down the steep slope toward the senator's complex. He stopped his vehicle in the parking lot across from the senator's office. Tom turned off the engine and reached over and placed his hand on Julie's shoulder. "What do we do next?"

"Tom, I'd love to have you in and talk, but I've got a big day tomorrow. I'm hard pressed right now—a deadline for putting together a trip to Africa."

"For the senator, I assume?"

"Yes, and he's taking some of his staff along, including me and the two interns."

"Wow! You've been there before, haven't you?"

"A couple of times. This time the senator is going to Togo. I visited there when I was a college student. Actually, I hitchhiked across the country."

"You what! A college girl hitchhiking in Africa sounds pretty dangerous to me."

"No more dangerous than your taking on a cold-blooded killer in your dining room. Remember what happened after your neighbor Cushing got murdered?"

Tom shook his head.

"You can talk, Hastings. Less than forty hours ago, you were being pursued by some sort of monster." She pointed her finger. "You were doing the same thing that Tom Cruise did in the movie *War of the Worlds*."

Tom smiled and shook his head again. "Yeah, but a girl all alone, hitchhiking on an isolated highway in Africa! I don't even want to know what your mother thought about that."

Julie laughed. "Fortunately, she didn't know—I never told her— she would've flipped."

"Maybe I should take you over to Stuart's cornfield and just let you loose," Tom said, lifting his chin.

"Sure, and cheer while the monster—or whatever you call it— runs over me."

"When does this upcoming trip to Africa take place?" Tom asked.

"In a couple of weeks. I'll be hopping busy, planning right up to take-off."

13

Tom CHOSE THE SINGLE LANE COUNTY ROADS on his way to Fargo to attend a computer seminar. The early Monday morning fog in late August appeared to be thickening as he crossed a county boundary. Flocks of gulls swarmed around a large farm implement, converting golden stubble into black dirt, and creating a sea of worms.

The terrifying experience Tom had experienced in the cornfield a few days ago wasn't forgotten but had been placed on a back burner. Tom decided to accept Stuart's explanation of why a monster machine and trucks with electronic equipment operated on his land. Occasionally at night, he'd wake up in a cold sweat, suffering from a dream in which he was being chased by a massive wheel.

Tom looked at his watch. The seminar began at 10:00 a.m. He felt relaxed knowing that he had about half an hour to spare after he arrived at the Doublewood Inn. He sat down by a small table in the dining room and sipped on coffee, reading the *Forum*.

Gads, he told himself, you would think that the *Fargo Forum* would have gotten hold of any news about the monster machine if it was indeed a project of the Department of Agriculture. Hmm, maybe it's up to me to give them a call.

———-

TOM GLANCED AT THE TIME. Only 10 minutes remained for the final seminar session of the day. He looked up at Nicole, who he had met earlier in the day, and noticed that her head tilted to one side, a give-away appearance of fatigue. She had responded vaguely, muttering something about a company called Delvo Industries when Tom asked who she worked for and why she participated in the seminar. I guess it wasn't any of my business, he thought.

Her blood-red, well-manicured fingernails caught Tom's attention for most of the day. Nicole's hazel eyes, enhanced with light blue eye shadow, glanced around the room a great deal as the day wore on. Her thin face and light brown hair made her very attractive, Tom thought.

Tom and Nicole sat next to each other during the lunch break. Nicole had told Tom that she lived alone in a condo in the south part of town. She said that her attraction to computers went beyond the boundaries of her position at Delvo Industries.

He noticed that she showed sudden interest when he told her that he lived on Border's Lake in Minnesota. "Border's Lake—you have a lake home there?"

"Yup—"

"Hey, I'm somewhat deaf when it comes to understanding what the speaker is saying most of the time. How about if I buy you a glass of wine at Applebee's?—and, you can teach me what I missed."

Tom turned and looked right into her eyes, her smile showing the tips of her pretty white teeth. He nodded. "I'd be glad to help you—if I can."

"Of course you can," she said, grasping his wrist lightly with his fingers.

The speaker at the podium cleared his throat. "That's all folks. I appreciate you all coming, and I hope you all learned something today."

A generous round of applause followed. Nicole separated her palms and said, "Where's Applebee's anyhow?"

"Which one do you have in mind? There are two of 'em."

"The original one—"

"Yeah, just a few blocks from here—east on thirteenth."

Nicole nodded, a tight smile forming on her face.

"How about if I meet you there in an hour?" Tom asked, hoping that she wouldn't back out.

She bunched a fist and brought it up to her lips. "Hey, I've got a better idea. Why don't you give me a little more time, and we could go out to the Cork?"

"The Cork! Yeah, I've been there before—many times when I used to live in Fargo."

Nicole smiled mischievously. "To simplify the evening, why don't you pick me up?"

"Yes—"

She touched her lower lip with the tip of one of her long red fingernails. "At my place—it's real easy to find."

———

TOM SAW THE GRAY NUMBERS ON A SIGN next to the door. He swung his SUV into the driveway and pushed the button to roll down the window. Tom stepped out and glanced around at the other structures nearby. Real nice neighborhood, he said to himself.

He took a deep breath and pressed the doorbell. I've done this so many times before, but I'm nervous as hell, he thought. Who knows what I'm getting into? His tension increased as he saw the door knob turn.

"Good evening, Mr. Hastings. Won't you come in?"

Awesome, he thought. She wore a long, dark green dress, which snuggled tightly on the hips. Her black high heels clacked as she walked on the foyer tile.

Nicole pointed at the gray sectional. "Would you like something—to drink that is?"

"Sure, some wine if you have it."

"What kind do you like?"

"Chardonnay, or some other kind of white wine. I'm not that fussy."

She had opened the refrigerator door and raised a bottle in front of her eyes. "How about some Lindeman's?"

"Great...thanks."

"What's your favorite brand of computer, Tom?" Nicole asked, sitting down on the other end of her sectional.

"Dell...I'm all Dell."

Nicole nodded and gently tilted her glass. "Yum." She took a second sip and set the glass down on the coffee table.

Tom looked around the room. He saw several ornately-framed, classic-looking prints embellishing most of the walls. "You like art, I see." Tom said, raising an open hand toward a wall.

"Yes, I sure do."

"So how long have you worked for Delvo Industries?"

"Only one year....I moved here from Indianapolis."

"What did you do in Indianapolis? May I ask?"

Nicole looked away. She hesitated. "Pretty much the same thing —"

She took a sip of wine and swallowed. "So tell me more about your place on Border's Lakes. What part of the lake is it?"

"I'm on the north shore of a long narrow bay," Tom said.

Nicole cocked her head. "On the north shore, huh?"

"Yes...why?"

"Is it near Senator McDougal's place?"

"It's across the bay and down a bit toward the closed end. On a clear day, I can see his boats from my deck."

Nicole nodded her head. "I'd like to see your place some day...."

Tom gulped.

"Well, shall we get going?" she asked.

——

TOM SAW A NEW SIGN AT THE FARGO CORK & CLEAVER. He turned off University Avenue and looked for a parking spot. Tom glanced at his date. She sat so still, her hands folded in her lap. She must trust me, he thought. We've only known each other for less than a day.

"There's a spot," Nicole said, pointing one of her blood-red nails.

"Uh-oh...too late," Tom said and continued driving slowly. "Aha, there's one."

Tom quickly exited after removing the ignition key and dashed around to open the door for Nicole. She swung her long legs across and planted her heels on the running board. Tom reached out a hand and assisted her out of the vehicle. She lightly grasped the inside of his elbow and followed him to the door. Tom opened the two doors ahead of her and motioned for her to pass. "Two for dinner," he told the hostess.

"Name please?"

He gave her his last name and said, "We'll wait in the bar area."

"Okay, I'll come get ya."

The restaurant consisted of several small rooms and coves, separated by a low wall and see-through dividers. The long, narrow room where they headed after putting in his name had an L-shaped bar with some high tables and a fireplace in the corner.

They sat at one of the high tables and Tom ordered a bottle of white wine.

Nicole looked around, her mouth opened partially. "Speaking of the devil, that looks like Senator McDougal sitting at that table across the hall."

Tom nodded. He had seen the senator on television and in the newspaper many times. "Do you have a specific interest in the senator?" Tom asked.

"Well, yes I do—sort of."

Tom blinked his eyes waiting for the rest of her response.

"My daughter Veronica has agreed to work for him—as an intern to begin with."

A reddish, radiant glow formed in the center of Nicole's cheeks. Tom took a sip of wine and saw a concerned expression in her hazel eyes. Nicole chuckled. "You'll be neighbors for a month or so...."

"You mean your daughter Veronica?"

"Yes....Until October sometime."

———

TOM ASSISTED HIS DATE OFF HER STOOL after the hostess came and announced that their table was ready. They followed her and got seated in a room adjacent to the senator's.

He watched Nicole bring a glass to her lips with her deep-red fingernails, both the same color.

Tom raised his eyebrows. "I really don't know the man, but I do know someone that works for him."

"Who's that?" she asked.

"Julie Huffman, an old friend of mine."

"Is she a blonde?" Nicole asked.

'Yes, she is. Do you know her?"

"No, I don't, but I think—"

Tom frowned.

"I know who she is. My daughter will be working closely with her."

Suddenly, they heard a loud voice coming from the next room where the senator and his wife were having dinner. Tom saw two men standing next to the senator's table. One of them, a short man with wide hips and wearing a wide-brim hat, waved and pointed a finger at the senator.

"Looks like the senator has a problem," Tom said.

Nicole nodded. "I've heard that he has a lot of them." Her face twisted slightly and she took a sip of wine.

Tom noticed a second man standing. Also dark-skinned, he appeared much taller, and had kinky black hair and a narrow face with a narrow-beaked nose.

Tom watched his date frown and take another sip of wine. He turned his head toward the senator's table. The tall politician had risen from his chair and towered over the finger-pointing man. Long, brawny fingers reached out and grasped the dark-skinned man's shoulder.

"What do you see?" Nicole asked anxiously.

"The two guys who've been giving your daughter's boss a bad time just left."

The waitress returned to take their orders. Nicole asked her a lot of questions, pointing at the menu often. She finally settled on a specific entré.

Tom ordered a half rack of ribs and a salad. He lifted the wine bottle out of the container and filled both glasses. "So how much did you get from the seminar today?"

"I didn't understand half of it—found it hard to concentrate."

"The guy up front did talk a little fast," Tom said.

"I'm a novice when it comes to computers, but I'm willing to learn," Nicole said, rotating her wrists and opening her palms.

"It takes time," Tom said.

Nicole laughed. "So tell me about your place—your home on Border's Lake."

———

THE WAITRESS SAID, "IS THAT ALL FOR YOU TWO?"

"Yup, it is. Here give me the bill," Tom said.

"Oh, no, Tom, let's share it. Actually, you taught me so much today that I should pay for it."

Tom laughed. "I appreciate you having dinner with me, Nicole. I'll take care of it—deductible, you know."

Tom put his arm around Nicole's waist as they walked out into the parking lot. He wished that his vehicle had been farther away...a mile away. He opened the passenger door.

"Thanks," she said and slid onto the seat.

As Tom walked around to his door, he wondered if she would invite him in when they got to her place. He inserted the key and started the engine. "Well, what do you think? Should we hit the night spots?" Tom asked laughingly.

"You must be kidding."

"Yes, I am. I bet you're plenty tired after taking in the seminar all day."

"Yes, I am tired and I appreciate the dinner—your company, too."

"There it is. It's easy to find," Tom said and turned his vehicle into her driveway.

He turned off the ignition, turned his head toward Nicole and said, "I've really enjoyed the evening, Nicole. I hope that we can do this again."

"Tom, I have found you to be a delightful person, but this time around, I would prefer we stop right here. You understand, don't you?"

"Yes, I do." Tom opened his door, stepped out and hurried around to the other side. Nicole had opened the door and he assisted her onto the driveway.

"Goodnight, Tom," she said.

Tom kissed her on the cheek. "Have a pleasant sleep, Nicole."

———

TOM DROVE HIS VEHICLE INTO THE PARKING LOT of the Sleep Inn in Fargo. He moved through the small lobby briskly and walked up the carpeted stairway, pausing at the top, looking back at the counter area. Ever since he had been almost run over by the monster in the cornfield, he looked behind himself frequently. He entered his room and went to bed immediately, enjoying the thoughts of spending the evening with a very attractive woman.

When morning came, he headed down to the lobby. "Good morning, Sandy," he said to the woman behind the counter.

The clerk with reddish-colored hair looked up. "Hey, Tom, good to see you again. What's up today?"

"I'm goin' home—had a computer seminar yesterday."

"Have you read the *Forum* yet? The police dragged a body out of the river this morning—a woman."

Tom dropped a dollar bill on the counter. "Would you give me some change and I'll get one?"

He walked into the vestibule and used his quarters to remove a *Fargo Forum* from the dispenser. He set it on a table in the coffee room, and poured himself a cup.

Woman pulled from river, Tom read. He continued with the article. *The body is that of a middle-aged woman. Her name is being withheld until relatives are notified.*

Tom folded up the newspaper. "See you next visit, Sandy."

14

"HI, ELLIE," TOM SAID TO THE CHECKOUT CLERK at Stillman's Super Market the next morning, and grabbed a *Fargo Forum* from the newspaper rack. He scanned the front page and his heart skipped a beat. Near the middle, Nicole's picture jumped at him like his neighbor's dog.

He laid the paper down on the counter stand along with a dollar bill. "Ellie, see this picture with this article? You're not going to believe it, but this person...."

Ellie said, "Thank you."

"Yeah, she looks a lot like someone who I had dinner with in Fargo a couple of nights ago."

Ellie looked up. "Tom! Not again! Haven't you had enough dead bodies the past couple of years?"

Tom didn't respond. He flipped to another page and continued to read the article. "Geez, Ellie, it says here that the cops suspect foul play."

"They'll probably be talking to you soon. Surely, someone else knew that you had dinner with the woman."

Tom shook his head, relieved after taking a closer look at the picture again. "Naw, this isn't her. It had me worried for a moment. Have a good day, Ellie."

———

TOM'S MIND BUSIED THINKING about what he had learned at the seminar as he drove across the railroad tracks toward his home. He tried to think about the most recent version of Excel and Word software, but his mind kept returning to his new friend, Nicole.

He had no doubt that the picture of the murdered woman he had seen in the *Forum* was not Nicole. Yet, he wished that he had called before he left. How can I call her when I don't have her phone number, he asked himself, hitting himself gently on top of the head. Geez, I hope to take Nicole out again, but I didn't even ask her. I don't even know her last name. Some dummy I am, he thought. Tom entered his house and put away his groceries before sitting down in front of his computers. He pressed the down-arrow key and the screen came to life.

While reading the Internet news and his email, Tom couldn't keep his mind from drifting to Nicole and how warm she felt. He shook his head. Ah, come on, Hastings, most of the women you meet become friends of yours because they want something, he said to himself.

He thought about his friend Jolene, and how she used him to find the killer of her father. That happened a couple of years ago, he said to himself, but it appears as if I haven't learned a thing. It's sure a coincidence that Nicole's daughter is going to work for the senator. Surely, that's not why she chose to go out with me, he thought. He stared at the monitor for a few moments.

I'm getting surrounded, he thought. The senator and Julie are over there...southeast. The so called Department of Agriculture is over there...northwest.

Tom chose not to share his brutal experience in the cornfield with Nicole. Surely, she doesn't have anything to do with that, he thought.

He sat and day dreamed for a few moments, seeing the massive wheels. One of them almost ran over me, he said to himself. His mind drifted to a few years ago. He had gone for a walk and found a good sized hill just south of Stuart's cornfield. It wasn't on Stuart's property, nor was it on his. He stared at the monitor.

———

THE WALK UP HIS GREENWAY WESTWARD took only a few minutes. Tom armed himself with his automatic pistol, camera bag and binoculars before leaving. His target was Martin's hill. He crossed the fence at his west property line and continued on into Martin's field of grasses, weeds and wildflowers. He stopped to admire a brilliant patch of goldenrods.

At the far border of the field, he walked along a tree line until he came to a path which led through a narrow band of trees. The afternoon is as quiet as a morgue, he thought. Tom smiled, hearing the loud roar of a motorcycle engine on the highway...so much for the quiet. He walked through an area dominated by high trees and reached a path that led up the slope of the high hill he had in mind.

Tom felt anxiety building as he neared the summit. He slowed his steps and peeked over the top. He could indeed see the barn. The two white trucks appeared to be in about the same place as before. He could only see the tops of their boxes.

He scanned the area with his binoculars. Tom saw four men standing near the barn. Two of them walked over to the massive door on the end of the structure. They pulled on handles and the door slowly opened. Tom held his breath when he saw an implement with massive wheels exit.

Geez, those wheels have to be three to four stories high, he said to himself, amazed. Slowly and soundlessly, the implement approached the cornfield. Its controls appeared to be managed by someone in a narrow glassed-in cab above the right side of the forward axle.

He saw the massive machine take a right turn and head southward. As it approached the end of the field, not too far a distance from the top of the hill, Tom lay down in the grass. He remembered what had happened when he was spotted during his last visit to the cornfield.

Tom could hear the same hissing sound that he had heard the last time he encountered the beast monster. The machine stopped at the end of the field and made a short turn, the four wheels looking as if they were at war with each other.

The front looks like a gigantic fish mouth, he thought. Something one would expect to see watching a science fiction movie. The massive machine turned on a dime and began moving on the same tracks it had just made.

Tom cleared his throat. Well, it does look like an experimental implement, he said to himself. Perhaps, I'm over- thinking this whole thing. Naturally, they wouldn't want someone snooping around.

He waited until the machine returned back to the southern edge of the field, near where he lay hidden on the hill, before taking a series of photographs. This should look mighty interesting on my computer, he thought.

He heard his camera beep, warning him that the batteries needed charging. He shut it off and placed it back into its case. Tom remained down in the grass, and continued to watch the machine go back and forth in the same tracks for another half an hour.

He could hear the hissing sound only faintly, and only when it made the turn near to him. It sounds like a snake in tall grass, he thought. Tom had never been a fan of monster movies in the past. I've got one as a neighbor, he said to himself, and began to creep down the southern side of the hill.

15

THE YELLOW TAXICAB PULLED UP AT THE CURB on Broadway in Fargo on a cool Wednesday morning in late August. A rear door opened and a dark-skinned man got out. He stepped onto the sidewalk carrying a tan briefcase. The taxi pulled away from the curb and the man walked toward the door of an office building. Tall and lean, Thor Zantro stood with his back against the outer brick wall, holding a briefcase in both hands.

Five minutes later, a second cab arrived and parked in almost the same spot. A wide-hipped man wearing a pin-striped suit exited. He pulled on the brim of his tan Stetson and waved at the man with a deformed left ear. Zudo Mante stepped onto the Broadway Street sidewalk in Fargo, North Dakota for his very first time. He smiled widely at Thor as they approached each other. They embraced and exchanged kisses on their cheeks.

"You have come at last. I have been anxiously awaiting your arrival," Thor said.

Zudo's eyes glistened. "We have much to discuss with the senator."

"It has been long since I have been home to Togo. I trust the mining is going well," the narrow-faced man said.

Zudo grasped both Thor's hands and brought them close to his chest for a moment. "Yes it is—and partially due to your good work here in America. We could not be successful without you. I pray for you every day."

"It is time for our appointment," Thor said.

They walked into the lobby of the office building and looked around. Zudo pointed. "The elevators."

———

GREG KURTZ, OWNER AND MANAGER OF KURTZ MANUFACTURING in West Fargo sat in an easy chair parked at an angle to Senator McDougal's desk. He skipped through the pages of a document that the senator had given him minutes earlier. His mouth opened partially when he saw the bottom line on the last page. "Five hundred beasts! That's a lot of moola."

The senator pointed his finger. "That's only for starters. I expect to get that number up to a million within a couple of years."

Greg leaned forward slightly in the chair, his dark brown eyes fixed on the senator. He began to speak, pausing to control his stutter. "I've got two people working the numbers to see what—the costs for each beast will be. Five hundred—that's going to take some planning."

He felt perspiration building up in his armpits. Greg's brain exploded, filling with wild ideas of a massive expansion.

Senator McDougal placed both palms down on his desk. "You will become one of the richest and most successful manufacturers in the nation, if not the world."

Greg's dark brown mustache quivered slightly as he thought about his next words carefully. "Who do I get paid by?"

The senator looked at his watch. "You will meet the man who is in charge soon. He is due any minute."

Greg Kurtz felt his heart rate increase. His entire life flashed across his eyes. His father had advised him against starting the manufacturing plant: too much debt...too much debt. This would solve it all. My father will be pleased, he said to himself.

He brushed his fingers over his well-manicured brown hair, careful to tap loose strands back into place. "Senator, I will need a contract and a substantial down payment."

"Consider it done. My attorneys have already started the paperwork. Your share will be exceedingly generous, believe me."

———

JULIE HEARD HER NAME CALLED. She had been working on the Togo itinerary all morning in an office next to the senator's. Isabelle appeared in her doorway. She tilted her chin upward and said, her voice firm and sensuous, "The senator wishes your presence in his office now, Julie—now."

"Thank you, Isabelle."

Julie felt pressured at times by the senator in the past week. It probably has something to do with the deal in Togo, she said to herself. I've noticed his hands tremble a lot lately. There's also been a stream of strange visitors since that Togo vote. I wish he would tell me what's going on. "Maybe this is it," she said and left her office.

She knocked on the senator's door gently and entered. She saw two dark-skinned men sitting in chairs to her left, and a tall man spread out in the easy chair next to the senator's desk. The two men stood. "Come on in, Miss Huffman. Gentlemen, I would like you to meet Julie Huffman. She doesn't know it yet, but I'm going to ask her to coordinate communications between the country of Togo and Kurtz Manufacturing."

The senator stood and walked around his desk. "Miss Huffman, meet Mr. Thor Zantro." He pointed. She shook his hand.

The man bowed. "My pleasure, madam."

The senator guided Julie to the other two men where she exchanged introductory greetings with Zudo Mante and Greg Kurtz.

He placed a hand on Julie's shoulder. "When Mr. Kurtz is finished here, I'm sending him to your office. He has some papers for you which will help get you started."

"Gentlemen, "Julie said. She smiled and walked out.

16

VERONICA LEWIS HAD GRADUATED FROM St. Mary's High School in Bismarck, North Dakota in May of 2005. She had experienced a merry-go-round life style during her last two years. An unwanted pregnancy angered her father to the extent that he was charged with "attempted murder" of a young man who he thought caused her to be with child. Veronica didn't have the heart to expose the man who was truly responsible for her pregnancy. He is married with four children, she kept saying to herself. I cannot wreck the lives of his wife and those children.

Her father paid for the abortion just before he was jailed on the criminal charge. Veronica's junior-year classmates supported her during the pregnancy and welcomed her back to school before the spring quarter ended. The next year, as a senior, she studied hard and nearly graduated with honors.

Blind faith intervened in June when she interviewed for an intern position with a U.S. senator. A local attorney and cousin of the senator recommended her for the position and she jumped with joy when the call came. She felt bubbles of tension popping up all over her stomach walls when walking into Senator McDougal's office in Fargo.

"Miss Lewis, I assume," the red-headed receptionist had said, smiling.

"Yes—"

"The senator will be with you in a moment. Please have a seat."

Veronica felt her heart rate increase. She took several deep breaths. Calm down, woman, she said to herself.

A door opened and a blonde lady smiled and beckoned with the fingers of her hand. "I'm Julie Huffman. Welcome to Senator McDougal's staff."

Veronica's jaw trembled as she said, "I'm Veronica Lewis."

She followed the woman into the senator's office. Standing behind a desk, she saw a tall gray-haired man. He smiled and winked. Veronica wasn't sure what that meant. The senator took two long strides, circled his desk and extended a long arm to his new employee. Veronica returned his smile and accepted his handshake, watching his eyes roam up and down the front of her body.

——

NICOLE LEANED FORWARD IN HER CHAIR and hung up the phone. "Yes!" she muttered loudly. She's in, or as good as in, she thought. Veronica will have access to his office. There's fifty thousand in it for me if she can get her hands on those blueprints. But, I...we...must be patient.

Lance, her boss, had called earlier in the day and set up a meeting for a week from Wednesday in Fargo. She strongly feared and didn't trust Lance and his cohorts, but felt the fifty thousand made the risk worth her while.

Nicole didn't know their exact motive, but her instructions were clear: her daughter, Veronica, had a list of the files that should be in the senator's office. She will make copies. I am to make close friends with Tom Hastings and learn as much as possible regarding the activities in the cornfield next to his property.

She shuddered thinking about the meeting which she had attended a week ago. It was held in a room on the fifth floor of the Radisson Hotel. Lance introduced her to three men. Holy buckets, they looked me over real good. The short, slim one with the stringy hair gave me the chills. His big eyes appeared to almost roll out of their sockets. Yikes!

Nicole opened a desk drawer and brought up a phone book. She scanned the New Dresden section for Tom Hastings's name.

——

TOM'S SPIRITS LEAPED TOWARD THE sky listening to Nicole's

soft-spoken voice. He didn't have any expectations at all after their cool goodnights following the seminar in Fargo. Tom didn't expect her to call him. This has got to be my lucky day, he said to himself, raising a fist into the air after hanging up the phone.

He had suggested Fireside restaurant in Big Lakes as their rendezvous place for dinner. She readily agreed. Tom felt totally stunned when she agreed to pick him up at his place. Hey, we can have some wine on the deck and get off to a great start, he thought.

Tom glanced at the calendar on his computer monitor. Friday is only two days away. I better get my house cleaned up. Calm down, he said to himself. I can easily do that on Friday morning. He walked out his front door and headed for the garage.

Tom slowed his vehicle on the county highway approaching the gravel drive that led to Stuart's farmstead. His eyes fell upon a gray van moving slowly away from the farmstead, headed for the county highway.

Tom thought the hatless driver was a man. The passenger had a baseball cap pulled down over his face. He, too, was a man. In his rear view mirror, Tom saw the van turn onto the highway and head his direction. Tom rounded Purgatory Curve and noticed the van had closed the gap between them, and the driver appeared to be pushing him to drive faster.

Tom drove across the railroad tracks and took a left. The van continued onto Main Street. Tom drove around the block and saw the van had parked in the Stillman's Supermarket parking lot. Tom parked in front of the hardware store and hurriedly exited his vehicle, wondering who the heck came in the van.

He passed by the post office and saw two men walk onto the sidewalk near him. One of them, the man wearing the baseball cap, glanced at him with bloodshot eyes. Tom cringed. He continued to walk and watched the two men enter the grocery store.

Tom walked onto the parking lot and stood next to the van. He looked for a logo or sign on the door. There isn't any, he said to himself. I thought they would be representing the department of agriculture.

Tom entered the grocery. "Good morning, Tom," he heard Ellie say. "What are you up to today?"

Tom picked up a newspaper and stepped over to check out. He narrowed his eyes. "Did you ever see those two men before—the one's who came in just before me?"

"Sure have. They come in darn near every day."

"Do you know who they are?"

Ellie shrugged her shoulders, moving her head slowly from side to side. She busied herself with the register. Tom made his way up and down the area next to the grocery carts, gazing up and down the aisles. Oh, the heck with it, he thought and headed out the door.

17

TOM'S HEART RACED AS HE WATCHED A CAR come up his driveway. He saw a dark brown Lexus sedan stop in front of his garage. Tom gasped seeing Nicole leave her car and walk down his sidewalk. She's dressed to kill, he said to himself, swallowing deeply.

She wore a red dress, bare at the neck and part of the shoulders. A gold pendent hung from a very thin chain. He noticed the long red fingernails as a hand reached out toward his doorbell. It rang.

Tom felt perspiration spread out over the doorknob as he grabbed it, turned and pulled.

He looked into her eyes and reached out his right hand. She grasped his fingers and closed the gap between them, snuggling tight to his chest.

"Ah—come on in, Nicole. Sure a nice evening, isn't it?"

"You feel so good, Tom. I...."

Tom nodded his head and motioned with his hand for her to be seated on a loveseat in his dining area. "Would you like a glass of wine, Nicole?"

"Sure would—what kind do you have?"

"Chardonnay—hope that's okay."

Tom's insides melted watching Nicole's warm, wide smile. He

opened the refrigerator door and poured two glasses almost full. After setting one down on the small table next to Nicole, he took a seat on a wooden rocking chair. They exchanged small talk until both wine glasses showed nearly empty.

Tom stood and carried the empties into the kitchen. He returned and said, "Should we get going?"

Nicole lowered the tone of her voice. "The sooner we get going, the better I will like it." She slowly ran the tip of her tongue between her lips.

Tom cleared his throat and asked, his voice quavering, "Do you want me to drive?"

Nicole smiled. "My car is sitting right out there. I'll be glad to."

———

THE FIRESIDE RESTAURANT IS A LOCAL LANDMARK PERCHED on a rise of land on the northeast shore of Big Lake. It had been recently remodeled, which included the addition of a summer bar and lounge area, both in a large room. Tom guided Nicole through the door and toward the hostess station. He requested a table in the main dining room by a window.

He looked down at Nicole and bit his lower lip to prevent it from trembling. "Hey, let's wait in the new lounge area. The hostess said there's going to be a fifteen minute wait."

Tom grasped her elbow and steered her into the next room. They sat down at a table. Nicole lightly worked her tongue over the inner surface of her lip after taking a sip of wine. "So how long have you had your home on Border's Lake?"

"Mighty long time—about thirty years or so."

"It doesn't appear as if you have any close neighbors. That drive down your roadway appears to be never-ending."

Tom smiled. "I like it that way. Actually, I do have neighbors: Pete and Lisa next to my roadway, and two places hidden from the county highway on my western border."

Nicole's eyes widened. "Oh really—hidden, huh?"

"Yup—there's Miller next to the lake. He's a summer resident only. Also, I am next to an unoccupied farmstead out by the northwest corner."

Nicole raised her eyebrows. "Who owns that property?"

"A friend of mine: Stuart Eldridge."

"Is he an older guy—younger—what?"

Tom chuckled. "A lot younger than me. Why do you ask?"

Nicole leaned forward. "Have I mentioned to you before that I have a daughter who currently lives in the senator's compound? She's been hired by the senator as an intern. Veronica is her name."

"Yes, I think that you told me that when we went out for dinner in Fargo."

"Oh, I guess I have. If you ever see a real big pontoon boat go by, my daughter may be on it."

"I've seen it go by many times—a bunch of people usually."

Nicole's eyes enlarged. "You're property is so unique. I bet you could get a ton of money for it."

Tom looked up at the ceiling. "I don't know what I would do if I sold my place. Where would I go? What would I do?"

"Oh my, did I strike a nerve? I'm sorry," Nicole said.

Tom shook his head. "Not one bit. No problem. Our table is ready. The hostess just waved."

"Oh, look at that view," Nicole said after they were seated.

A massive wave caused by a large speed boat at top speed caused the mast of a sail boat to tilt severely.

"Do you like boating, Nicole?"

"No, not really. I would much rather go for a long walk in the woods."

Tom swallowed a sip of wine and set his glass down. "In the woods, huh?"

"Yes, I love nature. Your place looks so ideal." Tom said anxiously, "Maybe you'd like to go for a walk sometime. I do have some interesting trails."

Nicole's face lit up. "Oh, I would just love that. When can we do it? Soon, I hope."

"How about tomorrow evening?"

"Yes—Yes, Tom. I would like that."

Tom's stomach rumbled all the way back to his home. Nicole turned the Lexus into the driveway and placed the lever in park. "Would you like to come in for a bit?" he asked.

"Tom, I've had a beautiful evening. I'm rather tired—and I am looking forward to our walk tomorrow. Is that okay?"

"Sure." Tom exited the car and walked around to the other side. He kissed Nicole lightly on the lips. "See you tomorrow."

———

TOM SAT ON A DECK CHAIR and watched Nicole's vehicle drive into his driveway. He checked his watch: 5:30. Right on time, he thought, smiling. His emotions had calmed considerably since watching her arrive for her initial visit yesterday evening. Tom felt disappointed that the evening ended so abruptly. He wished that she could've stayed longer.

Nicole smiled and waved after getting out of her car. She wore a dark blue warm-up outfit. The wide, white stripe up the side of the pant legs made her appear taller. Tom stood and walked toward her car. He gasped as she hugged him tightly.

She moved her body away but held onto his hands. Smiling widely she said, "I'm ready for the walk."

Tom swung a camera bag over his shoulder. "Okay, let's go."

The sun partially broke through a bank of gray, streaky clouds in the west. Two crows squawked a warning to others, and hurriedly left their prey, parking themselves in a tall aspen tree near Hastings's greenway. The freshly grown narrow band of Minnesota prairie grass and unwanted orchard grass led to the beginning of a trail, which ran along his western border.

They walked quietly for a few minutes, no one saying anything. Tom grabbed Nicole's hand and led her northward past the greenway to the beginning of a pathway. He stopped and pulled her close, kissing her on the lips.

"Oh my, Mr. Hastings. What does this mean?"

"I don't know—sorry, but I lost control of myself."

They kissed again. "Losing control once in awhile is good for one's spirit," she said.

Tom held her close, feeling his heart pounding against the inside of his chest.

He released her but held onto one hand. "The trail—we're supposed to go for a walk."

"Nice trail," Nicole said. "Nice everything."

They walked past the fields and into the woods. "I hope that we see some wildlife. There's lots of turkey and deer in this area," Tom said nervously.

"Oh, what's that screeching?" she asked.

Tom pointed. "Oh, that's a red-shouldered hawk. There's a pair of them that nest in the deep woods every year—over there."

They crossed a small, wooden-planked bridge and continued. The trail led up and over a rise and down to a grassy area. Nicole stopped. "That's an old barn over there, isn't it?"

Tom wondered how she knew that it was a barn when he could see only the top edge of it. He cleared his throat. "That's an old farmstead a friend of mine purchased a few years back. He tore down all the buildings but the barn. Right now you can only see the top edge of the roof."

Nicole tilted up her chin. "Cool."

Tom continued. "See that cornfield. According to my friend, the U.S. Department of Agriculture is conducting research on it."

"Really now! Why do you suppose they selected this field? There are so many—especially Iowa. Why here?" Nicole asked.

"Boy, I sure wouldn't know. But what I do know is that—there's a weird looking implement that occasionally wheels up and down the length of the field."

"Is it like a tractor then?"

"It has four humungous wheels and a large plastic tank in between them. The operator sits in a small glassed cab off to one side. Very strange looking rig, I must say," Tom said, extending his hands as far apart as they could reach.

"I sure would like to see that machine. Do you think they go out every day?"

Tom raised his right hand and stopped walking abruptly. "Prancer!

It's Prancer. See that gray shadow over there." He pointed.

"Who's Prancer?"

Tom brought his hand down and continued to gaze at a small clearing in the woods. "He's a friend of mine—a deer."

Nicole gave Tom a curious look.

He looked down at her and smiled lightly. "Yes, but—It's too complicated a story to attempt to explain."

Nicole chuckled. "Living out here by yourself—you make a lot of friends."

He nodded. "I'm rather shocked by how gray his hide has gotten. But, I suppose he's getting older like the rest of us."

Nicole laughed. "I asked you a question. Do you think the big machine is out there in that cornfield every day? Like right now?"

"Don't know, Nicole—don't know—I have a photograph of it back at the house."

Nicole turned and looked up into Tom's eyes. "Could I see it? I would love to." She grabbed one of his hands in both of hers.

"Sure."

————

NICOLE STARED AT EACH PHOTOGRAPH of the big machine on Tom's computer screen. How can I print these without rousing Tom's suspicion? she asked herself. She gazed toward the kitchen and saw Tom pouring wine into two glasses.

She got up from the chair and walked to the French door that opened onto the deck. "You sure have a nice view, Tom."

Tom smiled and handed her a glass. "Let's relax a bit. I hope you like this wine."

Nicole nodded and brought the glass to her lips. "It's delightful, Tom."

"Should we sit on the deck?" Tom asked. "It's still nice outside," he added.

Nicole rolled her eyes. "Sure."

Tom gestured toward a deck chair and Nicole sat down. He sat in the chair next to her. "Any plans for dinner tonight? Mary Ann's is just a hop and a skip away."

"Uh—I would love to, Tom, but I promised my daughter—"

Tom's face expressed disappointment. "Where is your daughter right now?"

"She is staying at Senator's McDougal's place—across the bay—over there," she pointed. "You remember, don't you? We talked about her a couple of times."

Tom bit his lower lip. "Oh sure—you had mentioned that she has been hired as an intern?"

"She has. I plan on staying with her tonight."

Tom emptied his glass. "Would you like another wine, Nicole?"

"No thanks, I've got to run. Say, Tom, would you do me a favor?"

"I'll try. What is it that you wish?"

"Those photographs you have of that unusual machine. I would like to show them to Veronica. She is a photography student and I would like to give her the opportunity to see them and comment."

"Sure, I can print one up for you."

"Could you do about four of them?"

"I suppose so. Just show me which ones you want."

They returned to his computer. Tom placed four sheets of photography paper in the printer. "You sit down and print up what you want, Nicole. I'll be right back."

18

VERONICA HUNG UP THE PHONE. She smiled and sat down at her small kitchen table on a Sunday evening in her apartment at the senator's compound. The black, plastic, zippered case, not much bigger than her hand, contained what she felt would satisfy her reason for taking the job in the first place, a key duplicating kit.

She pulled on the zipper and removed a small packet with different types of key shapes. The battery-run mechanism inside the case had a slot in one of its narrow ends. Simply placing a naked key inside resulted in an exact duplicate. She had been warned to always use new batteries. Got to pick up a bunch tomorrow, she said to herself.

Veronica thought about her most recent meeting with her mother and that other man...the one with the bulging eyes. They had emphasized that Julie Huffman would likely possess a spare set of keys to the senator's office. If not, she thought, I'll give Isabelle a try.

She glanced at her wrist watch. She's expecting me right about now, she thought. Gently closing the door, she walked to Julie Huffman's unit and tapped on the door. In moments it opened. "Come on in, Veronica," Julie said, smiling.

"Hi, Julie, I appreciate you seeing me this evening, and I'm so anxious to learn from you," Veronica said, watching Julie turn her head slightly, straining to hear.

"Have a chair. I'll get you something to drink. Would you like a coke?"

Veronica moved slowly past Julie's desk, scanning the drawers before sitting down on a loveseat across from the window that looked out at a wall of trees beyond the walkway.

"Here you are," Julie said, extending her arm and handing her a glass.

Veronica reached out. "Thanks. Some of the bushes out there are starting to turn color."

"It gets real beautiful out here this time of the year. Now what is it you would like to talk about? You mentioned something on the phone."

"Ah—I was wondering...."

"Yes," Julie said.

"Exactly, what will I be doing for the senator?"

"You'll be spending most of your time in my office—working on mailings and such. I do tons of correspondence, ya know—communicating with restaurants, airlines and hotels. I'll also need help in catching up the payables—invoices."

Veronica took a sip of her coke and stroked her hair away from her left eye. "I admit that I'm real nervous about tomorrow, my actual first full day on the job."

Julie smiled. "The first thing that I want you to learn is our computer system. According to your application, you've had lots of experience, so you should catch on quickly."

The phone rang. "Excuse me," said Julie, walking into her bedroom. "Hello."

Veronica quickly stepped over to the desk. Gently she pulled a small narrow drawer open—no keys. She shut it and pulled open the second drawer, cocking her head, listening to Julie's voice in the bedroom. "Bingo!" she whispered as her eyes feasted on a ring with four keys.

Veronica heard Julie say, "Okay, see you tomorrow." She quickly closed the drawer and returned to the loveseat. Now, at least I know where some of the keys are, she said to herself.

"Well, are you more relaxed now?" Julie asked after returning and stopping in front of the window.

Veronica stood. "Gotta' go now, Julie. Thanks for the coke."

Julie opened the front door. "Have a good night. See you on Monday."

Veronica nodded and stepped out onto the walkway.

———

VERONICA AWAKENED TO THE CACKLING CRIES of a covey of crows. It sounds like a convention outside, she thought, pushed aside the covers and glanced at the clock. Uh-oh, I've overslept. Better get up and get ready or I'll be late on my first day in Julie's office.

Isabelle Franks peered over her glasses when Veronica entered the senator's business suite. She didn't smile and pointed toward Julie's door.

Veronica smiled. "Good morning, Isabelle."

Isabelle nodded and returned to her papers. Veronica knocked on the door frame and entered. Julie was sitting at her with a phone snuggled to her ear. She pointed toward a chair.

Veronica sat down and looked around the office. The single, crank-out window behind Julie's desk was partially open. Three tall metal file cabinets lined the wall to Julie's left. Veronica wondered what the door next to the file cabinets accessed. Probably a closet, she thought.

The top of Julie's desk appeared well organized. A plastic multiple tray unit contained several items in the top tray, and only one in the bottom. The flat panel computer display, fronted by a keyboard, occupied the surface of the far end of the desk. An empty chair, directly behind, didn't appear to have much padding. Several framed photographs decorated the far wall. They look like travel pictures, Veronica thought.

Julie replaced the phone in its cradle and smiled. "Good morning, Veronica. How are you today?"

The intern forced a smile. "I'm ready to go to work, Julie."

"Oh, yes—the computer you will be working on is right over there. Why don't you take a seat? I'll be with you shortly."

Veronica walked around the desk, setting her purse down on the floor, and she sat down. Pressing on a key, the monitor sprang to life. She double-clicked the Internet Explorer icon. The *Fargo Forum* home page window appeared. One of the lead stories headlined: *Senator McDougal to visit Togo, Africa.* Oh, I'm going to like working here, she said to herself.

Julie had gotten up from her chair and stood behind the intern. "Okay, Veronica, please click the *Accounting* icon. Yes, you have it—good." Julie brought over a stack of papers. "These are bills which I want entered today. When you get those done, I have the senator's check register, which needs to be updated. How does it look?"

"Piece of cake!"

"Good. Let me know if you have any questions."

Veronica finished the bills within an hour. "I've got 'em done, Julie. What's next?"

Julie reached into a drawer and brought out a three-unit check register. She used a magic marker to mark a starting point. "I want you to start right here."

Veronica stared at the ring of keys in the open drawer. "Okay."

"I need to attend a short meeting in the senator's office. I'll be back shortly. Are you all right by yourself?"

Veronica looked up, a deep smile forming on her face. "You go right ahead. I can handle this."

She watched anxiously as Julie sauntered out the door, closing it behind her. Quickly, Veronica got up off her chair and opened the drawer. She stared at the key ring. Is this a good time? she asked herself.

Veronica looked at the door and hurriedly reached into the drawer and grabbed the ring, holding if tightly to her bosom. After closing the drawer, she set it down on her desk and leaned down to pick up her purse. Veronica quickly brought out a small screw driver and used it to pry the metal ring apart and remove all four keys.

Veronica plugged in her portable key duplicator, leaving it on the carpeted floor. She inserted the first key. Her heart thumped as the whirring sounded louder and louder: first key done. Veronica dropped the second key to the carpet. She hit her head on the edge of the desk trying to pick it up. Veronica's fingers succeeded and she placed it into the slot: second key done. Veronica finished the third key and sighed deeply, holding her breath, listening for the sound of feet walking in the other room: all four done.

She replaced the keys into their original positions on the ring and returned them into the drawer. Veronica wiped beads of perspiration from her forehead with a tissue and returned to the computer. Minutes later, Julie reentered the room.

Veronica kept her eyes on the display. "Looks like you're hard at it, Veronica."

The smiling intern sat back in the chair. "It's going well."

———

"MOTHER, I CAN'T BELIEVE THAT YOU DID IT—got those photos. How in heaven's name?"

Nicole laughed. "Hah, some people are easily manipulated—not a problem at all." She flicked a thumb into the air.

The two women sat at a table at Sunflower Hill in Big Lakes. Veronica looked at each of the four photographs several times. "Wow, what a monster."

"Isn't that something? I'd swear it's something from outer space,"

Nicole said.

Veronica looked around the room. She held up one of the photographs. "Just look at those wheels. They're as tall as this building."

Nicole chuckled. She took a sip of coffee.

"Okay there, Miss Expert. What about this?" Veronica said, opening her right fist exposing four keys.

Nicole's mouth popped open. "Oh, my gosh! Don't tell me!"

Veronica's wide smile exposed a perfect set of teeth. "These are gonna get me into the big guy's office."

Nicole stepped forward. She threw up her hand for a high-five and hugged her daughter. She pulled back and looked up into her dark eyes. "We're a great team."

"Well, I better get back to work, still a couple more days before the weekend," Veronica said.

19

LATE SUNDAY EVENING, VERONICA LOOKED AT HER WATCH. It's time, she thought. She unplugged her micro digital camera and placed it into her black leather purse. Zipping it shut, she raised the strap over her shoulder. Victoria walked over to her window and looked out. She couldn't see anyone.

Veronica opened the door and walked onto the walkway, looking around in all directions. Gently, Veronica closed the door and quickly walked toward the senator's office suite. Pausing short of the entry, she looked at the four keys in the palm of her hand. Hopefully this one, she thought, and placed it into the lock. It clicked and turned.

Veronica slipped inside quickly and closed the door. She hastened to the large front window and peeked outside. This is my lucky day, she thought, absolutely no one around. She walked to the senator's office door and placed a key in the lock. Wrong one, she said to herself, and quickly replaced the key.

"All right," she muttered. Moments later, she stood in the senator's office, not making a sound, interrupted only by the distant, rumbling sound of a freight train.

She allowed her eyes to adjust to the darkness. As she recollected, the senator's large oak desk had two large drawers on the right side. Veronica had noticed earlier that the lower one had a lock. She walked around the desk, knelt down and tried key number three: nothing happened. She tried key number four: again, nothing happened.

"Damn," she whispered. Julie doesn't have a key for the desk. But then, why should she, she asked herself. The senator's files are private. Where the heck would he keep the key? Surely, he wouldn't carry one around. Veronica smiled. I bet he keeps it hidden somewhere in this office.

She saw a windowless door next to a large window in the back wall. The darkness coming from the outdoors made the green curtains appear black. I could put the lights on if it wasn't for that window, she thought. Placing her nose against the glass, she noticed a wall of trees, just beyond a wooden railing deck. A splash of light, coming from a yard pole, lit up a section of the floor of a deck.

Veronica turned on her pen-flashlight and shone the light around the room. Where would I hide a key if this was my office? Where oh where? she asked herself over and over again.

She pushed the senator's desk chair aside and looked under the mat. Shaking her head slowly, she walked to a wall where several framed pieces of art work hung. Standing on her toes, she ran a finger over the top of each. Dang! Nothing!

She shone her light on the desk. The beam flashed across a metallic bust of Abraham Lincoln. Veronica leaned against the desk and placed her fingers around the shoulders of the heavy sculpture. She lifted it and placed it aside. Her beam of light exposed a single *gold key*. She felt like yelling with joy. I must control my emotions, she said to herself, suppressing a strong desire to make a lot of noise.

Veronica picked up the gold key and held it in her trembling left hand. Calm down, she said to herself. She reached up with her left hand and clamped her fingers around the shaking wrist. She hustled around to the front of the desk and placed it into the lock. Her heart stopped for a moment as her fingers made it turn.

She left the key in the lock and pulled the drawer open. Holding the flashlight in one hand, she flipped through the titles of each folder. Veronica took a deep breath and pulled out the one which read *Formulas*. She laid it on the floor and exposed the contents. Must be twenty sheets, she thought. Her fingers shook as she reached into her purse for the camera. I'm so close to the grand prize, she said to herself...must relax.

"Dang," she muttered after dropping the camera on the floor. She picked it up and flicked the switch. Uh, thank God, she said to herself and began to take pictures of each sheet. She completed the entire folder and placed it into the drawer.

I should make a copy of that key right now, she thought. Hesitating for a few moments, she returned to the file cabinet. Heck, I can make the duplicate when I'm done here.

Flipping through the other folders, she latched onto the one titled *OxyBeast*. Veronica laid it down on the carpet. She opened it and her beam lit up a photograph of a huge machine. She set the flashlight down and reached for her camera. Her body froze in its tracks as she heard some movement in the next room. The sound of soft footsteps frightened her—the door opened. Quickly, she flicked off the light, ducked her head and held her breath.

The overhead light came on. Veronica could hear someone breathing other than her own short shallow gasps. Both her hands shook, she rolled into a ball, taking longer, deeper breaths, exhaling into her blouse.

Her heart skipped a beat as she heard footsteps approach the desk.

———

JULIE HUFFMAN PEERED OUT THE BACK WINDOW of her apartment. Through a stand of trees, she saw dark, gray-blue waves rolling westward. Julie liked water and she flirted with the idea of making a walk down to the dock before going to her office. Her watch read 8:30 a.m.

Dressed in dark blue warm-up pants and a gray sweatshirt, she put on her tennis cap and opened the front door. Julie walked the same direction that she had used the previous day to get down to the dock. She hesitated at the upper landing, watching a boiling cloud of fog move by and blocking the view of the trees across the bay for a moment.

Grabbing the rail with her right hand, Julie used it to guide her way down to the dock. She smiled watching three loons feeding a short distance away. One of the large birds disappeared, diving under the water. A second loon went down. It appeared as if the big birds would not all dive beneath the water surface at one time. They're playing the loon game, she said to herself.

Julie stood on the first section of the dock and marveled at the view, no matter which direction she looked. The sun splashed its rays against the shoreline across the bay. She watched an eagle soaring above the tree line. Oh...another one. The long, wide wings spread out to their fullest, using the wind to effortless swoop and cut.

She looked westward and noticed the top of a stone chimney farther down on the opposite shore. That's Tom's, she thought and reflected on the times that she spent with Tom Hastings at his home. I sure enjoyed those nature walks...maybe again some day.

Julie walked next to the senator's canopied pontoon boat and stopped at the bench near the end of the dock. She looked into the water. What's that? Looks like someone's foot, she thought.

She moved closer. *It is a foot*...what am I thinking? she asked herself, wondering if she should scream. Julie looked away, up at the stairway and the large house up above. Do I dare look again? She did, and attempted a scream. The sounds never left her mouth.

Placing a hand over her lips, she gasped for air. Julie closed her eyes and opened them freshly—hoping the foot would go away. The wet, white stocking stretched tight over the foot moved—slowly up and down, keeping beat with the waves.

Her thoughts raced wildly. What should I do right now? She took another step and peeked over the edge. Julie saw a vague outline of a human body partially submerged. Strands of wet, dark hair danced on the water's surface. She shrieked and hastened toward the steps, taking them up two at a time.

Julie raced to her apartment and fumbled with her key, dropping it on the sidewalk. Sobbing quietly, she steadied her shaking right hand by grabbing it with her left. Picking up the key with her fingers, she unlocked the door and entered. Her thoughts continued to race. *Who should I call...the senator...911?*

She paced around the room. "Okay, now I've got it," she muttered. Grabbing the phone, she dialed *911*. Julie's voice crackled as she attempted to explain what she had seen down by the dock to the person on the line—"I found a body—my name is Julie Hoffman. I'm not sure of the address, but it's on the south shore of Border's Lake—the lake home of Senator McDougal."

After hanging up, she dialed the senator's house. One of his domestics answered. "The senator and his wife are not home. Please call Miss Franks if you have a problem."

"I just want you and others in the house to know—you'll be hearing sirens—soon. I can't say any more." Julie hung up.

She dialed Isabelle's number. It rang five times before the secretary's voice responded on the answering machine. After the beep, Julie took a deep breath, attempting to maintain stability in her voice. "Isabelle, this is Julie. I've just dialed 911. There's someone...." Julie grimaced. "Someone floating in the water—down by the dock."

Julie dialed yet another number. "Peter, are you up?"

"Barely."

"We've got a problem—well, you and I don't, but Senator McDougal sure does."

"Yeah, what happened?"

"Peter, are you sitting down?"

"Hey, I'm still in bed."

Julie took a deep breath. She stammered, "There is a dead somebody in the water—right next to the dock."

"A dead body?—you've got to be kidding. Are you sure that you didn't have a bad dream?"

"Peter, when you hear the sirens, you'll know it's for real."

———

PETER RAPIDLY DONNED HIS CLOTHES and opened his door. He dashed toward Julie's unit and heard the first siren. It sure sounds eerie coming through that fog, he thought, shivering.

Julie appeared in her doorway, her face convoluted, showing lines and streaks of dried tears. Peter hastened toward her and they hugged. "Who the heck do you suppose is in the lake?" he asked.

Her voice trembling and moisture filling her eyes, she said, "I don't know, Peter, but I'm pretty sure that it's a woman."

Peter narrowed his eyes. He looked at Julie. Who else is there? he asked himself. Is it Veronica? Jesus, God, please no, his mind tortured.

Peter looked toward the highway and saw flashing lights. "The body could have drifted over from somewhere else—perhaps not our problem."

Julie tightened her lips together. "I hope you're right, and we'll soon know."

The New Dresden Fire & Rescue vehicle roared into the driveway. Two occupants jumped out and trotted toward Julie and Peter.

"Hey!—someone called about a body!—down by the dock."

Julie pointed. "Yes, that was me. Follow that sidewalk. It's down there."

Peter watched the two-person crew hurry down the sidewalk toward the lake. He felt a chill as his ears picked up the sound of another siren.

20

TOM HASTINGS SAT AT HIS DINING ROOM TABLE on Monday morning. He watched a covey of geese, lined up in a long column, work their way toward the middle of the bay. Amazing, how they follow a leader like that, he thought. I wonder why they do it in the water. I can understand breaking wind for each other while flying.

Some of the fog that had blanketed the water earlier in the morning had lifted. Tom could now see the trees across the entire bay. He heard a siren and looked at his watch—it read 8:45 a.m. someone got stopped for speeding, he said to himself, smiling.

Tom noticed a set of flashing lights on the state highway as the vehicle passed by a break in the tree line on the other side of the bay. A few minutes later, he heard a second siren blaring and the vehicle headed in the same direction as the other. A third vehicle with flashing lights followed.

Tom went inside for another cup of coffee. He sat out in the deck for another hour when he heard a fourth siren in the distance. The intensity picked up and he noticed lights flashing in the area of an informal boat ramp, across the bay and down from his place. Geez, I wonder what the heck is going on over there, he asked himself.

Watching intensely, Tom saw a second vehicle drive down to the ramp. Tom set down his coffee, walked into his house, and returned with binoculars.

"Geez, they're moving a stretcher from a boat into an ambulance," Tom whispered. His thoughts filled with possibilities. I hope it's not Julie or someone I know. The sound of still another siren reached his ears. Shaking his head, he returned to his house.

Some of the fog had returned, partially obliterating the activity across the bay. Tom attempted to concentrate on the book he had been reading, but his curiosity got in the way.

He put on his jacket and walked out to the garage. After backing out his vehicle, he opened the passenger window and looked at the bay. The fog had cleared again and he saw a massive number of lights flashing. Shaking his head, he drove onto his roadway and headed for New Dresden.

Tom had just fished his mail out of his post office box when he glanced out the window and saw an emergency vehicle driving on Main Street, coming from the direction of Border's Lake. He stepped out onto the sidewalk and saw two more emergency vehicles pass down Main Street, including an ambulance.

"Wonder what happened this morning?" a man dressed in striped coveralls and a dirty, tan baseball cap said.

Tom looked at the man and said, "Dunno."

Tom walked to Stillman's Super Market and entered. "Why the serious look today?" Ellie asked.

"Someone must've drowned in Border's Lake this morning— lots of sirens and flashing lights. I'm not sure, but I may have seen them moving someone into an ambulance."

Ellie frowned. "Uh-oh, that don't sound good at all."

Tom checked out and paid for the items in his small grocery basket.

"Goodbye, have a good day," Ellie said.

Tom nodded. "See ya later." He walked over to the window, looking out onto Main Street. *I wonder if all the emergency vehicles are back by now.* He walked out onto the sidewalk and looked northward past the railroad tracks. *I bet they're all back,* he thought. *I'm gonna head over to Border's Café and see if Henry is there.*

———

MOST OF THE CHATTER IN THE CAFÉ STOPPED when Tom entered. He felt pleased seeing his friend Henry sitting at the usual table.

"I figured you'd show up today, Tom," Henry said, smiling.

Tom sat down. Henry's smiled disappeared.

"Okay, let's have it, Henry. What happened?"

"Our local fire and rescue team pulled a body out of our lake this morning."

"Yeah, I figured as much, since I saw some of the process when the fog cleared a little."

"That must have been quite the scene," Henry said.

"You know, Henry, I'm more interested in who it was they pulled out. I'm afraid to ask. I have a friend working over there."

Henry's voice deepened. "It wasn't your friend, Julie."

"That's a relief," Tom said. "Who was it then?"

"Senator McDougal's secretary. A woman by the name of Franks, Isabelle Franks."

Tom shook his head. "I didn't know her. I feel for what happened, but I'm sure glad it wasn't Julie."

Henry nodded. "I didn't know her either. I don't believe that she was from around here. Somebody said that she lived in Big Lakes."

———

TOM DROVE ACROSS THE RAILROAD TRACKS and headed for home. He removed his cap passing by the cemetery, thinking about his long-ago deceased wife, Becky. Tom slowed while turning up the hill of the township road that led to his roadway. Glancing to his left, he noticed two vehicles parked in the driveway of the home of his former friend, Maynard Cushing. The retired CIA agent was murdered in his home about three years ago.

He thought about the conflict that followed the death of Maynard. I darn near lost my life because of it...the murderer hired a hit man to do me in. I can still see that evil looking fish-faced, small man standing in my dining room with a knife in his hands. If it wasn't for a small loose carpet and my tennis racquet, the culprit may have gotten me. I got lucky.

Maynard's killer had eventually gotten caught on the Hastings's property with the help of Tom's neighbor, Pete, and four officers from the sheriff's department. It seems like so long ago, he thought. Yet, it's only been a couple of years or so. Maybe it's all over now, and trouble will stop following me around.

Tom parked his vehicle in the garage and carried his mail toward the house. He heard the phone ringing as he passed through the door. "Hello."

"Hi, Tom, this is Julie."

Tom gasped. She must be a basket case, he thought. "Hi, Julie, I understand you guys have had a tragedy over there?"

"Tom, we've had a serious accident. Senator McDougal's secretary drowned."

"Yes, Julie, I already know."

"You must have been in New Dresden, huh?"

"Sure was. It sounds as if you need some calming. Do you want to come over?"

"Yes, I sure do—be there in half an hour."

21

TOM FELT HIS HEART RACING as he hung up the phone. Warm memories of a relationship with Julie three to fours years ago had momentarily resurfaced. We had some darn good times, he said to himself. I've always regretted that it didn't work out. Oh well, life goes on.

He took a quick shower and dressed in a dark blue warm-up outfit. Tom glanced at his watch: 1:15. He sat down in his computer corner and waited.

Minutes later, Tom saw the movement of a vehicle drive up his driveway. He had been thinking about Julie and the trauma that she was going through.

He got up off the chair and jerked the door open, expecting Julie to be walking down the sidewalk. He stopped. That's not her car, he said to himself.

Two brown-clad police officers got out of a white car. That's a sheriff's car, he thought. He watched the two officers stand and look around for a moment. Then they proceeded toward him.

Tom recognized Sheriff Johnson. He's been here before, Tom said to himself.

He stood on the small deck in front of his door, knowing very well why the officers had come. It's because of my view, I think. Or perhaps they think that I know the victim...or because I know Julie.

The sheriff's hair appeared a little thinner since the last time they talked. Tom's thoughts flashed back to the previous year when this same man, his deputy and two other officers rescued him from a nearly fatal scene in Chilton Mills.

Tom walked up the sidewalk to greet the officers. "Hello, Sheriff Dave. I think I know why you're here."

"Mr. Hastings, this is Deputy Kelly Martin."

Tom shook hands with both men. He looked up at the taller officer. "Hello, Deputy. Welcome to my home."

"Quite the place you've got here," the deputy said.

"Tom, I know you're busy so we'll get right to the point. You may have already heard, but the body of one of Senator McDougal's employees was found in the bay there earlier this morning." He pointed.

"Yeah, I did hear about it."

The deputy squared his shoulders, spreading his legs slightly. "Did you hear any unusual sounds last night? Something different than usual. Like a scream—a yell?"

Tom's eyes picked up Julie's vehicle entering his driveway. "No, I didn't, but I did hear the sirens and saw the flashing lights early this morning."

The sheriff turned his head. "Well, looks as if you have company. We won't use up any more of your time. If you hear anything— anything at all—please call my office."

Tom nodded and reached out to accept the sheriff's card.

Julie had driven her vehicle past the sheriff's and parked in front of the garage. She met the sheriff and his deputy as she walked toward Tom's house.

Tom watched as Julie shook hands with them. Tom wasn't surprised that the officers spent time talking to her. She's living over there, he thought. They talked for a few minutes before Julie nodded her head and headed down the sidewalk.

Tom had taken a seat on the front deck. He watched anxiously as the officers got back in their car and Julie hurried toward him. He opened his arms and Julie melted into his embrace.

She coughed and cleared her throat. "Oh, Tom—I'm not sure what's going on. Let's have a drink—on the deck. I need some time— this really hurts."

Tom shook his head. He had never seen Julie's composure suffering to this extent at anytime previously. He poured two glasses of wine in the kitchen and took them out onto the lakeside deck. He noticed Julie wiping away tears as he handed her a glass. "You're really taking it hard, aren't you?"

She nodded and took a long drink from her glass. "Something is telling me that I shouldn't be working where I am. There's so much tension. Everyone feels it...." Julie lifted her wine glass again. "Well, except for Peter. Nothing ever shakes that guy up."

Tom frowned watching the strained look on Julie's face. "And worst of all...." Julie looked into Tom's eyes. "Worst of all—I found the body."

"Oh my God! That's awful. Do you want to talk about it?"

"No! I want to forget it."

Tom forced a smile. "So where was the senator when all this happened?"

"I'm not sure, Tom. I'm supposed to be in charge of all his travel plans, but about half the time, I don't know where he is. I think he spent the last few nights at his home in Fargo, though."

"I bet the sheriff you just met outside will be around to ask him a few questions."

"The sheriff! Oh, yes—one of his deputies—the one who was with him—he's already interviewed me and the rest of the staff."

Julie set down her glass. "I know I shouldn't be doing this. It will only lead to a headache in the morning, but could I please have another?"

Tom stood. "Sure, I'll be right back."

———

THE SUN'S RAYS LIT UP THE TREES ON THE OPPOSITE SHORE. "Isn't that beautiful?" Julie said, slurring her words.

Tom stood. "Hey, we better get something to eat. I'll fire up the grill."

He walked over to the Weber, opened the gas valve, and engaged the burners.

"Tom, do you remember the night we were out here and Mary Ann's house burned down? I'll never forget what the sky looked like." Julie laughed hysterically. "Yeah, the mother of all fireworks displays."

Tom frowned. "The fire was one thing—but I'd just as soon forget what else happened."

Julie laughed loudly. "Like, you mean the little weasel coming after you with a knife."

"Well, I know that you've had a lot of wine—and you've experienced high trauma—so you can laugh if you wish."

Julie stood. She wavered slightly, stepped over to Tom. They hugged and kissed.

Tom pulled away. "I better get those steaks on, Julie."

She smiled and dropped back into her chair. "How about a dip in the hot tub after dinner?"

"Sure, but we better wait until its dark."

Tom reentered his house and brought out a thick New York Strip steak. He dumped it on the grates and closed the lid.

———

THE THREE-QUARTER MOON HAD RISEN UP HIGH over the tree line when Tom closed and fastened the cover of his hot tub. Julie had gone inside the house. He carried in the two empty glasses. Hesitating at the refrigerator door, he opened it and brought out another bottle of wine. As the cork pulled loosed from the neck of the bottle, he heard the shower running.

I wonder what that means, he said to himself, visualizing Julie, water running down the sides of her head. Tom sat down on the loveseat after pouring himself a half full glass of wine. He got up and walked into the den to turn on the television. Tom found a Lifetime channel movie that looked interesting.

Minutes later, Julie entered the room, wearing one of Tom's robes.

Tom looked up. "Oh, I see you've visited my closet."

Julie placed a hand over her forehead. "Tom, I've got the feeling that I'm going to have a splitting headache. Could I go lay down on your bed?"

"Of course. How about a glass of water?"

"Ah—yeah—damn good idea."

Tom hastily got up off the couch and patted Julie on the top of the head as he walked into the kitchen.

"There you go. Maybe the headache will go away after a bit."

Julie forced a smile. "I hope so, Tom. Thanks." She turned and headed up the stairs.

Tom returned to his den and the movie. Half an hour later, he fell asleep.

He awakened in what seemed moments later. "Geez, I've been asleep for four hours," he muttered.

Tom shut off the television and headed up the stairs. Quietly, he opened the door to his bedroom. He looked for a bulge in the bedspread. There wasn't any, instead the covers had been pulled back.

"She's gone!" he whispered. Hurrying to a window that viewed his driveway, he looked out. "Her vehicle is gone, too."

Tom banged his fists together. "Darn! I guess she's done this before." Putting on his night clothes, he climbed under the covers.

22

VERONICA BURIED HER HEAD IN HER HANDS. The nightmare she had experienced on Sunday night grated heavily on her mind. She replayed the event over and over again as she sat on her living room loveseat.

The door to the senator's office opened. She heard it close and the sound of footsteps approaching the desk. A flashlight beam lit up part of the wall behind her. She remembered that her lungs had stopped functioning for an instant. She held her breath as long as she dared, then inhaled in short gasps, desperately hoping that the intruder wouldn't hear.

Veronica had placed a hand over her mouth when the footsteps stopped in front of the desk. Did I close the file drawer? she asked herself, panicking, but unable to move. Turning her head slightly, one of her eyes didn't see anything protruding from the desk. She felt relieved temporarily that she had closed it after all, but...the darn key is still in the lock, she thought, feeling the tension.

She had fought the urge to pull the desk chair toward her, thinking her hiding place would be more secure.

Veronica had realized that she didn't have much choice but to remain exactly where she lay. She heard the sound of someone chewing gum, a cough and the clearing of a throat. She fantasized a big brute of a monster standing there, waiting to devour her after she emerged from her lair.

Veronica remembered the tinkling noise, then the sound of a key turning. The gum chewing had stopped. Hurried footsteps moved away from the desk toward the door. Veronica risked a deep breath, and then heard the door creak as it opened slowly.

I couldn't control my lungs after hearing a loud thud, a screech, a high-pitched cry, and someone falling onto the carpet, she remembered. I gasped—thank God no one heard me. When the footsteps approached the desk right then, I felt sure the jig was up, and I was going to be exposed.

Veronica chuckled. When I heard the clunking sound on top the desk, I thought the next clunk was going to be on my head—but then, like a miracle, I heard rapid footsteps retreating. Then I heard a series of grunts. She squirmed on her loveseat and remembered what she felt like doing—taking a peek and seeing what the heck was going on....I didn't dare, she thought.

Then she heard a dragging sound—some more grunts, and the door slam shut. She had cleared her throat as quietly as she could, then pushed away the chair. Gads, I remember how my body wouldn't respond as I attempted to roll out from underneath the desk.

I panicked and imagined a massive cramp overtaking my entire body. I really had to talk to myself, to relax and get the heck out of there. I remember feeling the beads of perspiration forming on my forehead. My entire body seemed wet.

Finally, my knees moved beyond the confines of the desk frame and I stretched out my legs. My fingers hurt as I pushed down on the carpet and got up on my hands and knees. I felt numb but somehow crawled out from underneath the desk.

Veronica remembered getting up on her knees, grabbing the edge of the desk with both hands, and hoisting herself onto her feet. Jeez, I felt so sore and stiff.

She had used one of her sleeves to clear away the moisture from her eyes. Stooping down, she picked up her camera and laid it on the desk. She locked the file drawer and pulled the key out of the lock.

Veronica did a couple of knee bends, feeling the numbness leave her toes. She had twisted her body from side to side five times. Her eyes had adjusted to the dark enough to realize that the bust of Lincoln had been moved. She placed the key down on the desk in approximately the same position where she had gotten it earlier. Grabbing the bust with both hands she lifted it and set it down on top of the key.

I remember thinking about using the back door as an exit, but I didn't have a key for my own back door. She draped her camera strap over her shoulder and tip-toed to the front office door.

Veronica had opened it just enough to move her head partially through. She saw no one. Closing the door behind her, Veronica hurried toward the outside entry door and did the same. Again, there was no one in sight. She exited and walked quickly down the sidewalk toward her unit.

I thought that I was in heaven after getting back into my apartment and locking my door. I flung myself down and now here I sit.

———

VERONICA HAD TOSSED AND TURNED MOST OF THE NIGHT after her traumatic experience. Finally, just before dawn, she fell into a deep sleep. The shrieking sounds of sirens and vehicle noises awoke her mid-morning. She reached for her watch which lay on the small table. "Oh my heavens, I've overslept," she muttered and quickly got out of bed.

She drew a curtain aside and peeked out the window. My God, it's a sea of color out there, she said to herself, observing multitudes of flashing lights and bright red vehicles.

Veronica dressed hurriedly and brushed her hair before walking out onto the sidewalk. She felt uncertain as to what was going on, and she didn't want to appear conspicuous.

She walked quickly toward the conglomeration of vehicles and people. The first person who noticed her approaching raised an arm— Peter.

He moved from his position and stepped toward her. She grabbed both of his hands with hers. "Peter, I'm afraid of all this. What's going on?"

"You haven't heard?"

"Heard what?"

"Isabelle is dead."

"Oh, my God!" Veronica exclaimed.

Peter's face knotted, his chin lowered, and he stared at the sidewalk.

Veronica made two slow short steps toward him. She opened up her arms. They hugged—released and hugged some more.

She pulled away and looked into his eyes. "Peter, I'm lost."

"Hey, I'll get Julie. She'll be able to help you."

Tears streamed down both of Veronica's cheeks. Her mind and thoughts struggled with total disarray. I've had a multiple hit here, she said to herself. I didn't care squat for the leader of the pack, Isabelle. Yet, she's dead—murdered. I didn't see it—but I heard it— am I a witness? What do I do?

Veronica jerked—she felt a hand on her shoulder. Looking up, she looked into the eyes of Julie Huffman. They hugged. Julie's chest heaved intermittently. She's trying hard not to cry, Veronica thought.

While holding Julie tight, Veronica's thoughts drifted back to her cage under the desk—she was trapped. What do I tell the police? They will certainly interview me.

Veronica stared at the senator's office. She saw yellow strips of tape began at the door of Isabelle's apartment and stretched all the way to the senator's garages. She stiffened and thought, Jeez, I hope that I didn't drop anything lying under that desk. I bet they go over that room with a fine tooth comb.

"Veronica, are you all right?" Julie asked. "You seem so far away," she added.

Veronica pulled away and uttered, "My God, Julie, I don't know what to think—all those flashing lights—all the sirens."

Julie patted her on one side of the head. Veronica coughed, and she cleared her throat. "I'm fine—just not accustomed to all this action. I surely didn't expect this when I took this job."

Julie hugged Veronica again and looked toward the roadway. She watched another white police car come down the steep slope.

"That's the sheriff!" she heard someone say loudly.

Veronica felt snakes crawling around her stomach walls watching the two officers get out of their vehicle. She knew the investigators had arrived...what in heaven's name will I tell them? She saw them talking to another group of officers. Veronica felt the tension when one of them pointed at her and Julie.

Her heart fluttered as a tall, broad-shouldered officer approached. The officer stopped and looked at Julie. "I'm Deputy Investigator Martin. You live in one of those units over there?" he asked, pointing.

"Yes, I'm Julie Huffman and I'm in unit two. This is Veronica Lewis. You're in unit four, right, Veronica?" Julie asked.

Veronica nodded.

"Look, ladies. I need to interview both of you. Who's in number three?"

She pointed. "Peter Nelson. That's him standing over there—the young looking guy."

The deputy looked back toward the cluster of officers within the confines of the tape. "Would you give me half an hour? I would like to talk to each of you alone and in your units."

"Sure," Julie said. "I'll tell Peter," she added.

———

THE GENTLE KNOCK ON THE DOOR sent shivers up Veronica's spine. She and Julie had returned to their units several minutes ago after the fire and rescue vehicles began leaving the premises. She jumped up off the couch and opened the door.

"Hello again. Veronica Lewis, right?"

"Have a seat. Would you like something to drink?"

"No thanks. This won't take long."

The deputy asked the usual questions: *Where did you spend the night? Can anyone verify that? How well did you know Miss Franks? Did you hear any strange noises last night or early this morning? What time did you go to bed? Did you talk to anyone last night?*

"Thank you very much, Miss Lewis. Here's my card. If you think of anything that could possibly help us with this case, give me a call."

Veronica took the card and watched the deputy leave. She walked into her bedroom, picked up her cell phone and lay down on the bed. She punched in her mother's work number.

"Yes?"

"I'm going to tell you something, but you have to promise me that it will remain our secret."

"Veronica, what's happened?"

Methodically, Veronica told her mother what she had experienced the previous evening.

"I'm proud of you—you kept your cool—how did the photo's turn out?"

"Jeez, ya know, Mom, I haven't had a chance to look. I'll check 'em out after I hang up."

"You hang in there, sweetie—and, you're doing one heck of a job. My boss will be pleased. We will be paid well."

"Thanks, Mom. Love you."

"Love you, too."

23

SHERIFF DAVE JOHNSON OF BIG LAKES COUNTY paged through the medical examiner's preliminary report. He bit his lower lip. "Well, Kelly, what do you think?"

Deputy Kelly Martin had been hired as an investigator by the sheriff six months ago. He felt confident that the extensive training he had undertaken would help him, but the death of the woman on Border's Lake made him feel overwhelmed. It became his first case...dealing with a United States senator.

Sheriff Johnson stood four inches shorter than his deputy. The slightness of his body frame matched his narrow face and pointed jaw perfectly. His narrow shoulders stooped forward slightly, totally in contrast to Kelly's, whose broad shoulder filled a doorway. Dave combed his thinning blond hair straight back. The deputy's thick, black hair dangled slightly over his left ear. The sheriff's light blue eyes contrasted sharply with the dark brown ones of Kelly's.

"Dave, even though the medical examiner's report isn't conclusive, I'm 110 percent sure it's a homicide."

"Yeah, the dent in the skull doesn't fit a fall very well. She could've fallen and did that—but...."

"Dave, from what I learned about the woman, she rarely went near the water. What the heck would she be doing down at the dock at night?"

The sheriff sighed and shook his head slowly. "Yeah, it does bring up some serious questions." He read from the report: *cause of death— drowning likely, complicated by a blow to the head.*

The deputy nodded. "So the killer knocked the woman out with a blunt object. He or she then dragged the victim down hill and into the water."

Sheriff Johnson locked his upper incisors into his lower lip. "I'll be anxious to read the report on the fibers the boys found in the drag route—but they probably came from the victim's clothes.

"Also, the fingerprints on the door knobs—and the desk things. We need fingerprints taken off everyone that spent the night here on Sunday—and find the victim's missing left shoe."

The deputy smacked his lips together. "Yeah, it's probably at the bottom of the lake. I really don't think finding the shoe would help us much anyhow. What do you think?"

"You're probably right." The sheriff finished reading the second page and set the report down on the desk.

The deputy placed his hands on his hips. "What about the button we found under the senator's desk?"

"Oh yeah, it was a small white generic button, the type that you would see on a man's shirt or a woman's blouse. Probably came from the cleaning crew. The victim was hit over the head by the door, not anywhere close to the desk."

"Yes, but what if the killer was hiding under the desk?"

The sheriff frowned. "Well, it's possible. I suppose we should keep an eye out for a missing button. For right now, let's go over the details of your interviews—slowly. I want to hear exactly what everyone said."

Dave raised his hand. "Oh yes, but first I want to hear the background report on the victim."

Deputy Martin grimaced. He reached inside his jacket pocket and retrieved a notebook. Pulling his chair next to the desk, the deputy flipped a page and began. "Isabelle Franks lived alone here in Big Lakes. She originally comes from Arlington, Virginia, one of two children born to Ben and Emily Franks. She has a brother, Steve, living in Cambridge, Michigan. He flew down here to take care of arrangements.

"She met the senator while in college, during his first term. Isabelle has been working for him ever since, mainly as a secretary. According to a majority opinion of other employees, she has been the senator's most trusted and reliable employee.

"Miss Franks has never been married, but rumors say that she had a child during her college days. We can assume the child was put up for adoption as there has been no communication from a sibling other than her brother at this time.

"She has managed the senator's office at Border's Lake since it was built four years ago. When the summer office closes, she moves to the office in Fargo." The deputy put his notebook down. "Any questions thus far?"

Dave shook his head.

"Okay. Next is Julie Huffman: she's the senator's travel secretary and was apparently the last person to see the victim alive." The deputy frowned. His eyes lifted and looked at the sheriff. "That is except for the killer."

Johnson nodded.

The deputy looked at his notes and began to read. "*I went for a walk just before dark on Sunday evening. When I returned, I saw Isabelle Franks sitting on a bench in front of her unit.*"

Kelly pulled a sheet of paper out of his pocket. He unfolded it and pressed out some of the creases. He planted his finger "Right there: there are two sitting benches fronting the units. It was the closest one to the senator's office suite."

Sheriff Johnson nodded. "Go on."

Kelly continued reading. "*Isabelle did not look up from her book and didn't appear to see me.*"

"I asked Miss Huffman what she did the rest of the evening. She told me that she spent it watching television and went to bed about 10:00. She did not hear anything—unusual noises and such. Julie also claimed that she got along well with Franks and couldn't recollect anyone who didn't."

"Okay, Kelly—now tell me about the intern."

"Veronica Lewis joined the staff less than a month ago. She had been assigned to assist Julie Huffman last week."

"What's her background?' the sheriff asked.

"She graduated from a high school in Bismarck, North Dakota last spring. She is enrolled as a freshman student for the second quarter in Concordia College in Moorhead."

The sheriff held up his hand. "How did she get the job? Anyone pull any strings."

The deputy smiled. "Yes, according to the intern, a lawyer in Bismarck, a friend of her father's, convinced the senator to hire her."

"You don't happen to know the friend's name?"

"Yup, sure do—Jack McDougal."

"A relative?" the sheriff asked.

"Yup—cousins."

"Go on."

"The intern claimed to have spent Sunday evening alone watching television. She claims to have talked to her mother on the phone about 9:00 p.m."

"Who's her mother?"

The deputy turned a page. "Nicole Dunton. She owns and lives in a townhome in Fargo. She works for a company called Delvo Industries."

"What about this Peter kid?"

The deputy turned a page. His large brown eyes squinted. "Ah, he spent the evening watching television, so he said."

Dave nodded. "You didn't interview the domestics, though, did you?"

"No, I thought I would do that today when the senator and his wife return from Fargo."

The sheriff nodded. "Kelly, another subject, but do you remember the story about a race car blowing up at the track in Brainerd about a month ago?"

The deputy frowned. "Yup, the FBI investigated that one, didn't they?"

"Yes they did—and they concluded that there wasn't any foul play." The sheriff put both hands on the table. "Maybe a coincidence— first the senator's nephew—then the senator's secretary—it makes me wonder."

Kelly Miller stood and walked over to the sheriff's desk. He slapped a palm down on the surface. "Dave, I think we should talk to the judge. We need to search the employee's units."

"Okay, let's go see him."

24

SENATOR MCDOUGAL WATCHED OUT THE WINDOW at mid-morning on Tuesday, the day after Isabelle's body was found, as the white police car drove up his roadway and parked in the circular drive. "Looks like we have company, Aaron."

The politician's aide got up from his chair and walked to the window. "It's the sheriff himself—and that nosy deputy."

"Take it easy, Aaron, I have nothing to do with Franks's death. You know that."

"I know that—regardless, I don't like them snooping around."

Stella Robinson, the senator's chief of domestic aides, answered the door.

"Good afternoon, ma'am. I'm Sheriff Johnson and this is Deputy Miller. We are investigating the death of the senator's secretary. Could we come in? We have some questions."

"I'll let the senator know that you're here."

Deputy Miller raised a hand. "Ah, actually, it's you that we would like to talk to first."

She led the two officers to a sitting room where they sat down on a couch. "Coffee, or something to drink?"

"No thanks," the deputy responded. "This won't take long."

Deputy Miller asked her several questions, all very routine. Both the officers raised their heads when she told them of seeing a pair of headlights come up the roadway about 9:00 p.m. They became even more interested when she reported seeing a set of taillights leaving around midnight.

"Were you the only person present in the house that evening?"

"Yes, I was. The senator and his wife had spent the past three nights at their home in Fargo."

The deputy stood. "Would you call in the senator, please?"

Stella left the room.

A door opened. The senator spoke first, using his deep booming voice. "Hello, Sheriff Johnson. I don't believe that I've met your deputy."

The officers both stood and shook hands with the senator. "Now, what can I do for you two? My wife and I are both in shock regarding Miss Franks's death." The senator looked down at his watch. "Harriet is asleep right now. She didn't get any last night. I'm a little behind myself."

The deputy ran a thumb and forefinger over his chin. He turned the page of his notebook. "So you and your wife were at your home in Fargo the past two days. Is that correct?"

"Yes, it certainly is. Several people can verify that."

"That won't be necessary, senator. I believe you," the deputy said. He asked several more questions and closed his notebook. Glancing at the sheriff, he said, "That's all I have, Dave. How about you?"

The sheriff stood. "Thank you very much, Senator. I have no more questions, but we have one more request."

"What's that?"

Sheriff Johnson's face muscles tightened. He waved a folded document in front of him. "I need to search all of your employee's units."

"Why is all that necessary?"

"It's more or less routine. It's our job—I have a court order."

The senator frowned. "Very well, I'll give Julie Huffman a call—she'll make the units available for you."

The deputy said, "We need a key for each of the units in the event they aren't home—this includes the Isabelle Franks unit."

The senator opened a desk drawer and brought out a ring of keys. "They should all be here, Sheriff."

The senator saw the two officers out the door. He shook his head watching them walk quickly toward his office.

———

VERONICA HAD UPLOADED HER DIGITAL CAMERA images to her laptop. She flipped through twenty-six photos, not very pleased because over half of them were blurry and not readable. "Jeez, I'm going to have to do it again," she muttered. "But how and when?"

A rapid knock on the door jolted every brain cell in her brain. Who the heck is that? she asked herself and pulled the curtains back from her front window. Veronica saw two police officers standing on the sidewalk.

Her legs felt like jelly striding toward the door. It's that snoopy deputy again, she thought after opening the door.

"Miss Lewis, remember us? I'm Big Lakes County Deputy Martin and this is Sheriff Johnson." He extended a hand. "This is a search warrant. Would you please wait outside? It won't take very long."

Veronica moved aside and allowed the officers to enter. She stepped onto the sidewalk and left the door open. She stomped her right foot on the concrete and punched the side of her head with her fist. "Damn," she muttered. "My camera and laptop. What if they take them? I'm dead."

She peeked in the doorway and saw the sheriff approaching. "Miss Lewis, we're going to have to confiscate your camera and computer. Would you save what you were doing and shut it off?"

Veronica worked hard to keep her composure as she walked to her desk. She hoped the sheriff wouldn't notice her press the *Delete* button instead of *Save*. She quickly cleaned out the Recycle Bin and double-clicked the *Shut Down* icon.

"Do you have to take my camera? I need it this evening. All I have in it are some text documents the senator wanted us to read."

The sheriff nodded. "Okay, show me,"

Veronica held up the viewer and flicked through some of the images. She felt relieved because they appeared blurred.

"All right, then, we'll leave it."

She felt her face flush when the deputy held up one of her blouses. "Dave, look what I found in the closet!"

Johnson entered the room.

"A blouse with a white button missing!" the deputy exclaimed.

The sheriff looked directly at Veronica. "Miss, do you know what happened to that button?"

"No, of course not. Everyone loses a button once in a while."

Kelly said, "Nevertheless, we have to take the blouse with us. Hope that you won't mind."

Veronica felt like passing out. "No, of course not," she said, wondering how she ever got those words out.

She placed her camera in its case and walked outside. Ten minutes later, the officers exited her unit. The deputy continued on to the next unit. The sheriff paused. "Thank you, young lady. There's one more thing, though."

Veronica's voice trembled. "What's that?"

The sheriff pointed to a white panel which had just arrived. I want you to volunteer to be fingerprinted over there. You have the right to refuse, but we could get a court order to force you."

Veronica muttered, "Jeez, what next?" She threw up her hands and stomped toward the van.

25

Hans MUELLER STUDIED THE COUNTRYSIDE as he sat in the back seat of the senator's Lexus. Minutes earlier, they had passed through the city of Big Lakes and he marveled at the beauty of the glittering lake water.

We don't have lakes like this in Germany, he thought. A few miles later, a long, narrow body of water appeared to his left as the automobile scooted up a gradual incline, the height lined with pine and oak trees. Those we have, he mused.

The driver turned onto an exit ramp, leaving the main highway and driving onto a county highway. Hans observed more pockets of water as the vehicle negotiated a series of curves in the road. A series of rolling hills descended down to a large body of water. He knew enough English to properly read the *Border's Lake* sign.

He heard the clicking of a turn signal and the Lexus slowed and made a left turn onto a graveled country road. Shortly, the vehicle stopped in front of a gate manned by two armed guards. The gate opened and they took a sharp turn, exposing a large building, along with a trailer home and a white semi-truck. Hans looked beyond at a tall stand of corn.

The vehicle came to a stop next to the trailer home. Aaron Crier, the senator's number one aide, stepped out of the automobile on the passenger side. He walked around the vehicle and opened the rear door. "We've arrived, Hans."

Hans followed Aaron to a small door at an outside corner of the large building. My God, it's a barn...very much like in Germany, he thought. Very old, though. German barns are much more modern.

Aaron opened the door and Hans followed him in. The small room looks like an office, Hans thought. Aaron opened a second inside door and held it open. He nodded and gestured. Hans walked through and his mouth opened in amazement as he stared at the OxyBeast. "My God, it's enormous!"

Hans walked slowly to one of the huge wheels. He reached out and touched it...then, he gave it a kick.

Aaron laughed. "Hans, you've been briefed on the element zillium, right?"

"Yeah—I 'ave—magnificent!"

"I'm sure that you are aware of the significance of the connection between oxygen and zillium."

"I am excited—excited as any scientist could be."

"Now, don't get me wrong—the trial runs have been going well—but, recently—the energy level has been disappointing. That's precisely why we hired you, and I know that you have been working on formulas in the laboratory of Kurtz Manufacturing in West Fargo for the past two weeks.

"Mueller, we need you here to see the oxygen-zillium connection in action. There's a small bedroom available in the trailer. Let's move your things in there and you get some rest. You can begin your work in the laboratory first thing in the morning."

The scientist smiled and said, his German accent very evident. "Yeah, that is good,"

———

SENATOR MCDOUGAL ARRIVED AT THE BARN SITE the next morning at 10:00 a.m. His towering frame forced him to stoop slightly as he entered the barn door. His driver had remained in the car. Through the glass-walled laboratory, he saw Hans, the scientist and another person, dressed in fully-protected white body wear. Aaron, who had been sitting next to a small table, stood. "Good morning, Sean. Care for a cup?"

"Yeah, don't mind if I do. How's it going in there, anyhow?"

Aaron shook his head, smiling. "How the heck would I know? I don't understand any of this. They could be manufacturing a nuclear bomb in there and I wouldn't have a clue."

The senator pointed his finger. "Well, let's get Hans out here. I want to know what's going on."

Aaron walked over to the laboratory door. He pressed a button and spoke into a microphone. Hans Mueller's head turned. He nodded.

———

SENATOR MCDOUGAL LISTENED INTENTLY to Mr. Mueller's explanation. The bars of zillium they had been using were inadequate. They needed to be of a much greater in dimension for this large a machine. The smaller bars would work for an automobile, but not for an airplane, train or semi-truck.

The senator nodded and motioned for the scientist to return to work. "Aaron, we're going to have to import an updated version of zillium from Togo."

Aaron penciled some words into his notebook. He looked up.

"This creates a problem," the senator said. "We need to bring in the new zillium secretly. Do you remember a couple of years ago when we used that isolated port in Mexico?" he added.

Aaron smiled. "Yeah, I remember. That was cool."

"Would you arrange all the details, Aaron. I'll make it worthwhile. Confidentiality is imperative. I hate to think what would happen to my career if the opposing party would find out that we're smuggling in the element from Africa."

Aaron nodded and closed his notebook. "Sean, consider it done. Do you think that we should use the same route as before? To cross the Rio Grande, I mean?"

"That's a decision that you're going to have to make."

Aaron opened his notebook and penciled in more notations.

"Cripes, Sean, we could haul the Empire State Building over the border at that point, and the U.S. Border Patrol would be none the wiser."

26

JULIE FELT ESTATIC. The boarding for the flight from Minneapolis to Amsterdam went off without a hitch, in spite of what happened to Isabelle. She sat by the window, next to Peter, in the first-class section. The senator occupied a rear seat next to Hans Mueller. Aaron sat next to Veronica in the seats ahead of Julie's.

She had never flown KLM Dutch Airlines before and looked forward to the experience. Julie had flown Northwest Airlines on a non-stop previously and remembered that she had read two books during the flight.

She closed her eyes when the plane began roaring up the runway. Julie felt perfectly relaxed and excited about visiting the country, which she had seen during her college days. I wonder how much it's changed, she thought. I probably wasn't too smart hitchhiking like I did then...I'm a lot wiser now. Julie's mind drifted with the clouds. She experience feelings of weightlessness. Hell, I'm just as dumb now as I was then. Julie laughed quietly.

She felt confident with the arrangements that she had successfully made in advance. According to the schedule, which she stored in her briefcase, they should arrive in Lome after a stopover in Amsterdam the next day at 10:00 in the morning—2:00 a.m. our time, she said to herself, enjoying the weightless feeling as the huge plane banked eastward and ascended sharply.

When Julie opened her eyes, the plane had broken through the clouds and the rays of the sun lit up the tops of the heads on the other side of the aisle. She glanced at Peter, who appeared tense, his sparkling eyes dashing around from window to window.

Julie chuckled. She grabbed Peter's hand. "Relax, young man, we'll be there before you know it."

Half an hour later, the seatbelt warning light went out, and she unbuckled. She peeked over the top of her backrest, a wide smile frozen on her face. "Are we going to get fed or not?"

Senator McDougal looked up from a paper which he had been reading. "Julie, there's more to life than eating, ya know."

The hours passed by. Julie set her book *Pattern of Violence* down in her lap—a morbid story about a child abuser and killer in Minneapolis, known as the River Rat.

A SPATTERING OF AMSTERDAM CITY APPEARED through the clouds during the descent of the DC-10. Peter felt both excited and afraid. He didn't like flying but knew that he would be on the ground shortly. Surely, nothing bad will happen, he thought.

His legs felt like wax as they moved slowly along a line of people going through customs. This, too, shall pass, he said to himself, wondering how the heck he ever got into this situation.

The senator towered over him, his huge arms folded like a giant cross across his chest. Julie and Veronica walked ahead of the senator. Aaron talked to someone in low tones directly behind. Peter glanced backward. It's not the German who he's talking to. Hans Mueller's stubby body bobbed along directly behind Aaron.

Julie led the group toward their departure gate after they had cleared customs. Peter dashed ahead to catch up to her. "You know where you're going, Jewel?" he asked.

She smiled and pointed. "Sure do, young man. Our gate is down at the end of that corridor."

AMBASSADOR BODJONA OF THE TOGO REPUBLIC smiled so wide that the frontal surface of his back teeth showed. He had been a representative to the U.S.A. from the small nation for the past ten years. "Gentlemen and ladies, welcome to Togo."

The small gathering of Americans had just come down the steps of the aircraft, which had landed at Gnassingbe Eyadema International airport in Lome. The tall senator shook hands with the ambassador. He turned and introduced the other members of his party.

Fifteen minutes later, three of the Americans entered a room for a meeting with three representatives of the Togo government. The senator elbowed his chair off to the side and stood up. "Gentlemen, Mr. Mueller knows what he's talking about. The size and shape of the zillium bars need a major adjustment."

The Togo representatives sat stoically in their chairs. Only Hans Mueller and Aaron Crier of the senator's staff attended the closed-door meeting. The tall senator puckered his lips. "We need a truckload shipment immediately. Do you understand?"

———

JULIE, PETER AND VERONICA HAD THREE DAYS TO BURN. On their first free one, they walked in the direction of the ocean.

"What kind of trees are those?" Peter asked, attired in a light-colored pair of shorts and shirt, waiting to cross a highway at an intersection.

"Coconut trees," Julie said.

They hurried across the highway and wandered through rows of typical fishermen's dwellings. Julie removed her shoes and stockings and sloshed into a sea of find sand. "This feels so good," she said. "Isn't this amazing?"

"Wow, it's really hot," Veronica said, holding onto the wide brim of her straw hat.

Julie wiped the perspiration from her brow with a towel. "We're not too far from the equator, only a few degrees to the north."

"Is that why the sun is just about right over our heads?" Peter asked.

Julie laughed. "You're catching on, Pete."

They sat down in the sand allowing the waves to reach their knees at high tide.

Julie gathered her upraised knees in her arms. "Maybe we should sign up for a tour tomorrow. I hear there are sacred crocodiles in the Bapure River."

Veronica asked, "Is there a place around here where we could shop for souvenirs?"

Julie turned her head. "Yes, actually Arts Street and Rue Foch are both within walking distance. There are all sorts of shops and street vendors. Most of them carry authentic Togolese products."

"I want to go there. Can we do it today?" Veronica asked.

"Sure."

They shopped through the afternoon hours, returning to their hotel before dinner. While in the lobby, Peter studied a poster, which depicted an overview of Togo, along with the local geography:

Togo shares borders with Benin, to the east; Burkina Faso to the north; and Ghana to the west. The capitol, Lome, is located on the border with Ghana and on the shore of the Atlantic Ocean, which is directly south.

This building and the country are located on a narrow strip of land, which rises beyond coastal lagoons and swampy plains to an undulating plateau. Northwards, the plateau descends to a wide plain irrigated by the River Oti.

The central area is covered by deciduous forest, while grasslands stretch to the north and south. Near the eastern border, the River Mono runs to the sea.

You must visit the fetish market, with its intriguing voodoo charms, lotions and potions. We have three national wildlife parks, including the Fazao Park outside Sokode, the Keran Park near Kara, and the Fosse aus Lions (Lions' Den) near the northern town of Dapaong.

Have a great visit and we sincerely wish that you come again!

Day Two

THE TOURISTS SAW MANY LAGOONS AS THE BUS rolled northward through the swampy flatlands near the ocean. They noticed various water birds, including storks and cranes. The landscape changed to a chain of hills that eventually became the Atkora

Mountains, which traverse the central part of the country from Ghana in the southwest to Benin in the northeast.

The bus stopped at a village of scantily dressed people who decorated themselves with a generous amount of ornate metal. After crossing the mountains at about 2300 feet, they rode into the Oti River Valley where mango and other flamboyant trees dominated the landscape.

They saw endless miles of rolling hills of savannah. At times the hills disappeared and the road continued on through ranges of deciduous forest. Later in the day, the bus approached the central city of Bassar, which is adjacent to the Malfacassa forest.

From there, they employed a guide and toured the rocky hills of Malfacassa Mountain. Julie pointed. "Look! A waterbuck!"

"What's that over there by those funny looking trees?" Veronica asked.

"Uffta, that's a pack of hyenas," Julie said.

Peter imitated a lion's growl. "They look like weird dogs."

They toured one of the ancient iron smelting mines and witnessed endless acres of deforestation. Two hours later, the guide's vehicle stopped on a ragged road near a mountain top. "Get out, please," he said.

Julie walked to the edge of a cliff and used her binoculars to scan the massive valley below. "I see elephants!" she exclaimed.

Peter and Veronica rushed to her side. They took turns using the binoculars. "Just like the zoo in the Cities," Peter said.

Hours later, they returned to Bassar and spent the night in a motel.

Day Three

THE BUS TOOK THEM TO THE TOWN OF KARA, which is about 260 miles north of Lome. Again, they hired a guide, who drove them to the region of Mont Kalbye about ten miles north-east of Kara.

"This place is so beautiful!" Julie exclaimed. "Look what they make here. It's amazing."

The three tourists had stopped in the town of Landa, known for its craft markets.

Later they visited Pagouda, which is known for its music. Peter stood with his neck extended and his eyes bulging as they sat at a table watching and listening to spectacular, partially-clad dancers. Concurrently they enjoyed fufu, a popular ethnic food made by pounding yams in a pestle until it reached the consistency of baker's dough. The sauce that they spread over the fufu was flavored with palm nut.

The long bus ride back to Lome took all afternoon.

"I'm bushed," Peter said as they stepped off the bus in front of their hotel.

Julie gave him a gentle shove. "Well, Pete, did you see enough female anatomy?"

27

TOM HASTINGS HAD JUST RETURNED FROM HIS MAIL RUN to New Dresden. He laid two envelopes on his desk in the den and heard the answering machine beeping.

He pressed the play button and listened to a dreamy voice. "Hi, Tom, this is Nicole Dunton. My work number is 701-232-5498. Please return my call. Thank you."

Tom dialed the number.

"Hello, Delvo Industries, Nicole speaking. How may I help you?"

"Nicole, this is Tom. You called."

"Oh yes, I was wondering if you would do me a favor?"

Tom chuckled. "Well, I suppose so, but it depends on what it is."

"I need to get some of my things from my daughter's apartment in Senator McDougal's complex. Since she and most everyone else have flown to Africa, the guards at the gate will not let anyone in—and, I mean anyone."

Tom hesitated.

"It's worth a dinner at Mary Ann's this evening—please."

"You want to use my boat, don't you?"

"You're getting the idea, sweetie. How about it? It gets dark about 8:30. I could be out to your place by about 8:00."

"Well, okay, but I'm not going up there—the buildings. I'll just drop you off at the senator's dock."

"Oh, thank you, honey. I'll see you about 8:00."

Tom hung up the phone and remained sitting on the couch. "Geez, what the heck am I getting into now?" he asked himself, rapping his knuckles against the left side of his head. Her voice is setting me on fire.

During the rest of the daylight hours, Tom couldn't get his mind off Nicole Dunton. She's a beautiful woman, he thought. I could really go for her...yet, she's probably going to use me once again. Oh, what the heck! What have I got to lose?

———

TOM WALKED OUT TO HIS TENNIS COURT AT 7:30. He felt gladdened that the black flies and their relatives had left for the season. A slight breeze cooled his forehead as he walked onto the greenway, an extensive field of native grass about the size of three football fields.

He smiled watching the white, upraised tail of a deer as it leaped into the woods. Sorry that I interrupted your feeding, he said to himself. His stomach gurgled slightly from not having eaten since lunchtime. Tom looked forward to a dinner at Mary Ann's...if Nicole kept her promise...and they weren't both in jail. Stranger things have happened around here in the past, he thought.

"Kee-ya, kee-ya, kee-ya," a red-shouldered hawk screamed. Tom looked above the tree line to the north but didn't see one of his favorite predators. He glanced at his watch and felt the usual tightness in his stomach, thinking about his company, who could arrive at any minute.

Tom walked back toward his house, pausing at the garage, listening for the sounds of a vehicle approaching. I may as well wait inside the house, he thought.

A minute later, while walking down the sidewalk, he watched Nicole smile and wave as she drove by him, parking in his driveway.

She wore black slacks and a red plaid shirt. They met part way between the house and garage. As Tom had hoped, they embraced warmly. He looked into her eyes and she turned away.

"So what sort of trouble are you going to get me into, Nicole?"

She pulled herself away and swung an arm across her breasts. "Shouldn't be any trouble for you at all—it's not like say—we we're going to rob a bank."

Tom thought about the two times he went along with his previous friend Jolene. She talked him into raiding a farm building and the house—twice I fell for that. Twice I got into trouble. Oh well, I survived.

"So what are you thinking, big guy? You can simply take me over to the senator's dock with your boat, drop me off, and wait."

Tom muttered, "That doesn't sound too difficult. Well, let's get it out of the way. I'm starved."

Nicole placed a warm hand on his arm. "So am I."

Tom's 8-horsepower boat motor started on the second pull. He reversed the engine and backed away from the dock. Nicole sat on the front bench seat. She had a large black purse slung over her shoulder—her slacks snuggled up tight to her butt.

He rotated the control and the engine roared to full speed. When the senator's dock came into sight, he slowed the engine to a troll. "You're lucky—no lights down at the dock."

Nicole stood and grabbed onto a dock post as Tom shut off the engine. He snapped an adapter around a metal ring bolted to the dock frame. Nicole stepped from the boat onto the dock.

There's an eerie feeling down here, Tom thought, listening to the perpetual sounds of the small waves splashing onto shoreline rocks. He felt a deep-seated loneliness when Nicole walked away from the boat and disappeared into the night.

He heard Nicole hurrying up the wooden steps that obviously led to the senator's complex. The clop-clop sound of her shoes dissipated into the darkness above—then it became quiet. He shivered hearing the long, penetrating cry of a loon break the silence. An almost full moon peeked at Tom from a narrow opening between two eastern grayish clouds.

Tom looked at his watch. "Geez, she's only been gone three minutes," he muttered. I've got to relax, he said to himself.

His nervousness became even more apparent as more time passed. Geez, what if she doesn't come back? he asked himself. What the heck am I going to do?

"Zrrrrrr...zrrrrr...zrrrrr...." The loud, clattering alarm that went off seemed to be coming from all directions. Tom's back straightened. He grasped the rim of the boat with his left hand and the handle of the starting rope, his ears straining for the sound of footsteps. He pulled the rope—nothing happened. He pulled again and again. "Come on motor. Don't do this to me now," he muttered.

Pausing and catching his breath, he pulled again...again....

Finally, he heard the sound of footsteps coming down the stairway. Tom heard her speak, her voice low-pitched and quavering, "Tom— Tom, let's get the h.... otta here."

He grabbed the oars just as Nicole thumped onto a bench seat. "Nicole, the damn motor won't start. I've got to row back home."

"Oh great, but let's get the hell going."

Tom turned the boat around and grasped an oar firmly in each fist. He felt relieved when three of his strokes sent the boat toward his house.

"Is there anything I can do to help?" Nicole asked.

"Nothing! I have nothing else to paddle with. Use your hands if you wish."

Tom established a rhythm, feeling the boat move at a reasonable pace. He turned and saw a cluster of lights had come on by the senator's dock. He heard someone yelling...then the gurgling sound of a boat engine. Panic bounced off the insides of his stomach walls.

"Someone's started the speedboat! They're going to come after us!" Tom exclaimed, his heart thumping. He struggled with his breathing as he increased the rowing pace.

Tom altered his directions, heading the boat not for his dock but for a large weedy shallow area straight north, which he felt he could reach much sooner. Tom heard the unmistakable sound of the speedboat taking off.

"We're almost in the weeds, Tom. Hurry! Can't you row any

faster?"

Tom chose not to respond...fighting to subdue his feelings of disgust. Instead he used all the energy that he could muster to row as fast as he could. Who the hell is she talking to? he asked himself. It's been her idea all along.

The speedboat roared as it sped away from the dock eastward, and made a banking turn toward Tom's boat. As it leveled off and headed in his direction, Tom felt his chances of making a successful escape suddenly dimmed...row like hell or get caught.

Finally, he felt one of the oars strike resistance. Oh Geez, I'm in the weeds at last, he said to himself. The noise of the approaching speedboat forced him to row even harder, ignoring the intense pain in his arms and shoulders. Gads, the damn boat will be here in less than a minute.

Deeper and deeper into the weed bed, Tom rowed his boat. His arms felt exhausted and he felt the rapid thumps of his heart against his chest. Geez, I could have a heart attack, he thought. And for what? A good looking broad....

Removing one of the oars from its bracket, he stabbed it into the muddy bottom, and pushed hard, moving the boat deeper into the weeds. "Get down, Nicole! The damn boat is almost here!"

Tom dropped the oar and they both lowered their bodies as far as they could. Out of the corner of his eyes, he saw the tops of the weeds light up. The speed boat roared by and moments later Tom felt his boat heave rise and fall, over and over again.

"Now, what are we going to do?" Nicole asked. "This is almost funny," she added.

"We've got no choice right here—looks like we'll be late for dinner."

Nicole laughed hysterically.

———

MARY ANN'S RESTAURANT ON THE EAST SHORE of Border's Lake had a sparse crowd by the time Tom Hastings and Nicole Dunton entered. Tom looked at his watch. It read 9:45. "Well, at least they're still serving," he told Nicole after putting his name in for a dinner reservation.

The hostess led them to a booth which overlooked the lake. Tom assisted Nicole into her seat and sat across from her. Nicole gazed out the window. "Oh what a beautiful view, even if it's dark."

Tom smiled. "See that row of lights over there to your left? Just beyond is where a couple of nuts raided Senator's McDougal's property this evening."

Nicole's loud laughter drew the attention of a couple in the next booth. She placed a hand over her mouth. "Sorry, Tom, but the whole thing was rather hilarious."

Tom frowned, his thoughts remembering his panic on the dock...the motor...damn thing wouldn't start...the speed boat...the chase...the escape. He looked at the smiling face of his date and couldn't help himself. He laughed loudly. "I wonder what would have happened if they caught us? We might be in jail instead of sitting here."

Nicole placed a hand over her mouth, subduing a chuckle. A young man of less than 30 years walked up behind Tom. "Well, I see that you have some new company this evening."

Tom's head turned. "Hi, Jeremy. Hey, I want you to meet Nicole Dunton. She's here on business—from Fargo."

Jeremy chuckled and shook her hand. "Yes, I can see that. See you guys later."

Their dinner entrés arrived and they busied eating without conversation. Tom had one forkful of his torsk almandine remaining, some of his high from the wine depleting. He had mixed feeling about the evening...total delight with his beautiful date, but frustrations with his experience at the senator's dock. Oh what the hell, he thought and thrust his fork into the fish.

Suddenly, a new voice said, "You forgot something, miss!"

Tom pulled his hand back. A burly looking man stood by their booth. He dropped a small, black, plastic folder containing a single credit card on the table. "You should be more careful when breaking the law, and you're damn lucky that the card is expired."

Tom looked up into his large, green, blood-shot eyes. The

intruder's unshaven face made him look like a porcupine in disguise.

"And you, sir. I've got a message for you. Next time you bring someone over in your boat, we're going to blow you away. Do you understand?"

Tom's face muscles contorted. He searched for words, finally muttering, "I want you to leave us alone right now, or I'm calling the police."

"The cops—now that's a joke—how're ya gonna explain what you did? Deliverin' a thief to break into the senator's office—huh!" The man turned and walked away with a slight limp, the crotch of his baggy jeans at a level with his knees.

Nicole held a hand over her mouth. "I don't know what to say, Tom. This is entirely my fault. You had nothing to do with it."

Tom regained his composure. "Oh, but I did. I took you over there."

Nicole's mouth opened wide, her arms extending forward. She groaned, "Oh my gosh, I had two credit cards in that folder!"

28

SHERIFF JOHNSON LEANED FORWARD IN HIS CHAIR. "Kelly, I want you to listen to me. Last night I thought about asking the C.B.A. in St. Paul to help with this case—then I remembered Izzy Felton. She's had lots of experience. The two of you can make a great team."

Deputy Kelly Martin frowned deeply, sitting up straight, his back to the wall. He turned to look at Deputy Izzy Felton, who sat near him. Kelly forced a smile and said, "Welcome aboard, Felton."

Izzy nodded and smiled. Her dark brown pony tail bounced on a stiff collar that tightened firmly around her narrow neck. She wore large plastic-framed glasses, the thick lenses slightly distorting her sky-blue eyes. "Kelly, I have no intention of interfering with whatever you have done or are doing. I'm only interested in helping."

Kelly nodded curtly. "I appreciate the help."

Izzy's face lit up. "I'll do all I can. What have we got so far?"

Kelly inhaled and puckered his lips, blowing air through them. "A week ago, Sunday evening, about 10:00 p.m., the victim apparently surprised someone in the senator's office. She got whacked over the head with the—of all things, the bust of Abraham Lincoln. Anyhow, the blow must have knocked her out. She got dragged down to the lake and dumped into the water—drowning was the cause of death."

Kelly paused. He looked at Dave, then at his new partner. "Veronica Lewis's prints were all over the bust and—and get this— also all over both door knobs—she's the new intern."

The sheriff grinned devilishly and nodded his head. "There's more, Izzy. Kelly found a small white button under the senator's desk. Guess what he found in her closet—a blouse with a missing button, pretty much the same kind. The lab boys in Bemidji are working on that as I speak."

Sheriff Johnson leaned forward. "But—what we really lack is a motive by her—or any of the staff for that matter. Why would Lewis kill the secretary? She just started her job in early August."

Izzy glanced up from the folder lying on her lap. "Is the intern strong enough to drag another person that far?"

Deputy Kelly Martin shifted in his chair. "She's a big girl. I don't think that would have been a problem—and I think her story about putting her hands on the bust earlier in the week is full of holes. Whoever used the bust to strike Franks would have pretty much obliterated any previous prints. Hers, Veronica's, were clearly on top."

Izzy nodded. "Who had keys to the senator's office?"

Kelly leaned forward in his chair. "Lots of people: the housekeeper, Stella Robinson; the senator's travel coordinator, Julie Huffman; the victim, Isabelle Franks; and the senator himself."

Sheriff Johnson removed a pencil from between his front teeth. "An unknown vehicle came through the gate that evening just after dark. The housekeeper also reported a set of taillights leaving about midnight.

"Just to fill you in, Felton, right now the senator has full-time guards at the gate. Before the murder, his people had been using magnetic cards to open it."

Izzy extended her elbow, pushing knuckles against her belt. "I'll delve into the backgrounds of all the people you mentioned. Dave, I think you hit the nail on the head. We need to find a motive."

The sheriff nodded. "That's a great idea, Izzy. Well, we've got some time. The senator and his staff won't be returning from Africa until next week—on Friday they're expected. Hopefully, we'll have enough evidence by that time to make an arrest."

———

DEPUTY MARTIN WALKED TO THE DISPATCHER'S STATION after the meeting with the sheriff and Deputy Izzy Felton ended. He didn't feel enthused about the idea of Felton becoming part of the team. We really don't need her, he thought. Besides, there isn't much doubt in my mind that the intern did it...it could be over.

"Kelly, I have a call from one of Senator McDougal's gate men. Could you take it?"

"Sure." The deputy reached over the counter and grabbed the phone. "This is Deputy Martin. How can I help you?"

The rough sounding voice on the other end uttered, "We had an intruder attempt a break-in of the senator's office last night."

The deputy asked some questions. He nodded. "We'll be out there this afternoon to check it out."

Kelly returned to the sheriff's office and knocked on the door frame.

"Yeah, what's up?" the sheriff asked without looking up. He was going over some papers on his desk.

"Just got a call from the senator's gateman—there's been an attempted break-in of the senator's office."

The sheriff looked up, his blue eyes reflecting the ceiling light. "We better get out there as soon as we can." He looked at Izzy. "You're coming along."

Kelly frowned. His mouth opened slightly as if ready to object. "All right, Chief."

TWO WHITE SHERIFF'S CARS TURNED OFF the state highway and onto the senator's asphalt roadway. They pulled to a stop in front of the closed gate. Deputy Martin emerged from the driver's side of the lead car. He walked to the guard's cubicle. "Which one of you guys called us this morning?"

The burly guy raised his hand. "That would be me." He shook his head. "I'm sorry to tell you this, but I think that the alarm malfunctioned."

"What makes you so sure of that?" the deputy asked.

"Well, there really wasn't anyone around. Everyone but the housekeeper is gone."

"I think we will check it out anyhow. I need a key."

The burly man threw a ring of keys onto the small window counter. They bounced and fell onto the ground. Deputy Martin threw a disgusted look at the gateman and leaned down to pick them up.

Deputy Martin reentered the car. "Dave, the jerk has changed his mind, but then...."

"Then what?"

"We better check it out anyhow. I've got the keys."

Both white vehicles stopped in the parking lot across from the senator's office. Four uniformed officers approached the building. Deputy Martin had a key ready. He raised the other hand. "What's that down there in the bush?"

The deputy tunneled his hand down between the leaves of an evergreen shrub. He lifted his arm upward, grasping a green- stained plastic credit card. "Nicole Dunton. Now what the heck is this card doing here?"

He handed the card to the sheriff. "This name looks familiar."

Kelly placed a key in the door lock. He turned his head. "Who is Nicole Dunton? She's not listed as being a member of the senator's staff."

Dave held up a hand. "Don't touch that knob, Kelly."

He turned toward Izzy. "Call the office. I want this knob dusted for prints."

Kelly said, "Good idea, Dave. I won't touch it." He turned the key and used two fingers to grasp the shaft and opened the door. The alarm went off. He stepped in quickly, opened a small plastic door in the wall and turned a switch. The blare tailed off and went silent. "Sure seems to be working now."

———

TOM HASTINGS STRETCHED OUT ON HIS SECTIONAL IN THE DEN. He watched the Minnesota Twins play the Boston Red Sox. He jammed a fist into his left palm while watching Torii Hunter round the bases after hitting a three-run homer. The Red Sox pitcher kicked up a chunk of Agra line next to the pitching rubber.

The phone rang. "Hello."

He heard a rough-sounding voice. "Hastings. I need twenty thousand dollars or the sheriff will hear all about what happened on Saturday night."

"Who is this?"

"You'll hear from me soon." Tom heard a click.

Tom got up off the sectional and headed for the kitchen. He partially filled a glass with ice. Grabbing a bottle of brandy from a cabinet, he poured some into the glass, and topped it with water.

The baseball game ceased to hold his interest. He walked into the next room and sat down in his computer chair. This is ridiculous, he said to himself. So the sheriff finds out eventually that I delivered Nicole over to the senator's dock...big deal. "Sheriff Johnson is going to hear from me first thing in the morning," he muttered.

29

THE LIGHT GRAY MASONRY COURTHOUSE IN BIG LAKES also housed the Sheriff's Department of Big Lakes County. Tom parked his vehicle alongside a curb across the street. He didn't feel totally confident of his decision to report the blackmail to Sheriff Dave Johnson. However, he had already talked to him on the phone and scheduled an appointment.

Tom proceeded in the direction of the arrow which indicated sheriff's office. "Hello, I'm Tom Hastings, here to see Sheriff Johnson. I have an appointment."

"Have a seat, Mr. Hastings. He'll be with you shortly."

Five minutes later, a door opened and Sheriff Johnson entered the room. "Hello, once again, Hastings. Would you step into my office?"

Tom followed the sheriff and accepted a chair across from his desk. Dave took a seat in his swivel-padded black chair and placed his hands on top of his head. "What can I do for you, Tom?"

The skin around Tom's lips tightened. He explained his part in the incident of delivering Nicole Dunton to Senator McDougal's dock so she could recover personal effects from her daughter's apartment.

"Dave, once that alarm went off, instinct drove me into escaping at all costs. I didn't like what was going on, but believe me, it was the only thing to do—get the heck out of there."

Dave smiled. "I can understand that, and it doesn't look as if you did anything illegal. So Nicole Dunton is Veronica Lewis's mother. That sheds a new light on the entire case—of course that's nothing for you to be concerned about."

Tom took a deep breath. "Oh, but there is something for me to be concerned about: a man called me last night asking for twenty thousand dollars."

Dave's upper incisors sank slightly into his lower lip. "What! A blackmail threat? For what?"

Tom shook his head. "Really, Dave, I'm thinking the same thing. There must be a lot more going on than meets my eye. And if there is, why didn't the blackmailer call Nicole instead?"

"When did the guy say he's going to call back?"

"He didn't say, but I assume it will be soon."

"Well, what you did is not illegal, but what the caller did is— blackmail is a federal crime."

"What do you think that I should do?"

"For starters, you should have a recorder installed, tied to your phone. Secondly, don't agree to do anything until you talk to me first. I need to consult with my investigators."

Tom nodded.

"Here, take this card—it has my cell phone number. Call me anytime—anywhere."

——

TOM FELT RELIEVED AFTER TALKING TO THE SHERIFF. He drove right to Radio Shack and purchased a recorder. On his return trip home, he stopped in New Dresden, parking next to the curb abreast of Stillman's Supermarket. His thoughts returned to the gruff voice that he had heard on the phone—the blackmail call.

He got out of his vehicle and walked toward the post office, the skin of his hands wet from a light drizzle, which had dotted his windshield as he drove into town. Tom fished out his mail and turned in a package-notice slip in the business room. As he listened to Jerry's voice, he wondered if he had heard the mysterious gruff voice before. It could have been someone from up and down Main Street, he thought, maybe even the postmaster. No...it wasn't Jerry.

Ellie didn't have time to talk to him in the grocery store as she busied checking and bagging items from a nearly full cart. Tom paid her seventy-five cents for the *Forum* and headed out the door. There seemed to be more than the usual numbers of out-of-state license plates in the area as the month of August neared its end.

Tom's two offspring had both committed to visiting him during Labor Day weekend. Kris lived in Florida working as a flight attendant. She planned on flying to Minneapolis where Tom's son, Brad, and his daughter-in-law Terry would pick her up at the airport. Tom expected them to arrive on Friday. He looked forward to the visit.

30

TOM STRETCHED OUT AND WATCHED TELEVISION on Wednesday evening. He found it difficult to focus on a movie, turning his head frequently to glance at the phone. Tom had installed the recorder and felt confident that it would work.

When the phone finally rang, he jolted awake. Glancing at the clock, he saw it was 9:45. Tom flicked on the recorder switch and picked up the phone. "Hello."

He could hear breathing, but no one talked. "Hello," he said again.

"Tomorrow morning, you will go to your bank and get twenty packets of one-hundred dollar bills. Place the money in a white envelope and seal it. You drive to Big Lakes and enter Central Supermarket at exactly 10:30 a.m. Take a small shopping cart and proceed to the shelves of bagels just beyond the meat department.

"Pick up two packages from the lowest shelf nearest the outer corner and drop them into your cart. Underneath them you will find a sheet of paper with further instructions. Do as I say! Or else you'll be sorry!"

"Wait! How am I going to get that kind of money so quick?" The phone went dead.

Tom looked at the sheriff's card lying on the table. He punched in the numbers.

"Hello, Sheriff Johnson."

"Dave, this is Tom. The creep called back. I've recorded the message."

"Can you play it for me now?"

"Sure—hang on."

Tom pressed the *Play* button and lowered the phone to the recorder.

"Would you do that once more?" the sheriff asked.

"Sure."

"Okay, Tom. I want you to get the money as the man said. Follow his instructions. I'll have a team waiting at the supermarket. We'll catch this guy."

"But—what about the money? I don't have twenty thousand bucks. Why don't we use phony money?"

"Because after we catch the guy and he goes to trial, we don't want his lawyer to twist the jury's mind. If we use real money, we'll have an air-tight case."

Tom held the phone away from his ear for a moment.

"Hastings! Are you still there?"

"Yeah, I'm here—and thinking about the money. What if something goes wrong?"

"Tom, if we had plenty of time, I could get the cash—but I'd have to go through the commissioners—that would take days."

"Well, okay, I'll do it...."

"Tell you what. I'll have a couple of deputies waiting at the bank when you get there. They open at 9:00, don't they? I'm sure the bankers will cooperate."

———

THE PASSING OF NIGHT SEEMED TO TAKE FOREVER as Tom tossed and turned—over and over again. Cackling crows awakened him at close to 8:00 a.m. He felt tired but glad that he had at least gotten some sleep.

Shortly after 9:00, he backed his vehicle out of the garage and headed for New Dresden. He felt relieved when he spotted a deputy sheriff's car close to the bank. Tom parked and entered. He walked slowly across in front of the teller windows. Jane, the woman behind the last window, pointed. "Tom, they're waiting for you in Mr. Arnold's office, right back there."

He felt totally embarrassed entering the room. The bank president, Bill Arnold, stood. "Tom, this is Deputy Flicek. He's explained the entire matter and the bank will cooperate fully. I will need you to sign a document, though."

"A document—what kind of document?" Tom asked.

"This is routine, Hastings. Don't worry," the deputy said.

Tom glanced at the officer and back at the banker. "Where do I sign?"

"Right here, Tom."

Tom stared at the loan document and scribbled his name above a dark line. Bill reached into a drawer and brought out a bulky white envelope. He handed it to Tom. "Great, I see you have a jacket on. Does it have an inside pocket?"

"Yes it does—a big one, too."

"Okay, see if it fits," the banker said.

With ease, Tom pushed it into his pocket.

The deputy stood. "Soon as you leave, I'll follow you to Big Lakes. We don't want you to go into the market until exactly 10:30, though. You won't see any uniforms. We don't want to scare the guy off."

Tom padded the bulky area of his jacket. "Okay, deputy, let's get this over with."

———

TOM FELT THE STINGING PAIN of severe apprehension as he headed west out of New Dresden onto a county highway. He frequently glanced at the police car that followed behind. After turning onto the state highway that led to Big Lakes, he chuckled. "I won't have to worry about a speeding ticket today."

He thought about three years ago when he got stopped for speeding on this very stretch of highway...not once, but twice. Minutes later he arrived at the stoplight where the state highway intersected with a federal highway. He took a right and drove into the town of Big Lakes. After passing by downtown, he took a left into the parking lot of Central Market. The deputy's car that had been following him disappeared.

Tom parked his vehicle and opened the door. After stepping out, he reached his hand under his jacket, feeling the mass in his pocket. The creep is going to be in for a big surprise, he said to himself. Tom strode across the pedestrian crossing and stopped at the sliding glass entry doors. He looked back across the lot. Tom didn't see any bubble-topped vehicles. They're keeping their word.

Two pairs of elderly people had entered the main part of the store ahead of Tom. They all stopped to look at the items in the stock-up shelves, blocking the aisle. Tom's anxiety led him to say, "Excuse me, folks, but I need to get in there."

One of the women turned and said sarcastically, "What's the hurry? Is there a fire?"

Tom felt like laughing, but instead he rudely brushed by her and continued into the main part of the store. He knew very well where the market stored bagels, because he had been a frequent buyer of them in the past. Tom slowed his pace at the meat market aisle and looked around. He spotted Deputy Martin, in plain clothes, looking over the cheese selections. There're probably a whole bunch of deputies in here, he said to himself, feeling a bit more secure.

Tom rolled his cart straight ahead and turned left at the bagels. As the man instructed, he removed two packets from the bottom shelf and dropped them into the cart—he stared at the sheet of paper. Tom looked around again. He noticed that Deputy Martin had disappeared. He's probably hiding around the corner of the aisle, he thought.

He reached down. The paper read: *Go to the Prescription Counter immediately and give the attached prescription to the person behind the counter.*

What the heck should this have to do with a prescription? he asked himself, scanning the other shoppers in the area. No one appeared to be watching him. Tom reversed his direction and rolled his cart toward the pharmacy. He saw four carts and several shoppers mingling there. Tom scooted his cart past them and parked at the end of a colorful wrapping paper display.

He carried the prescription to the window. The woman behind it smiled. "Let's see what you have there?"

She continued to smile. "It'll only be a minute or two, sir."

Tom chided himself for not noticing the name of the recipient on the prescription. He returned to his grocery cart and stopped. Leaving it unattended, he walked to the next aisle. Tom didn't see anyone watching, but he could feel penetrating eyes burning a hole in his jacket.

He heard a loud woman's voice. "Your prescription is ready, sir."

Tom walked back to the window. The woman placed a white bag on the counter. He unfolded the top and peeked into it, seeing a small bottle. "How much do I owe you?"

"It's already been taken care of," the woman said and walked away.

Tom grabbed the bag and returned to his cart. He reached in and looked at the name on the label: *Amy Robinson*. I have no idea who that is, he said to himself, looking around again, wondering why he had been asked to do what he did. He looked in his cart, two bags of bagels and the white bag. What the heck should I do now?

Tom heard the sharp clicking of a woman's heels. An elaborately dressed shopper, moving very quickly, appeared from around the corner. She rolled her partially-full cart next to Tom and the clicking stopped.

Tom gasped when the woman reached into his cart and grabbed the prescription bag. She looked straight ahead and pushed the white bag up to his chest. Tom leaned back, startled by the raspy voice, "Throw in the envelope—Now!"

Tom reached into his inside pocket and followed the instructions. Before Tom realized what had happened, the woman had disappeared. He looked around, expecting to see a rush of officers. Tom muttered, "Where the heck are the cops?"

Tom left his shopping cart and anxiously hurried to the checkout area. He saw two men standing next to the wide glass exit doors, obviously police officers, he thought. He saw an elderly woman wearing a shawl over her head, using a cane and carrying a white bag, walk past them.

He didn't see either Deputy Martin or Sheriff Johnson. Then he saw someone running—Deputy Martin hastened to the two men by the door. They hurriedly talked and then two of them trotted toward the back of the store.

———

"I'M REALLY SORRY, TOM, BUT THE BLACKMAILER got clean away," Sheriff Johnson said to Tom out in the parking lot, next to his vehicle. "It's like he vanished into thin air."

Tom stared at the sheriff. "Oh, but it may not have been a man, sheriff. It seemed to me as if it was a woman."

Dave Johnson stared at Tom. "A woman! Okay, we better get back to my office. I need a full description from you."

"What about my money?"

"Don't worry, my entire staff of deputies here, along with the Big Lakes Police Department are watching the roads out of town. They have road blocks set up. I'll let 'em all know right away that the blackmailer could be a man or a woman."

Tom spent an hour in the sheriff's office. After he left, it took him forty-five minutes to leave town, his vehicle being caught in a long line of others getting stopped and searched. He felt genuinely ticked off. Tom thought about Nicole and how he had fallen for her charm...that's how the hell I got into this mess. I should know better by now. I'm no kid anymore.

31

JULIE ENJOYED A BEAUTIFUL VIEW of the English Channel as the DC-10 banked westward on a cloudless morning. "There's England," she said, nudging Peter's sleeve.

"At last, we're on the last leg. I like working for the senator, and especially with you, but I don't like air travel, period."

Julie chuckled. "Oh, Peter, you'll get used to it."

The senator sat next to Veronica on their final flight. They occupied two seats in the last row. Julie glanced out the window and then at Peter who stretched out next to her. She couldn't see the scientist, Hans Mueller, who sat directly ahead of her, but she did notice the top of the partially bald head of Aaron Crier. He sat in the seat just ahead of Peter.

Three hours later, Julie looked at her watch. This trip is really going fast. It won't be long and we'll see our coastline, she thought.

———

PETER YAWNED AND LOOKED AT HIS WATCH. Jeez, only four more hours and we should be in Minneapolis. He turned down the chance to order a free martini. Maybe I should have drunk it, then I would be more relaxed, he thought. Julie drank at least three of 'em. She's sound asleep.

He heard the door behind him swing open and the sound of fast moving footsteps. Peter knew in an instant that something was seriously wrong. The two dark-skinned men who hurried by him shouldn't be there. Peter straightened the back rest, watching them stop in front of the cockpit door, next to a stewardess.

One of them turned. Jeez, that's a knife in his hand! Peter exclaimed to himself, his heart jumping into his throat. He heard a yell and saw a red streak on the stewardess's neck. My God, that's blood! He watched the man give her a shove and she fell to the floor.

One of the men opened the door to the cockpit and entered. Peter's fear mushroomed, the weight in his stomach pulling his chest down. He visualized the airplane spinning out of control and falling to earth. He had moments to live before it splashed into the ocean.

Peter's eyes, full of fright, looked at Julie. She remained asleep. Those two men are terrorists, he said to himself.

Suddenly, his fear vanished. He became overwhelmed with a surge of adrenalin. His breathing had returned to normal. He visualized himself wearing white with a black belt around his waist.

Peter flexed his knees and got up off the seat. He felt steady and secure. He slowly walked toward the terrorist, seeing nothing but evil in his face. The terrorist's black, beady eyes widened, his evil smile irritating Peter to no end. Peter stared at the blade, held tightly by the lunatic's fist. It jerked upward...again...once more.

Peter didn't fall for the fakes and approached to within four feet of the terrorist. He studied the expression on his face, looking for a sign that would signal an attack. Peter bent his knees and planted his feet. Suddenly, he did a front push kick to the solar plexus.

The terrorist bent over forward. Peter felt another surge of adrenalin. He used his hand to do a hammer-fist to the radial nerve on the forearm. The weapon dropped to the floor. Peter did a knife-hand strike to the man's neck. The terrorist collapsed into a heap.

Peter looked around. A stewardess came through the cabin class door, her face wrenched with fear. Peter cupped his hands over his mouth. "Get help."

———

SENATOR MCDOUGAL'S CHIN JOLTED UPWARD. He feared the worst when seeing Peter get up from his seat and attack one of the dark-skinned persons who had just walked by. Shockingly the other one had gained access to the cockpit. "My God, we're getting hijacked!" he exclaimed.

He glanced at Veronica. Her brown eyes looked like a couple of basketballs. She clutched her throat with both hands. Sean reached out his hand. Veronica grabbed it and pulled herself close to him. He patted her on the shoulder and whispered, "It's going to be okay."

Suddenly, he saw Peter begin to attack the hijacker. In moments the intruder lay on the floor. He heard a shuffling noise and looked up to see Hans Mueller standing on his seat, waving his fists in the air.

Aaron Crier's usual poker-faced expression melted like snow at 60 degrees. Sean saw him sit on the edge of his seat, holding a hand up to prevent Hans from getting around him and entering into the fray.

Sean's feelings and respect for Peter elevated to a new high when he saw the second hijacker fall. "Come on, Aaron, Peter needs help in holding these guys down. The senator hastened over to where the first intruder lay and pressed his knee down on the waist. Aaron accepted a piece of rope from the pilot and begin to tie the hijacker's hands together as Peter dashed off and burst through the cabin door.

———

THE PILOT OF THE DC-10 FEARED THE WORST as the intruder pressed a blade against his skin just under his jaw. He felt no pain but could feel blood running down his neck. Damn, I wish we had a gun up here, he said to himself...I hate this helpless feeling.

"Chad, take over would you?" the pilot asked calmly.

He looked across the controls and saw deadly fear in his partner's face. The pilot thought about 9-11 and visualized the films that he had seen of two planes sticking out of the tops of the Twin Towers.

Suddenly, the door sprung open. The intruder turned his head and fell backwards onto the aisle. The pilot quickly got out of his seat and peered into the first class section. "Chad, radio emergency! Hijack attempt!" he exclaimed.

A young man was flailing at the intruder, knocking him to the floor. The pilot watched with awe, remaining calm, feeling respect and gratitude for having that young passenger aboard.

———

PETER HAD HURRIED TO THE COCKPIT. He yanked it open and grabbed the man's belt, pulling him back and out. The man recovered and took a swing at Peter with his blade. Peter quickly dodged backward, causing the terrorist to miss. He turned and did a back heel kick, the blow sinking into the terrorist's abdomen. He knife-handed a strike to the neck and the man fell.

Peter looked up at the pilot. "Will someone get some rope and tie this guy's hands behind his back?"

The pilot nodded, his face muscles and eyes expressing wonderment.

Peter turned around and saw two men sitting on the first terrorist's back, his stomach flat on the floor. A third man busied tying a rope around the wrists. Peter hurried to them, meeting their eyes, and placing a forefinger to his lips. He jumped over the fallen man and continued to the door leading into cabin class.

He had no idea how many more terrorist were on the plane. It didn't matter, he thought. My survival, as well as all others on this plane depends on me. There's no stopping now.

Peeking around the edge of a curtain, he saw a third terrorist standing in the middle of the aisle, holding a blade in each hand. A woman lay on the floor, blood oozing from her neck. A man near her sat on the front edge of his seat, totally helpless.

Peter ran down the aisle. The terrorist planted his feet and pulled back his right hand. Peter stopped a step short and faked a strike. The terrorist swung at him viciously. Peter ducked, stood quickly, and kicked upward into his attacker's groin. The terrorist shrieked in pain, both arms flailing loosely in front of him.

Peter showed him no mercy, chopping at his neck and kicking him in the stomach. The terrorist dropped to the floor. The man who had been sitting nearby gasped and picked up both blades.

"Is there a doctor in here?" Peter yelled.

———

BRAD AND TERRY SAT IN A LOUNGE AT THE AIRPORT, patiently awaiting the arrival of his sister Kris from Florida. "It's sure going to be good to see Dad's place again," Brad said, squeezing Terry's shoulder.

Terry reached up and grabbed Brad's wrist. "I'm looking forward to it, too. I just love that part of Minnesota."

"Wonder what's going on? Look at the TV," Brad said.

Terry pulled away her arm and set her magazine down. "Wow, a hijacking attempt thwarted on a flight from Amsterdam to Minneapolis."

Four people brandishing television cameras quick-stepped while passing. A minute later, two more groups of obvious media people moved by hurriedly.

Brad yawned. "Geez, I wonder when that plane from Amsterdam is due?"

A woman sitting across from them said, "Any minute. There's going to be a lot of people waiting down in the disembarking area. I hear a U.S. Senator is on the plane."

The loudspeaker blared. "Flight 302 from Miami, Florida has arrived at gate 23."

"That's Kris's plane," Terry said, standing.

Brad pointed. "She should be coming out of that gate right over there."

Meanwhile the television screen above their heads showed a reporter, wearing a trench coat, pointing at a maze of lights. The television cameras were aimed at a large airliner approaching. It came to a stop short of a gate. Several people pushed on the framework of a high stairway, moving it toward the plane.

Minutes later a group of armed police officers rushed up the steps. The door opened and they moved into the plane. The people in the lounge gathered directly in front of the screen. Brad and Terry had to stand so they could see.

Two police officers escorted a hatless person wearing shackles down the steps. Brad tightened his grip on Terry's arm. "Look, there's another one. There were two of 'em."

Terry exclaimed, "Three of them, Brad!"

They watched until the police officers and captives disappeared from their sight.

Moments later, the door opened again, and a tall, large man stepped out on the landing. He stopped and waved. Lights from the cameras were so intense that the view became distorted at times. The large man came down the steps followed by a very much younger and smaller guy. The big man got to the bottom. A microphone almost hit him in the mouth.

He spoke loudly and clearly. "This young man right here...." The large man turned and grasped the younger guy, placing a large hand on each shoulder. "He saved us from a disaster. Three terrorists attempted to hijack the plane. Peter, this young man here, is a tae kwon do black belt, and he took them all out." He pointed upward toward the plane. "We all owe him our lives."

32

JULIE LOOKED ACROSS THE AISLE OF THEIR VAN AT PETER in the next seat. My God, he's sitting there like nothing happened, she said to herself. His life will never be the same again. The media spent over an hour with him at the airport. It ain't over. When he gets home, the local reporters will be all over him. Why heck, I wouldn't be a bit surprised if he doesn't get a call from the president.

I wonder how Tom is reading into all this news. He doesn't like to fly either. Her mind drifted to the deceased Isabelle Franks. I'm not sure if I'm anxious to get back to the compound. Someone killed that poor woman. Perhaps the sheriff has got it solved by now. That would help us tremendously. We have so much work to do. Veronica will be a big help for me. She's a smart girl.

The van passed by the state reformatory in St. Cloud. Now, there's a depressing looking place, she said to herself. She thought about the three terrorists on the plane. There are some stupid goons out there. So many people have no brains, do something stupid and end up spending the rest of their lives in sickly places like this.

Julie closed her eyes as they got beyond St. Cloud. She opened them and saw a sign for a Little Falls exit. Another hour and a half, she thought. Gads, I used to drive this route a lot when I was special to Tom Hastings. It's never going to happen again. We are worlds apart...although, I did feel something the night that I got drunk...yuk...what a headache I had the next morning.

————

SHERIFF DAVE JOHNSON FELT LIKE HELL. He looked out the window of his car. His driver, Deputy Izzy Felton, turned the wheel to the right. They exited the highway at the New Dresden exit. He forced a smile. "Okay, Izzy, how am I going to explain the fact that the blackmailer got the money—and got clean away—in spite of the fact that we had the place surrounded—and under complete surveillance?"

She muttered, "Dave, things like this come with the job." Izzy turned toward him, a half smile on her face. "Frankly, I'm damn glad that I'm not in your shoes right now."

Dave ran fingers up and down the sides of his chin. He looked straight ahead.

Six miles later they turned onto a township road which led to the Hastings's home. "Look at those turkeys, Dave," Izzy said, slowing their vehicle.

She steered the car onto Tom's roadway, watching the woods and spaces in both directions, looking for deer.

Izzy turned the wheel and stopped the vehicle in Tom Hastings's driveway. "Well, let's get it over with."

She exited the car and stood by the door waiting for the sheriff to take the lead. He grimaced walking by her and continued down a sidewalk to the front door. He pressed the doorbell button. Moments later, it opened.

"Hello, guys, come on in," Tom said.

The two officers sat on the loveseat while Tom parked himself on a dining room chair.

"So what is it you want to talk to me about, Dave—as if I already didn't know?"

"First of all, I have to apologize to you, Tom. I thought we would catch your blackmailer easily. I was wrong."

Tom frowned. "You know, sheriff, I really don't know why I went along—with your scheme—it should have been county money at risk, not mine!"

"I understand your feelings, but getting the cash from the county would've taken too much time," the sheriff said. "I've talked to a couple of the county commissioners. There's a good chance they can swing a vote soon to include the loss in their budget. Please be patient—you will get your money back."

Tom's eyes lit up. "Really! Wow, that would be tremendous."

The sheriff crunched his lower lip with his upper teeth, smiling. "I can't say for sure, but it does look promising."

Tom nodded. "How's the murder investigation going?"

Izzy stared out a window that overlooked the lake. "Mr. Hastings, we are very close to making an arrest. As you probably know, the senator and his staff have been in Africa for the past few days. They are due to return today."

Tom held up a hand. "So you think that the killer is one of his staff who went on the trip?"

Sheriff Johnson's blue eyes rolled slowly. He nodded. "It will happen soon."

Tom thought of Julie. She's out as a suspect, he thought. Then there's the senator himself...his two interns. Could one of them be guilty?

––––

TOM ANXIOUSLY MAINTAINED SURVEILLANCE OF HIS DRIVEWAY, expecting the arrival of his children at any moment. His normal happy anticipation of family arriving had been somewhat degraded when the sheriff's car showed up...and without the money. I could lose twenty grand, simply for being a good guy. Geez, I wonder if I should tell this to Brad. He's going to have a fit.

The warm tingling sensation that Tom had been feeling intensified when he saw the vehicle coast up the driveway and come to a stop. They're here at last, he said to himself.

In the next few moments, he felt as if he had gone to heaven. Tom hugged his children tightly, Kris three times. "It's been a long time. How are you, Kris?"

"Just fine, Dad. You're looking great—so is your home."

Tom sat down and looked at his daughter. Her long blonde hair, parted in the middle, splashed the top of her shoulders. Her gleaming blue eyes resembled his former wife Becky's even more than in the past. He thought Kris's face had thinned since he had seen her last.

The four of them spent the next few hours visiting and reminiscing.

Brad grilled four steaks on the Weber.

The eating of dinner had ended and they sat on deck chairs sipping wine and coffee. Brad turned to his father. "I've heard that there is a senator living not far from you."

Tom pointed. "Yes, right over there, at that point."

Brad nodded. "I also heard there was a murder there lately."

Tom lifted his wine glass. After taking a sip, he set it down. "There was a drowning—the senator's secretary down by the dock. The sheriff's department is treating the case as a homicide, even though there haven't been any charges filed yet."

"Does the senator have a butler?" Terry asked, smirking.

Tom laughed. "No, but he has cooks and a housekeeper."

Terry smiled. "On television, usually the culprit is someone close to the victim."

"Well, I may as well level with you guys," Tom said, setting his glass down on the table. They all turned their heads, waiting for more. Tom explained the story about him motoring Nicole to the senator's dock, and the subsequent successful blackmail.

"Twenty thousand bucks! Dad, are you out of your mind?" Kris exclaimed. "Why did you ever pay it?" she added.

"It was the sheriff's idea."

Brad cleared his throat. "Dad, remember when you used to quote George Will about *bottomless naivety*?"

Tom puckered his lips. "I'll get the money back. Don't you worry. The sheriff has already talked to the county commissioners."

After an enjoyable weekend, Tom felt the usual sunken feeling as the taillights on Brad's vehicle blinked and disappeared beyond a bank of trees, heading up his roadway.

33

JULIE SHIFTED IN HER SEAT AS THE VAN TURNED OFF the state highway and onto the senator's roadway. She glanced around and noticed mostly glum looking faces. Jeez, we should all be delighted, getting home alive, she thought. I'll never forget what happened on that plane. She looked at Peter and smiled.

The van stopped in front of the gate. As it swung open, the attendant came out of the guard's cubicle and walked over. He leaned over, placing his face into the open window. "Welcome home, Senator. As you requested, I got rid of the media. There must have been thirty of 'em here a couple of hours ago."

Julie heard his booming voice. "Good work—we don't need that right now. Everyone's exhausted—we need rest."

The van nudged forward and made its way down the slope and onto the senator's circular drive. The brakes screeched lightly as it came to a stop.

Julie saw Peter open his door and hop out. He beat Gus to the senator's door, swinging it open. The driver opened the rear gate, and removed some of the luggage. Julie smiled watching Peter and Gus carry and roll pieces toward the senator's front door. That Peter is something else again, she thought. She glanced at Aaron's face. He looks worried.

Peter returned and got into the van. The senator stuck his head in the window and said, "Thanks for your help, all—especially you, Peter."

Julie watched the senator stride toward his front door. The van completed the short loop and continued toward the employee living units. When it stopped, the driver and Peter exited quickly, and removed the luggage from the rear compartment. Hans's short legs appeared stiff as he stepped out on the driveway and attempted to walk.

Veronica bumped against the scientist as she rolled her luggage toward her unit. "Sorry," she said.

Hans looked up at her. "We very lucky—very fortunate."

Gus's tenor-pitched voice warbled, "Have a good day to all you." He got back in the van and drove away.

Julie unlocked her door and smiled. She watched Peter graciously assist the elderly German with his luggage. Hans had not been satisfied with his accommodations at the barn, so he moved into unit number five, near the far end.

———

SENATOR MCDOUGAL STOOD AND STARED OUT his office window overlooking Border's Lake. "Aaron, I'm not so sure all this recent publicity is helping me: the murder of Franks and the attempted hijacking—we need to get all this behind us—as soon as possible."

"I don't know how we can do that, Sean. The media just doesn't stop calling. It's going to be up to you to keep the press conference Tuesday in Fargo short."

The senator blurted, "Damn, the press conference. I don't need that right now."

Aaron raised his hands into the air. "I could get it postponed, but that would only delay the inevitable."

"No, I'll go ahead with it. I can easily divert most of the issue—blaming some of it on the sheriff."

Aaron smiled. "Yes, that's what I like about you, Senator, you know your way around in a crowd."

———

DEPUTY KELLY MARTIN KNOCKED ON HIS BOSS'S DOOR FRAME and entered. "We got it—got it this morning—the button."

The sheriff looked up at his deputy, his mouth partially open. "And?"

"It's a match, Dave. The lab people are ninety-nine percent sure that the button found under the senator's desk came from Miss Veronica's blouse."

Dave swung his lower jaw from side to side. "So what do we conclude from that, Kelly?"

"That Veronica Lewis is our number one suspect. I think we have enough for an arrest."

The sheriff grated his upper and lower front teeth against each other. "I tend to agree with you, however—"

"However, what?"

"We lack motive. The button is a clue, but a good attorney will tear that apart. We mainly have the fingerprints on the vase and door knob—but then, she works in that office. Can you imagine what her lawyer would do with that?"

The deputy's chin dropped to his chest. "It's all we've got, Dave. A shaky arrest would be better than none."

"I'm going to sleep on it, Kelly. Let's continue this discussion after the weekend."

"Okay, Chief, see you on Monday."

34

STELLA ROBINSON DECIDED ON A BREAK. She had been watching a Lifetime movie on television. Stella rolled off the couch and headed for the refrigerator. After taking a sip from a plastic water bottle, she walked into her bedroom. Stella opened the bottom drawer and reached under a stack of sweaters.

She carried a white envelope back to the couch. Stella smiled widely counting the stacks of hundred dollar bills. She flipped through the stacks, again and again, as she had been doing frequently the past two days...pleasure flowing warmly through her body.

She laid the neatly bound packets in orderly rows on the seat next to her. The movie had resumed and she left the bills lying on the couch continuing to watch television. The phone rang, startling her from a touch of malaise. She fingered the money and stretched her torso across them to reach the phone sitting on a table. "Hello."

She listened intensely, nodding from time to time. "Okay, I'll see you then."

Stella smiled and began organizing the money into one stack. She slipped it back into the envelope and returned to the bedroom. After slipping the envelope under the sweaters, she returned to the movie.

Ten minutes later, a sharp knock on the front door startled her. She looked at the clock on the wall. "What's he doing here so early?" she muttered, shaking her head.

Stella slid off the couch and waddled to the door. She opened it. "What are you doing here? Huh!"

———

GUS OPENED THE VAN DOOR FOR VERONICA AND JULIE. Peter got in the back behind them. Aaron Crier, carrying a briefcase, walked out onto the circular drive. He got in the seat behind the driver. He said crisply, "Good morning, everybody."

Veronica and Peter muttered a response. Julie said crisply, "Good morning, Aaron."

Minutes later, the senator emerged from the house. Gus opened a door for him and he entered the van to several 'good morning' greetings.

Labor Day weekend is behind me, Julie thought, watching a gray squirrel scurry across the ditch bottom and head into a cluster of aspen. She reminded herself to charge the batteries in her camera as she looked for potentially favorable photography sites. The colors are gorgeous, she said to herself.

The sun had broken through a thin bank of gray clouds, sending shivering rays along the length of Loon Lake on the other side of the state highway. She shook her head at six ancient boiler pots displaying plants in someone's yard as the van turned onto a county highway and headed for U.S. Highway 10, which would take them through

Big Lakes, Audubon, Lake Park, Hawley, Moorhead, and across the
Red River into Fargo.

———

TWO BROWN-CLAD OFFICERS HEADED UP THE
ELEVATOR. It stopped at street level and they walked into a sheltered
parking area reserved for the sheriff's staff. Deputy Martin got behind
the wheel of the official sheriff's car. Dave Johnson sat down on the
passenger seat and closed the door. The phone rang.

"Yes," the sheriff answered. He listened for a few moments. "Send
an ambulance over there immediately! We're on our way! Oh, put
Deputy Izzy on alert. We're going to need at least four more deputies
at the senator's complex—and right away!"

Dave put the phone away. "We now have another reason to drive
out to the senator's place."

"What happened?" the deputy asked anxiously.

"An apparent attempted homicide...the head housekeeper, Stella
Robinson, was found unconscious in her apartment less than an hour
ago."

Kelly turned his head, his facial expression strained. "What about
the arrest of Veronica Lewis that we planned?"

"We're too late for that anyhow. She's in the senator's van headed
for Fargo." The deputy pressed the button that engaged the flashing
lights and siren.

Fifteen minutes later they pulled up at the senator's gate. The
gate had been open previously, and as they drove down the sloped
roadway, they could see that the ambulance had already arrived.

A female member of the senator's domestic staff ran directly to
the sheriff's car. She pointed. "I don't know what to do. Stella is
lying there. There's blood all over. I think she's dead."

The deputy and sheriff exited their vehicle. The sheriff said,
"Look, young lady—go back into the house—find someone to talk
to. Okay?"

The woman burst into tears. Dave poked his finger into Kelly's
shoulder. "Would you escort her back inside, please?"

The staff member bowed her head and accepted the deputy's hand on her arm. She stuttered, "Sheriff, I did just what you told me. I didn't let anyone near the apartment!"

The deputy said, "Good work, young lady. Was it you who found the victim—unconscious?"

"Yes, and it was awful—seeing her lying like that—blood splattered all over the carpet."

The deputy guided the woman through the front door, and hurried back to the Robinson apartment. The distant sound of sirens reached his ears as he approached the door. He looked back. A white police car, followed by another close behind, appeared on the down slope of the roadway.

Kelly waited next to the door of the apartment while a stretcher moved through the doorway. The attendants pushed it into the rear of the ambulance. One of the crew members remained in the rear of the vehicle as the ambulance hurriedly left the premises.

35

DEPUTY MARTIN AND SHERIFF JOHNSON CAME OUT the front door of Stella Robinson's apartment. The deputy leaned over and touched a red brick, one of many that made up the border of a flower bed. The bricks had been set into the soil vertically. He ran his fingers over the tops, moving along slowly.

"Aha, here it is, Dave."

The deputy pulled a single brick away from the border. He pointed. "This chipped area looks fresh. I bet what's spread out on the floor back in the apartment is a match to this."

The sheriff nodded. "Yeah, and look what's on the asphalt over there. We better get the lab boys out here. There's a trail of red masonry chips all over the place."

The deputy placed his hands on his knees and moved along in a crouched position, following the trail to where vehicles normally parked. He stood. "I better get back in there and get a couple of the guys. We need more tape."

"Hey, Dave and Kelly!" a deputy yelled from the doorway.

The two officers looked up and saw one of their staff holding up a white envelope.

Dave clapped his hands together. He met the deputy half way and grabbed the envelope. He peeked inside. "Well I'll be darned, looks like we may have Hastings's money back."

Half an hour later, the lab people had finished inside and they came out to examine the splatters of red-chips. They took photographs and swept up samples, placing them into plastic bags.

The sheriff and deputy walked back to their car. Deputy Martin said, "Looks like someone hit her over the head with the brick and then searched her place. After he came out, he placed the brick back into the border."

The sheriff nodded. "Huh, imagine how dumb he (or she) was, leaving footprints all over the place, not only on the carpet floor in there, but also on the driveway."

The deputy took a deep breath. "It's obvious that the attacker was looking for something, with so many drawers pulled out—and the cabinet doors open. It must have been the money. Perhaps the culprit had been interrupted and didn't get to complete the search. That's why the money was still in the drawer."

Deputy Izzy Felton came out the door of the apartment. She hesitated and then walked over to the Dave and Kelly. "Fellas, there's something really wrong here."

"What's that?" Kelly asked.

Deputy Izzy tightened her lips together. "I have the hunch that two people were in that apartment—not at the same time—one of them attacked the housekeeper—the other had a different reason for being there."

Kelly cleared his throat. "Izzy, hunches can be good, but we need facts."

Dave kicked a small stone into the flower bed. "Look, Izzy, I'm willing to listen. Give her a chance, Kelly. We have damn little going in this case right now."

Izzy smiled. "Thanks, Dave. I'll say no more right now. I need time to study the clues—yet—"

"Yet what!" Kelly exclaimed.

Izzy's eyes hardened into steely brown stones. The muscles in her face tightened. "Whoever struck the victim with the brick didn't do it as a reason to search her apartment."

Kelly tilted his head to one side. "Okay—now, how do you know that?"

"Because the brick chips between the victim and the door didn't have any footprints."

Kelly shook his head slowly. "I don't follow, Izzy."

"If you were the attacker, and you hit the victim over the head with a brick, the broken-off brick pieces would fall on top of your boot, leaving a bare area underneath. It wasn't there."

Deputy Kelly Martin threw up his arms.

Izzy stood on the tips of her toes. "One more thing, Dave."

"Yeah, what?"

"I'm going to take a couple of the boys and we are going to search that slope over there." She pointed.

Dave nodded. "It won't do any harm. Are you looking for anything specific?"

"When I read the evidence report for the Franks homicide, I noticed that one of the victim's shoes was missing."

Dave raised his eyebrows, shifted his jaw and glanced at the sheriff. "It won't hurt to look, deputy."

———

IZZY FELTON GRABBED SMALL BUSH BRANCHES to keep from sliding as she worked her way along the steep side hill beneath the staff living quarters. She looked down at Jake and listened to him. Those words would never be heard in a church, she thought, laughing.

What's that? she asked herself. Is that a shoelace? She slid downward and her boots stopped at the base of a bush. Reaching over, she tugged at the string. She felt resistance. Separating some of the branches, she looked down. "Uh-huh—uh-huh—Deputy Martin is going to be embarrassed. She saw a shoe. Working it out of the bush, she placed it into a plastic bag.

Smiling, she looked down at the other two men. "Hey, Jake, look at this." She held up the bag.

"What is it?"

"The missing shoe, I think."

"Good job, Izzy."

"I'm about all done up here—see you back above."

"Okay."

———

SHERIFF JOHNSON SMILED FROM EAR TO EAR when Izzy showed him the shoe. "Hey, take a look at this, Kelly. It sure looks like a match if memory serves me correct."

Deputy Martin held up the bag. He looked at the shoe. He looked at Dave. He looked at Izzy. "Okay, you win. It does look like a match, but we better make sure. Off to Bemidji it goes tomorrow."

"All right, deputies, now that we have the shoe, answer me this question. How did it get way over there?"

Izzy said, "There's no way anyone would have lost it while walking there. *Someone threw it!*"

Kelly said, "That would take a throwing arm as strong as say, Kirby Puckett."

36

TOM HASTINGS PARKED HIS VEHICLE IN HIS GARAGE. He had just returned from his get-the-mail trip to New Dresden. Tom heard the sirens earlier and guessed that the destination was the senator's place. He thought about giving Julie a call but decided to wait. Through a break in the trees across the bay, he saw the flashing lights of vehicles heading west on the state highway.

He walked out onto the deck to get a better look. His phone rang. Rushing back inside, he answered, "Hello."

"Tom, this is Sheriff Johnson. I've called you to let you know that we found your money."

"No kidding—wow! I'm flabbergasted."

"There's one little catch, though."

"What's that?" Tom asked.

"Your money is now evidence in a crime scene—an attempted homicide. Our lab people need to do a work-up on it before I turn it over to you."

"Attempted homicide!" Tom exclaimed and shook his head. "I'm afraid to ask—the name of the victim."

"A Stella Robinson, the senator's chief housekeeper," the sheriff replied.

"Is she hurt bad?"

"I'm afraid so. I'll tell you more when we bring your money over."

"Sure—good luck, Sheriff." Tom clicked the *Off* button on his phone, sitting and contemplating...torn between feeling good about getting his money back...and feeling awful that another person had been attacked. He punched in Julie's number. It rang six times without an answer. He hung up the phone. Oh, that's right, he thought. The senator has a press conference in Fargo this morning. She's probably there.

———

A MEETING ROOM IN THE DOUBLEWOOD INN IN FARGO had been selected for the press conference. Five microphones projected above the speaker's rostrum like golf club blades. Several members of the media had already gathered, some standing, some taking seats in the folding chairs.

Aaron Crier walked into the room. "All right, folks. Please have a seat. The senator will be with us shortly."

Several cameras, some on tripods, had been set up, spread out on the floor next to the chairs. Heavy footsteps sounded in the hall. Moments later the senator entered, followed by members of his staff. The senator walked stiffly to the podium. He waved to a maintenance person. The microphones all needed to be raised.

"Good morning," the senator said.

He proceeded to explain why he visited Togo, Africa. He talked about trading partners, the benefits for America by assisting less fortunate African nations. Fifteen minutes later, he stopped talking and raised his hand. "I'll take some questions now."

A young woman in the audience stood. "Senator, has there been any progress in solving the murder of your secretary?"

"Yes, there has, but you would have to talk to the sheriff of Big Lakes County about that. I have nothing to do with the investigation."

A thin-faced man with a dark narrow mustache stood. "Senator, it has been rumored that an arrest is imminent. Could you tell us who the suspect is? Is it a member of your staff?"

The senator flushed. His eyes darkened. "You call Sheriff Johnson—next."

A man in the far corner, to the senator's left, stood. "I heard some breaking news less than an hour ago. The police are investigating a second crime in your complex—another victim, as we speak, Senator. Could you tell us anything about that?"

The senator looked up at the ceiling. He turned toward Aaron Crider. Just then, a man came through the door. He walked over to Aaron and whispered in his ear. The senator waited anxiously to hear what his aide had to say. He listened.

The senator turned away from the podium and walked quickly toward the door, followed by his staff. He ignored the ever-increasing din of loud voices within the room. The senator continued moving briskly out into the lobby. He stopped and looked around, spotting his driver sitting on a lounge chair. He waved to his staff and headed for him.

"We're getting out now, Gus."

The driver jolted awake from his snooze. His eyes widened and he jumped out of the chair. "Okay, boss, let's go."

———

THE SENATOR HURRIEDLY LED HIS STAFF OUT THE FRONT DOOR of the motel. He placed a hand up toward approaching reporters. One of them managed to jam a microphone in front of the senator's face. The senator pushed it away. "Sorry, but I have an emergency to deal with."

Julie turned her shoulders, raised herself up on her tiptoes and looked up into the senator's eyes. "What happened, Sean?"

"Stella has been attacked! She's in the hospital!"

Julie's face turned white. "Oh no!—is it serious?"

"Yes, it is. Please get everyone into the van right now!"

"Shall do." Julie walked back toward the group. She talked to them, and they all hurried off.

Veronica grabbed Julie by the arm. "Julie, I'm going to have lunch with my mother across the street. I'll be back here by 1:00."

"No way, Veronica! Gus is getting us out of here right away."

"But I have this lunch date with my mother!"

"You'll have to change it. We have no choice. Please do as I say and go outside and get in the van."

The senator pulled a rear passenger door open, quickly got in, and slammed the door shut. The rest of the staff got in hurriedly. "Let's get out of here, Gus!" the senator exclaimed.

37

THE SOUND OF THE VAN'S WHEELS AGAINST the pavement droned on and on as the van sped back toward Border's Lake. Julie thought the trip would never end. There wasn't a sound or a smile for the last twenty miles, she thought. Finally, they turned onto the state highway. Their destination loomed directly ahead.

The gate opened as they approached. Julie got a glimpse of the hairy face. Jeez, that man looks awful, she said to herself. Those horrible looking green eyes....Ugh!

Holy smokes, four sheriff cars, Julie thought as the van slowed and entered the circular drive.

Gus got out first and opened the door for the senator, who hastened into his house. The van slowly moved to its second destination and parked next to the sheriff's vehicles across from the office. Julie stiffened when she saw two officers come out of her door.

She exited the van and hurriedly approached the officers. "What are you two doing in my apartment?"

"We have a legal search warrant, lady."

"I would like to see it!"

"Jake, go get the paper from Dave."

Julie picked up her case from the asphalt. "Oh, never mind."

The square-shouldered deputy said, "By the way, Miss Huffman, could you tell me why there are shoe tracks of red brick dust in your apartment?"

Julie looked straight into the deputy's eyes and exclaimed, "None of your business!"

The deputy chilled. "Getting a little testy, huh, lady?"

"Wait! I always go for a walk first thing in the morning."

"Did you go for a walk this morning?" the officer asked.

"Yes, I sure did."

"Where did you go and what did you see?"

Julie shrugged her shoulders. Her face colored. "I walked up the roadway for a bit but didn't see anything unusual. Why?"

"Thank you, Miss Huffman. We won't bother you any more right now—but be prepared for more questions later." The two officers walked toward the sheriff's vehicles.

————

THE SENATOR HAD BEEN ON THE PHONE for almost two hours after they had arrived back from Fargo on Tuesday evening. Then he sat in the living room, consulting with his aide for an hour. Sean looked at Aaron. "Damn, this is exciting. I wish the heck we didn't have to go to D.C. next week."

The senator shook his head and said, "Would you go get Hans?"

Aaron got up and left the room. The senator entered the dining room and walked behind the bar.

Minutes later, Aaron escorted Hans Mueller through the front door. He pointed. "In there, Hans. The senator is going to treat us to dinner."

They entered the room. The senator lifted a glass to his lips and swallowed hard. "Oh, hello, Hans, glad that you could make it."

The senator extended his hand to Hans. They shook. "Would you like a drink?"

"Yeah—yeah," the scientist said, smiling.

Aaron moved behind the bar. "What would you like, Hans?"

"A whiskey—straight up, as you Americans say."

Aaron smiled and poured from a bottle, almost filling a glass. He handed it to Hans. Then he poured himself another scotch and water.

A waitress appeared, coming from the kitchen. She carried a tray, filled with steaming pots. "It's all ready, sir," she told Aaron and distributed the steaming food on the table. The three men sat down and busied themselves eating their dinners.

Hans Mueller licked his lips. He set the fork down on his plate. "I tell you, Senator, the formula fine. Next week, Kurtz have vehicle ready." He smiled widely. "We take it for test ride."

"Here-here," Aaron said and raised his glass.

Hans swallowed and set his drink down. He looked at the senator. "I will need to access your files and update your records tomorrow, Senator...yes?"

The senator reached across the table and patted Hans's arm. "Be my guest—you just let me know when you wish to do it. You can use Julie's office."

Hans smiled widely. "As I mentioned previously, Senator, the formula is adjusted—it ready. I'm anxious, but confident—the test drive go fine. I need a ride to West Fargo after finishing here tomorrow."

The senator adjusted his tooth pick. "Consider it done, Hans."

———

VERONICA SMILED HEARING A WHISTLE as she crossed the street. She glanced to her left and briefly met the eyes of a young man peering at her through his open car window. She hurriedly walked toward the Sunflower Hill restaurant.

She entered and saw a hand waving near the rear of the dining room. Her mother stood and they hugged warmly.

"You look so awesome, Veronica. How are you?"

"I'm just fine—a little shaky after the press conference."

"Oh, what happened?"

"The senator's head housekeeper is in the hospital. She was attacked in her room last night. I heard that she hasn't recovered consciousness."

"Oh, how terrible!"

"I haven't much time. Let's order," Veronica said. "We need to go to the counter apparently."

They each selected an entree from a plethora of choices on a blackboard behind the counter. Nicole asked the waitress to hurry. Veronica took a table in the far corner where she had a great view of the sidewalk on Main Street, thanks to a row of large windows.

Nicole bent down low over the table. She placed a hand next to her face. "We need those copies from the senator's files—time is running out."

Veronica set her water glass down. "I have a new plan—"

"Yes, what's that?"

"I think it will work."

Nicole forced a smile and said, "I can't wait—please tell me."

"I'm going in the back door this time."

Nicole's eyes widened. "And...."

"I've asked around. The back door isn't supposed to have an alarm."

"Are you sure?"

Veronica nodded her head slowly. "It's a bit of a stretch as my back door drops off onto a steep slope—being there as a fire escape. Then I have to climb onto his deck at its highest point."

"Why can't you simply go around and take the steps?"

"The pole light—don't you remember, you thief?"

Nicole laughed. "I knew that I raised you strong for a good reason. Can you do it before next week?"

"I was thinking of this coming Sunday."

Nicole reached down into her purse. "Here's your new tool. This little camera will do the job a hundred percent better. Also this small light—you do have to plug it in, though."

"That shouldn't be a problem. There's an outlet under the desk."

"Yeah, you know that spot well, don't ya?" Nicole muttered, laughing quietly.

They finished their lunch and walked outside to the corner of the block. Nicole gave her daughter a hug as she waited for the light to change.

38

IZZY FELTON PLACED A HAND ON EACH HIP. She stood next to the sheriff's desk. Deputy Kelly Martin sat on a wooden chair, its top edge pressed against a wall.

Sheriff Dave Johnson had been reading from a report that Izzy had just laid on his desk. "Hey, Kelly, listen to this. Veronica Lewis played four seasons as a center fielder with her high school softball team."

He looked up and smiled. "In her senior year, she established a record—she threw out five base runners at home plate." The sheriff stretched out his fingers. "*Five!*"

Izzy smiled and nodded. She took a seat in an empty chair, her face beaming. "So how far do you think Veronica could throw a shoe, Kelly?"

The deputy cleared his throat. "Not sure, deputy, but she didn't have any brick dust in her apartment."

"So you've sort of changed your mind about arresting Lewis," Izzy said, smirking.

"I have to admit that I now have some doubts. It's the button that bothers me. If it was found lying by the door, I would think differently," Kelly said.

Izzy tightened her lips together. She braced her hand against the butt of her weapon. "The pieces in this puzzle, in either of these two cases, do not fit together, and as I mentioned before, I think it's for a very good reason."

Kelly leaned forward. "And?"

"It's like when your car quits working right. The mechanic finds the problem and fixes it. You go your merry way, and then behold, something else goes wrong. The mechanic finds a second problem."

Kelly and Dave listened intently.

"There were two problems with the car to begin with. It's the same with these two assault cases. There are two motives involved. An X and a Y. The Y is someone involved in a lesser way. The X is the killer."

Dave nodded. "So do we need to identify Y first before we go after X?"

Izzy nodded.

————

TOM PLACED HIS ARM AROUND JULIE'S SHOULDER as they walked toward the entrance of Mary Ann's restaurant on the Friday evening after Labor Day weekend. They both decided a bottle of wine and a nice dinner would help them relax. Julie's phone call and the news about Stella Robinson he had gotten earlier annoyed him. Geez, is Julie next, he thought.

"What do you plan on having for dinner?" Tom asked.

"Not sure...."

Tom opened the door and followed Julie inside.

She turned toward him. "A walleye fillet sure sounds good to me. How about you?"

Tom shook his head as they approached the hostess station. "You know, I'm really not that hungry—not right now, anyhow."

He talked to the woman and allowed Julie to pass ahead of him. They got seated in a booth by a window overlooking the lake.

"Here, Julie, why don't you order the wine?" Tom passed her a menu.

"No, I'd rather have you do it. My mind is not working well right now."

"Hi, Amanda," Tom said to the waitress. "Would you bring us a bottle of KJ?"

Amanda nodded. "I'll be right back."

An hour later, they had finished their entrés and the bottle of wine sat empty.

"What should we do now?" Tom asked.

"Tom, I feel like quitting my job—just too much. Two violent crimes right under my nose and to top it all off, I'm a suspect." She used a napkin to wipe a tear from her cheek.

"Huh? I bet Deputy Martin is on your case."

"Yeah, how did you know?"

"I've overheard them talking. The sheriff appears to have more patience. Like Hercule Perot used to say, *I suspect no one. I suspect everyone.*"

Julie laughed.

"Okay, Julie, what's your take on what's going on with the senator? His secretary has been murdered. His head housekeeper was almost murdered."

Julie shook her head. "It seems as if the sheriff and his deputies are living at the senator's complex. There's chaos and total confusion...."

Tom leaned forward. "This is a toughie question, but do you think the senator could be involved in any way—any way at all?"

"Doubt it, but I don't really know. The Togo trip he took was supposed to be to assure that the congressional appropriations go to the right place in that county—yet the senator didn't tour any facilities that will end up being benefactors. He spent most of his time meeting secretly with a handful of officials."

Tom shrugged his shoulders and said nothing.

Julie continued. "Then there was that late night conversation that the senator had with his aide, Aaron. I think everyone else was asleep on the plane but me. They talked about a new energy source—

something called zillium—or at least it sounded like that."

"Zillium?" Tom repeated. "Never heard of it."

"Apparently it all has something to do with a monster machine which runs up and down a cornfield."

Tom gulped.

———

TOM READ THE *FORUM* WITH GREAT INTEREST on Saturday morning. *Senator McDougal bolted a press conference held at the Doublewood in Fargo on Thursday. This reporter has learned that it was because his head housekeeper had been violently attacked and left for dead in her apartment. She is currently fighting for her life in the Meritcare Hospital Intensive Care unit.*

"Mind if I sit down?"

Tom looked up and smiled. His friend Henry had arrived for his daily lunch. Tom looked at his watch. "You're one minute late, Henry, or do I have to reset my watch."

Henry sat down and looked up at the board of lunch choices. "Ah, the croissant looks good today."

The waitress came. Tom continued to read the *Forum* as Henry ordered. Henry scratched above the right rim of his glasses with his thumb. "Now what's this I hear about you and some woman setting off an alarm at the senator's office?"

Tom's cheeks turned red.

Henry crooked a finger in the handle of his coffee cup waiting for an answer.

Tom shook his head. "Well, Henry, it really wasn't any big deal—ya know how the locals build everything up."

Henry laughed. "Okay then—just tell me what happened, and I'll let everyone know that it wasn't any big deal."

"Henry, it's just too darn complicated for me to even attempt to explain—but you can pass the word that I didn't do anything illegal."

Tom got up from the table, not daring to look around the room. He could feel the piercing stares as he walked over to the counter to pay his bill. Tom laid a bill down, looked straight ahead and walked out of the restaurant.

39

TOM KEPT TO HIMSELF FOR THE REST OF SATURDAY. On Sunday morning, he dashed into Stillman's Supermarket to pick up a newspaper. He quickly exited before anyone had a chance to even say hello.

Outside, he got into his vehicle and headed for his home, removing his cap as he passed the cemetery. What would Becky think of me now? he asked himself. Geez, all I did was a favor for the woman. So the alarm went off. It's no big deal.

As he drove into his garage, he thought about his twenty thousand dollars, and when the sheriff would bring it back to him. How come I got blackmailed? Why not Nicole? It was all her idea anyhow. She's the one who got me into trouble.

The Vikings opened their National Football season that afternoon against the Atlanta Falcons. He watched with disgust as they made error after error. How can that dumb tackle be offside three out of four plays? I don't understand. Grade school players are better disciplined than that.

The Vikings lost and Tom knew that going for a walk would be a sure way to forget the game. He put on his hiking shoes and pulled the strap of his camera bag over his shoulder. He looked at his watch. It read 4:45. Walking west, he stayed close to the broad band of tall trees that separated his greenway from the lake. Nearing his field of small evergreens, he stopped. A band of nine wild turkeys had spotted him and disappeared over a ridge.

He walked northward, picking up the main trail. The dead elm tree where he spotted a raccoon stuck in a hole up high a couple of years ago had totally collapsed. There goes a nice winter home for the coons, he said to himself.

As he walked, he thought about what Julie had said about a monster machine. I'll never forget something like that passing over me last month. Those wheels were absolutely humongous.

Tom stopped at a break in the trees where he normally could see Stuart's barn. He could only see the roof right now. The corn blocking his view had begun to lose its bright green color. He stopped and listened, hearing only the honking sounds from a distant pair of geese.

Tom crossed the fence and stepped into the corn. Should I be doing this? he asked himself.

Ah, what the heck...there's probably nothing or anybody over there anyhow. He walked between two rows of corn, heading toward Stuart's farmstead. Tom paused at the deep ruts that the monster machine had churned into the soil.

Geez, they're about five feet wide, he thought. The length of the corn stalks decreased as he approached the edge of the field. He saw the mass of the barn's roof and stopped to listen. Hearing nothing, he continued, taking deliberate steps.

Tom could clearly see the entire barn from between the seventh and eight rows of corn. What the devil is that? he asked himself, noticing a huge camouflaged dome-like structure off to his left, just beyond a narrow band of trees. He stepped closer. It looks like a bubble used for an indoor tennis court, he thought.

Tom listened as he stood between the third and fourth rows. He heard nothing except the occasional sound of a vehicle lumbering on the county highway. He took a step into the cleared area and heard the sound of an engine. Geez, someone is coming, he thought and quickly stepped back into the cornfield.

Tom's heart raced as he clumsily retreated, stopping and squatting down to remain hidden. He peeked over the top of the tassels and saw a truck with a huge white tank appear and slowly make its bumpy way over to the huge tent. It stopped. The driver turned it around and slowly backed toward the massive structure. The truck stopped rolling and two men got out. They connected a hose from the dome to the truck tank.

Tom ducked down and waited. He peeked again hearing a whirring sound. The sound stopped and he watched the two men remove the hose and got back into the truck. He heard the engine start and anxiously observed as the wheels rolled ahead. Tom stood when the truck disappeared from sight.

He listened to the chirping sounds of a flock of black birds that had invaded the branches of a bass wood tree. Tom watched the birds for a few minutes before walking back into the clearing. He looked around in all directions, cautiously moving toward the camouflage structure.

Tom stopped. He heard the rustling of leaves in the tall grass. He smiled watching a baby raccoon scurry toward the cornfield. Everyone's gone. I'm the only one here, he said to himself. Tom removed the strap from his shoulder and pulled his camera out of the bag. Moving back several steps, he began taking photographs.

Tom flicked off the camera switch and placed it back into the bag.

"Freeze!"

He didn't move...someone had yelled. Tom held his breath, his lungs almost bursting...he slowly turned his head. Tom looked into the barrel of an awful looking weapon. Behind it, next to the barn, stood a military man, his feet spread apart and planted firmly.

———

TOM SAW THE MAN'S LIPS MOVE. "Drop the camera, buddy," a gruff voice said firmly.

Tom bent his knees slightly and held onto the strap momentarily, allowing it to stretch before dropping it into the grass.

"Step away from it!" the man ordered, waving the barrel of the gun.

Tom took two steps to the side.

"Farther, buddy," the man said.

Tom walked a short distance away. The military guy quickly walked over to the camera and picked it up. He slung the strap over his shoulder. "All right, now we'll take a walk."

Tom hesitated.

The man shouted, "You'll do as you're told! Walk toward the

barn, and along the side all the way to the other corner."

The man followed, keeping the barrel pointed in Tom's direction. "Stop!"

Tom stopped at the corner of the barn. The military guy walked passed him, staying a few feet away. "Okay, buddy, open that door that's right around the corner."

Tom took one step and saw it...a small door. He grasped the knob and turned it.

"Open it!"

Tom pulled it open.

"Get yar butt inside...."

Tom obeyed and entered the small room. He saw a desk along the west wall flanked by a wheeled, black office chair. Two wooden chairs had been placed next to the opposite wall.

"All right, buster, open the far door."

Tom hesitated.

"Come on—git in there."

Tom opened the next door and entered another small room. He glanced back and looked into the threatening, ugly hole in the middle of the rifle barrel.

"Get down on the floor—hey, I'm talkin' to you."

Tom obeyed and got down on the floor next to two more wooden chairs.

"If ya know what's good for ya, stay right there," the man said, bringing up his rifle.

Tom watched his captor sit on the office chair. The man leaned the weapon against the wall next to the desk. He picked up a phone and punched in a number.

The man's head turned away for a moment as the chair swiveled and he talked.

Tom's heart almost stopped beating. He gasped. It's now or never, he said to himself.

Not making a sound, he rose from the floor and stepped quietly toward his captor. The man held a glass ashtray in his other hand, tapping the top of the desk. Tom moved silently and quickly, his body energized by the threat. The man turned his head just as Tom lunged at the office chair. Tom felt pain in his shoulder when he made contact and pushed with all his strength, driving the chair into a metal filing cabinet in the corner. The man shrieked.

Tom moved back quickly and picked up the weapon. Stepping back, he saw the man throw aside the chair. Tom lifted the weapon and aimed it at his abductor crouched near the desk.

"You get your damn hands up or I'll pull this trigger—I will, damn it. I will. "

"Okay—okay, you take it easy. No one has to get hurt," the man muttered in response.

Tom watched the man like a hawk as he worked his way to the opposite corner. "Okay, buster. Now you get into one of those chairs in the other room—Git!" Tom tightened his grasp on the weapon. "I want you to know, pretty boy, that I was a pretty darn good deer hunter in my day. I know how to shoot, so don't get any stupid ideas."

Tom held the rifle with his left hand, grasping a wooden chair with the other. He made certain his adversary remained sitting on the chair against the back wall in the second room. Tom closed the door and jammed the top rim under the knob. He shouted. "You stay put, buster. I'll be watching outside."

Tom walked out, thinking that he better leave quickly, or he could get into big trouble. What should I do with this weapon? He asked himself. I could dump it in the cornfield on my way back.

A voice from behind him shouted, "Drop it!"

Tom froze in his tracks. He turned his head saw two more men dressed in military fatigues. They stood a good distance apart, both aiming weapons at him. Tom dropped the rifle.

"Back away!" one of them yelled.

Tom took three steps to his right. He looked at the cornfield. Too far to run, he thought. I'm hooked.

One of the men entered the office. Moments later, he returned, along with Tom's original abductor. Tom looked at his face, noticing a red streak on his forehead and an ugly sneer. The man approached and didn't stop until their stomachs touched. "It's your turn," the man snapped.

"Hold it," one of the other men said. "We're going to call the sheriff, and we don't need complications."

Tom followed their instructions and returned into the back room of the office. He sat down on one of the two chairs. Geez, could I be lucky and they will actually call the sheriff? he asked himself, his spirits lifting.

He patiently waited while the leader of the three men talked on the phone. Tom watched a hairy arm hang up the phone. The man stood. He waved his hand. "Right this way, spy."

Tom followed him outside. The leader firmed up his jaw. "Okay, spy-man, we're walking out to the gate. Get going—now—follow the road ahead of you."

Tom didn't dare look back as he walked up the roadway, wondering if they were going to shoot him. He moved past a curve and saw the gate, the same one he had discovered a few days ago. Tom stopped and put his hands on a cross-arm, glancing back.

The lead man pointed. "You stand over there by that post."

Tom obeyed.

The man pressed a button and the gate opened. "You get on the other side and wait until the sheriff arrives—understand?"

Tom nodded his head and looked up at the sky. Could I be this lucky, he said to himself. The man closed the gate and leaned against it. He looked at his watch.

The two men stood there, saying nothing to each other. Ten minutes later, a white car approached. Tom recognized the bubble on top...a police car, he thought. The car stopped and a deputy emerged from the driver's side. Tom did not recognize him. He opened a rear door and walked toward the gate. He pointed at Tom. "That's him, huh?"

"It is—throw the book at him."

Tom gladly sat down in the back seat. He and the deputy didn't talk while the car turned around and headed for the county highway. I wonder what Julie's going to think about this, Tom thought, smiling.

Fifteen minutes later, the deputy's car arrived in Big Lakes. In another five minutes, it stopped in the sheriff's parking area.

TOM FOLLOWED ORDERS AND MARCHED down a narrow flight of metal steps. He grabbed his throat, stifling a retch from the smell of stale whiskey. The deputy directed him to a small table and chair. Tom sat down and stared at a single sheet of paper with the title of TENNESSEN WARNING.

Tom read: *Name of arrestee: Tom Hastings*; *You have been arrested by: Deputy Ben Mattlock; For the charge of: felonious trespassing of a Federal Secured Area.*

You are being detained in the Big Lakes Law Enforcement Center. I have a list of questions that I will be asking you. Before we begin the booking process, I am required to read to you....

Tom didn't hear a single word that the deputy said in the next few minutes.

The deputy, obviously irritated, asked. "Do you understand what I have read to you?"

Tom murmured, "It's clear as mud."

The deputy cleared his throat. "Will you answer my questions now?"

Tom nodded. "Anytime, deputy, but this whole mess could be cleared up if you called your boss."

"Sign here," the deputy said and placed a pen down on the table.

Tom wrote his name, the date, and also the time. He handed the deputy the paper. "I need a phone book."

The deputy signed the paper. "Okay, I'll see that you get one." He left the room with the paper in hand.

A portly man with long stringy hair and a bald top entered. "Clean out your pockets, including a billfold if you have one."

Tom stared at the man. He reached into his pocket and brought out a beer bottle cap. Tom laid it on the table. "That's all I've got— sort of a weak haul, huh?"

The jailer pointed his finger at Tom. "Don't get smart with me." He grabbed the beer cap and dropped it into a plastic bag.

The deputy re-entered the room, set a phone book on the table, and promptly left.

Tom opened the book to the yellow section. He flipped to the attorney's section and fingered the names until he reached Patrick

Levitt. Yes, he thought, that's who represented Jolene last year. "I need to make a call," Tom told the portly man.

The jailer pointed. "Use that wall phone over there—as long as it's not long distance."

Tom tried four times to reach the attorney. No one answered. He returned to his chair. "Take me away, jailer, I'm tired and need some sleep."

40

THE MAN STANDING ON THE BRIG yelled, "Land ho!"

The freighter, *Mol Dantoot*, crashed through the waves near the gulf coast of Mexico. It had left Togo, Africa, seven days ago and now approached the Port of Le Pesca.

Captain Melford Delfeen sat in his cabin, talking on the phone. "Thank you," he said and hung up.

He looked at his aide. "We've cleared customs thanks to some politics. That's going to save us a lot of time. How far are we from Le Pesca?"

"We should dock by nightfall."

"Good, it's time for a siesta."

———

MOL DANTOOT HAD BEEN SECURED TO THE DOCK for over an hour, and most of the crew had left the ship. The captain and two aides remained behind. They stood next to each other on a lower deck, pulling their collars up around their ears to protect against a biting wind.

One of the aides pointed. "There they come."

Two men walked up the dock, heading directly for the freighter. "Lower the ramp!" the captain yelled.

Slowly, the massive structure separated from the freighter, exposing a compartment where a single truck waited. The two crewmen secured it to the dock. The captain had left the ship and joined the rest of the crew on the planks. He examined papers presented to him by one of the visitors.

The captain waved to his crew people and nodded. The two visitors walked onto the ramp and entered the compartment. The eldest of the two got in the driver's side. He started the engine and drove the truck slowly onto the pier. The younger man waved through the passenger window as the truck turned a corner and disappeared around a building.

"My job is done," the captain said to his crewmen. "Bring on the rum."

———

SOL GOMEZ GLANCED AT HIS PARTNER, Jesus Rodriguez, who appeared to be sound asleep as they drove across the Mexican flatlands headed for Texas. Sol could only hope that they would get paid when they drove across the border. He had done this many times previously and felt confident that he could do it again. He did worry about the size of the truck a little, as he had never transported this large a vehicle across the border before.

He spotted the sign which told him they were less than a mile from the river. The town of Santa Maria spread out over the countryside near the border. He pulled the truck over on a side road and stopped. His partner, Jesus, shifted his body. Sol smiled. He could just as well sleep though all of this, Sol thought when he saw a lantern moving from side to side. It's safe.

Sol felt the truck lurch as the rear dual wheels spun slightly. He pressed the accelerator and knew that they had crossed. Driving without lights, Sol experienced a wall of fear building. Someday I will hit a tree, he thought and get caught. It would be all over—prison for life.

A few hundred yards ahead, he spotted a white object also moving from side to side. Sol removed his foot from the accelerator and tapped the brakes. Sol became temporarily blinded when a bright pair of headlights sprang up from nowhere. His door jerked opened.

A man yelled, "Out! Your work is done!"

Sol nudged his partner. "We are here, amigo."

They got out of the truck. Sol put out his hand. "Si, amigo—our money."

He accepted an envelope and got into the other vehicle. Sol watched out the window as two new drivers took their places in the truck.

———

JAY JUL SON SMILED AT HIS YOUNG PARTNER, Bill Korum. "We've got five days to get this box to Fargo. I can sure use the money."

Bill sat straight up. "I'll drive this truck all the way to Alaska for that kind of moola—more than I could make in a year working construction."

Bill was about to twist the cap off a bottle of beer. "Hey, not now!" Jay yelled. "You have to wait until we reach our destination."

"Where the hell is that?"

"Harlingen, Texas. We stay at a truck stop there, and head out first thing in the morning."

Bill threw up his hands. "Okay, I'll behave."

The truck's engine droned on for three hours before they saw the Harlingen sign. Jay turned the truck off the highway and parked in front of an Econo Motel.

The next morning, just after dawn, they switched to U.S. Highway 77 and continued northward. At Waco, Texas, Jay turned off on the Interstate Highway 35 exit and headed for Forth Worth. Mid-morning, he pulled into a rest stop. After they both visited the restroom, Jay turned the wheel over to Bill. "Stay on U.S. 35 all the way to and through Oklahoma City."

Jay nodded. After motoring through the big city traffic, he felt relieved. He saw the Guthrie sign but failed to notice the *All Trucks Must Exit* sign.

A siren jolted Jay from his sleep. "Holy Jesus, Bill, what did you do?"

"I didn't do nuthin'."

"You better pull over and stop. We're in enough trouble the way it is," an aggravated Jay said.

Bill pulled his foot off the accelerator and tapped the brake. The truck squealed to a stop on the side of the road.

Jay looked into his side view mirror. "Oh my God, there's a trooper walking toward us."

He heard a rap on the window and saw the uniform of an Oklahoma State Trooper. Bill shielded his eyes from the bright beam of a flashlight. He cranked the glass down.

"You missed the weigh station back there. Can I see your driver's license?"

"Yes, sir," Bill said and flicked through the cards in his billfold.

The officer took it and returned to his car. Minutes later he returned. "You need to follow me back to the weigh station. Do you understand?"

Bill nodded.

"You dope—how did you ever miss that sign?" Jay asked, spitting on the floor between his feet.

Jay shuffled through his leather pouch, searching for a number he was to call if they got into any trouble. "Here it is," he said.

The truck followed the patrol car onto a ramp and back around to the highway. It took 20 miles of driving to return to weigh station exit.

Jay got out first and approached the trooper. "Sir, would you have your superior call this number? We are on a special federal mission."

The trooper looked at him curiously, but he took the slip of paper. "You two gentlemen please come into the office."

Jay and Bill sat on wooden chairs for a whole hour. Finally, an officer came out of the meeting. "Okay, fellas, you can be on your way—but—please don't fail to stop at all the weigh stations on your way through Oklahoma."

Jay glanced at the darkened sky in the west as they drove through Kansas. Wichita remained over an hour away. "Looks like some tough weather ahead," he said.

Bill looked up from his magazine. "I've never seen the clouds so black," he said. "Maybe we should pull over, if you get a chance."

"I'm looking for a spot. Right now, I have to keep going."
Bill yelled. "Jay, look!"

Jay's eyes darkened with fear. He saw a black twister drop from the sky about a mile northwest of them. Jay took his foot off the accelerator and applied the brakes.

Some of the vehicles around them left the highway and drove into the ditches. People got out and lay on the ground. The truck screeched to a stop.

"Let's get out!" Jay exclaimed.

The two men left the truck and ran for a ditch next to the road. They dropped into the grass and laid down flat.

"Sounds like freight trains colliding!" Bill yelled, his voice blotted out by the earth-shattering noise.

He watched with mixed feelings of terror and awe when a vehicle became airborne in the dirt-laden sky. It twisted and turned for about the lengths of two football fields before dropping down to the ground. Jay marveled that the car sat down upright. The twister just missed our truck, he thought.

Jay got up on his hands and knees and watched a person get out of the vehicle. Whoever it was staggered for a few moments and began walking back toward the road. The poor guy is totally black, Jay said to himself. Oh my God, he fell down. Jay felt pain in his stomach watching the person struggle to his feet and plod ahead.

Minutes later after the cacophonic rumble ceased, they stood up. "Well, the truck looks okay," Jay said. He watched in awe as the survivor of the airborne-car continued to trudge toward the highway. Several people walked out to meet the blackened victim.

Jay heard a noise. "Holy God, there's another one coming!" he yelled, seeing a second black twister coming toward the road from the southwest. "Run! Hit the ditch!" he screamed.

The noise intensified and all visibility ceased as the air filled with dust and debris. Jay heard a sliding noise. "Oh no, the truck." he muttered. He heard the screeching sounds of metal grating against metal. Jay felt suction pulling on his body. His legs lifted. He grabbed the base of the tall grass with all his strength.

Jay's legs dropped and the suction ended. His eyes felt full of dirt. Suddenly it got quiet. Jay sat up and rubbed his eyes with his sleeves. "Are you okay, Bill?"

He heard a grunt. "I really don't know. My mouth is full of dirt."

Jay looked at their truck. It remained upright, but sideways across the road. He heard the engine running. "Holy Jesus, Bill, did you leave the truck running?"

They stood and swept the dirt off their clothes as well as they could. He saw vehicles scattered at all angles, some still on the road, and some in the ditch. "Come on, Bill, let's get outta here."

Jay got behind the wheel and tested reverse. The truck moved, allowing him enough space to lurch it forward. He steered it around scattered piles of debris and abandoned vehicles, almost sliding into a ditch. Jay drove for four miles before the highway returned to normal.

They pulled into Wichita, Kansas just before dark and spent the night, both exhausted. By early afternoon of the next day, they arrived in Salinas where they switched to U.S. Highway 81. They stayed on it the entire distance through Nebraska, entering South Dakota at Yankton on the fourth day.

Bill was behind the wheel when they reached Interstate 90 in South Dakota. "Turn right here," Jay said.

An hour later, they arrived in Sioux Falls where they picked up Interstate 29 and headed north. Seven hours later, Jay saw the Fargo sign. "We're darn near home."

Bill rubbed his eyes and looked out the window. "It's sure flat around here."

"After what we experienced in Oklahoma and Kansas, I'll take it anyway we can get it," Jay said.

Bill laughed.

Jay turned off Interstate 29 and onto the ramp which accesses Main Avenue in Fargo. He turned left at the stop light and headed for West Fargo. After crossing the Sheyenne River, he flicked the left-turn signal, approaching Eight Avenue. A minute later the truck pulled up at Kurtz Manufacturing.

"We made it. We're rich—rich, I tell you!" Bill shouted as he and Jay exchanged hi-fives.

41

VERONICA LEWIS PICKED UP HER CELL PHONE. The ten o'clock news had just ended, and she got more nervous with each passing minute. "Hello, Mother."

"How do you feel? Are you all right?"

"I feel damn nervous. You know what happened last time."

"Don't worry, sweetie, it won't happen like that again."

"How can you be so sure?"

"Trust me—it will go just fine. You have a much better camera—it shouldn't take long."

Veronica ran the edges of her front teeth back and forth, tightly against each other. "I might as well do it right now. There doesn't seem to be anyone around. I think Julie and Peter are both gone this evening."

"Great! Give me a call just as soon as you get back into your apartment. We need to meet tomorrow so I can pick up the camera."

"I only work until noon tomorrow, so we should be able to meet at Sunflower."

"Go, sweetie, go!"

———

VERONICA CHANGED INTO HER BLACK WARM-UP OUTFIT. She put on a pair of tight gloves and slung the camera over her back. Veronica opened her dresser drawer and brought out the four keys, held together with a tie. She walked to her rear door and made sure that the latch was set to unlock.

She opened it and listened. She heard the sound of a steady splash of waves against the pontoons and the irregular thumps of the boat against the bumpers. Gently, Veronica let herself down to the sloped ground. Her waist remained about even with the floor of her apartment after planting her feet.

Veronica scolded herself for not wearing shoes with more efficient grips. The tennis shoes had a tendency to slip on the stones which layered the slope to prevent erosion. Keeping a hand on the building, she eased herself past the first window. As she expected, the apartment didn't have any lights because Peter and Julie had driven to Fargo earlier. She passed by Julie's window and eventually the vacated apartment window of the late Isabelle Franks.

She raised both hands up and supported her body on the framework of the senator's deck. Flexing her knees, she readied for the pull-up at the shortest distance between the ground and deck.

Veronica placed a knee on the edge of the deck surface. Grabbing part of the rail with both hands, she hoisted herself up. Two massive efforts and she successfully swung over the top, thumping down lightly on the decking.

She got down on both knees to catch her breath. The light pole that lit up the walkway next to the office remained out of sight, guaranteeing her shadows. Standing up, she took a deep breath and walked softly toward the door.

Her left hand gripped the keys firmly. She held them up toward the walkway area background light, selecting a key that she had not used during her previous visit. She grabbed it between two fingers and slid it into the lock. Veronica turned the key and heard the door lock click.

Holding her breath, she turned the knob, then breathed a huge sigh of relief when no alarm sounded. She snickered remembering her mother's description of her ordeal—the night when she got Hastings to deliver her over to the senator's dock. "That alarm must have been heard for miles around," her mother had said. She stepped into the room and quickly made her way to the back of the desk. Pushing the chair aside, she plugged the cord of her special light into the outlet on the floor. She stood and walked around to the front of the desk, pleased that the soft light could hardly be visible from inside the room.

The previous Friday, Julie had called her into the senator's office. She noticed that a rather large, realistic miniature model of a John Deere tractor had replaced the bust of Lincoln. She also noticed the small tool box near the rear hitch.

Veronica smiled when she pulled up on the lid and felt the surface of a key. Men are so predictable, she said to herself. She walked around the desk and tried the key in the file cabinet. It worked perfectly. Pulling the key out, she got down on the floor and created a duplicate.

I better put the original back right away, she thought. Nice tractor. She placed her new creation into the lock and pulled the drawer open. Oh my, another file. She read the title on the tab, *Ford Mustang*.

Ten minutes later, she had completed all her photographs and returned the three files into the cabinet. Remaining on the floor, she flicked the back-arrow button on her camera and viewed all the photos. Jeez, they look great, she thought. Mother will be pleased.

She crouched and scanned the area under the desk, making sure that she didn't drop anything. Oh God, she said to herself. I darn near forgot my key. She turned the lock on the file cabinet door and dropped the key into her bag.

Veronica carefully opened the back door, flicked the latch, and closed it behind her. She heard voices. "Oh, God," she muttered, placing a hand over her fluttering heart. Quickly, she moved into the dark corner where she had entered. The voices seemed to be getting louder. Veronica's thoughts roared back to her previous experience under the desk. Oh no, not again.

I've got to get the hell out of here right now, she thought, securing the camera bag strap around her neck and scooting over the top of the rail. Her ankle twisted when she dropped to the stony slope. The voices had stopped. She moved silently and quickly, heading for her back door. She had come abreast of Peter's window when she slipped and fell down.

"Who's there?" a raspy voice yelled.

The voice sounded as if it had come from the walkway area. Veronica regained an upright position and painfully moved toward her door. She grimaced tasting the bile that had regurgitated from her stomach and settled on her tongue. Veronica placed a hand over her mouth and coughed, muting the sound.

She saw a flashlight beam traverse the inside of the deck rail. Veronica dropped to her knees and swung her body over slowly, lying prone. Dang, she thought. I feel every one of those blessed small stones underneath me, but I'll put up with damn near anything to get this job done.

She held her breath as a flashlight beam moved across the wall above her. Veronica worried that the sounds of her heart thumping and short, shallow breaths would give her position away. The beam of light danced back and forth across the side hill.

Suddenly, Veronica heard the thudding of footsteps on the deck. They came closer and closer, stopping at the rail. Her eye saw a beam of light on the leaves of a wild plant, only inches away. She didn't move, but knew that her mischievous adventure was about to end—damn, I have failed again, she thought.

She felt relieved when the footsteps retreated—the sound of them stomping on the wooden steps below turned defeat into victory. Veronica, ecstatic, patiently remained lying down until she heard the shuffle of feet dissipating in the distance.

Veronica slipped twice attempting to stand, the pain in her ankle intensifying. Keeping her body snuggled up to the wall, she edged toward her apartment. She could barely reach the knob, but successfully turned it and opened the door. Pulling herself up and in, she closed it. Veronica carried the camera bag into her bedroom and laid it on the bed. She walked to the refrigerator and grabbed a bottle of beer.

Her ankle buckled and she almost fell. "I can handle it," she muttered. "Mom will be so proud of me."

The first drag from the bottle felt like gold as it slid down her throat. Veronica experienced the pleasure of another deep swallow and headed for the couch. She placed the bottle on the coffee table and sprawled. Sharp raps on her door sent shivers up the length of her spine.

Who could that be? she asked herself, knowing that she wasn't expecting anyone. She stood and grimaced, feeling a sharp stabbing pain in her ankle, before walking to the door. The heavy raps repeated.

"Who's there?" she asked loudly.

"Ivan—the gatekeeper."

"What do you want?"

"I think that there's a prowler about. Are you all right?"

"Yes, I am."

"Would you open the door?"

"I don't think that's necessary. I'm in bed."

"I'd sure like to make sure. Someone could be forcing you, ya know."

"Please take my word for it. I'm alone and I'm fine."

Veronica listened and hoped—she finally heard the sound of slogging footsteps moving away from her door.

She sat down on the couch and punched in her mother's number on her cell phone.

"Hello."

"Mission Accomplished!" Veronica hissed.

"Oh you, sweetheart—are you okay?"

"Yes, meet me tomorrow at 3:00 p.m. at Sunflower Hill."

42

THE SHADOWS OF VERTICAL BARS DANCED for him on the opposite wall when Tom opened his eyes. He heard the unsteady hum of a ceiling fan in the jailhouse corridor. Tom looked down at his watch. Damn, they took it, he said to himself, frustrated.

I've got to get back to sleep, he thought, hearing the loud snores coming from the bunk in the cell next door. Tom tossed and turned for the next two hours before finally succeeding. He jerked awake to the sound of squeaking metal.

"Okay, Hastings, let's go," a voice said.

Tom sat up and rubbed his eyes. The stringy-haired jailer smiled, exposing a blackened tooth. Tom quickly got up off the bed and stood, hurrying out the door and following the jailer up the passageway. When he reached the room with the small table, he saw his belongings laying there—his watch and a beer cap. "Oh, you guys are really funny," he muttered.

A deputy appeared in the doorway, smiling. "You're the funny one. Follow me, sir."

Tom walked up the metal steps and followed the deputy through a door and down another hallway. The deputy stopped, opened a door, and directed Tom to enter.

Tom blinked when he entered the brightly lit room. "Good morning, Mr. Hastings," Sheriff Dave Johnson said, remaining behind his desk. A woman deputy sat on a chair by the wall. The sheriff leaned back in his chair and looked Tom in the eyes. "Tom, the Feds have agreed to forego the charges if you promise never to step onto their grounds again."

Tom nodded sheepishly.

"I would like to hear a firm commitment," the sheriff said.

"Yes, I will not trespass the cornfield again!"

"That's better. Have a seat."

Tom sat down on the remaining chair. "How can it be trespassing if they don't have any signs up saying so?"

The sheriff laid a paper down on the desk and dropped a fist on it. "I need you to sign this. They do have warning signs up—the area is mostly fenced, except for that corner where you got in. Why did you do it anyhow?"

"Sheriff, I do a lot of photography. For years and years, I've wandered onto the lands surrounding me. Never before have my neighbors ever complained. AND! The land belongs to my friend, Stuart Eldridge. AND! Someone over there took a shot at me."

Sheriff Johnson's facial expression deepened. "I suspected that you may have been the one. One of the officials from over at the site said one of his guards fired a warning shot at a trespasser."

"Huh!" Tom exclaimed. "It sounded mighty close to me."

"Hastings, my hands are tied together on this matter. As far as I know, it's a federal project. Your neighbor had made an agreement with the federal government, allowing them to run some experiments on corn. I have no control over that. Now please sign the damn paper!"

Tom leaned over the desk and scribbled his signature.

"You need to date it, too."

Tom picked up the pen and wrote down the date. "I don't have a vehicle. How do I get home?"

The woman deputy raised her hand. "I'll give you a ride. My route today goes out that way anyhow."

"Tom, this is Deputy Izzy Felton."

Tom nodded and raised a hand up slightly.

The sheriff opened a drawer. "Oh, I almost forgot. This is yours, Tom."

Tom reached out and grabbed a large brown envelope.

"Remember the money you lost in the grocery store. We got it back from Bemidji on Friday."

"Well now, at least I've got something to smile about."

The sheriff laughed loudly. He recovered and said, "I hope you had a good night. Now, I've got work to do. Please stay out of trouble."

He handed Tom the envelope and placed a hand over his mouth, trying to suppress another burst of laughter.

Tom stood and walked toward the deputy who had opened the door. He turned back toward the sheriff, but decided not to comment, waving instead.

————

TOM HAD BEEN ALLOWED TO RIDE IN THE PASSENGER SEAT of the deputy's car. The communications systems crackled several times before they reached the city limits of Big Lakes. Ten minutes later, the deputy turned off the U.S. highway and onto the county road that led to Tom's home.

"Where do we turn, Hastings?" the deputy asked.

"It's the first main left turn after passing by the lake," Tom said and glanced at Stuart's blue Jet Ski mounted on a lift.

The deputy slowed. "That's it," Tom said.

She turned the vehicle left.

"Bear to the right," Tom added.

The car drove up a steep rise and slowed for a farmer's truck turning onto the road from a field. "My number is just ahead," Tom said.

When the car stopped in Tom's driveway, the deputy stepped out of the car. She stood and placed a notebook on the hood. "Hastings, the reason that I volunteered to give you a ride home is because I want you to look at some pictures."

"Pictures of who or what?" Tom asked.

"I want you to tell me if any of these photos look like the woman who picked up the blackmail money from you at the grocery store."

Tom flipped two of them and readily placed his finger on a third. "That's her right there."

"Are you sure?"

"Dang right, I'm sure. Who is it?"

"It's the second victim...the one who's still in the hospital."

Tom tilted his chin. "But if she was assaulted for the money, how come they didn't take it?"

"You should be a detective, Hastings. That's exactly what we have to figure out."

———

TOM FELT A CHILL AS HE LEFT HIS HOUSE, walking toward the garage. A gusty wind played havoc with the dry, colored leaves of the higher branches of his tall oak trees. He saw clusters of them play the wind like an eagle's wings before settling on the ground. He backed his vehicle out of the garage and drove up his roadway, an occasional large orange leaf bouncing on his windshield.

He felt uplifted glancing at the money package lying on the passenger seat next to him, in spite of spending the night in jail—his first time ever. Why shouldn't I feel good? he asked himself. My money has been returned. I've survived a military attack. Tom lifted his hat while passing the cemetery. "Thanks, Becky," he muttered.

Tom parked in front of the barbershop, his thoughts on Floyd Pella who passed away during the winter. He was quite the guy...sort of kept an eye on things on Main Street. I'm sorry that he's gone,

Tom thought. Oh well, the new barber, Kelly, will do just fine—women barbers are getting more and more common all the time.

Tom entered the bank and spotted Lois Haugen, one of the bank employees, sitting at her desk in an area next to the tellers. "I need to see Bill," he said.

Tom took a seat in the waiting section and picked up a magazine. Five minutes later, Lois came around the corner. "Bill will see you now."

Tom marched behind her and entered Bill Arnold's office. "Good morning, Tom."

Tom walked right to the desk then pushed the package toward the banker. Bill smiled. "I think I know what you have there."

Tom sat down.

Bill removed the white envelope from the brown package and peeled open the flap. He pulled out the stack of bills and laid it on the desk. Bill looked at the door. "Lois, would you come over here and do a count."

Tom and Bill chatted while Lois worked. Tom glanced at her occasionally, focusing on her busy fingers dancing over the calculator. She went through the bills a second time.

"There's two thousand missing," she said.

Tom frowned. "What?"

"I've done it twice. One more time perhaps?"

Bill leaned forward. "Lois, get Jane in here. I want both of you to count it."

Tom walked out of the bank with mixed feelings. He still owed two thousand dollars...but, the bank is going to notify Sheriff Johnson...and hopefully, I'll get it back. He forced a smile walking toward Border's Café . Sure beats owing the full twenty, he thought. He paused on the ramp that accessed the door of the restaurant. Tom stood and watched a freight train rumble through town. When the last box car disappeared from sight, he entered.

———

TOM LOOKED AT THE WALL CLOCK in the restaurant. It read

10:59. He looked out the window and saw someone crossing Main Street. He looked up at the clock again. It read 11:00. The door opened and Henry entered. Right on time, Tom said to himself.

Tom felt glad to see Henry but there was something about the businessman's expression that made him uncomfortable. Henry stopped to chat with two men before heading for the corner where Tom sat.

Tom nervously snapped the newspaper open and tried to read. His worries reminded him of as a boy, sitting in a confessional waiting for the little window to open. Finally, he heard Henry's footsteps.

Henry pulled a chair out and looked at the menu listings on the wall. He sat and smiled from ear to ear.

Tom glanced away "Okay, so I spent the night in jail," Tom said. "I suppose it's all over town."

Henry laughed. "By this afternoon, it will be old news."

Tom took a sip of coffee. "I've been photographing the area around me for years. Stuart knows that. He still works for you, doesn't he?"

"Yes, he does. He told me the federal government paid him quite a bit of money to give up his land for one year."

Tom laid his fork down. "There's one thing that especially bothers me, Henry."

"What's that?"

"There aren't any Department of Agriculture signs around his place. The trucks and vehicles that I saw don't have any official logos, either."

Henry's grin fizzled. "Hmm, that does sound strange."

"Does Stuart ever talk about what's happening on his land?"

"No, he doesn't—well, one day, he...."

"He what?" Tom asked anxiously.

"He said, 'Sometimes, I wonder if it's really the Department of Agriculture that I'm dealing with.'"

———

TOM TURNED HIS VEHICLE ONTO THE CEMETERY roadway and stopped near the wrought-iron gate. He opened it and walked slowly up the center path toward his former wife's grave, stopping near her stone marker. He puckered his lips and tapped the top of the marker with his hand.

He gazed at a large marsh beyond the cemetery, the tall reeds partially hiding floating coveys of Canadian geese. This would make a great photograph, he thought, looking at the landscape in all directions from the knob of the small hill he stood on. The colors are spectacular. The wind he had experienced earlier in the day had abated, leaving only the sounds of distant vehicles on the highway.

Tom heard squealing brakes. He looked at the highway and saw an automobile approaching on the county highway from the southwest. He watched it slow down and turn onto the cemetery roadway. The vehicle stopped next to his SUV and no one got out. He stared at it, feeling tension building. I wonder why they're still in the car, he thought. I've seen many vehicles stop at the cemetery before, but some one *always gets out.*

Suddenly, he saw two men walk through the gate, stopping just inside the wrought-iron fence. They both wore trench coats with the collars pulled up. The one with glasses wore a gray hat. The other was hatless. They don't look as if they belong here, he thought, his feelings of apprehension intensifying because he had never seen them or their vehicle before. *Those men are here to do me harm.*

Tom thought about his pistol tucked away in the glove compartment. He looked at the ground next to a nearby oak tree, hoping to see a big stick to use for a club. Tom walked over to the tree and scanned the field beyond. He didn't see anything that even came close to resembling a weapon.

He walked back to his wife's stone, occasionally shooting a glance at the gate. Each time, one of them would quickly turn away. They're watching me for sure, he thought.

Suddenly, Tom heard the sound of another vehicle on the county highway. Tom celebrated when it turned and drove up to the gate, parking behind the other two vehicles. He saw a senior man and woman get out.

Quickly, Tom took off, walking fast, heading for the gate. He looked straight ahead and noticed that the two seniors had entered the cemetery and continued moving along inside. Tom nodded at the couple as he passed by them, quickly walking toward his vehicle. He held his breath passing the two men by the gate. Jerking the door open, he got in, started the engine, and headed toward the county highway.

43

AARON CRIER DROVE THE WHITE GMC ENVOY. His boss, Senator McDougal, sat next to him. He glanced into the rear view mirror, hoping to see the black Ford Explorer right behind. He smiled. Right on, he thought.

He flicked the left-turn signal arm and drove through a green light onto Main Avenue, heading for West Fargo. "This is a big day, Sean."

"I sure hope so. I'm a little nervous, probably because the two Texas guys got the truck here just in the nick of time."

"Yeah, I heard they had quite the time—stopped by the highway patrol—survived a pair of tornados in Kansas."

Sean laughed. "It may have been tough to explain to the authorities if the zillium plates were scattered all over Kansas."

The West Fargo city sign appeared. He glanced through the rear-view mirror again. "The boys are still behind us. When did you decide to hire those guys in that Ford?"

"A murder—an attempted murder—trespassers! Are you kidding? I think someone out there wants a piece of my action. I decided that I needed body guards."

Aaron stopped the vehicle for a red light on Sheyenne Street. A minute later, he turned left onto Eighth and slowed, waiting for the black Explorer to catch up. He brought the vehicle to a stop in front of Kurtz Manufacturing.

The senator unbuckled his seat belt. "Would you go check and see if they're ready. I want to spend as little time as possible out here."

Aaron nodded and exited the vehicle. He walked toward a single door and paused. An oversized door in the corner of the building opened. He heard the sound of a diesel engine and saw the front hood of a semi-truck drive slowly through the door. A camouflaged Ford Mustang, secured with chains around the axles, bounced slightly as the rear wheels of the truck crossed a bump at the door.

Two men followed the truck out of the building. Aaron saw Hans Mueller and another person wearing a helmet and racing jacket. Aaron waved at Hans. The German sauntered towards him and the racing guy got into the truck.

"Hello, Hans, you want to ride with us?"

"Sure," Hans muttered, his thick hair tussling after catching a gust of wind.

"Hello, Hans," the senator said as the scientist took a seat in the back. "Let's go, Aaron. The truck is leaving."

The senator turned his head and looked over at Hans. "Did you get the problem fixed?"

Hans smiled widely. "Goot—very goot, Senator."

———

A WOODEN, OPEN-AIR GRANDSTAND TOWERED over the north straightaway of the dirt race track. The Mustang had been removed from the flatbed and rolled onto the track by two workmen, the truck driver and a helmeted guy.

The senator, Aaron and Hans walked into the bleachers and took a seat ten rows up. Sean looked up at the sky and watched a jet trail elongate as it moved in the direction of Minneapolis. He worried that something would go wrong. He had talked to his concerned accountant on Friday. Six million in debt is a lot of money, he thought, but I didn't have any choice. This is an opportunity sprinkled with gold, my one chance to become powerful and famous.

No one spoke as the helmeted guy opened the driver's side door and entered the Mustang. Sean held his breath waiting for the engine to start. He heard a "murr...murr...murr...." Thank God it started, he said to himself.

The Mustang rolled forward, picking up speed as it approached the turn.

"Wow, look at it go!" Aaron exclaimed.

Sean gasped. The Mustang slowed while heading east on the far side. It gained some speed, but slowed again, as it approached the area in front of the grandstand. Hans rose from his seat. He waved and hurriedly stepped down to the ground. The Mustang had stopped and the driver exited.

Hans stiffly hurried onto the track. He pushed up an arm. The driver raised the hood. Hans leaned against the fender, his head disappearing for a time.

Minutes later, the scientist backed off and nodded. The driver closed the hood and got back into the vehicle. The engine started and the Mustang quickly gained speed as it raced toward the west turn. The speed increased again on the far straightaway, then it slowed slightly while taking the curve.

The senator raised both arms in the air and yelled. "Aaron! He's got it!"

Sean saw Hans jumping up and down and waving frantically as the Mustang sped by, continuing to increase speed. "God, Aaron, he must be doing at least a hundred and fifty."

Aaron Crier raised a fisted hand above his head. He tapped the senator on the shoulder. "By Heavens, Sean, we've made it. Look at that Mustang go."

———

TEARS CAME TO AARON'S EYES as he thought about his son, lying in a rest home, his brain comatose for six years, the result of a motorcycle accident. *Now I'll finally have the resources to take him to Europe and get treated by the world's most successful specialist in the field. All that's happened has been worth it,* he thought. *Once I get the money, I'll establish as many miles as possible between me and the ambitious nut sitting next to me.* He looked at his watch as the Mustang sped up the near straightaway, beginning its final lap.

The senator stood and looked down at Aaron. "Let's get down

there. We have some celebrating to do."

————

TWO MEN AND A WOMAN STOOD on a weathered wooden stand near the livestock barns. The men each watched with binoculars. The shorter one of the two lowered his. "Would you like to take a look, Nicole?"

"Sure." She rotated the adjustment slightly and found her target. The car whizzed around the track, and didn't make a sound. "Wow, I've been at car races and the noise has always been obnoxious. Not a sound over there—and the car's floating around that track like a space ship."

The taller man brought his arms down. "Well, we know it works. Are you sure that your daughter has copies of all the mechanisms?"

"Yes...."

"We can depend on that, then," the man said sternly.

"Well, I haven't seen them, but she assures me that they turned out great."

Nicole looked at her watch. "As a matter of fact, I have to get going. I'm meeting Veronica in Big Lakes in a couple of hours. She will have the original camera and the photos. I'll have multiple copies made right away, and should get back here by nightfall."

Nicole saw the bulgy-eyed guy staring at her...she shivered.

44

VERONICA PARKED HER VEHICLE NEXT TO A CURB directly in front of Sunflower Hill and the Big Lakes Mall. She grabbed the camera bag and exited her car. She gazed up and down the sidewalk before locking the door.

The mall in Big Lakes occupied an entire city block. The stores on Main Street had a double access—inside the mall, plus the sidewalk.

She pulled the mall door open and walked to the counter in Sunflower Hill. She looked around and didn't see her mother in the restaurant section. Veronica walked into the adjoining gift shop. A gentle tap on her shoulder startled her. She turned. "Oh, it's you, mother."

They ordered and Nicole carried a number three marker to the table farthest away from the counter. Veronica laid her camera bag on the table and sat down, her beaming smile meaning only one thing. Reaching into the bag, she grasped the camera and quickly passed it to her mother.

Nicole placed the camera into her purse. "So on the phone you mentioned that it didn't go all that smoothly, huh?"

The smile disappeared from Veronica's face as she gazed toward the far wall, the muscles in her face tensing. "No, not at all...."

Nicole patiently waited for her daughter to continue.

Veronica rubbed the tip of her nose with two fingers. She brought the hand down to her lips. "Don't turn around, Mom! I think that whiskered man next to the window by the counter is watching us."

Nicole leaned forward and placed her left palm over the corner of her mouth. "Who is it? Do you know?"

"I think it's that nosy gatekeeper...."

Nicole laced her fingers behind her head. "The green-eyed monster?"

"Yes! I'm quite positive it was he who tried to catch me last night."

———

TOM'S ENJOYED LISTENING TO THE SOUND OF his John Deere Garden Tractor mower blade chewing up leaves after he returned from lunching in New Dresden. He touched the brakes lightly, steering the machine down to the slope between his house and the lake.

A short distance to the east, he saw the senator's large pontoon boat moored across from a brightly colored speed boat. After already spending one night in jail, he thought he would never mess with any of his neighbors again.

He felt confused, still thinking about the conversation with Deputy Izzy earlier that morning. The cleaning lady must have seen him and Nicole when they made their escape after the alarm went off. Why would someone knock her down and not take the money?

Tom remembered looking into Deputy Izzy's eyes. She has that solid look of confidence, he thought. It dawned on him that the things going on at Stuart's barn were somehow related to the murder and attempted murder. Izzy didn't say that, but Tom had that gut feeling.

The sheriff put on a show of being upset with me, Tom thought. He looked away several times, obviously trying hard not to laugh. I wonder what Julie knows.

After completing the mowing, he drove the garden tractor into his garage and turned the key. He heard the usual-engine backfire. It sounds just like a gunshot, he thought. Maybe I shouldn't be so casual around my place. Who were those two men at the cemetery?

He walked into the house and locked the door. Reaching up onto a shelf in the closet, he grabbed the pistol and holster and set them on the desk. Tom punched in the senator's Border's Lake office phone number. "Come on, Julie, pick it up," he whispered.

"Senator McDougal's office," a feminine voice answered.

"Julie, is that you?"

"Yes it is, Tom." She laughed. "What's on your mind, jailbird?"

———

THE LOT AT MARY ANN'S HAD ONLY FOUR VEHICLES parked when Tom and Julie drove up. She had driven her car to his place, since he didn't want to mess with the gateman...or with anyone else over there.

She parked her convertible next to a blue pickup truck. Tom hustled around to the other side of her vehicle and opened the door. "Thanks, you've always been such a gentleman."

Tom smiled and said, "Jailbird at your service, ma'am."

Julie laughed. "You should write a book about all your experiences. Maybe even two books."

"Let's sit at the table by the fireplace," Tom said, grabbing Julie's arm.

They sat down and Tom looked around. He didn't see anyone he knew except the staff members. "Half a carafe?" the bartender said, holding up an empty.

Tom looked into Julie's eyes. She smiled.

"Yup," Tom said, nodding at the bartender.

"Good evening," Terri the waitress said and set down two menus. "I'll be back. I see Randy is getting you some wine."

"Thanks," Tom said. "I think we know what we want, Terri."

The waitress took their orders and left.

"So tell me what happened," Julie anxiously said.

Tom spared no details as he explained his walk through the cornfield and his subsequent capture by armed military-like guards.

"Military!" Julie exclaimed.

"I'm not sure how you're going to take this, but I think the cornfield and the monster machine have something to do with your boss—and perhaps the murder of Franks—and the clubbing of the cleaning woman."

Tears built up in Julie's eyes. "Oh, Tom, I've been thinking it over—and getting more scared by the day. Something very mysterious is going on. I've thought about leaving—so many times."

"Right now, nothing would surprise me. There seems to be a huge black cloud hanging over us," Tom said.

Julie picked at her eyes with a tissue. "Speaking of cleaning ladies, the senator has hired a new head. It's not a lady, it's a guy."

"A guy head cleaning lady—that's a new one."

"No—a head cleaning person."

Tom smiled. "Oh."

Fifteen minutes later, Terri returned to remove their plates and replace them with two steaming cups of coffee.

Julie blew into the cup and took a sip. "Tom, I'll be gone for the next two weeks. I hope that you don't get into too much trouble."

"I hear you're all flying to Washington."

"That's right. Most of is work, but I'm looking forward to showing Peter and Veronica the sights, especially the Washington Monument and Jefferson Memorial."

Tom smiled. "The same Peter who whipped the terrorists on the plane?"

"Yup."

"Taking him along is like insurance. There are tons of derelicts hanging around the mall. Peter will watch over you gals like a Saint Gabriel."

Julie's face sobered. "As long as I live, I shall never forget Peter and his dashing courageous attack on the terrorists. Our grandchildren will read about him in their history books."

"Julie, what do you think of the gateman at the senator's complex?"

She shook her head. "He scares me. I can't imagine why the senator wants such a gross looking and mean-spirited character around."

"He's gross all right, and I wouldn't be a bit surprised if he doesn't have two thousand dollars of my money," Tom said, his voice building up steam at the end.

Julie frowned. "Could be, but I've never seen the gook hanging around Stella's apartment. It could be someone else that partnered in your blackmail case."

Tom's eyes widened. "Speaking of gooks—"

"Yes."

"There were these two guys at the cemetery—they were dressed like characters out of *The Godfather*."

Julie reached out her fingers and set them on top of Tom's hand.

Tom forced a smile. "I think they came to see me—but I escaped cleanly when an elderly couple showed up."

Julie withdrew her hand. "Did you notify the sheriff?"

Tom shook his head. "One more trip over there and they'll probably throw me in jail for good."

Julie laughed.

Tom scratched an eyebrow with his middle finger. "Well, there's hope. The sheriff has a new deputy. Her name is Izzy and she seems to be right on top of the case. Perhaps it will be solved by the time you get back," Tom said.

"Izzy, now there's a name."

They left the restaurant and Julie drove Tom back to his home.

"Would you like to come in for a bit?" Tom asked.

"I would like to, but morning is going to come very early. We need to be at the airport by 11:00 a.m. That means leaving at close to 5:00."

Tom leaned over and kissed Julie through the open window. He pulled back and looked into her blue eyes. The glass slid slowly upward. He felt butterflies flying around in his stomach watching her car disappear around the bank of trees.

45

THE ACTIVITY ON THE SIXTH FLOOR OF MERITCARE HOSPITAL in Fargo quieted dramatically after visiting hours ended at 8:30. The floor's head nurse, Lydia, tapped her fingers on the counter at the station. She glanced at her fellow worker, Blanche, who sat at her desk filing her nails.

"Now why the heck do we need to move the patient from 640 to 610?" she grumbled. "We just brought her up from Intensive Care a couple of hours ago."

Blanche shook her head. "Two sheriff's deputies came up here this afternoon. They had this paper, signed by a sheriff in Minnesota. The order said to move her to a different room."

Lydia shrugged her shoulders. She threw up her hands and walked up the corridor. She entered room 640 and looked around. Uh-oh, they forgot the patient's bag. Lydia picked it up and headed toward 610. Just before turning the corner, she heard footsteps behind her. She stopped and turned, seeing no one. Lydia rounded the corner and heard the footsteps again. She backed up and peeked around the corner. Again, she saw no one.

Oh that poor dear, Lydia thought, gently placing a palm across Stella Robinson's forehead. She felt something move. Stepping back, she looked at the patient. She placed two fingers on Stella's hand. Lydia's heart stopped beating for a moment. She felt the hand move. "Oh my goodness, she's comin' out of it," she muttered.

Lydia pulled out the patient's folder. She flicked the top of the ball point pen and wrote down an entry. Lydia looked at her watch and entered the time: *9:45 p.m.*

On her way back to the station, she pondered calling Stella's doctor. Well, she's not really awake, she said to herself. The doctor went home only an hour ago. When she approached room Lydia's former room 640, she heard a noise inside.

Lydia peeked into the room, seeing no one, but hearing heavy breathing. She heard a shuffling sound...then a burst of bright light...then darkness. Lydia fingers desperately pawed at the knob as her feet buckled, and she fell into a heap.

————

PETER CLOSED THE VAN DOOR BEHIND JULIE AND VERONICA. He got in on the other side, just behind them. He glanced at the narrow band of yellow and orange in the eastern sky. It's brightening by the minute, he thought.

The door behind the driver opened and Aaron Crier entered. Peter heard him mumble something at Julie and Veronica. The senator opened the opposite door. He ducked his head and peeked in. "Good morning, everyone."

Peter chuckled hearing the varied guttural responses. I've got the feeling that no one appreciates getting out of bed before sunrise, he said to himself. It doesn't bother me. I'm looking forward to spending some time in the capitol.

Gus started the engine. The van backed up slowly and turned. Gus drove it forward and turned left. The engine groaned as he pressed the accelerator to take it up the steep slope. Peter noticed the open gate. He saw a hand waving behind the glass of the cubicle. Ivan's at work early, he thought.

Ten minutes later, they cruised eastward on U.S. Highway 10, headed for the Cities. "Coffee anyone?" Aaron Crier asked, turning his head.

"I'll have some," Julie said.

Peter closed his eyes. Another reason I'm glad that we're heading for Washington is to get away from this nest of trauma. One death and perhaps another, plus all those rumors setting up questions in my mind: W*as the senator illegally involved with agents from Togo? Why weren't I and Julie permitted to go to West Fargo yesterday?*

Peter felt certain that Julie felt the same tensions that he did. I'm afraid that she's going to quit, he thought. I would miss her a lot. She's a person who I can trust.

———

DEPUTY IZZY FELTON SAT AT HER DESK on Tuesday morning. She had arrived at work early, well rested, and hoping to take advantage of the senator and staff's absence. I missed something over there, she said to herself.

One of the women from dispatch poked her head into the room. "Izzy, there's a call for Sheriff Johnson from the sheriff of Cass County in North Dakota. He said it's urgent."

"Okay, I'll take it."

"Deputy Izzy Felton here. How can I help you?"

Izzy's frame stiffened as she listened.

"Yes, sheriff, I'll tell him just as soon as he comes in. I'm sure he will get back to you."

Izzy hung up the phone. She got up from behind her desk and walked out the door over to the dispatch section. "Fran, would you let me know right away when Dave gets in?"

The dispatcher nodded.

46

SHERIFF JOHNSON SAT ON THE EDGE OF HIS DESK. So someone may have made an attempt on Stella Robinson's life if we hadn't moved her to a different, unregistered room."

"Damn!" Deputy Kelly Martin uttered loudly from his chair by the door. "We've got a scene from *The Godfather* movie going on over there."

Izzy placed her hands in her pocket and paced. "The nurse is conscious and going to be okay, but I'll stake my life on it: if Stella Robinson had been in that room, it would have been all over for her."

The sheriff stood. "I sure agree with that. Thanks for the idea, Izzy. I should have thought of it myself."

"Dave, I want to have another look around at the senator's spread. Is our search warrant still in effect?" Izzy asked.

"That it is," The sheriff said, looking across the room at Kelly. "I want you to go along."

Izzy's lips tightened together. "Kelly, I'll be ready to go in about an hour. How about you?"

Deputy Martin nodded.

———

KELLY MARTIN ROLLED DOWN THE WINDOW of their police car after stopping at the gatekeeper's station. He held out the search warrant to the attendant. The gate slowly opened.

"That guy in there is something else. He's definitely on my suspect list," Izzy said. "I'm serious about that, Kelly."

"Yeah, I know you are," Kelly said and drove through the gate and down the steep slope.

He turned right at the driveway and parked in the lot across from the senator's office. They got out, Izzy holding a ring of keys in her hand. "Where do you think we should start, Kelly?"

"How about Stella's apartment?"

"Good, but I think someone else has taken it over."

"Oh, all right, let's do the drag trail."

"Good idea, Kelly. I really haven't spent much time on that section anyhow."

Izzy held onto the railing with one hand as she eased herself down the slope. The grass, still bent, identified the path where the body of Isabelle Franks had been dragged. Izzy moved slowly and methodically, stopping occasionally to move obstructive grasses and wild plants.

Half way down the slope, her eyes fixed on a short northern prickly ash shrub. During a previous search, clothing fibers had been removed from some of the thorns. She saw that some traces of fibers still remained. Looking up, she said loudly, "Kelly, do you have a cutter in your belt?"

He nodded and snapped open one of his cases. "Here, catch," he said.

Izzy knelt by the plant and severed the base with the cutters. She tossed them back up to Kelly and worked her way to the rail where she laid the plant on the deck. She turned to return and saw Kelly down on one knee.

"Izzy, look what I've got." His gloved hand held up a pair of glasses.

"I'll be right there."

"Just like an evasive piece in a jig-saw puzzle—it's not there and then it is," Kelly said. He had gotten a plastic bag from his pocket and dropped the glasses into it. "One of the lenses is intact, the other is shattered." He held the bag up to the cloudless sky for Izzy to see.

"So now we have to determine if they belonged to the victim. Because if they didn't, this find could be a major, major breakthrough," Izzy said.

The two deputies spent another hour working the slope. Wearily, they walked up the steps and to their vehicle. "What do you think,

Izzy? Are these lenses the simple magnifying type or are they prescription?"

"When we get back to town, let's take them over to an optometrist. I know one on Washington Avenue."

Kelly paced back and forth. "You know, Izzy, I think we should check out the Franks apartment. We need to know if she wore glasses."

"I definitely agree," Izzy said. "Let's go, I've got the key right here."

———

THE FRANKS'S APARTMENT HAS THAT CLASSIC SMELL, Izzy thought as she entered, Kelly right behind her. "There's something about the smell of an apartment after someone has been murdered," she said. "It lacks—the human smell," Izzy added, the floor creaking as she stepped into the middle of the room.

"I'm going to boot her computer. I want to see a list of her vendors," Kelly said.

"I bet you're going to look for an optometrist, aren't you?" Izzy asked, smiling.

Kelly pressed the computer button. "Meanwhile, would you check her bedroom again? Anything to do with reading glasses—even empty cases."

Kelly sat down on the computer chair while Izzy walked into the bedroom. The Windows icons appeared and he double-clicked the *Money* icon and loaded her accounting software.

"Jackpot!" he heard a yell, coming from the other room.

He turned and saw a smiling Izzy, holding up an empty eyeglasses case.

Kelly pointed toward the monitor. "She sees a Doctor Morrison in Big Lakes." He watched as Izzy dropped the case into a plastic bag.

"This is going to hurt our case if the glasses I found belonged to the victim," Kelly said.

"Yup—and if they don't, then we have a major clue—who else on our suspect list wears glasses, or gets treated for eyesight problems?" Izzy said.

She tapped the top of her head. "Kelly, let's contact television media and get copies made of recent press conferences or events where the senator and his staff appeared—say the last six months. The pictures should show us who wears glasses."

"What about the senator himself?" Kelly asked.

"Yup—and the senator, too."

———

IZZY AND KELLY LISTENED INTENTLY to Dr. Morrison as he explained the difference between so called 'cheaters' and true prescription glasses.

"There's no doubt that these are prescription, and very expensive, too, I might add," the doctor said, peering at the item lying on his desk.

"Is it possible that you could find out what the prescription is?" Izzy asked.

"Yes, we happen to have a new piece of equipment, actually new technology. It's called a Lensometer."

Kelly's face beamed with excitement. "Doctor, we want this done right now if possible, before we have to send the glasses to our crime lab in Bemidji. Is their some way we could do it without touching the frame or lens?"

"Yes, there is. I'll wear gloves and the center of the lens will rest on a glass-like surface."

Kelly looked at Izzy. She nodded. "Okay, doctor let's give it a try."

"Please follow me."

The two deputies entered a room behind the reception desk. Dr. Morrison put on a pair of gloves. He took the glasses over to an instrument labeled as a Digital TOPCON CL-100. He snapped a switch on and placed the lens on a glass base. The small screen above came alive. It read:

LS +75

C-1.25

A 112
ADD +2.75

"What do those numbers mean?" Kelly asked.

The first one, LS, records the sphere, C is the cylinder, A is access, and ADD stands for power."

"Thanks," said Izzy. "I guess it isn't that important for us to know the technological details right now. Mainly, we need a copy so we can compare it to a suspect's eye correction numbers."

"No problem," Doctor Morrison said and pressed another button. A small printout emerged from a slot. He handed it to her.

"Thanks so much, Doctor. You have no idea how much you have helped," Kelly said.

They walked outside and got into their car. Kelly flicked the turn signal. "We've got a ton of work to do, Izzy."

Izzy chuckled. "Tell me about it."

———

THE SHERIFF OF BIG LAKES COUNTY and his two deputies watched the screen intently as a cameraman kept his finger near the *Control* button.

"Stop!" Kelly exclaimed. "Play that again."

The tape showed Senator McDougal reach into his pocket and place a pair of glasses onto his face.

"Look how narrow they are," Izzy said.

"Continue," Sheriff Johnson said.

The senator read from a document on the podium. When he finished, he took his glasses off. Reaching into his shirt pocket he brought out a case and placed the glasses into it.

"That's it, folks," the cameraman said. "It's all over."

"Let's get back to my office," the sheriff said.

"We need to know the optical history of other staff members," Izzy said after sitting down on a chair.

Dave Johnson gulped down a swallow of water. "That will be possible when the senator returns from Washington."

Kelly stood. "I agree with Izzy. If the glasses from slope do not belong to the victim—major breakthrough."

Dave's blue eyes brightened. "Then all we need is to find out where they came from and we have ourselves a killer."

Kelly nodded, his eyes gleaming. "I've got an interesting scenario theory for you to contemplate."

"Go on."

"Okay, consider this: the senator has something going with his intern, Veronica. Isabelle Franks catches them playing games in his office. That's how Veronica loses a button under the desk." Kelly tapped himself on top his head with a fist. "He hits her over the head with the Lincoln bust. The senator swears Veronica to secrecy and drags the body down to the lake and makes sure that she drowns. His chief cleaning lady witnesses the drag through her window. She confronts him later. He smacks her down—thinks that she's dead. He wears a disguise to Meritcare Hospital in Fargo on Monday night. Remember now, the senator didn't leave for D.C. until Tuesday morning."

Dave clasped his hands together, setting them down on the desk. "It's possible, Kelly, but we need a lot more evidence than we have. If the eyeglasses belonged to Franks, you don't have much of a case against the senator."

47

NICOLE GLOWED WITH GLEE AS SHE COUNTED THE MONEY. Veronica can now tell the senator to fly a kite when she gets back tomorrow. She's going to get forty thousand from this pile...and I get one hundred and sixty thou. Veronica's share is going to get her through college. What if she doesn't want to quit? Nicole asked herself. She shrugged her shoulders and muttered, "So what!"

Nicole chuckled while thinking about the first offer...fifty thousand sounded good at the time, then things happened, she thought. The unexpected picture of the OxyBeast, and my good fortune to meet

Tom Hastings changed everything. Her chuckle notched up into a deep laugh when she visualized the poor man rowing across the bay frantically after hearing the speedboat motor start up—my God, I've never heard raspy breathing like that before, she thought.

The clincher that won her extra money was the detailed blueprint of the Ford Mustang. We also got the best of Hans Mueller...and to top it all, we don't have to pay him a nickel.

———

VERONICA FELT UPLIFTED WHEN THE PILOT AN-NOUNCED the beginning of their descent. We'll be down in half an hour, she thought. I wish my mother would pick me up at the airport. Instead I have to ride four hours in that creepy van.

I can't wait to see the money, she said to herself, glancing over at Julie. The tour of the capitol mall was spectacular, but I felt glad when the senator finished his final session. I hope that he didn't mean anything by it when he patted me on my butt and laughed.

Her thoughts drifted to the Smithsonian Institute and the Space Museum. The Charles Lindberg plane hanging from the ceiling was something...and the small capsule that John Glenn sat in while he circled in space around the earth...the first man ever.

What I really liked the best, though, were the statues of the horses and Civil War heroes, she thought. My favorite was the one of Stonewall Jackson. I've always liked horses and fancy saddles.

She looked out the window and saw the colorful treetops. There are more trees down there than in all of western North Dakota, she thought. Minutes later, she heard the screeching sound of rubber on concrete.

"Hey, Peter, we made it," Veronica said, reaching across the top of the backrest and tapping him on the head.

She peeked back between the seats and saw the face of Aaron Crier. That man has a mission, she thought. He has that faraway look in his eyes...total contrast to the senator, whose stares take me apart.

———

AARON CRIER LOOKED FORWARD TO GOING HOME. He thought about his newly found friend Carlita. I've just been through two of the most boring work weeks in my life. Politics has always been my bag, but things have changed. She's all I've ever wanted in life...someone to love.

He thought about the brochures which they had been studying. I could easily spend the rest of my life on a Caribbean island with Carlita, but first I need to take care of my son and see that he gets treated by the specialist in Europe.

Aaron glanced at the senator. Poor devil, Aaron mused. He thinks that he's going to be the next Bill Gates. The roof is going to cave in on that guy.

My plan is going well, he said to himself and yawned. Almost too well...I can't believe that I've gotten away with everything...so cleanly.

The jet liner came to a stop at the gate. He heard the sound of the engines dissipate to a drone...then the noise stopped all together. A woman stewardess came through the doorway from coach class. "How's everyone doin'? We're gonna be getting off shortly. Please check your belongings."

She's got a nice shape, Aaron thought, but not nearly as sexy as Carlita's. I would commit suicide if I ever lost that woman. She is absolutely everything to me. The passengers ahead of him stood and moved into the aisle.

Aaron stood and reached up into the baggage compartment. He pulled out two bags. "I've got 'em both, Sean."

The senator nodded and stood. It took only three minutes for the first class section people to leave the plane. He led the walk down the tunnel, carrying only his coat. Aaron, carrying two bags, tried to keep up with him. They were followed by the two smiling members of his staff, Julie and Peter.

48

DR. MORRISON SMILED WHEN THE TWO DEPUTIES walked into his office. He shook hands, first with Izzy and then with Kelly. "What can I do for you today? Ah, I've only got one chair in here—sorry."

Izzy's eyelids fluttered. "Hey, no problem—we'll stand. This won't take long."

The doctor's face muscles tightened. "Did the information from the other day help you out any?"

Kelly nodded. "Yes it did, but now we have a more sensitive issue to discuss, so I hope that you can help us."

Doctor Morrison's smile died like a cell phone battery sometimes does.

Izzy looked up at the ceiling. The skin around her lips tightened. "Doctor, in our continuing investigation of a homicide, we have learned that an Isabelle Franks was a patient of yours."

The doctor's face remained serious. "I'll have to check my records...."

Izzy forced a smile. "Doctor, this may be uncomfortable for you, but we absolutely need to know whether the prescription for the lens that we brought in last week—is the same as the one you use for your patient Isabelle Franks?"

The doctor looked up at the ceiling. He took a deep breath. "Your request bumps against doctor-patient confidentiality—but since the patient is deceased—and you likely could force me to divulge the information via a subpoena, I will check and see."

The doctor left the room. Izzy looked at Kelly and murmured, "This is it. The direction of our entire case depends on what he's going to tell us."

The doctor returned, walked over to his desk but remained standing. "The glasses *do not belong to Isabelle Franks*. She actually had been in here for a repair less than a week before—well before she met with misfortune."

The doctor reached into a drawer. "Here they are, just like new."

Izzy and Kelly looked at each other. "What do you think, Izzy?"

She rubbed the sides of her chin. Thinking for a few seconds, she said, "I don't think they would do us any good, Kelly."

"You can have them if you want—they're no good to me. Her insurance will pay for them."

"Well, okay, it won't hurt anything," Izzy said and reached out to take the glasses. She handed them to Kelly who opened an evidence bag.

The deputies thanked the doctor and returned to their car.

———

HIS FAVORITE HIGH TABLE APPEARED AVAILABLE when Tom Hastings entered Mary Ann's on Saturday evening. He looked around the room but didn't see any threatening looking people. Tom thought about the two men he had seen at the cemetery and the pistol he had placed in his glove compartment.

He felt lonely since Julie left for Washington. Tom looked forward to her return tomorrow, the final Sunday in September. Tom knew that he would miss her nearness when the senator and his staff vacated their summer residence in early October. Oh well, Fargo isn't that far away, he thought.

He took a seat and glanced up at the television. Ugly, he thought, looking at a *Shaggy Dog* commercial that ended with a long tongue filling most of the screen. Carrie came by and took his wine order. "Say, Carrie, could you get me the remote?"

The tall, pretty, young waitress smiled and returned moments later, laying the remote on his table. Tom glanced to his left and his thoughts drifted to two years previous when he had met Jolene at that very same table.

Fate would have it that her paternal father had been killed in a

New Dresden train crash, resulting in her leading him into some swashbuckling, risky adventures. Geez, we almost got blown up in that machinery building on the victim's farm by a jerk of a nephew and his dishonest sheriff of a father.

"Here's your wine," Carrie said.

Tom smiled. "Thanks."

He wondered how Jolene was doing in Kansas City. Our lives were never intended to be spent together. We were just a blip in history. Tom found an Atlanta Braves baseball game on the television.

Tom glanced toward the hostess station. He felt uneasy when his eyes locked on a light-brown straw hat. The short wide-hipped man wearing it had a dark skinned, round-cheeked face with a blunt nose.

Another dark-skinned man appeared. He stood much taller and had a very narrow face. The two men were escorted by the hostess to a booth in the far corner. Tom suspected that those two men were enemies and had something to do with the mysterious cornfield...but they were not the same people who he had seen in the cemetery.

———

SHERIFF JOHNSON PULLED HIS NECKTIE LOOSE and unbuttoned his shirt at the top. His two investigators had pulled their chairs up next to his desk. "Let's go over each suspect, one at a time."

Kelly said, "Okay, I'll start with Veronica Lewis."

"Fine," the sheriff said. "Go ahead and read what you have down there."

She is a strong girl and can throw. I believe she is very capable of throwing a shoe—that distance.

Her fingerprints were found on the assault weapon in the Franks case.

She was present, in her apartment, when Robinson was assaulted.

A button from her blouse was found under the senator's desk.

She doesn't own or use reading glasses. However, her mother, Nicole, who has visited her frequently, does wear prescription reading glasses.

Dave looked at Deputy Izzy. "What do you think?"

The dark-eyed female deputy sighed. "I think that Veronica is a likely Y, but not an X. She's somehow tied to the case but didn't commit murder or assault—she's mixed up in it somehow—we haven't heard the whole truth from her."

Izzy put up a hand. "I have something for you guys to think about. We only have Veronica's word that she doesn't own or wear reading glasses."

The sheriff puckered his lips. "Go on, Kelly."

Julie Huffman was also in her apartment when both assaults took place.

It is unlikely that she could throw a shoe that far.

She wears contact lenses, but she does use prescription reading glasses. As a matter of fact, she uses them often.

Many fragments of the second assault weapon, the red brick, were spread around her carpet in her apartment.

She discovered the first victim.

"What do you think of Julie as a suspect, Izzy?" the sheriff asked.

"I don't think Miss Huffman is either an X or a Y."

Dave looked at Kelly.

"I disagree—Miss Huffman may be our dark horse. I think that she could be either an X or Y."

"Why?" Dave asked.

"Opportunity: she's in a position to know everything—she wears reading glasses—red-brick dust was found in her apartment—she's a tennis player—she could heave a shoe pretty far underhanded, I bet."

Dave puckered his lips. "Interesting, Kelly. Who's next?"

Kelly continued:

Senator McDougal was gone from the house the evening of the first assault, but he could have easily left his home in Fargo and committed the crime and gotten back.

He does wear prescription eye glasses when he reads.

I doubt that he could throw a shoe very far, but it's always possible, especially underhanded.

"I think that the senator could be both an X and a Y," Izzy said.

Kelly jerked his head to the side. "How could you be both an X and a Y?"

"Sorry, what I meant was he could have been either one."

Kelly nodded.

Tom Hastings lives just across the bay and can easily access the senator's compound, as he did one evening...and got into trouble.

He wears glasses all the time, no reading glasses.

He could never throw a shoe that far overhanded, but just as the senator, he likely could underhanded.

None of his fingerprints have been found in the office or Stella's apartment.

He acts like some sort of espionage agent regarding the Department of Agricultural experiments in the cornfield next to his property. It has cost him one night in jail.

Izzy scoffed. "Kelly, I don't think that he's even a possibility for a Y. So he agreed to boat Veronica's mother over one night. He simply falls for pretty women real easy—and that gets him into trouble."

"What about the gatekeeper and the van driver?" the sheriff asked.

"The van driver lives in Big Lakes. He checked out okay—being with his wife on the first night, and also the second night. There just isn't any evidence linking him to the assaults."

"And the gatekeeper Ivan—whatever his last name is?"

"He lives with his mother in New Dresden, who told us that her son was home all evening the night of the first assault."

"What about the second?"

"He has no alibi for that one, but there's nothing else."

Izzy put up a finger. "Did we ever check for any red brick dust in the cubicle, out at the gate?"

Kelly shook his head.

"Hmm, I wonder. Maybe it's not too late. I bet the floor in there never gets cleaned. I see Ivan as a strong possible Y. I strongly suspect that he was the guy who called Hastings demanding twenty thousand—I bet he and Stella were in cahoots."

"Anything else?" the sheriff asked.

Kelly shook his head.

Izzy raised a hand again. "There's possibly one more person. It's likely remote, but the senator's aide, Aaron Crier, has been known to hang around a lot—meetings and such."

The sheriff nodded. "Let's find out if he's been a quarterback, or if he wears prescription reading glasses."

Kelly looked down at his report. "I have two more names here. Hans Mueller and Peter Nelson."

Izzy chuckled. "Peter could likely throw a shoe clear across the bay, but not a single bit of evidence points to him—besides what the heck motive could he possibly have?"

Izzy's laugh tailed off. "Peter Nelson is one of the cleanest young men I've ever met."

The sheriff waited for Izzy to say more. "I believe that's true with Julie Huffman, too. She has a great background. Where's the motive?"

Izzy interrupted, "That's the whole case in a nutshell. The motive! I think the secret lies there. If we find a motive, we find the killer."

The sheriff nodded. "Well, guys, the next step is to do some checking on Aaron Crier. That's going to be tough because he lives in Fargo."

Kelly said, "We have some good contacts over there. I'll see what I can do."

"Good, consider this meeting over."

49

JULIE LOOKED AT THE COLORED LEAVES OF THE TREES as the van slowed and stopped at the gate. She yawned and secretly wished that she was back in Africa. Her desire for travel grew with each year that she was alive. Jeez, we're stuck here and in Fargo for at least a couple of weeks, she thought.

I wonder what Tom's been up to since I've been gone. He doesn't travel much but he sure seems to know how to get into trouble.

She stood outside the van, watching her fellow staff members quietly walk toward their units. Their fatigued looking frames tell the story, she thought. The two weeks were certainly tedious and tiring. She watched while Peter pulled his case into his room. We're a worn out bunch.

―――

PETER HAD LEFT ONE BAG OF POPCORN IN THE MICROWAVE too long, resulting in a smoky room. He returned to the couch and continued to watch television. When he finished the corn, he carried the bowl to the kitchen and opened both rear and front windows. Wow, I need some air, he thought.

He walked outside to the eastern end of the building. The last two units were both dark: number five vacated recently by Hans Mueller, and number six empty all summer.

According to the senator, we'll all be out of here in another couple of weeks, he said to himself. At least we can enjoy the fall scenery for a time. He started back for his unit when he heard two persons talking somewhere in back of the four parked vehicles.

Curiosity got the best of him and he quietly approached the first one, working his way slowly toward the sounds, but remaining in the shadows. There were only two cars apart when he recognized one of them.

Peter crouched and listened. Oh my God, what are they saying? he asked himself, feeling his heart thumping against his chest. Someone on the senator's staff is plotting to steal the zillium energy discovery. Peter didn't know what to do. Should he expose himself and demand an explanation?

His decision was made for him as a massive arm hit him from behind, knocking him to the ground, his head smacking off the side of a vehicle. His mind recovered momentarily and he felt a rope burning his wrists as it twisted around, over and over. A bit later, he smelled duct tape and whined quietly as a strip was pressed against his mouth, then a palm smacked him on the lips...his tongue edged forward, tasting blood.

His attacker grabbed him by the waist and dragged him to the rear of a vehicle. Peter banged his head on the carpet as he was shoved into the rear of a van. He felt his legs being tied together and heard a door slam shut.

———

THE WOMAN SITTING IN THE PASSENGER SEAT held a cell phone up to her ear. She talked in low tones, explaining to her boss what had just happened. She nodded a few times and said, "Uh-huh—okay—okay."

She put the phone down and said, "We're off to Fargo."

The driver drove the vehicle up the slope and onto the state highway. "Where in Fargo?" he asked.

"Best take him to my place. I have a utility room that will serve as a perfect cell if we make some adjustments."

"Why don't we just finish him off and dump him in the lake?"

"The boss doesn't want another body around for the cops to investigate. He says we need to keep him alive for at least a couple of days."

50

MONDAY MORNING CAME TOO SOON, Julie thought as she put the final touches on her face and walked outside. She needed a break before the 10:00 meeting that the senator had arranged. It was to be held in his office and visiting media had been invited.

She casually strolled down the walkway toward the office. The parking lot had several more vehicles parked than usual. Julie entered.

She saw Aaron Crier sitting stiffly upright near the senator's desk. Several people who she had never seen before were seated in chairs lined up in four rows. She looked around and didn't see Peter or Hans Mueller.

She sat down on a chair next to the wall and rubbed her eyes. God, I'm tired, she said to herself.

The senator's voice startled her into reality. "Folks, I thank you for showing up this morning. I have a very important announcement to make. On Monday, the day after Halloween weekend, I am going to host a press conference at the Fargo Dome in Fargo, North Dakota. The purpose of the event is to announce a spectacular breakthrough in the use of energy to fuel any type of vehicle. I expect the CEO's of all major automobile manufacturers in the whole world to be present— and I mean the *whole world*. They will get a first-hand view of what's going to change the way we use fuel—forever.

"I'm not going to spend more time on details at this time. If you want the full scoop, you will need to drive to the Fargo Dome on the Monday that I specified. That's all for now."

Julie's tongue tasted the unused toothpaste on the inside of her lower right molars. She felt tightness in her neck and a throb in her right-side frontal sinus. It's getting worse with each passing day, she thought. Looking around, she wondered where Peter was... probably overslept.

————

TOM HASTINGS WATCHED A SMALL FLOCK of fast moving ducks sweep by his dock and land in the shelter of a weedy, shallow bay beyond his house. He had heard in New Dresden the previous day that Senator McDougal and his staff had returned from Washington. He wondered if Julie would call.

It's been a long two weeks. I'm tired of going out to dinner alone, he said to himself, walking out onto his deck with a cup of coffee. He looked toward the senator's dock. The pontoon boat and speed boat hadn't moved in weeks. He watched a single leaf flutter down from a towering basswood tree. It got caught in a series of air currents and appeared to be searching for a place to land.

I'm sort of like that, he thought. I'm searching for a place to land, too.

————

JULIE REMAINED SITTING ON HER SEAT and listened to the excited voices of the media people who attended the conference. She knew that the senator had hit a home run. I know what my job will be, she thought. I'll have the arrangements for the Fargo Dome event dumped in my lap. Meanwhile, I have double duty...being in charge of travel arrangements, and acting as his Border's Lake secretary.

Some of the media people began leaving. She saw two of them talking to Aaron Crier. The senator had exited quickly and likely returned to his house.

Where's Peter? she asked herself. He never misses anything like this. Finally, the last of the media people had left. Veronica and Aaron stood by the door talking. Julie got up and walked over to them. "What do you suppose happened to Peter?" she asked.

Aaron looked down at her. "Probably slept in—he looked pretty tired on that van yesterday."

Julie frowned. "That's not like him at all. I better go check him out."

She left the senator's office and walked over to Peter's door. She knocked—no response. She knocked again, louder—again, no response. She turned her head and placed her ear nearer the door—hearing nothing.

Julie's concern grew more intense by the minute. She returned to the senator's waiting room. Aaron and Veronica sat on two adjoining chairs close to the senator's desk, talking to each other.

Julie tapped lightly on the door frame and entered. "Aaron, I'm really concerned. Peter didn't respond to my knock. Would it be all right if I had housekeeping open the door?"

Aaron nodded. Julie hastened out of the office and walked quickly to the housekeeping apartment. She knocked and a man responded. "Are you Stella's replacement?" Julie asked.

"Yes, I am. What can I do for you?"

"I need to get into Peter Nelson's apartment. He didn't show up for a meeting this morning."

The man shrugged his shoulders. Julie added, "I have Mr. Crier's permission."

"All right, then."

The housekeeper stomped ahead with Julie following close behind. He held up a ring of keys. Selecting one, he placed it into the lock and turned it. The door opened.

Julie pushed by him and entered. "Peter, are you there?"

She walked into the bedroom. The bed didn't appear to have been slept in and his empty travel bag lay on the covers. She checked the kitchen area and saw an empty popcorn bag on the counter near the microwave. A wooden bowl with sticky popcorn hulls lay in the sink.

She looked back at the door. The housekeeping man stood there with his hands on his hips. Julie walked toward him and said, "Thank you for opening the door," and moved past him and hurried toward the office. She rushed in and noticed that Veronica and Aaron had not moved from their chairs.

"Aaron, Peter is gone!"

51

Aaron Crier shook his head. "Look, Julie, we have no idea where Peter went. Calling the sheriff would be premature. He's been missing for only a few hours. Besides the senator wouldn't appreciate it—there's been enough of that around here lately."

The look of frustration on Julie's face sliced through the room. She almost lost it, noticing that Veronica bit her lip to suppress a smile.

Turning around, she left the room, slamming the door behind her. She entered her office and plunked down on her desk chair. Julie shook her head. What should I do? she asked herself. Should I call the sheriff? If I do, I'll catch heat from the boss.

She picked up the phone. "Hi, Tom, how are you this morning?"

"Well, I'm alive—and I'm glad to know that you are, too."

"Tom, I need to talk to you. Are you free for lunch?"

"Sure, the leaves can wait—something else has happened, I can feel it."

Julie looked at her watch. "How about if I meet you at William's Pub—say in half an hour?"

"Sure. See you there."

———

Tom put on his cap and walked outside. He glanced eastward toward the senator's complex. I wonder what's going on now. Julie sounded pretty frustrated.

He walked out to the greenway and stood by the tennis court for a few minutes. Geez, Julie's been here all summer, but hasn't come over to play even once. Maybe that'll change. He looked at his watch and walked hurriedly back to the garage.

He braked when seeing two small deer sprint across his roadway as he drove toward the township road. Wow, the sun is shining...I'm meeting Julie for lunch...something tells me this is going to be a good day, he thought.

Tom parked across from the post office and looked around for Julie's car. He didn't see it. Time to get the mail, he thought and strode across Main Street. Before entering, he looked toward the tracks and saw a brownish convertible approaching. It jumped when crossing the tracks. Julie is here, he thought.

He saw her sitting in a booth by the window when he entered William's Pub. Smiling faintly, she raised her hand in greeting. Tom stopped next to her and stooped to kiss the top of her head. He sat down next to her.

"You look troubled, miss."

"Tom! Peter has disappeared!"

———

TOM SCRATCHED HIS LEFT EAR listening to Julie's recollection of the previous evening. "Geez, call the sheriff. For heavens sake, what's holding you up?"

"I talked to Aaron Crier, the senator's top aide. He said to wait until at least tomorrow. Peter could show up with a perfectly good explanation."

"Geez, considering all the other stuff that has gone on there recently, you would think that he would call the sheriff right away."

"Crier said that it could embarrass the senator, and the call may be unnecessary."

"That attitude is unbecoming of a professional. Do you want me to call the sheriff? I think that I have become a friend of one of the investigative deputy's."

"Would you, Tom?"

"Sure, likely she will have some ideas as how to proceed."

Julie dumped her napkin on the table. "I'm sorry to rush you, but I feel every minute could make a difference."

"I read ya—let's go."

Ten minutes later, Tom had Deputy Izzy on the phone. She listened intently. "Tell you what, Mr. Hastings, Kelly and I will go down there in an unmarked car. Our search warrant is still effective. We will remain as inconspicuous as possible. Thanks so much for the tip."

Tom hung up the phone. He stared out the window, thinking deeply. What if Peter got hijacked by friends of the terrorists? They could be doing it for revenge—after the airplane incident. That's clearly over my head, he thought, troubled.

52

KELLY SLOWED THE CAR as they approached the senator's gate. "I'm afraid that we have to bother you again, sir," Kelly said through the open window.

Ivan eyed them suspiciously. "I don't think that the senator's expectin' ya."

Kelly opened the door and exited. He bumped his chest against the cubicle and looked Ivan straight in the eye. "I have a search warrant here. You are ordered by a judge to let us through."

"Let me see that paper."

Kelly handed it to him. "Well."

Ivan nodded. "The senator isn't going to like it."

"Fella, we have the law to uphold. It don't matter if someone don't like it—and that includes you. Now open that damn gate or I'll get a dozer to do it."

"Well, ya don't have to get huffy 'bout it." The gate slowly opened.

Izzy saw the senator's house and compound appear as they begin their descent down the slope. She realized immediately that they would have another obstacle to overcome when a man came out of the house and hurriedly walked toward the parking lot. The bugger in that cubicle gave them a call, Izzy said to herself. Good thing that we have the paper or we'd be rejected.

Kelly stopped their car when it came abreast of the man. "Can I help you?" the tall man asked.

"You're Aaron Crier, aren't you?" Kelly said.

"Yes, I am, and who might you be?"

"I'm Deputy Martin of the Big Lakes Sheriff's Department, and my partner is Deputy Felton. We're here to search another room." Kelly handed him the paper.

"I and the senator are of the understanding that you people had finished your search, and we were all done with you."

"Mr. Crier, there have been two felonious crimes committed here on these grounds. We will not be through until the perpetrator or perpetrators are brought to justice."

"Which unit do you plan to search?"

"Unit three, I believe. A Peter Nelson is staying there."

Crier shrugged his shoulders. "I guess that I can't stop you."

Kelly parked the vehicle in the visitor's lot across from the senator's office. They got out and walked up the walkway toward Peter's unit. They could see the face of Julie Huffman just beyond the curtain of the window next door.

Izzy pulled out the key chain. "She's the one who got Hastings to call us, Kelly."

They searched unit number three thoroughly, but found nothing unusual. They did get the name and phone number of Peter's parents in Red Wing. Izzy led the way outside, and Kelly followed and closed the door.

Izzy had her eyes focused on the asphalt as they slowly approached their vehicle. "Whoa, what's that over there?" she asked.

She walked quickly between two other vehicles and stooped low, picking up an object. "A cell phone—I wonder. She placed it in a plastic bag. "Let's get going. I'm anxious to check this out. If it belongs to Peter Nelson, we're on to something."

Kelly frowned. "Izzy, let me have a look at that. I thought I saw something."

"Sure." She handed the plastic container to her partner.

"Look! The back side—that looks like blood!"

Kelly handed it over to Izzy. She held it up into the light. "Jeez, you're right. Damn, I almost feel like driving straight to Bemidji."

"We've got to cool it. This is all very sensitive. Politics, you know," Kelly said.

Izzy turned and stared at Kelly. "We've got blood. We need something from Peter. Hey, I've got it. I'm going back in and get his toothbrush."

Izzy returned in two minutes. She got in the car and her door slammed shut. Kelly looked at his partner. "What would the senator think of us if we taped the door?"

"The hell with the senator! Let's do it!" Izzy exclaimed.

———

IZZY COULDN'T WAIT TO CHECK OUT the cell phone. She requested and successfully got the sheriff to assign a deputy to deliver the new evidence to Bemidji—with a special request that they get DNA results as soon as possible.

Before the deputy left, she and Kelly had played with the mechanism and determined that the cell phone belonged to Peter. The blood sample along with Peter's toothbrush and the resulting DNA tests should verify what we already know, she thought. That type of evidence is critical during a court trial.

What do we do about it? she asked herself. Who do we talk to? The senator and his aide have returned to Fargo. Only Julie Huffman and the domestic staff remain, plus the ugly gatekeeper. Peter has been missing less than 24 hours.

She laid her head between her hands and lowered her elbows to the top of the desk. She heard a knock and looked up. Sheriff Dave Johnson stood there—the blank expression on his face resembling a dry wash cloth. He stepped into the room. "Izzy, there's not much we can do right now, but wait until tomorrow. Then I suppose we start another round of questioning."

"How can we question the senator? He's in Fargo—so is Aaron Crier, his aide."

Dave bit his lower lip. "We'd have to see the judge again— get extradition—or we could call the senator and have him and his aide volunteer. But regardless, we cannot do it today. I don't even want to call the kid's parents. We may be worrying them needlessly."

Izzy frowned. "I bet we'll be calling them soon. I can see someone losing a cell phone, but not with blood all over it."

The sheriff nodded. "I bet you're going to have a tough night, thinking about this."

"Yes, I'm afraid so. Anything on the Crier background investigation yet?"

"No, I'm afraid not. The Cass County people are going bananas searching his background. They said it's like one dead end after another."

53

PETER WOKE UP WITH A FIERCE HEADACHE and the bumpy highway wasn't helping any. It took him a couple of minutes to regain his thought process and realize his situation. He tried moving a hand around his body and felt the rope. The numbness in his feet improved slightly after moving his toes for a period of time.

Peter faintly remembered the parking lot incident and being slid into a vehicle. He turned over slightly to reduce the pain in the right shoulder. By relieving one area of discomfort, he created another, in his rib area. Then his forehead rubbed against the carpeted floor, feeling sore. I've been cut, he thought.

Suddenly Peter realized that he had been blindfolded. He heard voices: a man and woman, he thought...a driver and a passenger. If only I could move my arms. Peter attempted to find a sharp structure to rub the rope against. Shifting his body, he managed to drag himself sideways, getting closer to a window. Peter ran his fingers against the side wall—all smooth.

"Hey, how are ya doin' back there?" he heard a gruff voice yell from the front—laughter followed.

Adrenalin rushed through Peter's body. I'm going to make that bum wish he had never said that, he said to himself, anger building with each passing moment. I've got to conserve my energy. On television shows, the bad guys always make a mistake. And when they do, I need to be ready.

Peter felt the van slow, more than it had previously since he had awoken. Reflections from lights darted and dashed across the sections between the windows. Some of them penetrated through the cloth loosely wrapped around his eyes. We have to be going through a town, he thought—Hawley.

The speed of the van increased, telling Peter that the van had driven past the outer limits of the town. For just a moment his brain felt a spirit of peace. He imagined large rolling white clouds drifting overhead and sleep came.

Peter awoke when the vehicle stopped with a jolt, his discomfort so gross that any alternative would appeal to him. He lay still and heard a rear panel swing open.

He felt hands grab his ankles and his body rub on carpet as he was pulled backward. He intentionally did not react, remaining as mute as possible. His body fell to the ground, his head catching the edge of the compartment bed. Peter's mouth opened to say *ouch*, but he maintained control.

Peter didn't move a muscle as he lay on the ground. He felt two huge arms wrap around his body. He heard a door open. Someone had lifted him up by the shoulders, pulling him up a short stairway. By the smell of a kitchen, he knew that he had entered someone's house.

He heard muted voices and felt his body lurch as his carrier dragged him down a long stairway. The movement stopped. "Put him in there," Peter heard, finding his hostility difficult to live with. Peter kept his body limp as he bumped up against something metallic, finally falling into a heap. He listened to the sounds of a power drill, and the scraping of something heavy against the floor. "It's done," someone said.

Peter heard footsteps coming into the room. He felt his arms being jerked, and he heard the slicing sounds of a knife blade. His arms became free. Moments later, the ropes around his legs had been removed. He felt the pain of the tape being jerked away from his mouth. The blindfold came off. Peter couldn't see.

A door slammed shut and the room went dark. The ensuing quiet temporarily relaxed all the muscles in his body. Minutes later, he felt like a tiger, ready to spring. Peter got up on his knees. He felt like a caged animal, but....

Peter staggered around the room. The dizziness he felt caused him to lose his balance. Both his hands fell against a flat structure, a wall, he thought. His fingers slowly probed the edges of what he thought might be a door. Peter's confidence increased when his finger felt a light switch. He pushed it upward. The lights came on, temporarily causing severe pain in his head, forcing him to close his eyes. Cautiously, he partially opened one. He saw a washer and dryer. What the heck is this? he asked himself. Am I in a laundry?

A half an hour had passed before his eyes adjusted to the surroundings. He remained sitting. I am indeed in a laundry room, he said to himself. Peter got to his feet, his legs shaky at best. He took a step and saw a toilet in a small room next to the dryer—ah, my lucky day—a half-bath.

Peter staggered into the room and flicked on the light switch. His hand reached up to feel his aching temples that had been gnawing at him for hours. Returning to the main door, he sought relief from the brightness of the room by turning off the light. My God, what's happened to me? Where am I? Peter asked himself.

54

JULIE STEPPED OUTSIDE AND WALKED down to the dock. She felt so all alone. She had noticed a light on in the housekeeper's apartment. Everyone else had left. She watched the amazingly bright, round sun touch the tree line in the west. Her thoughts focused on

Peter...a gut feeling telling her that her fellow worker was a victim of foul play.

She looked up at the senator's house, the windows glaring bright from the setting sun. It towered over the water like a light house she had witnessed in the Carolinas. Only the upper part of the sun remained visible as she glanced at Tom Hastings's place and his rock-veneered fireplace chimney, the highest point of his house.

The sun had disappeared and Julie shivered. I need to talk to somebody, she thought, otherwise I could go ballistic this evening worrying about Peter. Only the tops of the tallest trees on the western edge of the peninsula captured the fading rays of the sun.

She looked into the water at the end of the dock, vividly remembering the toes of the white sock sticking out. She shook her head, grabbed and pressed in her cheeks with her thumb and forefinger. Turning, she hurried up the wooden steps.

After emerging from the walkway, she felt secure, seeing only her vehicle and the housekeeper's in the parking lot. Julie locked the front door behind her and headed for the refrigerator. She brought out a bottle of wine and poured some in a glass.

Julie sat down on the couch and took three long gulps from the glass. She picked up her cell phone and punched in Tom's number.

———

TOM SAT CONTENTLY IN HIS DEN. The Atlanta Braves were playing the Cardinals in St. Louis. The Cards had already qualified for the playoffs. Atlanta had won 13 consecutive division championships but they would need a win to clinch number 14. The phone rang. "It's me, Julie."

"Hi, Julie, what's up?"

"Tom, I am so uptight, there's no way that I can sleep a wink over here. Do you mind if I come over?"

"You're always welcome here, Julie. I hope that you like baseball."

"I'll see you in about fifteen minutes."

Tom removed his .38 pistol from the top of his computer desk and placed it into a drawer. He interpreted Julie's request as being one of urgency. Something has happened over there, he thought. "I'll soon know," he muttered, watching Julie's convertible drive past his window.

He met Julie at the door. They hugged warmly and Tom directed her out onto the deck. He brought out two glasses of wine. "Relax. I can see that you've got somethin' on your mind—hey give yourself a break first."

"Thanks, I needed this," she said.

Tom gulped the rest of his wine down, stood and walked over to the rail. "It looks peaceful over there, right now."

"Yeah, that may be, but I wonder what it's like where Peter is. I have this awful feeling that I will never see him alive again."

Tom stepped over to Julie's chair and filled her wine glass. "I don't quite agree with ya. From what I've read about that young man, he's one mighty tough fella."

"I hope you're right, but every day I worry more."

The full moon rose above the tree line to the east as Tom and Julie continued to sip white wine.

She stood and staggered a little. "Tom, would it be okay if I spent the night? I don't think—not in any shape to drive."

"Sure."

They went inside and Tom insisted that Julie use his bed. She attempted to smile as she worked her way up the stairs. He sat down on the sectional in the den, turned on the television, and continued to sip wine.

The phone rang. "Hello," Tom said. He heard breathing on the other end. "Hello," he said again.

Tom heard a raspy voice. "You quit messin' with that broad or you're a dead man—understand?"

"Who is this?"

"You stay away from her and the others—you keep yar nose clean—get it?"

"Look, you're drunken threats will get you nowhere. I can protect myself," Tom said.

Click.

55

SHERIFF JOHNSON AND HIS TWO INVESTIGATOR deputies all arrived at work early the next morning. He had gotten off the phone with the housekeeper at the senator's house. His first call had been placed to Julie Huffman, but she hadn't answered.

"It's official, guys. Peter Nelson qualifies right now as a missing person. Izzy, I want you to get some help out front. I want my whole staff involved. We need to create a document report with Peter's picture on it—distribute it all over the county—Fargo, too."

"Yes, sir," Izzy said and left the room.

"Okay, Kelly, let's have the latest on Crier."

"I'll wait until Izzy gets back. She needs to hear this."

Dave's eyebrows raised and his blue eyes increased in size. He nodded.

Izzy returned to the office minutes later. She sat down. Dave nodded to Kelly. "Okay, let's hear it."

"Aaron Crier is apparently living under an alias name. Right now, we have no clue as to his background. The earliest record we have on him is when he was hired by the senator. That was five years ago.

"He lives with a woman by the name of Carlita in an apartment complex north of West Acres in Fargo— known as Park Avenue. His woman is actually a citizen of Costa Rica. She is here on a three year visa permit."

Kelly paused. He looked at Dave. He turned his head and looked at Izzy, his face beaming. "Our man *uses reading glasses.*"

The sheriff craned his head forward anxiously.

Kelly's smile faded and he continued. "They traced his optometrist to a doctor in West Fargo, a Doctor Levitt. Now get this. Crier had been in the optometrist's office recently. He had lost his reading glasses and *ordered a new pair!*"

The sheriff grabbed his phone. "Sarah, get busy and call FBI headquarters in St. Paul. Ah, yeah—try to reach Agent Brown. I want to talk to him. If he's not available, give Agent Crenshaw a ring."

Dave hung up the phone. "We're finally getting somewhere."

One of the dispatch women poked her head into the room. "Kelly, you've got a call from Bemidji."

The deputy hurriedly left the room. He returned a minute later and stood in the doorway. "Dave, Izzy, the blood on the cell phone we found in the parking lot—its DNA matches the toothbrush." Kelly snapped his fingers. "It's Peter's—he's been kidnapped—or worse yet, dead!"

———

PETER WOKE UP IN THE DARK. His body ached all over, even though he had padded the floor with layers of sheets he found on the shelves above the washer and dryer. He ran his fingers over his forehead and felt the Band-Aid that he had found in the medicine cabinet. He had washed the wound with warm water the night before, almost passing out looking at the gap. By pressing the two cut edges together, he hoped that he could avoid a scar.

He flicked on the main light switch and noticed a narrow box lying on the floor next to the door. Peter opened the box—pizza! His stomach growled and he yearned for food. He hadn't eaten since making popcorn in his apartment. Taking the box, he sat in the corner of the room and ate the whole thing.

Peter sat there and studied the door...it really wasn't a door...it looked like a solid wall had been installed there recently. The narrow slot near the bottom had apparently been cut out to fill his trough—just like my father used to do with his cows. I don't suppose it would do any good to try to knock it down, he thought. He edged up next to it and pushed—there wasn't any give whatsoever.

Peter looked around the room. At least I've got a toilet and water, he said to himself. Otherwise this could get real ugly. The walls all appeared to be finished with dry wall plaster. I imagine the wall opposite the door is up against concrete. He hopped onto the dryer and lifted one of the ceiling tiles. He saw the plywood...double based, I bet.

The side walls are my target, he thought...but which one. This room could be in a corner of the house. I assume that the utility room is in a basement. I need a tool.

Peter muttered, "The plunger in the bathroom!" He moved quickly and brought it back with him. How can I ever penetrate the wall with this blunt end? he thought. He examined both the washer and dryer for any sort of sharp edge—no luck.

56

JULIE'S HEAD THROBBED SLIGHTLY AS SHE WALKED out to the parking lot at 9:00 a.m. the next morning. The message on her cell phone had been perfectly clear. The senator wanted her at his office in Fargo by 11:00 a.m. She smiled trying to remember what had happened the night before. Gads, we must have gone through a couple of bottles, she said to herself.

She placed her card into the slot at the gate. No one manned the cubicle this morning, she noticed. She had hardly driven onto the state highway when she met a patrol car. She saw the lights flash for a moment. Uh-oh...just a warning, must be my lucky day. Julie focused on the speedometer until she reached Highway 10.

The image of Peter's bright brown eyes and ruddy cheeks returned. The wine she had drunk the previous night temporarily diverted attention away. She put her cruise on 75 and headed toward Big Lakes.

An hour later, she arrived in Moorhead, crossed the Red River bridge and took a right on Fourth Street. She parked in the ramp behind the complex where the senator had his office. After getting out of the car, she appreciated the coolness of the late September day. It helped clear her head as she walked toward the elevators.

Julie entered the reception room. Della pointed toward the senator's door. Julie entered. Several people sat on chairs in the room listening to the senator. "Good morning, Julie," the senator interrupted. "Good morning, everyone," she said.

There remained one empty chair and she sat down. Julie met the eyes of Aaron Crier who sat in a chair next to the senator's desk. Jeez, he looks evil, she thought.

The senator outlined his plans for the upcoming press conference to be held at the massive Fargo Dome. His face filled with pride when he announced that he expected the CEO's of all the major automobile manufacturing plants in the world.

The staff members who sat in the room had all been appointed as committee chair people. Aaron Crier walked around the room and handed each of them a multi-page document.

"We've only got three days," the senator said and stood. The people began rising. One by one they walked out of the room, until only the senator, Aaron and Julie remained.

The senator looked at her. "What's the latest on Peter?"

"According to what I heard on the radio on the way down here, there is a massive search going on by the Big Lakes Sheriff's department, as well as local police. The television stations have been posting his picture. Likely, he will make the front page of the *Forum* tomorrow."

"Thanks, Julie. Let's all pray for his safe return. Have his parents been notified yet, I wonder?"

"I would give Sheriff Johnson a call and ask him. If they haven't done it by now, perhaps it would be in your best interests to do it yourself."

Julie looked at the senator's face and thought he looked like a puppy dog for a moment, before he assumed his usual firm look. She frowned and slightly tilted her head. The senator looked away. "Now, if you excuse me, I have work to do—and so do you, Julie. There's a stack of papers on your desk. Veronica has been in there all morning, already working on the arrangements."

Julie stood, and then turned and clicked her heals as she walked out of the room.

———

PETER FELT HIS STRENGTH RETURNING. He spent part of each day working out, using the exercises, which he had done during his tae kwon do sessions. He used a paper towel to wipe off the perspiration from his forehead, and looked up at the two vertical marks in the wall. This is my third day in captivity, he thought and grabbed a finger file, which he had found in the medicine cabinet, to carve in a third one.

He had attempted to use the file as a whittling device, but it failed miserably. He returned to the half-bathroom and put the file back in the medicine cabinet, hesitating before he closed the mirrored door—he stared at the metal frame.

Peter yanked and pulled until he twisted the hinges of the small door away from the cabinet. He pried on the jointed corner of the metal frame with the file and successfully pulled it away from the mirror. Rubbing a finger across the edge of the glass, he felt the sharp edge.

He walked back into the main room, taking the plunger and glass door with him. Peter propped the sheets against the wall and sat down. He whittled for five minutes before blisters formed on his fingers. Peter stopped and held his hands up. He got up and brought back a roll of Johnson & Johnson bandages and tape.

Within minutes, he had succeeded in creating a makeshift glove for his right hand. An hour later, he set down the glass door and felt the end of the plunger handle with his fingers. He nodded, excited about the possibilities.

Peter sat and rested his hands for a few minutes, staring at the walls around him. Which wall should I try first? he asked himself. The half-bath and washer both needed water pipes, which would likely be installed in an inside wall. Peter laid the plunger on the washer and hoisted himself on top of the dryer. Holding the rubber end with both hands, he drove the sharpened end into the drywall.

Excited, Peter repeated the jabs over and over until he had successfully created a six inch diameter hole. I better take a break or my heart isn't going to be able to handle the hyper, he thought.

Peter slid off and stepped back for a minute, staring at the hole, fathoming his escape. He pulled aside the insulation and saw the gray liner of the drywall panel on the other side of the wall. Peter crawled back up on the dryer and drove the wooden handle into the two walls over and over again.

He set the handle down and put his perspiring head between his hands to slow his breathing and heart rate. Looking up, he placed a hand into the wall and begin pulling large chunks of plaster away. Five minutes later, he had successfully whacked out a large area in the inner wall.

Crouching and leaning in farther, he pulled out more chunks of insulation and plaster. Perspiration ran down his forehead as he continued to poke and tear the material away. Wiping his eyes with a sleeve, he continued his assault until the spaces appeared large enough for him to crawl through.

———

AGENT BILL BROWN'S STUBBY FINGERS pushed the car door shut. He smiled widely at his partner, Agent Susan Crenshaw. They had just arrived at Big Lakes from their headquarters in St. Paul after receiving a call from Sheriff Dave Johnson. Streaks of gray interloped his pine cone-colored, crew cut.

His wide-shouldered frame humped slightly as he approached the elevator, followed by the portly-hipped Crenshaw, whose brown eyes appeared larger than average. A gold tie in the back of her head secured a bushy pony tail of thick, brown hair.

They took the elevator down a floor and entered the sheriff's office reception area. The woman behind the desk smiled. "Can I help you?"

They showed her their ID's. She stood and smiled. "I'll open the door for you."

"You didn't waste much time," the sheriff said when they entered his office. "Have a seat." He picked up the phone. "Send in Kelly and Izzy."

The introductions had a festive flavor as hands shook and pleasant words were exchanged. The sheriff had two extra chairs brought into his office. After everyone sat down, he looked at Kelly. "Okay, would you give the two agents a rundown of where we're at?"

Deputy Kelly Martin had the floor for close to five minutes. The two agents nodded their heads from time to time, their faces serious.

Bill Brown spoke first. "Since we haven't had a ransom demand, it's rather difficult to determine how to proceed. It sounds as if you've done enough investigating at the compound. Now, it's time to have a serious chat with the senator and his aide."

He glanced at Crenshaw. "That means a call to Fargo, and an appointment for today."

She nodded.

The sheriff picked up his phone. "Get me Senator McDougal's office." He hung up and licked his lower lip.

Izzy had been sitting quietly throughout Kelly's report. Her eyes gleamed, reflecting light from the ceiling fixture. "I think Fargo is where everything is going. I'm so thankful that you two are here. We have no authority in that county."

Bill Brown leaned forward in his chair. "You're correct, Izzy, but we could deputize you and Kelly, and you could come along. You would only have to change badges."

Izzy's face brightened. "I'm positive that Peter got transported to Fargo, and don't ask me why, but I just know."

The sheriff nodded. "Hopefully, we'll have him back soon. God bless the young man, a national hero in the least."

57

SENATOR MCDOUGAL'S FACE TURNED WHITE. He hung up the phone. "Get Julie in here," he said briskly to Aaron. "Damn, two FBI agents are coming over here today. They'll be here this afternoon." He looked at his watch.

"You've got nothing to hide, senator," Aaron said, placing the top of his pen partially into his mouth.

"I don't need all this right now. I haven't got a damn thing to do with Peter disappearing. For Christ sakes, he probably ran off on his own."

Aaron put a finger to his lips. Julie appeared in the doorway. "You want to see me, Senator?"

"Ah yes, have a seat, Julie." The senator stood and paced back and forth in back of his chair for a few moments. He pointed at her. "I want you to call my cousin Jack in Bismarck. Tell him that it's an emergency and I need him as soon as possible—like early afternoon."

Julie nodded, appearing confused.

The senator continued. "Two FBI agents are going to be here later today. I want you to be at the reception desk when they come. You are to tell them that I've been called away on an emergency and my attorney will answer all their questions."

Julie's skin on her forehead creased and reddened. "Are you sure that you want me to do this?"

"Damn right. Please do as I say."

Julie looked at Aaron. He looked away. She looked back at the senator. He glared at her. "Okay, I'll do it."

———

PETER CRAWLED THROUGH THE SPACE and dropped onto the carpeted floor of a bedroom. His felt dizzy and thought about the box of food lying by the door in the laundry room. I need food in my stomach—too late now, he thought.

He knelt and buried his head between his hands and arms for a few moments. Standing up, he spotted a basement window. That's my ticket, he thought, his mind fighting the vertigo, encouraging his muscles to move.

He walked quietly to the open door of the bedroom. He peaked beyond into a sitting room where he saw a tan sectional facing a wide screen television. Peter gently closed the door, hearing a click. He pressed his ear against it, straining to hear any movement beyond.

All is quiet, he thought.

Looking around the room, he moved a lamp and doily off of a bed stand table. Grabbing it, he set it down upright under the window, pushing down to test its stability. Peter placed a knee on the stand, and elevated himself until both knees perched securely on the surface. Using the wall for support, he stood.

Peter grabbed the latch on the window, turned it, and pulled it open. By jiggling it, he managed to secure it open. He eyed the frame of the screen. I should be able to push that out, he thought.

Suddenly, he heard the door open behind him.

————

THE TWO FBI AGENTS CAME THROUGH THE DOOR. Julie looked up and smiled. "Good afternoon, gentlemen, can I help you?"

They showed her their ID's. "I'm Agent Brown of the FBI. This is Agent Crenshaw. We're here to see the senator."

"I'm sorry, but the senator has been called away because of an emergency, however his attorney will answer any of your questions."

She looked away for a moment, then met the eyes of Agent Brown. He doesn't appear very pleased, she thought. She noticed that Crenshaw had rolled her eyes and her face reddened. "Mr. Jack McDougal and the senator's aide are waiting for you." She pointed at an open door.

Agent Brown nodded and said, "Thanks."

They disappeared through the door and Julie breathed a sigh of relief when she heard it close. She got up from behind the desk and returned to her office. Veronica appeared to be busy. "Veronica, I'm taking my work next door—probably be there for a while."

Julie returned to the reception room and tried real hard to focus on her work. Forty-five minutes later, the door opened and the agents walked right through without saying a word.

Jeez, after the Dome press conference and dinner at the country club, I'm going to resign. I can't take this any more.

Aaron stepped into the reception room. "You did fine, Julie."

She touched her lips together and blew lightly. "Pooh."

Aaron smiled. "Don't worry, it will all be over real soon. I'm headed home."

Julie watched him walk out into the corridor. "I wonder what he meant by that?" she asked herself, pulling on strands of blonde hair which had slid over one of her eyes.

Julie looked at her watch. "I'm closing this joint, and right now."

She grabbed her handbag, locked the door behind her and headed for the parking ramp. She drove to her apartment and filled the tub with hot water. Julie lulled herself into dreamland, enjoying the soothing hot water, gently working her hands through the bubbly soap. After putting on her nightclothes, she grabbed her cell phone and punched in a number.

"Hi, Tom, I've got a favor to ask you."

58

TOM WORRIED THAT HE HAD AGREED TO SOMETHING that he would be sorry for as he walked through his front door. So Julie wants me to be her date at the country club, he said to himself. He carried the strap of his camera bag over his left shoulder. Next to the camera, he had placed a half pint of brandy. He planned on stopping at his favorite bench on his property.

He walked out to his greenway and stood next to a tree. Tom patted the holster that he had strapped on minutes earlier. He felt guilty not telling Julie or anyone else about the threatening phone call. Maybe I'm not taking the call and the men at the cemetery seriously enough, he thought. But then, why am I carrying this gun?

Something is really wrong, he said to himself. Julie didn't sound like her usual self. Tom walked along the tree line next to his greenway. When he reached the end, he took a left and walked along a curved path, glancing at the blue water beyond the trunks of tall trees.

He walked along his western border, lined by two rows of tall spruce and pine trees. Tom chuckled. Maybe I should give that cornfield one last run, he thought. Naw, I better not, the sheriff's got enough problems right now...and I have a date to keep.

He reached the bench and placed a padded seat down to sit on. He opened his bag and lit his pipe. After several successful puffs, he grabbed the small bottle and took a sip of brandy. He licked his lips and smiled. Life is good for the moment, he thought.

I've got a whole week in which to behave before joining Julie at the Country Club in Fargo, he said to himself. Heck, I may as well go early that day and take in the big event. It's free. Then, I'll have a night out in Fargo.

———

TEARS STREAMED DOWN PETER'S CHEEKS. He felt like a dog on a lease. I swear that I'm going to get even with that guy, he said to himself. I was so close. Another few seconds and I would have been out that window. He cried softly.

Before Peter could get off the night stand in the bedroom, a big brute of a man hit him across the legs with a poker. He fell to the floor. The pain in his legs couldn't match the pain in his heart. He had gotten caught again...by the same guy. "He's going to pay some day, I swear," he mumbled.

The next thing Peter felt was the rope being tied around his wrists, which had been pulled behind his back. "If you would've behaved, this wouldn't have been necessary," the brute said.

———

SHERIFF DAVE JOHNSON FELT DEEP frustration. A United States senator had successfully thwarted his investigation. The FBI Agents tried to meet with the politician but failed. He looked up at the calendar. Twelve days had passed since Peter Nelson had disappeared. He felt no closer to solving the case at this moment than the day Peter vanished.

Bill Brown entered. "Crenshaw will be along in a few minutes." He walked to the opposite wall, noticing several hanging portraits of previous sheriffs. Looking up for a moment, he turned and walked toward a chair. Before sitting down, he banged his fist against the paneled wall. "Sorry, but I'm frustrated."

Dave nodded. "You're not the only one."

Susan Crenshaw entered and sat down next to Brown, her face drawn, a look of defeat in her eyes.

"Good morning, Susan," Dave said.

She nodded.

"Soon as Kelly and Izzy get here, which should be shortly," Dave said and glanced at his watch, "we'll go over our strategy and you guys can be off to Fargo. The press conference is set for 3:00 p.m. If you get out of here by 1:00, you shouldn't have any trouble getting in."

Izzy entered. "Good morning, all." She sat down without saying more.

Kelly came in right behind her. Bill stood and handed each of them a badge. The officers discussed possible strategies for half an hour. Dave looked at his watch. It read 12:45 p.m.

"You guys better get going. I'll have a phone with me all day. I hope to hear good news."

Dave followed the four officers out of the room and down the stairway. He stood by the door watching them get into the FBI vehicle. Kelly sat in the passenger seat next to Bill Brown. The two women officers sat in the rear seats. Dave's eyes watched the vehicle drive out into the street and take a right. "God speed," he whispered.

59

THE PEOPLE OPERATING THE CONNING TOWER at Fargo International Airport had never seen anything like it. Wave after wave of private luxury air jets landed. They began arriving shortly after dawn. "That's number two hundred fifteen," Corey said.

"According to what I have down here, we have about seventy-five more to go—and four jetliners full of press corp," Blaine added.

By noon, the final visiting aircraft had landed and the crew in the Conning Tower breathed a sigh of relief. "Jeez, they all made it down," Corey said.

———

TOM HASTINGS GLANCED TO HIS RIGHT as he drove across the Red River of the North on the First Avenue Bridge. He saw the water down below and remembered the days that he used to snowmobile on that river. He took a right and headed into North Fargo.

The press conference should be interesting, he thought. The *Forum* reported that morning that the airport expected at least two hundred extra planes. The event had been scheduled to commence at 3:00 p.m., but Tom decided to arrive early and enjoy the scenery. Geez, imagine the CEO's of General Motors, Ford and Toyota, he said to himself. You have to hand it to the senator, he thought. The big guy has it going today. He felt amazed that the murder of the Franks woman, the assault on the housekeeper and the disappearance of Peter Nelson all took backseats to the event at the dome.

Tom thought about his experiences in the cornfield earlier. There's no doubt that the press conference is all about what's been happening there, on Stuart's land. He sobered considering the possibility that the crimes at the senator's compound were related, too.

No matter if I don't see Julie at the dome, I know where the country club is, he thought. Tom took a left on Nineteenth Avenue, crossed Tenth Street and took a left on University. He spent the next half an hour waiting in line to buy a parking ticket. I thought this was supposed to be free. Oh well, Fargo needs the money, he thought. The *Forum* articles and editorials write about the cities' needs almost every single issue.

"Ten bucks!" Tom exclaimed. He paid the kid and sped toward an open spot.

I wonder if the NDSU Bison have ever had a crowd as big as this one, he thought. He entered the door and followed the crowd. The chairs in front of the stage had already filled. He decided to climb into the bleachers. He selected a seat near an exit.

Tom watched uniformed escorts bring in guest after guest, all of them being seated in the chairs below. One of them wore a turban. He saw a large group of Orientals. "This is going to be somethin'," he muttered.

"You got that right," a man sitting next to him said. "It could mean the end of the oil cartel empire," the stranger added.

Tom checked his watch. Almost an hour to go and this place is about full, he thought. Where are they going to put everybody? The atmosphere sounded like ten million crickets in one pond. He felt fortunate to have brought his small set of binoculars. He scanned the podium...Geez, there she is...my Julie. The senator had not made his grand entrance yet.

———

PETER HAD TRIED FOR DAYS TO CUT THE ROPE from around his wrists using the edge of the toilet seat—total failure. His adversary had removed the medicine cabinet door. He heard something drop to the floor by the door. My lunch is here. By swinging his legs, he managed to crawl to the box. The rope tied around one of his ankles wouldn't allow him to move an inch farther.

He opened the box with his teeth and smudged up his entire face eating like a two-month-year-old. My mother should see me now, he thought. Why am I laughing? Peter worked his way back to the toilet seat. He stood and used a spare amount of toilet paper wiping off his face.

Feelings of despair drove him into a state of temporary depression when he returned to his pad of sheets at the far wall.

He closed his eyes. There, he said to himself. Please help me, God.

Peter looked up at the wall. He had used the file to place his thirteenth mark into the drywall, earlier in the day.

———

TOM LOOKED AT HIS WATCH. He jerked to attention as the band on the other side of the bleachers erupted loudly into song. He recognized and appreciated the old classic, "Stars and Stripes Forever." Tom felt tears building in his eyes by the time the band stopped—a dynamic clang by three pairs of cymbals.

He saw a man dressed in a tuxedo dash to the podium, grabbing the mike with a sense of authority. "Ladies and Gentlemen!" The man moved two steps to his left and pointed. "Let's hear it for the Shanley High School band."

The crowd cheered.

Drums rolled. "And now, ladies and gentlemen—our United States of America—Senator—Sean McDougal!"

Trumpets blared. Many people stood. Tom watched in awe.

The senator flapped his hands for quiet. Some of the people continued to clap. The sounds faded like the dissipating rumbling of a freight train when it leaves the outskirts of a small town. The tall man grabbed the microphone. "Welcome!"

More applause followed.

Tom's mind became absorbed in the sensationalism of the presentation. The senator talked about the high price of gasoline. "It's hard on everyone," he said.

He placed a finger to his mouth. "I want you all to watch the screen very closely."

A camouflaged automobile appeared in the center. A race driver with a helmet in his hand walked toward it. He raised a fist into the air, then he got in. "Folks, this 2004 Mustang is powered by oxygen."

The car took off and cameras followed it around the track. The crowd watched, shouting words of support and acceptance, interrupted by an occasional, resonant yelp.

When the film ended, the lights came on and uniformed attendants passed out packets of information to each row at the floor level.

The band played another number. He didn't recognize it, but when they finished, Tom clapped and clapped. Suddenly, his mind drifted back home...to the cornfield...to the monster he had seen in the field...the armed guards...his night in jail. His hands remained suspended in the air in front of him. My God...Department of

Agriculture, my foot!

He searched for Julie with his binoculars. He saw the empty chair where he had seen her earlier. Gads, she's probably in the washroom throwing up, he thought.

60

PETER'S SPIRITS STRUCK A NEW LOW. They're going to kill me, he thought. For some reason, they're keeping me alive right now. There's no hope. I'm lost. Only a miracle could save me now.

He lay still for a few minutes. Don't give up, his inner thoughts demanded. The door...the hole in the wall...the ceiling—all dead ends, but there has to be a solution.

Peter lifted his chin. He thought about his adversary, the man with the ugly, gruff voice. The same man who cracked my legs with a poker. He split open my forehead back there at Border's Lake.

He heard a toilet flush upstairs and jerked his head to one side. Peter got to his knees and shuffled over to the half-bath. He entered and sat on the back edge of the stool with his back firmly against the tank. He used his fingers to easily lift the lid off the tank then Peter swung his frame and released the lid as close to the floor as he dared. It dropped with a thud. He listened for a few moments, hearing nothing.

He dipped his hands into the cold water, his fingers seeking something sharp. "Ouch," he muttered.

Back and forth, he worked the rope around his wrists against an edge. Several minutes later, his back hurt so much that he pulled out his hands and got off of the stool. He felt encouraged when several strands loosened in the rope. Peter took a deep breath and got back on the stool, placing his body in a more comfortable position. The cold water in the tank relieved his sore and bloody wrists.

An hour later, he got off the stool again. The rope around his wrists had loosened. Suddenly, he freed his right hand and brought both arms to the front of his body. Peter twisted his shoulders and swung his arm in all directions to rid his extremities of the numbness.

His fingers didn't have the dexterity to untie the tight knots around his left wrist. Peter returned to the stool and saw the sharp edge. He kneaded the strands feverously until they begin to break loose. Minutes later, he shook off the rope and elevated his hand into the air.

Using the fingers of both hands, Peter successfully untied the rope, freeing his ankle. The hole in the wall above the dryer had been closed off by a metal bed frame. Peter grunted while pushing on the frame. It hardly moved. Changing his position, he used the back edge of the dryer as support and drove his shoulder into the obstruction. It moved about a foot, allowing enough space for him to slide his entire frame into the room. By simply bending over, the bed slid away.

He moved past the bed and over to the door. I've been here before, he said to himself. This time, I'm going on the attack. I don't care what kind of weapon my adversary has. Peter confidently moved through the door into the sitting area of the lower level.

Peter took each step methodically, preparing to fight in an instant if someone opened the door. At last he reached the top and twisted the doorknob slowly. He heard a click and pushed the door open. Moments later, he stood in the kitchen, listening for anyone.

Suddenly, he heard a sound in the next room. He moved his frame into ready position and waited. No one came. Peter moved silently to the doorframe, taking up a standing position against the wall. Shaking off the snakes crawling around in his stomach, he peeked into the room.

He heard the sound of a glass being set down on a table. Peter saw the back of the head of an elderly woman sitting on a couch. She had a glass in her hand. A partially full whiskey bottle sat nearby, on the coffee table.

Peter stood quietly for what seemed to him like eternity. He looked around and listened, expecting the brute to show up at any moment.

Instinctively, he charged into the middle of the room, and assumed attack position. The woman looked up at him and smiled. "Hello," she said. "Would you like a drink?"

Peter shifted his stance quickly, several times, expecting the enemy. He saw no one.

The woman continued to smile at him. "They're all gone, ya know."

Peter cleared his throat. "Who are you talking about? Where have they gone?"

She took another drink from the glass. "Oh, both Lem and Stan left for the country club."

Peter began to relax a little. "Where's your phone?"

She pointed.

"I need a phone book."

"In the drawer."

He opened the only drawer to the small cabinet and saw what he wanted. He dialed a taxicab company number. "What's your address, lady?" Peter asked.

Her head slumped against the back of the couch. Peter noticed two envelopes lying on the counter in the kitchen. He grabbed one.

"I'm at 3520 Seventeenth Street South."

Peter hung up the phone and hurried outside. It seemed like hours to him before the cab arrived.

———

"THAT WAS QUITE THE PRODUCTION," Izzy said from the back seat. Bill Brown drove, attempting to work his way out of the dome parking lot.

Susan Crenshaw sat in the front passenger seat. She turned to look at Izzy. "This may be a wild goose chase today, but somehow we feel that by showing up for these two events, it will help solve this case."

Bill Brown said, "We'll have to remain on the sidelines during the entire event. It could get long. We've already heard a lot of bull so let's everyone be patient."

Kelly Martin sat with his hands behind his head. "I'm rather enjoying this—remaining totally inconspicuous. Besides, now I can tell my grandkids that I was a former FBI Agent."

Susan laughed. "If you noticed, local police enforcement showed massive presence at the Dome, but I'm not so sure we'll see that at the country club. It's a private place, you know."

Bill uttered words not usually heard in churches when a red Camry cut in front of him.

Finally the four officers arrived at the country club. Susan exited the vehicle first. She stood and stretched. "Luxurious looking place."

All four entered the first door. They looked around, attempting to make an assessment of the layout. Farther in, a man dressed in a tie and sport coat met them. He pointed. "The event is in there."

Bill brought up his badge. "FBI. Please remain calm. We are here only as a precaution."

The man nodded and walked toward the dining room. He whispered something into another man's ear and pointed back toward the bar.

A cell phone jingled. Kelly plucked one from his belt. "Yes, Dave," he said quietly. "Uh-hm—uh-hm."

Kelly turned and walked away from the group toward a window. He nodded a few times and clipped the cell phone back on his belt.

He walked back quickly. "Izzy, I just talked to Dave. The Robinson woman has regained consciousness."

Izzy's eyes broadened. "Did she say anything?"

"Her only words thus far have been 'cry.'"

"Cry!" Izzy exclaimed.

"Yeah, cry."

Izzy scratched her forehead, deep in thought. She looked over at Kelly. "Cry, or Crier...."

———

TOM WALKED INTO THE FIRST DOOR AT THE COUNTRY CLUB feeling very uneasy. He assumed the banquet would take place in the main dining room and walked in that direction. He saw four people standing off the side in the bar area. "It's Izzy!" he muttered. "What's she doing here?"

Deputy Izzy Felton smiled and nodded, placing a finger vertically against her lips. Tom smiled lightly and nodded noticing a broad, stocky man with a crew cut standing next to her. He noticed the other deputy, Kelly Miller. Oh my gosh, that other woman...that's Susan Crenshaw, also an agent.

Suddenly, his uneasiness lifted, knowing that the FBI and other law enforcement were present.

"Can I help you, sir?" a male maitre d' asked.

"Yes, I'm a guest of one of the senator's staff."

"Name, please?"

"Tom Hastings. I'm meeting Julie Huffman."

"I'll show you where your table is. If you wish you can help yourself at that bar over there until she arrives."

Tom followed him into a large room with a huge chandelier hanging from the ceiling. He felt honored but a little nervous when he saw that he would sit near the head table. Geez, I need a drink real bad, he thought and headed for the bar.

61

SENATOR MCDOUGAL'S LIMOSINE pulled up at the second entrance to the country club. Gus, the tall, lanky driver quickly emerged first. He opened the door behind him and assisted Mrs. McDougal out of her seat and onto the asphalt surface. The senator opened his door and walked around the front, joining his wife.

Gus opened the rear door. Julie extended her hand. She smiled widely. Aaron Crier had gotten out of a back seat. He assisted Carlita, his special friend from Costa Rica.

"Come on, folks, let's go in and begin the celebration," the senator said and tucked his arm into a space between his wife's waist and elbow.

———

"NO, DON'T PARK BY THE DOOR," Peter said when the cab driver stopped. "Keep going and drop me off farther back in the lot."

The cabbie shrugged his shoulders but responded. Peter got out. "I have a problem. I've just escaped a kidnapping and have no money, but I can pay you in minutes if you wait here."

"Look, Buster, I've heard that one before. Now pay me or I'll call the cops."

"That's just what I want you to do—call the cops," Peter said and quickly walked away.

He slithered away from the cab, moving to an area shadowed by a row of trees. Peter stepped behind one of them. He watched vehicle after vehicle arrive and drop off passengers.

A dark blue van pulled up. Two rugged looking men got out. The van rolled away and parked in a far corner of the lot. Peter stared at the men...something looked familiar with one of them. The two men paused by the door. They stood off to the side as others arrived and entered.

———

TOM HEARD THE SOUND OF LOUD VOICES. He turned to look. Geez, she looks nice, he said to himself, watching Julie walk in with a group of people, among them, the senator and his wife. He noticed tall Aaron Crier with a woman who he had never seen before. Gads, she's beautiful...that long dark hair and slinky dress is something else again, he thought.

Tom got off his barstool and sauntered toward the new arrivals. His heart raced when Julie turned toward him and smiled. She reached out for his hand. Tom smiled and kept his voice down during the introductions. He felt intimidated when the senator's big hand squeezed his. Minutes later, Tom looked into the cold eyes of Aaron Crier. His hand felt cold and strong.

Tom felt his heart flutter after meeting Carlita. Her soft-spoken voice sounded like something from heaven. He looked away, escaping the blackish-brown eyes that looked deep into his. He gasped and coughed lightly after holding his breath for a few seconds.

Next, Julie introduced him to Veronica. He shook her hand and said, "I've already met your mother."

Veronica smiled. "Yes, I know. She's told me all about you."

Tom extended a hand to Nicole, standing next to her daughter. They clasped lightly, her dispassionate expression sending him a strong message.

An elegantly-dressed waiter approached with a tray. Julie and Tom each grabbed a champagne glass. They tapped the glasses together. "Here's to your future, Julie," Tom said.

Julie's expression firmed. "This is likely my last hurrah with the senator," she whispered.

Tom took a sip of his champagne. He narrowed his eyes and looked around. He couldn't see the bar area from where they stood. He did see two burly looking men standing in the main entry alcove. Probably more cops, he thought.

"All right, folks, let's get seated," the deep resonant voice of the senator announced.

Tom looked at the long table along the east wall. He saw the senator pull out a chair for his wife, continuing to stand, visiting with the mayor of Fargo and other dignitaries. Tom recognized North Dakota's other senator, who took a seat next to Mrs. McDougal.

"Come on, Tom, we're sitting over there." Julie pointed.

Tom followed her, taking a seat at an eight-place table. Next to Julie sat Aaron Crier and his date, Carlita. Veronica sat down next to Tom's left. Her mother took a chair next to her.

A couple of minutes later, the senator stood. He clinked a bread knife against a water glass. "Attention, please. I would like to thank everyone for coming." He raised his champagne glass. "I toast the future!"

"Hey! Hey!" Someone yelled at a corner table.

The senator talked for about a minute. "Please, everyone, enjoy your meal." He sat down.

62

PETER HEARD THE SOUND OF GLASSES CLINKING as he stood by the corner of the building, remaining out of sight. Spending 13 days in captivity hardened his patience level intensely. But he thought that the sooner he made his move, the better the likelihood he would succeed. Yet, he decided to wait until most of the people finished with their dinners. Perhaps the two men in the vestibule would leave by then.

He saw a police car turn off the street and drive through the country club approach. It slowly made its way around the lot. Peter could see two officers in the vehicle when it passed through a lighted area. I bet the cab driver called to complain about me. Maybe I should give up this ridiculous scheme and confess to them, he thought. The car continued out of the lot and disappeared from sight.

I'm not going to be satisfied until I've had justice, he said to himself, firming up his resolve. Those people have made me suffer enough. It's time for them to be exposed for what they really are.

Peter's chest tightened when the two men in the vestibule came out of the door and lit up cigarettes. Peter almost went bananas when he saw their faces. The burly one is my tormenter! I owe him big time, he said to himself, feeling his heart thumping against his chest.

Peter took a deep breath. He moved around the corner and approached the two men quickly.

The burley man turned. "You—how the hell did you get out?" He raised his right arm, sliding his hand under the open jacket.

Peter moved quickly. He executed a roundhouse kick to the man's ribs. Before the gruff-voiced man could recover, Peter let his momentum propel him in a circle and as he came around, he caught the man on the side of his face with a spinning back fist.

The second man crouched, his hands out in front. Peter feigned a kick. The man lunged forward. Peter hook-kicked him in the thorax flank. He followed with a spear fingers thrust into his enemy's eyeball. The man howled with pain. Peter landed a spinning-hook kick into the groin. The man dropped to his knees. Peter hurriedly reached inside the man's jacket and pulled out a pistol.

He crouched by the burly man and used his left hand to pick up the man's head by his hair. Peter held his face close to his. "Take a good look—a real good look. It's your turn." Peter slapped the man until he felt dizzy. Regaining his composure, Peter reached inside the man's jacket and removed his gun.

While his victims lay groaning on the ground, Peter ran until he reached the trees. He reached back with his arm and threw the guns as far away as he could.

When he returned to the door, he saw the police car turn into the parking lot again.

Peter held his chin high and burst through the second door, the one accessing the banquet room. He marched toward the head table, stopping next to Aaron Crier.

———

TOM GRABBED JULIE'S WAIST AND EXCLAIMED, "Geez, Julie, it's Peter!"

He felt her frame tense and jerk forward as she looked up. Tom glanced at the head table and saw everyone staring at Peter. The senator stood, planting his palms on the table. Tom saw his befuddled expression, his mouth partially open.

Tom turned his head toward Julie, seeing her face radiate delight and happiness. Tom saw the poker-faced Aaron Crier frown, his facial expression deepening to a look of despair.

Veronica, just like Julie, smiled wide. He saw her raise a fist in the air, her thumb straight up. Nicole, as did the senator, looked confused.

Peter pointed his finger at Aaron Crier and said loudly, "Folks, this is my kidnapper and the murderer of Isabelle Franks!"

All talk in the large room ceased, everyone staring at the intruder. The only sounds in the next few moments were those of throats clearing and an occasional gasp.

Aaron leaped to his feet and glared at Peter. Tom saw a wild-animal look in the aide's eyes as he reached inside his sport coat. Tom stopped breathing when Aaron pulled out a gun and pointed it at the intern.

The mayor and senator McDougal both stood. "Don't anybody try anything!" Aaron yelled, his voice screeching like a hawk.

Aaron backed away from Peter. Tom dreaded the possibility that the intern was going to be killed. Suddenly, Aaron grabbed Julie, jerking her out of her chair. His fingers clutched at her hair, twisting her head. The barrel of his gun pressed against her neck. "If anyone tries to stop me, she dies!" he yelled.

Tom remained glued to his seat, totally petrified. He glared at a white mark in Julie's skin, her blue eyes wide open and displaying the terror expressed by so many around the room. His eyes fixed on the gun in Aaron's hand. He's hurting her, but Geez it's only four feet from my head, he thought.

I know that if I try to interfere, I could die right here, he said to himself. He thought of Izzy and the other officers who he had seen upon entering the club—we need them right now.

Suddenly, Peter moved quickly and ran toward Crier.

"BOOM!" Tom saw Julie place a hand over her ear, and close her eyes, her facial skin scrunched up like the surface of a pumpkin.

The horrifying sound of shrill screams resonated off the ceiling and walls. The acrid smell of burnt gun powder reached Tom's nostrils. In an instant he could see that the bullet had missed Peter as the young intern twisted and turned. Peter sprang off his feet, flying through the air. "BOOM! BOOM!" Two more shots.

Tom gasped when he saw Peter drop to the floor. Tom got down on his knees, grabbing his chair and holding it up as a shield. He heard Veronica scream, "Mother!" Tom saw a red splotch the size of a baseball in the middle of Nicole's chest.

Tom looked up at Julie's eyes. They reminded him of a wounded deer he had witnessed so many times in the past. Her eyes lowered and met Tom's, her lower jaw trembling out of control.

"DROP THE WEAPON!" Tom heard someone yell from the other side of the room. He turned his head and saw Izzy crouched, a large pistol in both hands. He saw three other guns in the hands of the three officers. They had moved apart from each other. Agent Brown leaned forward, his legs spread apart and planted like tree trunks.

"DROP IT NOW!" Izzy yelled again.

Tom saw Aaron's arm tighten on Julie's neck, pulling her tight. Her face reddened and Tom shuddered hearing the sound of her throat heaving. Aaron pulled Julie toward the wall, now about ten feet from Tom.

Tom didn't dare move for fear of getting shot. Aaron pulled Julie a little farther, keeping her between himself and the four armed officers.

"Nobody else move!" Aaron yelled, keeping a sturdy arm around Julie. He dragged her slowly toward the door. Tom noticed that most of the other people had dropped to the floor, some had crawled underneath tables.

He looked at Julie's face. The redness had disappeared and he saw something that reminded him of the look of a cornered animal. She stared at the floor where Peter lay bleeding. He saw her eyes widen. Good God, she's going to try something, Tom thought, feeling totally helpless and mortified.

Tom thought about the cornfield. It worked there...*he charged his captor and drove him into a file cabinet.* He took three short breaths—THE TIME IS NOW! His mind commanded. Tom pushed the chair aside, stayed low and planted the edges of his shoes into the carpet and charged, his life flashing through his mind. I could die any second, he thought.

One step: still alive, he thought. A second step: no shot yet. A third step: his arms and elbows out front. He looked up and saw Julie raise her right fist into the air. Tom felt pain in his neck as his forehead and right cheek slammed into her shoulder, driving Aaron and her toward the wall.

"BOOM!"

Plaster bits falling from the ceiling landed on top of Tom's head.

He heard Crier gasp as Julie's elbow struck him in his stomach. A fourth step: Julie's feet went out from underneath her and she slid away, dropping to the floor. A fifth step: Tom's shoulder sunk deeply into Crier's stomach.

"BOOM!"

Tom felt excruciating pain in his left ear and the hot barrel of the gun against the side of his head just as they hit the wall. Crier screeched and gasped for air. Tom stretched his legs and in one last major effort slammed both of his elbows against Crier's right shoulder. He heard the gun slam against the plaster.

Tom heard another yell. "DROP IT NOW!"

He held his breath and the next moment seemed like eternity before Aaron's fingers released the gun. It bounced off Tom's left shoulder and thudded onto the carpet.

Heavy footsteps thundered across the floor as the four officers rushed toward Crier and Hastings. Tom felt the arms of one of them pulling him away from Crier. He looked up into Crier's glassy eyes and saw desperation and sadness. For an instant, Tom felt sorry for him.

Tom's feet went out from underneath him and he dropped to his knees next to where Julie lay. He glanced toward Peter and watched in horror as Peter's blood soaked into the carpet. Tom looked up and saw Agent Brown pull Crier's arms behind him. He heard the unmistakable clinking sound of handcuffs.

"Julie, are you okay?" Tom muttered in her ear. He saw blood on the side of her forehead, her eyes closed. Tom slid an arm underneath her neck and lifted slightly. She didn't respond.

Tom had gotten up on his feet, feeling dizzy. He lowered his head and saw Deputy Izzy Felton kneel down by Julie's side. Peter didn't move. Tom heard and saw two Fargo Police officers come through the outside door, weapons drawn.

Agent Crenshaw and Kelly had left the prisoner and rushed over to the victims. Veronica sobbed profusely holding her mother in her arms. Agent Crenshaw shook her head.

Minutes later, Tom heard the sound of multiple sirens. The door burst open and a massive number of white-clad medics and police officers entered. He pushed aside the chair and moved to where Julie and Peter lay.

Geez, Julie looks like she's still unconscious, he thought, as he peered over the shoulders of a medic. I better stay the heck out of their way. Tom walked back to the table and sat down.

Mayhem and confusion followed for the next few minutes at the country club—a mixture of screams and shouts.

Tom sat on the chair knowing there was nothing he could do to help. The Fargo mayor stood by the wall, appearing distraught, talking to a police officer. Senator McDougal, his hair disheveled, joined them.

The first stretcher moved toward the door. That's Peter, Tom thought. He noticed that Aaron Crier had been removed from the room. The two FBI agents had left as well and Tom felt sick when he saw Izzy assist the medics in rolling Julie's stretcher out the door.

He saw Veronica being administered to by two women. They had gotten her to sit down. She held a hand over the lower half of her face, peering at the third stretcher as the medics readied it for departure.

Tom kept wringing his hands and feeling remorse for what had happened. He looked up into the eyes of Deputy Izzy. He cleared his throat and managed to speak. "How does it look for everyone, Deputy?"

She scratched her right eyebrow. "It's hard to tell, Hastings. Julie took a real blow to the head. She's still unconscious. Peter was hit with a bullet in the stomach area—we can only hope that they get him to the hospital in time."

The deputy sighed deeply. "Hastings, that was a damn fool thing you did—but I have to admit that it worked."

Tom shook his head. "I don't know what happened—I looked into Julie's eyes—I had to do something."

Izzy nodded. "I'm glad to see that you're all right, but it doesn't look good for your friend Nicole. She took a bullet in the chest."

———

TOM DROVE SLOWLY TO THE HOSITAL. He didn't cherish the thought of a speeding violation, not now—even though his mind filled with anxiety, worried about his friend Julie and the others.

Grabbing a ticket from the parking lot dispenser, he parked his vehicle and eagerly crossed the street. At the receiving desk, he stood and waited until one of the woman hung up a phone. "I need to check on a patient. She just got here about an hour ago. Her name is Julie Huffman."

The woman looked up. "Are you a next of kin?"

"No, I'm not, but I'm a friend and she has no relatives in this area. She was brought in by ambulance from the country club."

"Just a moment."

Tom waited anxiously while the woman walked through a door. Glancing at the wall clock, it read 8:45.

The woman returned. "Julie Huffman is being examined in emergency. See that door over there?" She pointed.

Tom nodded.

"Take a right, go almost all the way to the end, then take a left. You will see the sign. Someone over there should be able to help you," she added.

Tom said, "Thanks," and hurriedly followed her directions. Within a minute he arrived at the emergency station.

Tom repeated his request. "She's being examined by a doctor right now. Please have a seat, and I'll let them know someone is waiting."

Almost a full hour went by before Tom was asked to follow a nurse through a door. She stopped and pointed. "Miss Huffman is in there."

Tom, overwrought, walked into the room and saw Julie lying in bed with her eyes closed. She had a bandage pasted to her temple above the right ear. He saw a nurse standing at the foot of the bed, writing on a clipboard. She looked up. "Is Miss Huffman family?"

"No, but I'm a very good friend and was with her when she got attacked earlier this evening. She has no family or relatives in this area, so I'm going to look after her."

"I see." The nurse returned the clipboard into its slot. "Well, we gave her sedation a few minutes ago, because she has a headache. We don't have the x-rays back yet. The doctor is coming back within the hour and we should have the results then."

Tom walked over to the bed. He grasped Julie's hand and felt movement in her fingers. He wasn't certain but he thought that he saw the faint hint of a smile. He moved his head closer to hers. "Julie, you're going to be fine."

Again, he felt her fingers move.

"You can wait in the room if you wish," the nurse said.

———

TOM DOZED OFF AFTER SITTING BY JULIE'S SIDE FOR AN HOUR. He woke up and looked at the clock—11:30.

He looked around and no one else was in the room. He got up and walked over to the bed. Julie appeared to be in a deep sleep.

He grasped her hand and said softly, "I'm going now, but I'll be back tomorrow." Tom kissed her on the forehead and whispered, "See ya later, kid."

Tom walked out of the room. He stopped when he saw Mrs. McDougal and Izzy Felton sitting across the corridor. He knew right then that things were not going well with the other two victims. Izzy had an arm around Mrs. McDougal's shoulders. The senator's wife buried her head in her own hands.

Tom walked over slowly, really not wanting to hear the news. Izzy looked up. "How's Julie doing?"

"She's doing okay right now. The doctor said that she has contusions in her skull. According to the nurse, all her vital signs look good."

"Tom, we've lost Veronica's mother. She died about half an hour ago."

Tom lowered his head. "And how about Peter?" he asked anxiously.

"He's been in the operating room since he got here. Other than that I know nothing."

"Geez, that's too bad about Nicole. What happened to Veronica?"

"She's with a social worker. I would imagine she's going through hell right now."

Tom nodded. "Where's Kelly, your partner?"

"He's with the two FBI agents. They took Mr. Crier to the sheriff's office. I imagine there's a lot of paperwork and catching up to do."

"Are they going to pick you up?"

Izzy looked at her watch. "I'm going to call Kelly in a few minutes and find out how they're doing. I do have a ride if that's what you're worried about."

"Time for me to go home," Tom said. "Good night, Izzy—Mrs. McDougal," he added.

———

THE NEXT MORNING TOM MADE COFFEE and checked out the Internet news. He double-clicked and read about the shootout at the country club in Fargo.

He set his coffee down on the table, staring at the monitor.

I'll have to check on Julie and Peter later this morning, he thought. "Uh-oh," he muttered while rounding Purgatory Curve. His speedometer read 42 miles per hour. Tom touched the brakes and felt relieved that he didn't see a deputy's car by the railroad tracks.

He got his mail and entered the grocery store. He stopped next to the newspaper rack. The *Forum* headline read, *Night out in Fargo*. He picked up a copy and got in line behind a woman customer. "Twelve-fifty, please," the check-out person said and looked up. "Hello, Tom, what's new with you? I'm surprised that you weren't in Fargo last night."

Tom shook his head and laid three quarters on the counter. "But I was there, Ellie—right in the middle of it all."

The woman customer hesitated as she picked up her bag. She looked at Tom and frowned before leaving.

"You were there!" Ellie exclaimed.

"Yup, I was there all right—a night out in Fargo."

EPILOGUE

Two Days Later

SHERIFF DAVE JOHNSON'S FACE reflected his mood. His beaming smile lit up the room. He sat behind his desk and glanced around. Izzy, Kelly, Bill and Susan reacted as if they had just scored a touchdown.

"So Izzy, we caught X. Now tell us about the Y's."

"Yes, X is in jail. Aaron Crier worked for a secret group of people who were determined to steal the senator's good fortune. They operated through a phony company with the title of Delvo Industries.

"Actually, neither Nicole nor Veronica had been aware that they were indirectly working with Crier—but he knew exactly what they were up to. I suppose Crier didn't want them to know that he was a traitor.

"Poor Isabelle Franks overheard a conversation between Aaron and one of his cohorts. She had witnessed him entering the senator's office suite that evening—and followed him with the intention of challenging him—you all know what happened.

"Stella Robinson witnessed Crier dragging Isabelle down the slope. She attempted to blackmail Crier, such as she and Ivan successfully did to Hastings—but they demanded a lot more money.

"Ivan was definitely a Y. Fortunately for him, Crier did not know that he and Stella were in cahoots. When Ivan discovered Stella's body, he thought she was dead. Ivan desperately searched for Hastings's money. He left the apartment hastily because he heard a noise in her bathroom—Crier may still have been there.

"Veronica was also a Y. She didn't witness the attack on Isabelle, but she did hear it, while hiding under the desk. Between her and her mother, they made three attempts to steal information from the senator's files—and finally succeeded.

"If Peter survives, and the last I heard was that he will, both he and Stella will be witnesses at Aaron Crier's trial. The defense for the traitorous aide doesn't have much of a chance."

Izzy set the paper down on her lap. Bill Brown stood. "Well, Susan, shall we get going?"

Two Weeks Later

TOM PUT HIS HAND ON JULIE'S, sitting across from her at Spanky's restaurant. He smiled at Jeremy Hanson, the owner, as he walked by. "Hey, Jeremy, I see you've changed the name of your place—nice."

"Yup—good to see Julie back," Jeremy said and walked away.

"Well, what's your plan, Julie, now that you've resigned your position with Senator McDougal?" Tom asked.

"Well, first of all, I'm thrilled that Peter's going to be all right. I talked to his mother yesterday and the young spunk is sitting up in bed already."

Tom pulled his hand away and laughed. "Peter is one tough kid. So what's next for you?"

"I'm not sure, Tom, but I've given notice on my Fargo apartment."

Tom sighed. "I can't imagine you not having a plan, Julie."

"Well, to tell you the truth, I've been thinking of buying a place in Florida, somewhere in the Bradenton area."

Tom frowned. I wonder what she would say if I asked her to marry me, he thought. She'd probably turn me down, knowing that I couldn't possibly keep up with her travel needs. Still....

Three Months Later

STELLA ROBINSON HAD RECOVERED FROM HER COMA and sat across from her attorney's desk. They were busy planning for a defense against two charges of blackmail and conspiracy.

The cubicle and the gate had been removed from the senator's property. The former gatekeeper, Ivan, had lost his two thousand dollars gained from the Hastings's blackmail at a casino and was never heard from again. He is posted as *Wanted for conspiracy and blackmail* by the Big Lakes Sheriff's Department.

THE SUN EMERGED ABOVE THE RIM OF TREES to the southeast for the first time since before Christmas, sending spikes of shadows over the snow-covered bay. Tom Hastings, cup of coffee in hand, looked out his window on a mid-January day.

He thought about the C-span television program that he watched the previous day. His friend Julie testified for two hours before a senate committee investigating the McDougal-Togolese financial relationship.

After listening to two days of testimony, Tom thought that the senator was in big trouble. He also thought that Julie would never return to Border's Lake. His spirits momentarily lifted thinking about the good times that the two of them had had over the years. It's all done...I'm totally alone again.

Well, not exactly alone, he said to himself, watching a gray squirrel attack his tube-like bird feeder. He couldn't believe that the aggressive rodent would take the risk of plunging its entire torso into the tube, clawing at the thistle feed. Tom was angry because the feeder was the fourth one that he had purchased within the last month.

Tom eyed his pellet gun, loaded and leaning against the wall near the door. I hate killing animals, he thought, but....

He returned to the kitchen to refill his coffee cup. Tom felt glad that the squirrel had vacated the feeder when he returned to his dining room table. I wonder, he thought, what the new year has in store for me this time around. Tom chuckled thinking about the barn and cornfield.

The phony Department of Agriculture project is gone, he said to himself. The corn has been harvested and the field is covered with snow. The plastic bubble is gone. Hans is gone. The military guys are gone. I can now safely go for a ski run or walk.

"It's time to go into New Dresden for the mail," Tom muttered. He put on his jacket and stood by the door, staring at the artistic glitter in the icicles, hanging from the roof, between him and the bright sun. Life goes on, he thought and smiled, backing his vehicle out of the garage.

One Year Later

AARON CRIER SAT ON HIS JAIL CELL BUNK in Stillwater, Minnesota, realizing that he would spend the rest of life there. He saddened thinking of his son, who had passed away three months earlier. At least he's at peace. Aaron missed Carlita, who had moved back to Costa Rica. Aaron shook his head from side to side slowly...I simply lost my head.

Trying to out-fox the senator doesn't bother me, he said to himself...but, taking a gun to the country club and shooting two people...what was I thinking?

He placed fingers on his forehead. Damn, I was only hours away, he thought. Our flight was scheduled to leave for Costa Rica at 6:00 a.m. Five million dollars was supposed to be deposited to my account in Switzerland. I had a flight scheduled for my son and an accomplice in two days. They were heading for Europe for treatment...it was all set...my God, I blew it.

Four Years Later

REPRESENTATIVE-ELECT PETER NELSON RAISED HIS ARMS to silence a screaming audience at the St. James Hotel in Red Wing, Minnesota. He had won the election and the right to represent the district in the Minnesota legislature.

His campaign had focused on an energy-based platform, which would eventually make it a law in Minnesota to forbid usage of oil-based energy products in all common vehicles such as SUV's, trucks, motorcycles and cars.

Peter became one of the youngest persons, at the age of 22, to ever get elected. He left the podium and began making it through a handshaking, backslapping circle of friends and supporters. He opened his arms to Julie Huffman, who had been his successful campaign manager. "Great job, Julie!"

Sean McDougal's face beamed with pride. He had regained his dignity after being forced to resign from the United States Senate—oxygate, the media called it. He and his wife resided permanently at their lake home on Border's Lake in Minnesota. They had created a sanctuary for despondent boys and girls.

After an hour of congratulatory scenarios, Peter whispered in Veronica's ear, "Time to go."

They hugged and he kissed her on the cheek. The ring finger of her left hand sparkled as she touched her fiancé on a shoulder.

"Your car is waiting, sir," a parking lot attendant said outside.

Peter got behind the wheel and turned the key. He smiled hearing the hissing sound of the engine. "We better fill up, Peter," Veronica said from the passenger seat.

Peter pulled the shiny, black-colored vehicle into an oxy station. He got out and opened a metal flap behind the rear wheel. He pulled on an adapter and plugged it into the pump, listening to the hissing sound. Thirty seconds later, a speaker voice said, *"FULL."* The mini marquee read, *"Your Account has been charged Twelve Dollars and fifty three cents. Thank You!"*

$16.95 EACH
(plus $3.95 shipping & handling for first book,
add $2.00 for each additional book ordered.
Shipping and Handling costs for larger quantites available upon request.

PLEASE INDICATE NUMBER OF COPIES YOU WISH TO ORDER

_____ BLUE DARKNESS _____ PURGATORY CURVE

_____ THE TOWERS _____ GRAY RIDERS

_____ DANGER IN THE KEYS _____ SLEEP SIX

_____ NIGHT OUT IN FARGO

Bill my: ❑ VISA ❑ MasterCard Expires _____

Card # _____

Signature _____

Daytime Phone Number _____

For credit card orders call 1-888-568-6329
TO ORDER ON-LINE VISIT: www.jmcompanies.com
OR SEND THIS ORDER FORM TO:
McCleery & Sons Publishing · PO Box 248 · Gwinner, ND 58040-0248

I am enclosing $_____ ❑ Check ❑ Money Order
Payable in US funds. No cash accepted.
SHIP TO:

Name_____

Mailing Address _____

City _____

State/Zip _____

Orders by check allow longer delivery time. Money order and credit card orders will be shipped within 48 hours. This offer is subject to change without notice.

RECENT RELEASES

Great Stories of the Great Plains Vol. 2 - *Tales of the Dakotas*
There really is only one place in which you can relive the events of the great past that make up the history of North and South Dakota and that is in your mind. And that is our job, to set the stage for your imagination to take you on journeys into the history of this great region. With our books and radio show we try to bring to life, in your mind, the events that have made the Dakotas the great place they are to live in today. Written by Keith Norman - Author of *Great Stories of the Great Plains - Vol. 1* and *Great People of the Great Plains - Vol. 1* (144 pages)
$14.95 each in a 6x9" paperback.

It Really Happened Here & There
This takes off where Ethelyn Pearson's "It Really Happened Here!" left off... More entertaining stories and true accounts: The Mystery of the Headless Hermit, Herman Haunts Sauk Centre, Hunting Trip Gone Wrong, The Swinging of Thomas Brown, Moltan Hell Created Creeping Molasses Disaster, Preachers Do Too!, Skinned Alive, Run Into A Blizzard or Burn!, Life and Death of Ol' Mother Feather Legs, How the Dakotans Fought Off Rustlers, and much more!!!! Written by Ethelyn Pearson - Author of *It Really Happened Here!*
(136 pages) $24.95 each in an 8-1/2 x 11" paperback.

Great People of the Great Plains Vol. 1
25 Biographies of People Who Shaped the Dakotas
This is the second book for Keith Norman and the first in this series.   Keith has always had an interest in the history of the region. His radio show 'Great Stories of the Great Plains' is heard on great radio stations all across both Dakotas. For more information on the radio show and a list of his current affiliates check out Norman's website at www.tumbleweednetwork.com. Written by Keith Norman (124 pgs.) $14.95 each in a 6x9" paperback.

History of Sargent County - Volume 2 - 1880-1920
(Forman, Gwinner, Milnor & Sargent County Veterans)
Over 220 photos and seven chapters containing: Forman, Gwinner and Milnor, North Dakota history with surveyed maps from 1909. Plus Early History of Sargent County, World War I Veterans, Civil War Veterans and Sargent County Fair History.
Written by: Susan Mary Kudelka - Author of *Early History of Sargent County - Volume 1* (224 pgs.)
$16.95 each in a 6x9" paperback.

History of Sargent County - Volume 3 - 1880-1920
(Brampton, Cayuga, Cogswell, Crete, DeLamere, Geneseo, Harlem, Havana, Rutland, Stirum & Other History)
Over 280 photos and fifteen chapters containing: Brampton, Cayuga, Cogswell, Crete, DeLamere, Geneseo, Harlem, Havana, Rutland and Stirum, North Dakota histories with surveyed maps from 1909. Plus history on Sargent County in WWI, Sargent County Newspapers, E. Hamilton Lee and bonus photo section.
Written by: Susan Mary Kudelka - Author of *Early History of Sargent County - Volume 1* (220 pgs.)
$16.95 each in a 6x9" paperback.

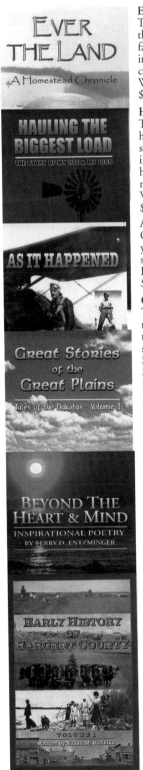

Ever The Land - *A Homestead Chronicle*
This historical chronicle (non-fiction) traces the life of young Pehr through his youth in the 1800's, marriage, parenthood and tenant farming in Sweden; then his emigration to America and homesteading in Minnesota. Multifarious simple joys and woes, and one deep constant sorrow accompany Pehr to his grave in 1914. Written by: The late Ruben L. Parson (336 pgs.) $16.96 each in a 6x9" paperback.

Hauling the Biggest Load - *The Story of My Life & My Loss*
This is an unusual story because of the many changes that have happened since the author's birth in 1926. In May 2002, he lost his son, John, in a car accident. None of those other experiences seemed important anymore... Richard needed something to try and take his mind off that tragedy. "I thought I had hauled some big loads in my life but I never had to have a load as big as this one." Written by: Richard Hamann (144 pages) $14.95 each in 6x9" paperback.

As It Happened
Over 40 photos and several chapters containing Allen Saunders' early years, tales of riding the rails, his Navy career, marriage, Army instruction, flying over "The Hump", and his return back to North Dakota. Written by Allen E. Saunders. (74 pgs) $12.95 each in a 6x9" paperback.

Great Stories of the Great Plains - *Tales of the Dakotas - Vol. 1*
The radio show "Great Stories of the Great Plains" is heard on great radio stations all across both Dakotas. Norman has taken some of the stories from broadcasts, added some details, and even added some complete new tales to bring together this book of North and South Dakota history. Written by Keith Norman. (134 pgs.) $14.95 each in a 6x9" paperback.

Beyond the Heart & Mind
Inspirational Poetry by Terry D. Entzminger
Beyond the Heart & Mind is the first in a series of inspirational poetry collections of Entzminger. Read and cherish over 100 original poems and true-to-the-heart verses printed in full color in the following sections: Words of Encouragement, On the Wings of Prayer, God Made You Very Special, Feelings From Within, The True Meaning of Love, and Daily Joys. (120 pgs.) $12.95 each in a 6x9" paperback.

Early History of Sargent County - *Volume 1*
Over seventy photos and thirty-five chapters containing the early history of Sargent County, North Dakota: Glacial Movement in Sargent County, Native Americans in Sargent County, Weather, Memories of the Summer of 1883, Fight for the County Seat, Townships, Surveyed Maps from 1882 and much more.
Written by Susan M. Kudelka. (270 pgs.) $16.95 each in a 6x9" paperback.

Terrorists Among Us
This piece of fiction was written to "expose a weakness" in present policies and conflicts in the masses of rules which seem to put emphasis on business, money, and power interests at the expense of the people's security, safety and happiness. Shouldn't we and our leaders strive for some security for our people? Written by Carl Aabye & R.J. Letnes. (178 pgs.) $15.95 each in a 6x9" paperback.

THE HASTINGS SERIES

Blue Darkness *(First in a Series of Hastings Books)*
This tale of warm relationships and chilling murders takes place in the lake country of central Minnesota. Normal activities in the small town of New Dresen are disrupted when local resident, ex-CIA agent Maynard Cushing, is murdered. His killer, Robert Ranforth also an ex-CIA agent, had been living anonymously in the community for several years. Stalked and attached at his country home, Tom Hastings employs tools and people to mount a defense and help solve crimes. Written by Ernest Francis Schanilec (author of The Towers). (276 pgs.) $16.95 each in a 6x9" paperback.

The Towers *(Second in a Series of Hastings Books)*
Tom Hastings' move to Minneapolis was precipitated by the trauma associated with the murder of one of his neighbors. After renting a high-rise apartment in a building known as The Towers, he's met new friends and retained his relationship with a close friend, Julie, from St. Paul. Hastings is a resident for less than a year when a young lady is found murdered next to a railroad track, a couple of blocks from The Towers. The murderer shares the same elevators, lower-level garage and other areas in the high-rise as does Hastings. The building manager and other residents, along with Hastings are caught up in dramatic events that build to a crisis while the local police are baffled. Who is the killer? Written by Ernest Francis Schanilec. (268 pgs.) $16.95 each in a 6x9" paperback.

Danger In The Keys *(Third in a Series of Hastings Books)*
Tom Hastings is looking forward to a month's vacation in Florida. While driving through Tennessee, he witnesses an automobile leaving the road and plunging down a steep slope. The driver, a young woman, survives the accident. Tom is totally unaware that the young woman was being chased because she had chanced coming into possession of a valuable gem, which had been heisted from a Saudi Arabian prince. After arriving in Key Marie Island in Florida, Tom meets many interesting people, however, some of them are on the island because of the Guni gem, and they will stop at nothing in order to gain possession. Desperate people and their greedy ambitions interrupt Tom's goal of a peaceful vacation. Written by Ernest Francis Schanilec (210 pgs.) $16.95 each in a 6x9" paperback.

Purgatory Curve *(Fourth in a Series of Hastings Books)*
A loud horn penetrated the silence in New Dresden, Minnesota. Tom Hastings stepped onto the Main Street sidewalk and heard a freight train coming and watched in horror as it crushed a pickup truck that was stalled on the railroad tracks. Moments before the crash, he saw someone jump from the cab. An elderly farmer's body was later recovered from the mangled vehicle. Tom was interviewed by the sheriff the next day and was upset that his story about what he saw wasn't believed. The tragic death of the farmer was surrounded with controversy and mysterious people, including a nephew who taunted Tom after the accident. Or, was it an accident? Written by Ernest Francis Schanilec (210 pgs.) $16.95 each in a 6x9" paperback.

Gray Riders *(Fifth in a Series of Hastings Books)*
This is a flashback to Schanilec's Hastings Series mystery novels where Tom Hastings is the main character. Tom's great-grandfather, Thomas, lives on a farm with his family in western Missouri in 1861. The local citizenry react to the Union calvary by organizing and forming an armed group of horsemen who become known as the Gray Riders. The Riders not only defend their families and properties, but also ride with the Confederate Missouri Guard. They participate in three major battles. Written by Ernest Francis Schanilec. (266 pgs.) $16.95 each in a 6x9" paperback.

Sleep Six *(Fifth in a Series of Hastings Books)*
Revenge made Birdie Hec quit her job in Kansas City and move to New Dresden, Minnesota. A discovery after her mother's funeral had rekindled her memory of an abuse incident that had happened when she was six years old. An envelope containing six photographs, four of them with names, revealed some of her mother's abusers. Birdie moved into an apartment complex in New Dresden, using an anonymous name. She befriended three other women, who were all about the same age. While socializing with her new friends, Birdie scouted her potential victims. She plotted the demise of the four men whom she had definitely recognized...
Written by Ernest Francis Schanilec (250 pgs.) ISBN: 1-931916-40-3
$16.95 each in a 6x9" paperback.

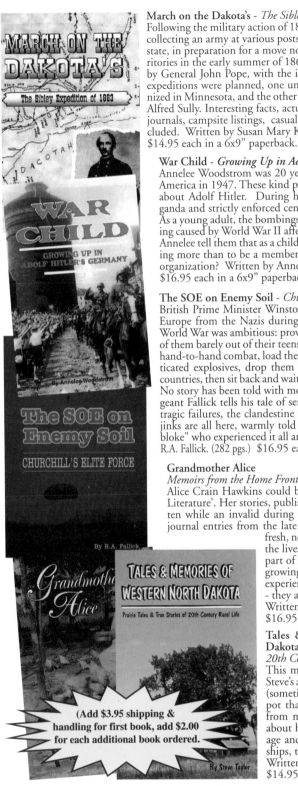

March on the Dakota's - *The Sibley Expedition of 1863*
Following the military action of 1862, the U. S. government began collecting an army at various posts and temporary stockades of the state, in preparation for a move northwestward to the Dakota Territories in the early summer of 1863. The campaign was organized by General John Pope, with the intent to subdue the Sioux. Two expeditions were planned, one under General H. H. Sibley, organized in Minnesota, and the other under the Command of General Alfred Sully. Interesting facts, actual accounts taken from soldiers' journals, campsite listings, casualties and record of troops also included. Written by Susan Mary Kudelka. (134pgs.) $14.95 each in a 6x9" paperback.

War Child - *Growing Up in Adolf Hitler's Germany*
Annelee Woodstrom was 20 years old when she immigrated to America in 1947. These kind people in America wanted to hear about Adolf Hitler. During her adolescence, constant propaganda and strictly enforced censorship influenced her thinking. As a young adult, the bombings and all the consequential suffering caused by World War II affected Annelee deeply. How could Annelee tell them that as a child, during 1935, she wanted nothing more than to be a member of Adolf Hitler's Jung Maidens' organization? Written by Annelee Woodstrom (252 pgs.) $16.95 each in a 6x9" paperback.

The SOE on Enemy Soil - *Churchill's Elite Force*
British Prime Minister Winston Churchill's plan for liberating Europe from the Nazis during the darkest days of the Second World War was ambitious: provide a few men and women, most of them barely out of their teens, with training in subversion and hand-to-hand combat, load them down with the latest in sophisticated explosives, drop them by parachute into the occupied countries, then sit back and wait for them to "Set Europe Ablaze." No story has been told with more honesty and humor than Sergeant Fallick tells his tale of service. The training, the fear, the tragic failures, the clandestine romances, and the soldiers' high jinks are all here, warmly told from the point of view of "one bloke" who experienced it all and lived to tell about it. Written by R.A. Fallick. (282 pgs.) $16.95 each in a 6x9" paperback.

Grandmother Alice
Memoirs from the Home Front Before Civil War into 1930's
Alice Crain Hawkins could be called the 'Grandma Moses of Literature'. Her stories, published for the first time, were written while an invalid during the last years of her life. These journal entries from the late 1920's and early 30's gives us a fresh, novel and unique understanding of the lives of those who lived in the upper part of South Carolina during the state's growing years. Alice and her ancestors experiences are filled with understanding - they are provacative and profound. Written by Reese Hawkins (178 pgs.) $16.95 each in a 6x9" paperback.

Tales & Memories of Western North Dakota *Prairie Tales & True Stories of 20th Century Rural Life*
This manuscript has been inspired with Steve's antidotes, bits of wisdom and jokes (sometimes ethnic, to reflect the melting pot that was and is North Dakota; and from most unknown sources). A story about how to live life with humor, courage and grace along with personal hardships, tragedies and triumphs. Written by Steve Taylor. (174 pgs.) $14.95 each in a 6x9" paperback.

(Add $3.95 shipping & handling for first book, add $2.00 for each additional book ordered.)